P9-DOE-262

NORA ROBERTS

THE MacGREGORS
DANIEL ~ IAN

Published by Silhouette Books

America's Publisher of Contemporary Romance

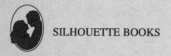 SILHOUETTE BOOKS

THE MacGREGORS: DANIEL~IAN

Copyright © 1999 by Nora Roberts

ISBN 0-373-48390-2

FOR NOW, FOREVER
Copyright © 1987 by Nora Roberts

IN FROM THE COLD
Copyright © 1990 by Nora Roberts

CONTENTS

FOR NOW, FOREVER   9

IN FROM THE COLD   241

THE MACGREGORS

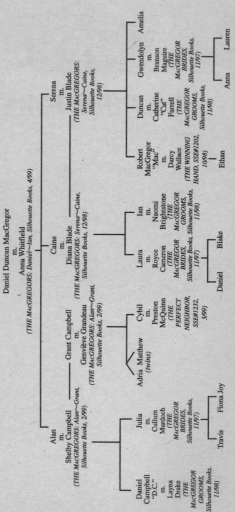

Daniel Duncan MacGregor
m.
Anna Whitfield
(THE MacGREGORS: Daniel~Ian, Silhouette Books, 4/99)

Alan
m.
Shelby Campbell
*(THE MacGREGORS: Alan~Grant,
Silhouette Books, 2/99)*

Grant Campbell
m.
Geneviève Grandeau
*(THE MacGREGORS: Alan~Grant,
Silhouette Books, 2/99)*

Caine
m.
Diana Blade
*(THE MacGREGORS: Serena~Caine,
Silhouette Books, 12/98)*

Serena
m.
Justin Blade
*(THE MacGREGORS: Serena~Caine,
Silhouette Books, 12/98)*

Daniel Campbell
"D.C."
m.
Layna Drake
*(THE
MacGREGOR
GROOMS,
Silhouette Books, 11/98)*

Julia
m.
Cullum Murdoch
*(THE
MacGREGOR
BRIDES,
Silhouette Books, 11/97)*

Adria   Matthew
(twins)

Cybil
m.
Preston McQuinn
*(THE
PERFECT
NEIGHBOR,
SSE#1232,
3/99)*

Laura
m.
Royce Cameron
*(THE
MacGREGOR
BRIDES,
Silhouette Books, 11/97)*

Ian
m.
Naomi Brightstone
*(THE
MacGREGOR
GROOMS,
Silhouette Books, 11/98)*

Robert
MacGregor
"Mac"
m.
D'arcy Wallace
*(THE WINNING
HAND, SSE#1202,
10/98)*

Duncan
m.
Catherine "Cat" Farrell
*(THE
MacGREGOR
GROOMS,
Silhouette Books, 11/98)*

Gwendolyn
m.
Branson Maguire
*(THE
MacGREGOR
BRIDES,
Silhouette Books, 11/97)*

Amelia

Travis   Fiona Joy

Daniel   Blake

Ethan

Anna

Lauren

FOR NOW, FOREVER

Prologue

"Mother."

Anna MacGregor clasped hands with her son as he crouched at her feet. Panic, fear, grief surged through her and met a solid wall of will. She wouldn't lose control now. She couldn't. Her children were coming.

"Caine." Her fingers were icy as they tightened on his, but they were steady. Her face was almost colorless from the strain of the past few hours, and her eyes were dark. Dark, young and frightened. It flashed through Caine that he'd never seen his mother frightened before. Not ever.

"Are you all right?"

"Of course." She knew what he needed and brushed her lips over his cheek. "Better now that you're here." With her free hand she gripped Diana's as her daughter-in-law sat beside her. Wet snow clung to Diana's long dark hair and was already melting on the shoulders of her coat. Anna took a long breath before she looked back at Caine. "You got here quickly."

"We chartered a plane." There was a little boy inside the grown man, the attorney, the new father, who wanted to scream out a denial. His father was invulnerable. His father was the MacGregor. He couldn't be lying broken in a hospital. "How bad is he?"

She was a doctor and could tell him precisely—the broken ribs, the collapsed lung, the concussion and the internal bleeding, which her colleagues were even now struggling to stop. She was also a mother. "He's in surgery." She kept her hand tight on his and nearly managed to smile. "He's strong, Caine. And Dr. Feinstein is the best in the state." She had to hold on to that and to her family. "Laura?"

"Laura's with Lucy Robinson," Diana said quietly. She knew well what it was like to hold emotions in. Slowly she massaged Anna's fingers. "Don't worry."

"No, I'm not." This time Anna managed the smile. "But you know Daniel. Laura's his first granddaughter. He'll be full of questions when he wakes up." And he would wake up, she promised herself. By God, he would.

"Anna." Diana slipped an arm around her mother-in-law's shoulders. She looked so small, so frail. "Have you eaten?"

"What?" Anna gave a tiny shake of her head then rose. Three hours. He'd been in surgery for three hours. How many times had she been in the operating room, fighting to save a life while a loved one agonized in these plastic waiting rooms, these cold corridors? She'd struggled and studied to be a doctor to ease pain, to heal—to somehow in some way make a difference. Now, when her husband was hurt, she could do no more than wait. Like any other woman. No, not like any woman, she corrected herself, because she knew what the operating room looked like, what it sounded and smelled like. She knew the instruments, the machines and the sweat too well. She wanted to scream. She folded her hands and walked to the window.

There was a will of iron behind her dark, quiet eyes. She'd use it now for herself, for her children, but mostly for Daniel. If it were possible to bring him back with sheer desire, she would do so. There was more to doctoring, much more to healing, she knew, than skill.

The snow had nearly stopped. The snow, she thought as she watched it fall thinly, had caused the roads to be slick and treacherous. The snow had blinded some young man, caused his car to spin out of control, and crash into her husband's foolish little two-seater. Her hands balled into fists.

Why weren't you in the limo, old man? What were you trying to prove with that flashy red toy? Always showing off, always... Her thoughts trailed away, going back in time. Her hands unclenched. Wasn't that one of the reasons she'd fallen in love with him? Wasn't that one of the reasons she'd loved and lived with him for nearly forty years? Damn you, Daniel MacGregor, no one can tell you anything. Anna pressed her fingers to her eyes and nearly laughed. She couldn't count the number of times she'd said that to him over their lifetime together. And adored him for it.

The sound of footsteps had her whirling, bracing. Then she saw Alan, her oldest son. Daniel had sworn before he had ever had a child that one of his offspring would be in the White House. Though Alan was close to making the oath reality, he was the only one of her children who took more after herself than their father. The MacGregor genes were strong. The MacGregors were strong. She let herself be folded in Alan's arms.

"He'll be glad you're here." Her voice was steady, but there was a woman inside her who wanted to weep and

weep. "But he's bound to scold you for bringing your wife
out in her condition." Anna smiled at Shelby and held out
a hand. Her daughter-in-law with the fiery hair and soft
eyes was big with child. "You should sit down."

"I will if you will." Without waiting for an answer,
Shelby led Anna to a chair. The moment Anna sat, Caine
put a cup of coffee in her hands.

"Thank you," she murmured and sipped for his sake.
She could smell it, strong and hot, feel it scald her tongue,
but she couldn't taste it. Anna listened to the ding of the
electronic pages, the quick slap of rubber-soled shoes on
tiled floor. Hospitals. They were as much her home as the
fortress Daniel had built for the two of them. She'd always
felt comfortable in them, confident in their antiseptic halls.
Now she felt helpless.

Caine paced. It was his nature to do so—to prowl, to
stalk. How proud she and Daniel had been of him when
he'd won his first case. Alan sat beside her, quiet, intense,
just as he'd always been. He was suffering. She watched
Shelby slip a hand into his and was content. Her sons had
chosen well. Our sons, she thought, trying to communicate
with Daniel. Caine with his quietly strong-willed Diana,
Alan with his free-spirited Shelby. Balance was needed in
a relationship almost as much as love, as much as passion.
She'd found that. Her sons had found that. And her daughter...

"Rena!" Caine was across the room, holding his sister.

How alike they look, Anna thought vaguely. So slim, so
bold. Of all her children, Serena came closest to matching
Daniel's temper and stubbornness. Now her daughter was
a mother herself. Anna could feel Alan's quiet strength beside her. They're all grown. When did it happen? We've
done so well, Daniel. She closed her eyes for only a mo-

ment. She could allow herself only a moment. *You wouldn't dare leave me to enjoy it all alone.*

"Dad?" With one hand Serena held on to her brother; with the other, she gripped her husband.

"Still in surgery." Caine's voice was rough with cigarettes and fear as he turned to Justin. "I'm glad you could come. Mom needs all of us."

"Momma." Serena went to kneel at her mother's feet, as she always had when she needed comfort or conversation. "He's going to be fine. He's stubborn and he's strong."

But Anna saw the plea in her daughter's eyes. *Tell me he's going to be all right. If you say so I'll believe it.*

"Of course he's going to be fine." She glanced up at her daughter's husband. Justin was a gambler, like her Daniel. Anna touched Serena's cheek. "Do you think he'd miss a reunion like this?"

Serena let out a shaky laugh. "That's just what Justin said." She smiled, seeing that Justin already had an arm around his sister's shoulder. "Diana." Serena rose to exchange an embrace. "How's Laura?"

"She's wonderful. She just got her second tooth. And Robert?"

"A terror." Serena thought of her son, who already worshiped Grandpa. "Shelby, how are you feeling?"

"Fat." She flashed a smile and managed to conceal the fact that she'd been in labor for more than an hour. "I called my brother." She turned to Anna. "Grant and Gennie are coming. I hope it's all right."

"Of course." Anna patted her hand. "They're family, too."

"Dad's going to be thrilled." Serena swallowed over the fear that had lodged in her throat. "All this attention. And then there's the little announcement Justin and I have to make." She looked at him, willing her courage to return. "Justin and I are going to have another baby. Have to insure the line. Momma—" her voice broke as she knelt down again "—Daniel will be so smug about it, won't he?"

"Yes." She kissed both of Serena's cheeks. She thought of the grandchildren she had, of those she would have. Family, continuity, immortality. Daniel. Always Daniel. "He'll consider it all his doing."

"Wasn't it?" Alan murmured.

Anna fought the tears back. How well they knew their father. "Yes. Yes, it was."

There was more pacing, murmuring, hand-holding as the minutes dragged by. Anna set her half-finished cup of coffee aside, cold and unwanted. Four hours and twenty minutes. It was taking too long. Beside her, Shelby tensed and deliberately began to breathe deeply. Automatically Anna placed a hand on the mound that was her grandchild.

"How close?"

"Just under five minutes now."

"How long?"

"Couple of hours." She gave Anna a look that was a little excited, a little terrified. "A bit more than three, actually. I wish I could've timed it better."

"You've timed it perfectly. Do you want me to go with you?"

"No." For a moment, Shelby nuzzled into Anna's neck. "I'll be fine. We're all going to be fine. Alan—" she held out both hands wanting to be hauled to her feet "—I'm not going to have the baby at Georgetown Hospital."

He drew her up gently. "What?"

"I'm going to have it here. Very soon." She laughed a bit when he narrowed his eyes. "Don't try logic on a baby, Alan. It's ready."

The entire clan clustered around her, offering help, advice, support. In her calm, efficient way, Anna summoned a nurse and a wheelchair. With little fuss she had Shelby settled. "I'll be down to check on you."

"We're going to be fine." Shelby reached over her shoulder for Alan's hand. "All of us. Tell Daniel it's going to be a boy. I'm going to see to it."

She watched as Shelby and Alan disappeared behind elevator doors just before Dr. Feinstein walked into the hall. "Sam," Anna exclaimed and was on him in seconds.

At the doorway of the waiting room, Justin held Caine back. "Give her a minute," he murmured.

"Anna." Feinstein put his hands on her shoulders. She wasn't just a colleague now or a surgeon he respected. She was the wife of a patient. "He's a strong man."

She felt hope surge and willed herself to be calm. "Strong enough?"

"He lost a lot of blood, Anna, and he's not young anymore. But we've stopped the hemorrhaging." He hesitated, then realized he respected her too much to evade. "We lost him once on the table. In seconds, he was fighting his way back. If will to live counts, Anna, he's got a hell of an edge."

She folded her arms around her chest. Cold. Why were the hallways so cold? "When can I see him?"

"They'll be bringing him up to ICU." His hands were cramping after hours of delicate work. He kept them firm on her shoulders. "Anna, I don't have to tell you what the next twenty-four hours mean."

Life or death. "No, you don't. Thank you, Sam. I'm going to talk to my children. Then I'll come up."

She turned to walk back down the hall, a small, lovely woman with gray threading through her deep sable hair. Her face was finely lined, her skin as soft as it had been in her youth. She'd raised three children, worked her way to the top of her profession and had spent over half of her life loving one man.

"He's out of surgery," she said calmly, calling on the control she'd been born with. "They're taking him to Intensive Care. They've controlled the bleeding."

"When can we see him?" The question came from several of them at once.

"When he wakes up." Her tone was firm. She was in charge again, and being in charge was what she did best. "I'm going to stay here tonight." She glanced at her watch. "He may float in and out a bit, and he'll be better knowing I'm there. But he won't be able to talk until tomorrow." It was all the hope she could give them. "I want you to go down to Maternity and check on Shelby. Stay as long as you like. Then go back to the house and wait. I'll call as soon as anything changes."

"Mother—"

She cut Caine off with a look. "Do as you're told. I want you rested and well when your father's ready to see you." She lifted a hand to Caine's cheek. "For me."

She left her children and comfort to go to her husband.

He was dreaming. Even through the drugs, Daniel knew he was dreaming. It was a soft world full of visions, tapestried with memories. Still, he fought it, wanting, needing to orient himself. When he opened his eyes, he saw Anna. He needed nothing else. She was beautiful. Always beautiful. The strong, stubborn, coolheaded woman he'd first admired, then loved, then respected. He tried to reach out but couldn't lift his hand. Infuriated at his weakness, he tried again, only to have Anna's voice float smoothly over him.

"Lie still, darling. I'm not going anywhere. I'm staying

right here and waiting.'' He thought he felt her lips on the back of his hand. "I love you, Daniel MacGregor. Damn you.''

His lips curved. His eyes closed.

Chapter One

An empire. At the time he'd turned fifteen, Daniel
MacGregor had promised himself he'd have one, build one,
rule one. He always kept his word.

He was thirty years old and working on his second million with the same drive that had earned him his first. As
he always had, he used his back, his brains and pure guile
in whatever order worked best. When he'd come to America five years before, Daniel had had the money he'd saved
by working his way up from miner to head bookkeeper for
Hamus McGuire. He'd also brought a shrewd brain and
towering ambition.

He could have passed for a king. He topped six four with
a build bold enough to suit his height. His size alone had
kept him out of a number of fights, just as his size had
seduced some men into challenging him. Either way was
fine with Daniel. He was reputed to have a temper, but he
considered himself a mild sort of person. Daniel didn't
think he'd broken more than his share of noses in his day.

He didn't consider himself handsome, either. His jaw was long and square, and running along its right edge was a scar that he'd gotten when a loose beam had toppled down on him in the mines. As a sop to his vanity, he'd grown a beard in his teens. A dozen years later it remained, deep red and well trimmed around his face, blending with a mane of hair that was too long for fashion. The combination made him look both fierce and royal, which pleased him. His cheekbones rose high and wide, and his mouth appeared surprisingly soft in its cushion of wild red hair. His eyes were a deep brilliant blue that lit with humor and goodwill when he smiled and meant it, just as they cooled to frost when he smiled and didn't.

Imposing. That was one adjective used to describe him. Ruthless was another. Daniel didn't care how he was described as long as he didn't go unnoticed. He was a gambler who played the odds boldly. Real estate was his wheel, and the stock market was his game table. When Daniel gambled, he played to win. The chances he'd taken had paid off. And when they had, he'd taken more. He never intended to play it too safe, because with safety came boredom.

Though he'd been born poor, Daniel MacGregor didn't worship money. He used it, wielded it, played with it. Money equaled power, and power was a weapon.

In America he found himself in a vast arena of wheeling and dealing. There was New York with its fast pace and hungry streets. A man with brains and nerve could build a fortune there. There was Los Angeles with its glamour and high stakes. A man with imagination could fashion an empire. Daniel had spent time in both, dabbled in business on either coast, but he chose Boston as his base and as his home. It wasn't simply money or power he sought, but style. Boston with its old-world charm, its stubborn dignity and its unapologetic snobbishness suited Daniel perfectly.

He'd come from a long line of warriors who had lived as much by wit as by the sword. His pride in his line was fierce, as fierce as his ambition. Daniel intended to see his line continue with strong sons and daughters. As a man of vision, he had no trouble seeing his grandchildren taking what he'd molded and building on it. There could be no empire without family to share it. To begin one, he needed the proper wife. Acquiring one, to Daniel, was as challenging and as logical as acquiring a prime piece of real estate. He'd come to the Donahues' summer ball to speculate on both.

He hated the tight collar and strangulating tie. When a man was built like a bull, he liked his neck free. His clothes were made in Boston by a tailor on Newbury Street. Daniel used him as much because his size demanded it as for the prestige. Ambition had put him in a suit, but he didn't have to like it. Another man dressed in the elegant black dinner suit and pleated silk shirt would have looked distinguished. Daniel, in either tartan or dress blacks looked flamboyant. He preferred it that way.

Cathleen Donahue, Maxwell Donahue's eldest daughter, preferred it, as well.

"Mr. MacGregor." Fresh out of finishing school in Switzerland, Cathleen knew how to serve tea, embroider silk and flirt elegantly. "I hope you're enjoying our little party."

She had a face like porcelain and hair like flax. Daniel thought it a pity her shoulders were so thin, but he, too, knew how to flirt. "I'm enjoying it more now, Miss Donahue."

Knowing most men were put off by giggles, Cathleen kept her laugh low and smooth. Her taffeta skirts whispered as she positioned herself beside him at the end of the long buffet table. Now, whoever stopped for a taste of truffles or salmon mousse would see them together. If she turned her head just a fraction, she could catch a glimpse of their reflection in one of the long narrow mirrors that lined the wall. She decided she liked what she saw.

"My father tells me you're interested in buying a little piece of cliff he owns in Hyannis Port." She fluttered her lashes twice. "I hope you didn't come here tonight to discuss business."

Daniel slipped two glasses from the tray of a passing waiter. He'd have preferred Scotch in a sturdy glass to champagne in crystal, but a man who didn't adjust in certain areas broke in others. As he drank, he studied Cathleen's face. He knew Maxwell Donahue would no more have discussed business with his daughter than he would have discussed fashion with her, but Daniel didn't fault her for lying. Rather he gave her credit for knowing how to dig out information. But while he admired her for it, it was precisely the reason he didn't consider her proper wife material. His wife would be too busy raising babies to worry about business.

"Business comes second to a lovely woman. Have you been to the cliffs?"

"Of course." She tilted her head so that the diamond flowers in her ears caught the light. "I do prefer the city. Are you attending the Ditmeyers' dinner party next week?"

"If I'm in town."

"So much traveling." Cathleen smiled before she sipped her champagne. She'd be very comfortable with a husband who traveled. "It must be exciting."

"It's business," he said. Then he added, "But you've just returned from Paris yourself."

Flattered that he'd been aware of her absence, Cathleen

almost beamed. "Three weeks wasn't enough. Shopping alone took nearly every moment I had. You can't imagine how many tedious hours I spent in fittings for this gown."

He swept his gaze down and up as she'd expected. "I can only say it was well worth it."

"Why, thank you." As she stood, posing, his mind began to drift. He knew women were supposed to be interested mainly in dresses and hairstyles, but he'd have preferred a more stimulating conversation. Sensing she was losing his attention, Cathleen touched his arm. "You've been to Paris, Mr. MacGregor?"

He'd been to Paris and had seen what war could do to beauty. The pretty blonde smiling up at him would never be touched by war. Why should she be? Still, vaguely dissatisfied, Daniel sipped the dry bubbling wine. "Some years ago." He glanced around at the glitter of jewels, the sparkle of crystal. There was a scent in the air that could only be described as wealth. In five years he'd become accustomed to it, but he hadn't forgotten the smell of coal dust. He never intended to forget it. "I've come to prefer America to Europe. Your father knows how to throw a party."

"I'm glad you approve. You're enjoying the music?"

He still missed the wail of bagpipes. The twelve-piece orchestra in white tie was a bit stiff for his taste, but he smiled. "Very much."

"I thought perhaps you weren't." She sent him a slow, melting look from under her lashes. "You aren't dancing."

In a courtly gesture, Daniel took the champagne from Cathleen and set both their glasses down. "Oh, but I am, Miss Donahue," he corrected, and swept her onto the dance floor.

"Cathleen Donahue continues to be obvious." Myra Lornbridge nibbled pâté and sniffed.

"Keep your claws sheathed, Myra." The voice was low and smooth, by nature rather than design.

"I don't mind when a person's rude or calculating or even a bit stupid—" with a sigh, Myra finished off the cracker "—but I do detest it when one is obvious."

"Myra."

"All right, all right." Myra poked at the salmon mousse. "By the way, Anna, I love your dress."

Anna glanced down at the rose-colored silk. "You picked it out."

"I told you I loved it." Myra gave a self-satisfied smile at the way the folds draped over Anna's hips. Very chic. "If you'd pay half the attention to your wardrobe as you do your books, you'd put Cathleen Donahue's nose out of joint."

Anna only smiled and watched the dancers. "I'm not interested in Cathleen's nose."

"Well, it isn't very interesting. How about the man she's dancing with?"

"The red-haired giant?"

"So you noticed."

"I'm not blind." She wondered how soon she could make a dignified exit. She really wanted to go home and read the medical journal Dr. Hewitt had sent her.

"Know who he is?"

"Who?"

"Anna." Patience was a virtue Myra extended only to her closest friends. "Fe fi fo fum."

With a laugh, Anna sipped her wine. "All right, who is he?"

"Daniel Duncan MacGregor." Myra paused a bit, hoping to pique Anna's interest. At twenty-four, Myra was rich and attractive. Beautiful, no. Even at her best, Myra knew she'd never be beautiful. She understood beauty was one route to power. Brains were another. Myra used her brains. "He's Boston's current boy wonder. If you'd pay more attention to who's who in our cozy little society, you'd recognize the name."

Society, with its games and restrictions, didn't interest Anna in the least. "Why should I? You'll tell me."

"Serve you right if I didn't."

But Anna only smiled and drank again.

"All right, I'll tell you." Gossip was one temptation Myra found impossible to resist. "He's a Scot, which is obvious I suppose from his looks and his name. You should hear him talk, it's like cutting through fog."

At that moment, Daniel let out a big, booming laugh that raised Anna's eyebrows. "That sounds as though it would cut through anything."

"He's a bit rough around the edges, but some people—" she cast a meaningful look at Cathleen Donahue "—believe that a million dollars or so smooths out anything."

Realizing that the man was being weighed and judged by the size of his bank balance, Anna felt a twinge of sympathy. "I hope he knows he's dancing with a viper," Anna murmured.

"He doesn't look stupid. He bought Old Line Savings and Loan six months ago."

"Really." She shrugged. Business only interested Anna when it involved a hospital budget. Sensing the movement to her left, she turned to smile at Herbert Ditmeyer standing with an unfamiliar gentleman, "How are you?"

"Glad to see you." He was only a few inches taller than Anna and had the lean, ascetic face of a scholar, with dark hair that promised to thin in a matter of years. But there was a strength around his mouth that Anna respected, and he had a sense of humor it took a sharp wit to understand. "You're looking lovely." He gestured to the man beside

him. "My cousin, Mark. Anna Whitfield and Myra Lornbridge." Herbert's gaze lingered just a moment longer on
Myra, but as the orchestra began a new waltz, he lost his
nerve and took Anna's arm. "You should be dancing."

Anna matched her steps to his naturally. She loved to
dance, but preferred to do so with someone she knew. Herbert was comfortable. "I heard congratulations are in order—" she smiled up into his dependable face "—Mr. District Attorney."

He grinned. He was young for the position but had no
intention of stopping there. If he hadn't considered it bad
form, he might have told Anna of his ambitions. "I wasn't
sure Boston news traveled as far as Connecticut." He
glanced to where Myra was dancing with his cousin. "I
suppose I should have known better."

Anna laughed as they twirled around another couple.
"Just because I've been out of town doesn't mean I don't
want to keep up with what's happening here in Boston. You
must be very proud."

"It's a beginning," Herbert said lightly. "And you—one
more year and we'll have to call you Dr. Whitfield."

"One more year," Anna murmured. "Sometimes it
seems like forever."

"Impatient, Anna? That's not like you."

Yes, it was, but she'd always managed to conceal it so
successfully. "I want it to be official. It's no secret that my
parents disapprove."

"They might disapprove," Herbert added, "but your
mother doesn't have any trouble mentioning you're in the
top ten percent of your class for the third year running."

"Really?" Surprised, Anna thought it over. Her mother
had always been more apt to praise her hairstyle than her
grades. "I'll have to be grateful for that then, though she

still harbors the hope that some man will come along and make me forget about operating rooms and bedpans.''

As she spoke, Herbert turned her. Anna found herself looking directly into Daniel MacGregor's eyes. She felt her stomach muscles tighten. Nerves? Ridiculous. She felt the quick chill that raced down her spine and up again. Fear? Absurd.

Though he still danced with Cathleen, he stared at Anna. Stared at her in a way that was designed to make a young woman's cheeks flush. Anna stared back coolly while her heart raced. Perhaps it was a mistake. He seemed to take it as a challenge and smiled very slowly.

With a detached admiration, she watched him maneuver. Catching the eye of another man on the edge of the dance floor, Daniel gave a quick, almost imperceptible signal. Within moments, Cathleen found herself dancing in the arms of another man. Anna braced herself for the next step.

With the ease of experience, Daniel weaved through the dancers. He'd noticed Anna the moment she'd begun to dance. Noticed, then watched, then calculated. As soon as she'd glanced over and had given him that coolly appraising stare, he'd been hooked. She didn't have the stature of Cathleen, but seemed small and delicate. Her hair was dark and looked as warm and soft as sable. Her eyes matched it. The rose hue of her dress set off her creamy skin and smooth shoulders. She looked like a woman who would fit easily into a man's arms.

With the confidence he carried everywhere, Daniel tapped Herbert's shoulder. ''May I cut in?''

Daniel waited only until Herbert had relinquished his hold before he clasped Anna and swirled her back into the dance. ''That was very clever, Mr. MacGregor.''

It pleased him that she knew his name. It pleased him as well that he'd been right about the way she'd fit into his arms. She smelled like moonbeams, soft and quiet. "Thank you, Miss…?"

"Whitfield. Anna Whitfield. It was also very rude."

He stared a moment because the stern voice didn't fit the quietly lovely face. Always one to appreciate a surprise, Daniel laughed until heads turned. "Aye, but I go with what works. I don't believe I've seen you before, Miss Anna Whitfield, but I know your parents."

"That's very possible." The hand holding hers was huge, hard as rock and incredibly gentle. Her palm began to itch. "Are you new to Boston, Mr. MacGregor?"

"I'll have to say yes because I've lived here only two years, not two generations."

She tilted her head a bit farther so that she could keep her eyes on his. "You have to go back at least three not to be new."

"Or you have to be clever." He twirled her in three quick circles.

Pleasantly surprised that for his size he was light on his feet, Anna relaxed just a little. It would be a shame to waste the music. "I've been told you are."

"You'll be told so again." He didn't bother to keep his voice low, though the dance floor was crowded. Power, not propriety, was his forte.

"Will I?" Anna cocked a brow. "How odd."

"Only if you don't understand the system," he corrected her, unsinged. "If you can't have the generations behind you, you need money in front."

Though she knew it was true, Anna disliked both forms of snobbery. "How fortunate for you society has such flexible standards."

Her dry, disinterested voice made him smile. She wasn't a fool this Anna Whitfield, nor was she a silk-coated barracuda like Cathleen Donahue. "You've a face like the cameo my grandmother wore around her neck."

Anna lifted a brow and nearly smiled at him. The look made him realize he'd said no more than the truth. "Thank you, Mr. MacGregor, but you'd be better off saving your flattery for Cathleen. She's more susceptible."

A frown clouded his eyes, and he looked fierce and formidable, but it cleared quickly, before Anna could gauge her reaction. "You've a cool tongue in your head, lassie. I admire a woman who speaks her mind...to a point."

Feeling aggressive for no reason she could name, Anna kept her gaze directly on his. "What point is that, Mr. MacGregor?"

"To the point where it becomes unfeminine."

Before she'd anticipated his move, Daniel swung her through the terrace doors. Until that moment she hadn't realized just how hot and stuffy the ballroom had become. Regardless of that, Anna's normal reaction with a man she didn't know would have been to excuse herself firmly and finally and walk back inside. Instead, she found herself stopping just where she was, with Daniel's arms still around her, the moonlight pouring over the flagstones and warm roses scenting the air.

"I'm sure you have your own definition of femininity, Mr. MacGregor, but I wonder if you keep it in tune with the fact that we're in the twentieth century."

He enjoyed the way she stood in his arms and subtly insulted him. "I've always considered femininity a constant thing, Miss Whitfield, not something that changes with years or fashion."

"I see." His arms seemed to fit around her a bit too easily. She drew herself away to stroll to the edge of the terrace nearest the gardens. The air was sweeter there, the moonlight dimmer. The music became more romantic with distance.

It occurred to her that she was having a private conversation, one that might have been approaching an argument, with a man she'd only just met. Yet she didn't feel any urge to cut it short. She'd taught herself to be comfortable around men. She'd had to. As the only woman in her graduating class, Anna had learned how to deal with men on their own level and how to do so without constantly rubbing against their egos. She'd gotten through the first year of criticism and innuendos by staying calm and concentrating on her studies. Now she was about to enter her last year of medical school, and for the most part, Anna was accepted by her colleagues. She was perfectly aware, however, of what she would face when she began her internship. The stigma of being labeled unfeminine still stung a bit, but she was long resigned to it.

"I'm sure your views on femininity are fascinating, Mr. MacGregor." The hem of her dress skimmed the flagstone as she turned. "But I don't think it's something I care to discuss. Tell me, what is it exactly that you do in Boston?"

He hadn't heard her. He hadn't heard anything from the moment she'd turned back to face him. Her hair swung softly just at her white, smooth shoulders. In the thin rose-colored silk, her body looked as delicate as fine china. The moonlight filtered over her face so that her skin was like marble and her eyes as dark as midnight. A man hears nothing but the thunder when he's struck by lightning.

"Mr. MacGregor?" For the first time since they'd stepped outside, Anna's nerves began to hum. He was huge, a stranger, and he was looking at her as though he'd lost his senses. She straightened her shoulders and reminded herself she could handle any situation that came along. "Mr. MacGregor?"

"Aye." Daniel pulled himself out of his fantasy and stepped closer. Oddly Anna relaxed. He didn't seem as dangerous when he stood beside her. And his eyes were beautiful. True, there was a very simple genetic reason for their shade. She could have written a paper on it. But they were beautiful.

"You do work in Boston, don't you?"

"I do." Perhaps it had been a trick of the light that had made her look so perfect, so ethereal and seductive. "I buy." He took her hand because personal contact was vital to him. He took it because part of him wanted to be assured she was real. "I sell."

His hand was warm and as gentle as it had been when they'd danced. Anna drew hers away. "How interesting. What do you buy?"

"Whatever I want." Smiling, he stepped a bit closer. "Whatever."

Her pulse accelerated, her skin heated. Anna knew there were emotional as well as physical causes for such things. Though she couldn't think of them at the moment, she didn't back away. "I'm sure that's very satisfying. That leads me to believe you sell whatever you no longer want."

"In a nutshell, Miss Whitfield. And at a profit."

Conceited ox, she thought mildly and tilted her head. "Some might consider that arrogance, Mr. MacGregor."

She made him laugh with the cool, calm way she spoke, the cool, calm way she looked even when he could see traces of passion in her eyes. She was a woman, he thought, who could make a man wait on the doorstep with bouquets and heart-shaped boxes of candy. "When a poor man's arrogant it's crude, Miss Whitfield. When a man of means is arrogant, it's called style. I've been both."

She felt there was some truth in his words but wasn't

willing to give an inch. "Strange, I've never felt arrogance changes with years or with fashion."

He took out a cigar as he watched her. "Your point." His lighter flared, highlighting his eyes for one brief instant. In that moment, Anna realized he was dangerous after all.

"Then perhaps we should call it a draw." Pride prevented her from stepping back. Dignity prevented her from continuing what was, despite logic, becoming interesting. "Now, if you'll excuse me, Mr. MacGregor, I really must get back inside."

He took her arm in a way that was both abrupt and proprietary. Anna didn't jerk away, and she didn't freeze; she merely looked at him as a duchess might look at a dust-covered commoner. Faced with that serene disapproval, most men would have dropped their hand and mumbled apologies. Daniel grinned at her. Now here's a lass, he thought, who'd make a man's knees tremble. "I'll see you again, Miss Anna Whitfield."

"Perhaps."

"I'll see you again." He lifted her hand to his lips. She felt the soft, surprising brush of his beard across her knuckles, and for a moment, the trace of passion he'd seen in her eyes flared full blown. "And again."

"I doubt we'll have much occasion to socialize, as I'll only be in Boston for a couple of months. Now, if you'll excuse me—"

"Why?"

He didn't release her hand, which troubled her more than she could permit to show. "Why what, Mr. MacGregor?"

"Why will you only be in Boston for a couple of months?" If she were running off to get married it might change things. Daniel looked at her again and decided he wouldn't allow it to change anything.

"I go back to Connecticut at the end of August for my last year in medical school."

"Medical school?" His brows drew together. "You're not going to be a nurse?" His voice carried the vague puzzlement of a man who had no understanding of, and little tolerance for, professional women.

"No." She waited until she felt him relax. "A surgeon. Thank you for the dance."

But he had her arm again before she could reach the door. "You're going to cut people open?" For the second time she heard his laughter boom out. "You're joking."

Though she bristled, she managed to make it appear she was simply bored. "I promise you I'm much more amusing when I joke. Good night, Mr. MacGregor."

"Being a doctor's a man's job."

"I appreciate your opinion. I happen to believe there is no such thing as a man's job if a woman is capable of doing it."

He snorted, puffed on his cigar and muttered. "Pack of nonsense."

"Succinctly put, Mr. MacGregor, and again, rude. You are consistent." She walked through the terrace doors without looking back. But she did think of him. Brash, crude, flamboyant and foolish.

He thought of her as he watched her slip into the crowd. Cool, opinionated, blunt and ridiculous.

They were both fascinated.

Chapter Two

"Tell me everything."

Anna set her purse on the white linen cloth and smiled at the hovering waiter. "I'll have a champagne cocktail."

"Two," Myra decided, then leaned forward. "Well?"

Taking her time, Anna glanced around the quiet, pastel restaurant. There were half a dozen people she knew by name, several others she knew by sight. She found it cozy, safe and serene. There were times in the rush and fury of classes and studies when she longed for moments like this. There would be a way somehow, someday to have both in her life. "You know, the one thing I miss about living in Connecticut is having lunch here. I'm glad you suggested it."

"Anna." Myra saw no reason to waste time on polite chatter when there was news ready to break. "Tell me."

"Tell you what?" Anna countered, and enjoyed the flash of frustration in her friend's eyes.

Myra took a cigarette out of a thin gold case, tapped it

twice, then lit it. "Tell me what happened between you and Daniel MacGregor."

"We had a waltz." Anna picked up her menu and began to scan it. But she caught herself tapping her foot as the music crept back into her head.

"And?"

She shifted her gaze over the top of the menu. "And?"

"Anna!" Myra cut herself off as their drinks were served. Impatient, she pushed her cocktail aside. "You were out on the terrace with him, alone, for quite some time."

"Really?" Anna sipped her champagne, decided on a salad and closed the menu.

"Yes, really." With calculated flamboyance, Myra blew smoke at the ceiling. "Apparently you must have found something to talk about."

"I believe we did." The waiter returned, so Anna ordered her salad. Seething in frustration, Myra ordered lobster Newburg and told herself she'd fast through dinner.

"Well, what did you talk about?"

"I seem to remember one of the topics was femininity." Anna took another casual sip but wasn't quite able to conceal the anger that leaped into her eyes. Seeing it, Myra put out her cigarette and perked up.

"I assume that Mr. MacGregor has some definite opinions on the subject."

Anna sipped again, savoring the taste of the champagne before she set her glass down. "Mr. MacGregor is an opinionated boor."

Thoroughly pleased, Myra cupped her chin in her hand. The little veil attached to her hat fell just below her eyes but didn't conceal their enthusiasm. "I was nearly certain about the opinionated, but I would have bet heavily against the boor. Tell me."

"He admires a woman who speaks her mind," Anna continued, firing up, "to a point. To a point," she repeated with a quick unladylike snort. "That point stops wherever it conflicts with his outlook."

A little disappointed, Myra shrugged. "He sounds like any other man."

"It's men like him who see women as subsidiary to their manhood." Sitting back, Anna began to tap her fingers in a slow, steady rhythm on the white cloth. "We're fine as long as we're baking cookies, diapering babies and warming the sheets."

After choking on a sip of champagne, Myra swallowed. "My goodness, he did get under your skin in a very short time."

Deliberately Anna drew herself back. She detested losing her temper and reserved the privilege for something of real importance. She reminded herself that Daniel MacGregor didn't fit the bill. "He's rude and arrogant," she said more calmly.

Myra gave it a moment's thought. "That may be," she agreed. "But it's not necessarily a mark against him. I'd rather be around an arrogant man than a stuffy one."

"Stuffy he's not. Didn't you see that maneuver he pulled on Cathleen?"

Her eyes lit up. "No."

"He signaled to some man to cut in while they were dancing so he could cut in on Herbert and dance with me."

"How clever." Myra beamed approval, then laughed at Anna's expression. "Come on, darling, you have to admit it was. And Cathleen's much too involved with her own charms to have noticed." Myra gave a sigh of pleasure as her lobster was served. "You know, Anna, you should be flattered."

"Flattered?" She stabbed at her salad. "I don't see why

I should be flattered that some enormous, self-important dolt of a man preferred to dance with me.''

Myra paused to appreciate the scent of the lobster. ''He's certainly enormous, and he may be a dolt, but he is important. And in a rough sort of way, he's attractive. Obviously, from the way you've brushed others off, you aren't interested in the smooth, sophisticated type.''

''I have my career to think of, Myra. I don't have time for men.''

''Darling, there's always time for men.'' With a laugh, she took another forkful of lobster. ''I don't mean that you have to take him seriously.''

''I'm glad to hear that.''

''But I don't see why you should just toss him back.''

''I have no intention of reeling him in.''

''You're being stubborn.''

Anna laughed. One of the reasons she was so fond of Myra was that her friend saw things clearly—her way. ''I'm being myself.''

''Anna, I know what becoming a doctor means to you, and you know how much I admire what you're doing. But,'' she continued before Anna could comment, ''you're going to be in Boston for the summer, anyway. What's the harm in having an attractive escort who's obviously going places?''

''I don't need an escort.''

''Needing and having are two different things.'' Myra broke off the corner of a roll and swore to herself she'd only eat half of it. ''Tell me, Anna, are your parents still pressuring you about your decision to go into medicine? Are they still lining up eligible men to change your mind?''

''They've already lined up three potential candidates for my hand this summer.'' She had to convince herself to be amused and nearly managed it. ''At the top of the list is the grandson of my mother's doctor. She thinks his connection to medicine might influence me."

"Is he attractive?" Myra waved away the question at Anna's scowl. "Never mind, then. My point is that your parents are going to continue to toss all of these men your way, hoping something sticks. But—" she added a bit of butter to her roll "—if you were seeing someone…"

"As in Daniel MacGregor."

"Why not? He certainly seemed interested last night."

Anna took the roll Myra had buttered and bit into it. "Because it's dishonest. I'm not interested."

"It might keep your mother from inviting every single man between twenty-five and forty over to your house for tea."

Anna let out a long breath. Myra had a point there. If just once her parents would understand what it was she needed, what she was striving for… *For your own good.* How many times had she heard that particular phrase? *If* she ever married and *if* she ever had children, those four words would never come out of her mouth.

Anna was well aware her parents had stopped arguing about her going to medical school only because they'd been certain she'd be out again before the end of the first semester. If it hadn't been for Aunt Elsie, Anna was aware she'd probably never have managed medical school at all. Elsie Whitfield had been her father's eccentric older sister—a spinster, who had made her money, some said, bootlegging whiskey during prohibition. Anna could hardly fault her however the money had been earned, since Aunt Elsie had left her a legacy large enough for tuition and independence, with no strings attached.

Don't marry a man unless you're damn sure of him, Anna remembered Elsie advising. *If you've got a dream,*

go after it. Life's too short for cowards. Use the money,
Anna, and make something out of yourself, for yourself.

Now she was only months away from the dream—graduation, her internship. It wasn't going to be easy for her parents to accept. It would be harder still when they learned she intended to begin her internship at Boston General— and that she didn't intend to live at home while she was doing it.

"Myra, I've been thinking about getting my own place."

With the fork halfway to her mouth, Myra stopped. "Have you told your parents?"

"No." Anna pushed away her salad and wondered why life was so complicated when so many things seemed clear to her. "I don't want to upset them, but it's time. I'm a grown woman, but they're never going to see me as one while I'm living in their home. Also, if I don't make the break now, they're going to expect me to go on living with them after I graduate."

Myra sat back and finished what was left of her champagne. "I think you're right. I also think you'd be wise to tell them after it's a fait accompli."

"So do I. How would you like to spend the afternoon apartment hunting?"

"I'd love it. Right after some chocolate mousse." She signaled the waiter. "Still, Anna, that doesn't solve the problem with Daniel MacGregor."

"There isn't any problem."

"Oh, I think you can depend on one. Chocolate mousse," she told the waiter. "Don't spare the whipped cream."

In his newly decorated office, Daniel sat behind an enormous oak desk and lit a cigar. He'd just completed a deal in which he'd bought the lion's share of a company that would manufacture televisions. Daniel calculated that what was now a novelty would become a staple in the American home in a matter of years. Besides, he enjoyed watching the little box himself. It gave him a great deal of satisfaction to buy something that entertained him. Still, his biggest project at the moment was revamping the teetering Old Line Savings and Loan to make it the biggest lending institution in Boston. He'd already started by extending two major loans and refinancing several others. He believed in putting money into circulation where it could grow. The bank manager was horrified, but Daniel figured the man would bend or find other employment. In the meantime, Daniel had some research to do.

Anna Whitfield. He knew her family background because her father was one of the top attorneys in the state. Daniel had nearly retained him before he'd decided to go with the younger, more flexible Herbert Ditmeyer. Now that Herbert had been elected district attorney, he might have to do some rethinking there. Maybe Anna Whitfield's father was the answer. He'd just about decided that Anna was.

Her family home on Beacon Hill had been built in the eighteenth century. Her ancestors had been patriots who'd started a new life in the New World and had prospered. The Whitfields were, and had been for generations, a solid part of Boston society.

Daniel respected nothing more than a strong lineage. Prince or pauper didn't matter, just strength and endurance. Anna Whitfield came from good stock. That was Daniel's prime prerequisite for a proper wife. She had a head on her shoulders. It hadn't taken him long to learn that, though she was studying something as odd as medicine, she was at the top of her class. He didn't intend to pass along soft brains to his children. She was lovely. A man looking for a wife and a mother for his children had to appreciate beauty. Especially that soft, creamy sort.

She also wasn't a pushover. Daniel didn't want a simpering, blindly obedient wife—though he did expect a woman to respect the fact that he called the shots.

There were a dozen women he could woo and win, but none of them had presented him with that little bit extra. A challenge. After one meeting with Anna, Daniel was certain she would give him that. Being pursued by a woman flattered the ego, but a challenge—a challenge fired the blood. There was enough warrior in him to look forward to the fight.

If he knew one thing, it was how to lay the groundwork for a takeover. First, he found out his opponent's strengths and weaknesses. Then, he played on both. Picking up the phone, Daniel kicked back in his chair and began.

A few hours later, Daniel was struggling with the knot in his black, silk tie. The only problem with being wealthy, as far as he could see, was having to dress the part. There was no question that he presented an imposing figure in dress black, but he never stopped straining against the restrictions. Still, if a man was out to sweep a woman off her feet, he was ahead of the game if he did it in his Sunday best.

According to his information, Anna Whitfield would be spending the evening at the ballet with friends. Daniel figured he had his accountant to thank for talking him into renting a box at the theater. He might not have put it to much use thus far, but tonight would make up for all that.

He was whistling as he walked down the stairs to the first floor. Most people would have considered his twenty-room house a bit overindulgent for one man, but to Daniel, the house, with its tall windows and gleaming floors, was a statement. As long as he had it, he'd never have to go back to the three-room cottage he'd grown up in. The house said what Daniel needed it to say—that the man who owned it had success, had presence, had style. Without those things, Daniel Duncan MacGregor was back in the mines with coal dust ground into his skin and reddening his eyes.

At the foot of the stairs, Daniel paused to bellow, "McGee!" He got a foolish surge of pleasure at the way his voice bounced off the walls.

"Sir." McGee walked down the long hall, erect and unbending. He'd served other gentlemen in his time, but never one as unconventional or as generous as MacGregor. Besides, it pleased him to work for a fellow Scot.

"I'll need the car brought around."

"It's waiting for you outside."

"The champagne?"

"Chilled, of course, sir."

"The flowers?"

"White roses, sir. Two dozen as you requested."

"Good, good." Daniel was halfway to the door before he stopped and turned around. "Help yourself to the Scotch, McGee. You've got the evening off."

With no change of expression, McGee inclined his head. "Thank you, sir."

Whistling again, Daniel went outside to the waiting car. He'd bought the silver Rolls on a whim but had had no cause to regret it. He'd given the gardener the extra job of chauffeur and had pleased them both by outfitting him in a pearl-gray uniform and cap. Steven's grammar might be faulty, but once he was behind the wheel, he was the soul of dignity.

"Evening, Mr. MacGregor." Steven opened the door, then polished the handle with a soft cloth after he'd closed it again. Daniel might have bought the Rolls, but Steven considered it his baby.

After settling himself in the quiet luxury of the back seat, Daniel opened the briefcase that was waiting for him. If it took fifteen minutes to drive to the theater, it meant he had fifteen minutes to work. Idle time was for his old age.

If things went according to plan, he'd have that piece of property in Hyannis Port by the following week. The cliffs, the tough gray rock, the tall green grass reminded him of Scotland. He'd make his home there, a home he already imagined in his mind's eye. There'd be nothing to compare with it. Once he had it, he'd fill it with a wife and children. So he thought of Anna.

The white roses were spread on the seat beside him. The champagne was cased in ice. He only had to sit through the ballet before he began his courting. He picked up a rose and sniffed. The scent was quiet and sweet. White roses were her favorite. It hadn't taken him long to find that out. It would take a hard woman to resist two dozen of them, a hard woman to resist the luxury he'd offer her. Daniel dropped the rose back with the others. He'd made up his mind. It would only be a short time before he made up hers, as well. Satisfied, he sat back and closed the briefcase as Steven pulled up in front of the theater.

"Two hours," he told his driver, then on impulse picked up one of the roses again. It wouldn't hurt to start his campaign a bit early.

The scene in the lobby of the theater was one of glitter and silk. Long sweeping dresses in pastels contrasted with dark evening suits. There was a glow of pearls, a sparkle of diamonds and everywhere the feminine scent of perfume. Daniel wandered through the crowd, not so much aloof as preoccupied. His size and presence coupled with his casual manner had fascinated more than one woman. Daniel took this with a smile and a grain of salt. A woman who was easily fascinated would be easily bored. Wide mood swings weren't what a wise man looked for in a mate. Especially when the man was prone to them himself.

As he strolled through the crowd, he was distracted now and again and stopped with a friendly word or greeting. He liked people, so it was an easy matter for him to socialize, whether in the lobby of the theater or in the pits at one of his construction sites. Since he was first and last a businessman, he was comfortable talking about one thing while thinking of something entirely different. He didn't consider it dishonest, merely practical. So while he stopped here, paused there, he kept a sharp lookout for Anna.

When he saw her, he was struck just as hard and just as fast as he'd been at the summer ball. She wore blue—pale, pale blue that made her skin glow as white as new milk. Her hair was swept up and back with combs so that her face was unframed and more like his grandmother's cameo than ever. He felt a pang of desire, then something deeper and stronger than he'd expected. Still, he waited patiently until she turned her head and their eyes met. She didn't, as another woman might have, blush or flirt but simply met his stare with a calm, appraising look. Daniel felt the excitement and challenge of the game as he moved to her.

In a move that was too smooth to be considered rude, he homed in on her and ignored the group around them. "Miss Whitfield, for the waltz."

When he offered her the rose, Anna hesitated, then saw there was no polite way to refuse. Even as she took the rose, its scent drifted to her. "Mr. MacGregor, I don't believe you've met my friend, Myra. Myra Lornbridge, Daniel MacGregor."

"How do you do?" Myra offered her hand, carefully sizing him up. He looked her directly in the eye, his own eyes cool and cautious. Myra discovered that, though she wasn't certain she liked him, she respected him. "I've heard a great deal about you."

"I've had some business with your brother." She was smaller than Anna, though rounder. One look told Daniel she'd be formidable but interesting.

"That's not who I heard it from. Jasper never gossips, I'm afraid."

Daniel sent her a quick grin. "Which is why I like doing business with him. You enjoy the ballet, Miss Whitfield?"

"Yes, very much." She sniffed the rose involuntarily, then annoyed with herself, lowered her hands.

"I'm afraid I haven't seen many and don't seem to get the full impact." He added a rueful smile to the charm of the rose. "I'm told it helps if you know the story or watch with someone who truly appreciates ballet."

"I'm sure that's true."

"I wonder if I could ask you a great favor."

Warning signals flashed and made her narrow her eyes. "You can ask, of course."

"I've a box. If you'd sit with me, maybe you could show me how to enjoy the dancing."

Anna only smiled. She wasn't so easily taken in. "Under different circumstances I'd be glad to help you out. But I'm here with friends, so—"

"Don't mind us," Myra cut in. Whatever devil prompted her to interfere urged her further. "It's a shame for Mr. MacGregor to sit through *Giselle* without really appreciating it, don't you think?" Eyes wicked, she smiled at Anna. "You two run right along."

"I'm grateful." Daniel looked at Myra, and his eyes, which had been cool, warmed with humor. "Very grateful. Miss Whitfield?"

Daniel offered his arm. For one quick, satisfying instant, Anna considered tossing his rose on the floor and grinding it underfoot before stomping away. Then she smiled and tucked her arm through his. There were better ways of winning a match than tantrums. Daniel led her away, tossing a wink at Myra without breaking stride. Myra caught it and Anna's scowl with the same aplomb.

"Isn't it odd to hold a box at the ballet without being able to appreciate it?"

"It's business," Daniel told her briefly as they walked up the stairs. "But tonight I'm sure I'll get more than my money's worth."

"Oh, you can count on it." Anna swept through the doors and took her seat. Carefully she set the rose across her lap and allowed Daniel to remove the ivory lace wrap she'd tossed on as an afterthought. Beneath it, her shoulders were bare. Both of them became aware of how stunning the lightest touch of flesh against flesh could be. Anna folded her hands and decided to pay him back by giving him exactly what he'd asked for.

"Now, to give you the background." In the tone of a kindergarten teacher reciting *Little Red Riding Hood*, Anna told him the story of *Giselle*. Without giving him a chance to comment throughout the lecture, she went on with everything she knew about ballet in general. Enough, she thought, to put a strong man to sleep. "Ah, here's the curtain. Now pay attention."

Satisfied with her tactics, Anna settled back and prepared to enjoy herself. She couldn't concentrate. Within the first ten minutes her mind wandered a dozen times. Daniel sat quietly beside her, but he wasn't cowed. Of that she was certain. She thought that, if she turned her head only a few inches, she'd see him grinning at her. She looked straight ahead. She'd deal with Myra, she thought grimly, for boxing her in with a red-bearded barbarian. And she wouldn't look at him. She wouldn't, she promised herself, even think about him. Instead, she'd absorb the music, the color, the dancing of a ballet she loved. It was romantic, exciting, poignant. If she could only relax, she'd forget he was there. Deliberately she took five deep breaths. Then he touched her hand, making her pulse jolt.

"It's all about love and luck, isn't it?" Daniel murmured.

She realized that, barbarian or not, he understood and, from the quiet tone of his voice, that he appreciated. Unable to resist, she turned her head. Their faces were close, the lights were dim. The music swelled and crested over them. A little piece of her heart weakened and was lost to him. "Most things are."

He smiled, and in the shadowed light seemed incredibly virile, incredibly gentle. "A wise thing to remember, Anna."

Before she could think to resist, he linked his fingers with hers. Hands joined, they watched the dance together.

He kept close during intermission, catering to her before she could prevent him. Somehow he maneuvered her until it was too late to make excuses and rejoin her friends for the last half. As she took her seat after the intermission, Anna told herself she was simply being polite by remaining in his box until the final curtain. It wasn't a matter of wanting to be there, or of enjoying herself, but of good manners. She managed to sit primly for five minutes before she was again caught up in the romance of the story.

She felt the tears come as Giselle faced tragedy. Though she kept her face turned and blinked furiously, Daniel gauged her mood. Without a word, he passed her his handkerchief. She took it with a little sigh of acceptance.

"It's so sad," she murmured. "It doesn't matter how many times I see it."

"Some beautiful things are meant to be sad so we can appreciate the beautiful things that aren't."

Surprised, she turned to him again with tears still clinging to her lashes. He didn't sound like a barbarian when he spoke that way. Somehow, she wished he had. Disturbed, Anna turned back for the final dance.

When the applause died and the lights came up, she was composed. Inside, her emotions were still churning, but she blamed that on the story. Without a sign that she'd been moved, she accepted Daniel's hand as he drew her to her feet.

"I can honestly say I've never enjoyed a ballet more." In the courtly manner he could draw out without warning, he brushed his lips over her knuckles. "Thank you, Anna."

Cautious, she cleared her throat. "You are welcome. If you'll excuse me, I have to get back to the others."

He kept her hand in his as they walked from the box. "I took the liberty of telling your friend Myra that I'd see you home."

"You—"

"It's the least I can do," he interrupted smoothly, "after you were nice enough to educate me. It made me wonder why you hadn't thought of going into teaching."

Her voice cooled as they walked down the stairs to the lobby. He was laughing at her, but she'd been laughed at before. "It isn't wise to take on responsibility for someone else without asking first. I might have had plans."

"I'm at your disposal."

She didn't lose her patience often, but she was close. "Mr. MacGregor—"

"Daniel."

Anna opened her mouth, then closed it again until she was certain she could be calm. "I appreciate the offer, but I can see myself home."

"Now, Anna, you've already accused me of being rude once." He spoke cheerfully as he maneuvered her to his car. "What kind of man would I be if I didn't at least drive you home?"

"I think we both know the kind of man you are."

"True." He stopped just outside the door, where a few people still loitered. "Of course, if you're afraid, I'll get you a cab."

"Afraid?" The light came into her eyes. Passion, fire, temper, it didn't matter, Daniel was learning to love it. "You flatter yourself."

"Constantly." With a gesture, he indicated the door Steven was holding open. Too angry to think, Anna stepped inside and was struck by the warm, sultry scent of roses. Gritting her teeth, she swept them into her arms so that she could sit as close as possible to the far door. It only took an instant for her to realize Daniel was too overwhelming to make the distance viable.

"Do you always keep roses in your car?"

"Only when I'm escorting a beautiful woman."

She wished she had the heart to toss them out the window. "You planned this carefully, didn't you?"

Daniel drew the cork out of the chilled champagne. "No use planning if you're not careful."

"Myra tells me I should be flattered."

"My impression of Myra is that she's a smart woman. Where would you like to go?"

"Home." She accepted the wine and sipped to steady her nerves. "I have to get up early in the morning. I'm working at the hospital."

"Working?" He turned to frown at her as he settled the bottle back in its bed of ice. "Didn't you say you had another year before you'd finished your training?"

"Another year before I have my degree and start my

internship. Right now, my training also includes emptying bedpans.''

"That's nothing a young woman like you should be doing.'' Daniel tossed back the first glass of champagne and poured another.

"I assure you, I'll take your opinion for what it's worth.''

"You can't tell me you enjoy it.''

"I can tell you I enjoy knowing I've done something to help someone else.'' She drank again and held out her glass. "That may be difficult for you to understand, since it is not business. It's humanity.''

He could have corrected her then. He could have pointed out that he'd donated enormous funds toward setting up medical services for the miners in his region of Scotland. It wasn't something his accountant had advised, but something he'd had to do. Instead, Daniel focused on the one thing designed to make her furious.

"You should be thinking about marriage and a family.''

"Because a woman isn't able to handle anything more than a toddler tugging on her apron while another's growing under it?''

His brow lifted. He supposed he should be used to the blunt way American women phrased things. "Because a woman's meant to make a home and a family. A man has it easy, Anna. He only has to go out and make money. A woman holds the world in her hands.''

The way he said it made it difficult for her to spit back at him. Struggling for calm, she sat back. "Did it ever occur to you that a man doesn't have to make a choice between having a family or having a career?''

"No.''

She nearly laughed as she turned to look at him. "Of course, it didn't. Why should it? Take my advice, Daniel, look for a woman who doesn't have any doubts about what she was meant to do. Find one who doesn't have windmills to battle.''

"I can't do that.''

She had a half smile on her face, but it faded quickly. What she saw in his eyes sent both panic and excitement rushing through her. "Oh, no.'' She said it quickly and drained her glass. "That's ridiculous.''

"Maybe.'' He cupped her face in his hand and watched her eyes widen. "Maybe not. But either way, I've picked you, Anna Whitfield, and I mean to have you.''

"You don't pick a woman the way you pick a tie.'' She tried to summon up both dignity and indignation, but her heart was beating much too fast.

"No, you don't.'' He found the sudden breathlessness in her voice arousing and skimmed a thumb along her jaw to feel the warmth. "And a man doesn't treasure a piece of cloth the way he'll treasure a woman.''

"I think you've lost your mind.'' She put her hand to his wrist, but his hand didn't budge. "You don't even know me.''

"I'm going to know you better.''

"I don't have time for this.'' She looked around, frantic, and saw they were still several blocks from her home. He was a madman, she decided. What was she doing in the back of a Rolls with a madman?

Her unexpected jolt of panic pleased him. "For what?'' he murmured, and stroked a thumb down her cheek.

"For any of this.'' Perhaps she should humor him. No, she had to be firm. "Flowers, champagne, moonlight. It's obvious you're trying to be romantic, and I—''

"Should be quiet for just a minute,'' he told her, and decided the point by closing his mouth over hers.

Anna gripped the roses in her lap until a thorn pierced

her skin. She never noticed. How could she have guessed his mouth would be so soft or so quietly clever? A man of his size should have been awkward or overbearing when he wrapped his arms around a woman. Daniel gathered her to him as if he'd done so countless times. His beard brushed her face and sensitized her skin while she struggled to remain unmoved. Her fingers itched to comb through his beard, and she reached for him before common sense could prevent it.

Something hot and fierce leaped inside her. Passion she'd kept firmly controlled, strictly in bounds strained free to make a mockery out of everything she had once believed of herself. If he were mad, then so was she. With a moan that was part protest, part confusion, she gripped his shoulders and hung on.

He'd expected a fight, indignation at the least. He'd thought she might pull herself away and level one of those cool looks to put him in his place. Instead, she pressed against him and made his impulsive demand flare like a torch in high wind. He hadn't known she could peel away his control with such delicate fingers and leave him stripped and vulnerable. He hadn't known she would make him want with such gut-wrenching desire. She was just a woman, one he'd chosen to complete his plans for success and power. She wasn't supposed to make him forget everything but the feel and taste of her.

He knew what it was to want—a woman, wealth, power. Now, with Anna pressed to him, with the scent of roses filling his head and the taste of her filling his soul, she was all those things in one. To want her was to want everything.

She was breathless when they drew apart, breathless, aroused and frightened. To combat her weakness, Anna fell back on dignity. "Your manners continue to be crude, Daniel."

He could still see the dregs of passion in her eyes, still feel it vibrating from her, or himself. "You'll have to accept me as I am, Anna."

"I don't have to accept you at all." Dignity, she told herself. At all costs, she needed to preserve some semblance of dignity. "A kiss in the back seat of a car means nothing more than the time it takes to accomplish it." It wasn't until that moment that she realized they were parked in front of her house. How long? she wondered. If color surged into her cheeks, she told herself it was anger. She fumbled with the door handle before the driver could come around and open it for her.

"Take the roses, Anna. They suit you."

She only looked over her shoulder and glared. "Goodbye, Daniel."

"Good night," he corrected, and watched her run up the walk with the pale blue dress swirling around her legs. The roses lay on the seat beside him. Picking one up, he tapped it against his lips. The bloom wasn't as soft as she was or as sweet. He let it fall again. She'd left them behind, but he'd just send them to her in the morning, perhaps with another dozen added. He'd only begun.

His hand wasn't quite steady when he picked up the bottle of champagne. Daniel filled his glass to the rim and downed it in one long swallow.

Chapter Three

The next morning Anna was at work at the hospital. The time she spent there brought her part pleasure, part frustration. She'd never been able to explain to anyone, neither her parents nor her friends, the excitement she felt when she walked into a hospital. There was no one who would understand the satisfaction she gained from knowing she was part of it—the learning and the healing.

Most people thought of hospitals with dread. To them, the white walls, glaring lights and smell of antiseptics meant sickness, even death. To Anna, they meant life and hope. The hours she spent there each week only made her more determined to be a part of the medical community, just as the hours she spent each week poring over medical books and journals made her more determined to learn everything there was to learn.

She had a dream that she'd never been able to share with anyone. To Anna, it was both simple and pretentious: she

wanted to make a difference. To accomplish her dream, she
had to devote years of her life to learning.

Working as a layman, sorting linen, dispensing magazines, she still learned. Anna watched interns drag themselves through rounds after snatches of sleep. A great many
of them wouldn't make it to a residency no matter how
high their marks had been in medical school. But she
would. Anna watched, listened and made up her mind.

She learned something else, something she was determined never to forget. The backbone of the hospital wasn't
the surgeons or the interns. It wasn't the administrators,
though they dispensed the budget and made the policies. It
was the nursing staff. The doctors examined and diagnosed,
but the nurses, Anna thought, the nurses healed. They spent
hours on their feet, walked miles of corridor each day.
Whatever hat they were wearing—clerk, maid, cleaning
woman or comforter—Anna saw the same thing: dedica-
tion, often laced with fatigue. The interns were run ragged
to weed out the weak. The nursing staff was just run ragged.

It was then, the summer before her last year of medical
school that Anna made herself a promise. She would be a
doctor, a surgeon, but she would be one with a nurse's
compassion.

"Oh, Miss Whitfield." Mrs. Kellerman, the senior nurse,
stopped Anna with a brisk hand signal, then finished filling
out a chart. She'd been a nurse as long as she'd been a
widow, twenty years. At fifty she was as tough as iron and
as tireless as an adolescent. Kellerman was as gentle with
her patients as she was hard on her nurses. "Mrs. Higgs in
521 was asking about you."

Anna shifted the stack of magazines she carried. Five
twenty-one would be her first stop. "How is she today?"

"Stable," Kellerman answered without looking up. She

was in the middle of a ten-hour shift and hadn't time for chitchat. "She spent a restful night."

Anna bit back a sigh. She knew Kellerman would have checked Mrs. Higgs's chart personally and could have given her exact information. She also knew Kellerman's opinion of the system. Women were meant to function in certain areas, men in others. There was no crossover. Rather than question Kellerman, Anna walked down the hall. She'd see for herself.

The blinds were open in Mrs. Higgs's room. Sunlight poured through and slashed brilliantly over white walls, white sheets. The radio was on low. Mrs. Higgs lay quietly in the bed. Her thin face was lined more deeply than it should have been on a woman not yet sixty. Her hair was thinning, the gray dull and yellowing. The spots of rouge she'd applied that morning stood out like fire on her pale cheeks. Though her color made Anna apprehensive, she knew everything was being done that could be done. At the end of each of her frail hands, Mrs. Higgs's nails were tinted deep red. It made Anna smile. Mrs. Higgs had told her once that she could lose her looks, but never her vanity.

Because the woman's eyes were closed, Anna shut the door quietly. After setting down her magazines, she walked to the chart at the foot of the bed.

As Kellerman had said, Mrs. Higgs was stable—no better, no worse than she had been for more than a week. Her blood pressure was a bit low and she was still unable to hold solid food, but she'd passed the night comfortably. Satisfied, Anna moved to the window to draw the shades.

"No, dear, I like the sun."

Anna turned and found Mrs. Higgs smiling at her. "I'm sorry. Did I wake you?"

"No, I was dreaming a bit." The pain was always there,

but Mrs. Higgs continued to smile as she held out a hand. "I was hoping you'd come by today."

"Oh, I had to." Anna took a seat beside the bed. "I borrowed one of my mother's fashion magazines. Wait until you see what Paris has in store for us for the fall."

With a laugh, Mrs. Higgs turned off the radio. "They'll never top the twenties. That was fashion with daring. Of course, you had to have good legs and nerve." She managed a wink. "I did."

"You still do."

"The nerve, not the legs." Sighing, Mrs. Higgs shifted. Anna was up immediately to rearrange her pillows. "I miss being young, Anna."

"I wish I were older."

Mrs. Higgs sat back, weak, and let Anna arrange her covers. "Don't wish the years away."

"Not years." Anna sat on the edge of the bed. "Just this next one."

"You'll have your degree in the blink of an eye. Then there will be times you'll miss all the work and confusion you went through to get it."

"I'll have to take your word for it." Efficient and unobtrusive, Anna took her pulse. "Right now, all I can think about is getting through the summer and starting again."

"Being young is like having a wonderful gift and not being quite sure what to do with it. Do you know the pretty nurse, the tall one with the red hair?"

Reedy, Anna thought as she moved her fingers from the woman's wrist. She recalled from the chart that Mrs. Higgs wasn't due to have medication for an hour. "I've seen her."

"She was helping me this morning. Such a sweet thing. She's getting married soon. I liked hearing her talk about her sweetheart. You never do."

"I never do what?"

"Talk about your sweetheart."

There were a few tired-looking flowers in a glass next to the bed. Anna knew one of the nurses must have brought them in, because Mrs. Higgs had no family. Leaning over, she tried to perk them up. "I don't have one."

"Oh, I don't believe that. A lovely young woman like you must have a handful of sweethearts."

"They distract me when they line up at my door," Anna told her, then grinned when the older woman chuckled.

"Not far from the truth, I imagine. I was only twenty-five when I lost my husband. I thought, I'll never marry again. Of course, I had sweethearts." A little dreamy, a little sad, Mrs. Higgs stared up at the ceiling. "I could tell you stories that would shock you."

With a laugh, Anna tossed back her hair. The sunlight slanted across her eyes, making them deeper, warmer. "You couldn't shock me, Mrs. Higgs."

"I was a dreadful tease, I'm afraid, but I had so much fun. Now, I wish…"

"What do you wish, Mrs. Higgs?"

"I wish I'd married one of them. I wish I married one and had children. Then there'd be someone who'd care and remember me."

"You have people who care, Mrs. Higgs." Anna reached for her hand again. "I care."

She wouldn't give in to the pain, or worse, the self-pity. Mrs. Higgs gave Anna's hand a quick squeeze. "But there must be a man in your life. Someone special."

"No one special. There is a man," Anna continued in a cooler tone. "He's just a nuisance."

"What man isn't? Tell me about him."

Because the tired eyes had brightened, Anna decided to humor her. "His name is Daniel MacGregor."

"Is he handsome?"

"No—yes." Anna shrugged her shoulders then dropped her chin on her hand. "He's not the kind of man you'd see in a magazine, but he's certainly not ordinary. He's more than six foot, about six three, I'd say."

"Big shoulders?" Mrs. Higgs asked, perking up.

"Definitely." She had decided to make him sound larger than life for Mrs. Higgs's sake, then realized she didn't have to exaggerate. "He looks like he could heft two grown men on each one."

Delighted, Mrs. Higgs settled back. "I always liked big men."

Anna started to scowl, then admitted to herself that her description of Daniel was better for Mrs. Higgs than the Paris fashions. "He has red hair," she continued, then waited a beat, "and a beard."

"A beard!" Mrs. Higgs's eyes brightened. "How dashing."

"No…" The image of Daniel came to her mind much too easily. "It's more ferocious. But he does have lovely eyes. They're very blue." She frowned again, remembering. "He tends to stare."

"A bold one." Mrs. Higgs nodded approval. "I could never abide a wishy-washy man. What does he do?"

"He's a businessman. A successful one. Arrogant."

"Better and better. Now, tell me why he's a nuisance."

"He won't take a simple no for an answer." Restless, Anna rose and walked to the window. "I made it very clear to him that I wasn't interested."

"Which has made him determined to change your mind."

"Something like that." *I've picked you, Anna Whitfield. I mean to have you.* "He's sent me flowers every day this week."

"What kind?"

Amused, Anna turned back. "Roses, white roses."

"Oh." Mrs. Higgs gave a sigh that was young and yearning. "It's been too many years to count since someone sent me roses."

Touched, Anna studied her face. Mrs. Higgs was tiring. "I'll be glad to bring you some of mine. They do smell wonderful."

"You're a sweet child, but it's not the same is it? There was a time…" Her words trailed off, and she shook her head. "Well, that's passed now. Perhaps you should take a closer look at this Daniel. It's never wise to toss away affection."

"I'll have more time for affection after I finish my internship."

"We always think we'll have more time." With another sigh, Mrs. Higgs let her eyes close. "I'm betting on Daniel," she murmured, and drifted off to sleep.

Anna watched her a moment. Leaving Mrs. Higgs with the sunlight and the magazine from Paris, Anna left, closing the door behind her.

Hours later, Anna walked out into the afternoon light. Her feet were tired, but her spirits were high. She'd spent the last part of her shift in maternity, listening to new mothers and holding babies. She wondered how long it would be before she'd be in on a delivery and share in bringing in new life.

"You're even lovelier when you smile."

Startled, Anna spun around. Daniel was leaning against the hood of a dark blue convertible. He was dressed more casually than she'd seen him before, in slacks and a shirt open at the collar. As the light breeze ruffled his hair, he grinned at her. He looked, though she hated to admit it, wonderful. While she hesitated, trying to gauge the best way to handle him, Daniel straightened and walked to her.

"Your father told me you'd be here." She looked so... competent, he decided, in the dark skirt and white blouse. Not as delicate as she'd looked in the rose or blue gowns, but every bit as lovely.

In a casual gesture, she tucked her hair behind her ear. "Oh. I didn't realize you were well acquainted with my father."

"Now that Ditmeyer's district attorney, I needed another lawyer."

"My father." Anna struggled with a surge of temper. "I certainly hope you haven't retained him because of me."

Daniel's smile was slow and easy. Yes, every bit as lovely. "I don't mix business with personal matters, Anna. You haven't answered any of my calls."

This time she smiled. "No."

"Your manners surprise me."

"They shouldn't, considering your own, but in any case, I did send you a note."

"I don't consider a formal request for me to stop sending you flowers communication."

"You haven't stopped sending them, either."

"No. You've been working all day?"

"Yes. So now, if you'll excuse me—"

"I'll drive you home."

She inclined her head in the cool manner he'd come to wait for. "That's very kind of you, but it isn't necessary. It's a lovely day and I don't live far."

"All right, I'll walk with you."

She discovered she was gritting her teeth. Deliberately Anna relaxed. "Daniel, I'm sure I've made myself clear."

"Aye, that you have. And I've made myself clear. So—" he took both of her hands in his "—it's just a matter of seeing which one of us holds out the longest. I intend for it to be me. There isn't any harm in our getting to know each other better, is there?''

''I'm sure there is.'' She began to see one of the reasons he was so successful in business. When he chose, the charm just oozed out of him. It wasn't every man who could lay down a challenge with a friendly smile. ''You have to let go of my hands.''

''Of course…if you'll take a drive with me.''

The light came into her eyes. ''I don't respond to bribes.''

''Fair enough.'' Because he was coming to respect her and because he still intended to win, he released her hands. ''Anna, it's a lovely afternoon. Take a drive with me. Fresh air and sunshine are good for you, aren't they?''

''They are.'' Where was the harm? Maybe if she humored him a bit, she'd be able to convince him to put his considerable energy elsewhere. ''All right, a short drive then. You have a beautiful car.''

''I like it, though Steven pouts whenever I go out without him and the Rolls. Pitiful thing for a grown man to pout.'' He started to open the door for her then stopped. ''Do you drive?''

''Of course.''

''Fine.'' Daniel drew the keys out of his pocket and handed them to her.

''I don't understand. You want me to drive?''

''Unless you'd rather not.''

Her fingers curled around the keys. ''I'd love to, but how do you know I'm not reckless?''

He stared at her a moment then burst into delighted laughter. Before she realized it, he swung her up and in two dizzying circles. ''Anna Whitfield, I'm crazy about you.''

"Crazy," she muttered, trying to straighten her skirt and her dignity when her feet touched the ground again.

"Come along, Anna." He plopped into the passenger seat with a wicked grin. "My life and my car are in your hands."

With a toss of her head, she rounded the hood and took her own seat. Unable to resist, she sent him a coolly wicked smile. "A gambler are you, Daniel?"

"Aye." He settled back as the engine sprang to life. "Why don't you head out of town a bit? The air's fresher."

A mile, she told herself as she pulled away from the curb. Two at the most.

Soon, they had somehow gotten ten miles out of town and laughing.

"It's wonderful," she called over the wind. "I've never driven a convertible before."

"Suits you."

"I'll remember that when I decide to buy one of my own." She caught her bottom lip between her teeth as she negotiated a curve. "I just might look into it soon. I'll be moving into an apartment closer to the hospital, but a car is handy."

"You're moving out of your parents' home?"

"Next month." She nodded. "They didn't object as much as I'd anticipated. I suppose the best thing I ever did was to go to college out of state. All I have to do is convince them they don't have to furnish it for me."

"I don't like the idea of you living alone."

She turned her head briefly. "That isn't an issue, of course, but in any case, I'm a grown woman. You live alone, don't you?"

"That's different."

"Why?"

He opened his mouth, then shut it again. Why? Because,

although he didn't worry about himself, he'd worry about her. However, that wasn't a reason she'd accept. He'd learned that much about Anna. "I don't live alone," he corrected her. "I have servants." Smug, he waited for her argument.

"I don't think I'll have room for any. Look how green the grass is."

"You're changing the subject."

"Yes, I am. Do you often take afternoons off?"

"No." He grumbled a bit, then decided to let it drop. He could always check out her apartment for himself and make certain it was safe. If it wasn't he could damn well buy it. "But I decided catching you at the hospital was the only way to see you alone again."

"I could have said no."

"Aye. I was betting you wouldn't. What do you do in there? You can't stick needles and knives in people yet."

She laughed again. The wind smelled delicious. "For the most part I visit patients, talk to them, pass out magazines. I may help sort or change linen if they need me."

"That's not what you're going to school for."

"No, but I'm learning nonetheless. Doctors or even the nurses can't give patients a lot of personal attention, simply because of lack of time and too much volume. I'm free to do that now, if only for a short while. And it helps me understand what it's like to lie there hour after hour, sick, uncomfortable or just bored. I'm going to remember that when I start my practice."

He'd never thought of it just that way before, but he did remember the lingering illness that had taken his mother when he'd been ten. He remembered, too, how difficult it had been for her to be confined to bed. The sickroom smell was just as clear to him now as the scent of the mines.

"Doesn't it bother you to be around sick people all the time?"

"If it didn't bother me, I wouldn't feel the need to be a doctor."

Daniel watched the way the wind tossed her hair back away from her face. He'd loved his mother, had sat with her every day, but he'd dreaded facing her illness and watching her fade. Anna, young, vital, was choosing to spend her life facing illness. "I don't understand you."

"I don't always understand myself."

"Tell me why you go into that hospital every day."

She thought of her dream. Why would he understand when no one else did? Then she thought of Mrs. Higgs. Perhaps he could understand that. "There's a woman in the hospital now. A couple of weeks ago they operated, removed a tumor and part of her liver. I know she's in pain, but she hardly ever complains. She needs to talk, and I can give her that. It's all the doctoring I can do now."

"But it's important."

She turned to him again, and her eyes were dark and intense. "Yes, to both of us. Today she was telling me that she wished she'd married again after her husband died. She wants someone to remember her. Her body's giving up, but her mind's so sharp. Today I was telling her about you—"

"You talked about me."

She could've bitten her tongue. Instead, Anna carefully explained. "Mrs. Higgs got on the subject of men, and I told her I knew one who was a nuisance."

He took her hand and kissed it. "Thank you."

Fighting amusement, she increased her speed. "Anyway, I described you. She was impressed."

"How did you describe me?"

"Are you vain as well, Daniel?"

"Absolutely."

"Arrogant, ferocious. I don't know if I remembered to include rude. The point is, if I can sit and talk to her for a few minutes every day, bring a little of the outside world into her room, it makes it easier. A doctor has to remember that diagnosis and treatment aren't enough. Maybe they're nothing at all without compassion."

"I don't think you'll forget that."

She felt a tug at her heart. "You're trying to flatter me again."

"No. I'm trying to understand you."

"Daniel..." How did she deal with him now? She could handle the arrogance, the flamboyance, even the demands. But how did she deal with the kindness? "If you really want to understand me, you'll listen to me. Earning my degree, starting my practice aren't just the most important things in my life. For now, they're the only things. I've wanted this too long, worked too hard to be distracted from it by anything or anyone."

He trailed a finger down her shoulder. "Are you finding me a distraction, Anna?"

"It isn't a joke."

"No, none of it is. I want you to be my wife."

The car swerved as her hands went limp on the wheel. Hitting the brakes, Anna came to a screeching halt in the middle of the road.

"Does this mean yes?" Because he enjoyed the blatant shock on her face, he grinned.

It took her another ten seconds to find her voice. No, he wasn't joking. He was insane. "You're out of your mind. We've known each other a week, seen each other a handful of times and you're proposing marriage. If you go into business deals with this kind of abandon I can't understand why you're not bankrupt."

"Because I know which deal to make and which to toss

out. Anna—'' he reached out and took her shoulders ''—I could have waited to ask you, but I don't see the point when I'm sure.''

''You're sure?'' With a long breath she tried to control the chaos of emotions inside her. ''It may interest you to know that it takes two people to make a marriage. Two willing, dedicated people who love each other.''

He dismissed that. ''There are two of us.''

''I don't want to get married, not to you, not to anyone. I have another year of school, my internship, my residency.''

''I may not like the idea of you becoming a doctor—'' nor was he convinced she'd pull it off ''—but I'm willing to make some concessions.''

''Concessions?'' Her eyes went nearly opaque with temper. ''My career is not a concession.'' Her voice was entirely too calm, too quiet. ''I've tried to be reasonable with you, Daniel, but you simply don't listen. Try to get this through your head. You're wasting your time.''

He drew her closer, aroused by her temper, infuriated by her rejection. ''It's mine to waste.''

Not as gently as he had before, nor as patiently, he crushed his mouth to hers. She might have resisted; he didn't know. In that moment Daniel was too absorbed in the needs churning inside of him, the emotions swirling through him to be aware of compliance or objection.

Her lips were warmed from the strong sun, her skin soft from whatever female magic she performed on it. He wanted her. It was no longer a matter of his choosing or his planning. Desire overwhelmed, enclosed and ruled him.

This is how she'd thought he would be: strong, demanding, dangerous, exciting. She couldn't make herself object, though she knew it should have been simple. Cold. How could she be cold when her body had so suddenly turned to fire? Unfeeling. How could she not feel the sensations racing through her? Despite all logic, despite all will, she melted against him. In melting, she gave more than she'd known she had. She took more than she'd known she wanted.

She'd want again. While her blood thudded frantically in her head, she knew it. As long as he was near, as long as she could remember his touch, she'd want again. How could she stop it? Why did she want to? There were answers. She was sure there were answers if only she could find them. It was logic she needed, but the weakness took over until she was lost in the power they made together.

When strength returned, it was entwined with passion. But passion, she could control. Fighting regrets, Anna pulled away. She straightened in the seat and stared directly ahead until she was certain she could speak.

"I'm not going to see you again."

The first prick of fear surprised him. Daniel shoved it away and turned her face toward his. "We both know that's not true."

"I mean what I say."

"I'm sure of it. But it's not true."

"Damn you, Daniel, no one can tell you anything."

It was the first time he'd heard her lash out in anger, and though she quickly controlled herself, he saw that her temper was something to respect.

"Even if I were in love with you, which I'm not," she continued, "nothing could come of it."

He twisted a lock of her hair around his finger and released it. "We'll just wait and see."

"We won't—" She broke off and jumped as a horn blared. A car bumped along beside them. The elderly man driving paused long enough to glare at them and shout something that was lost under the sound of his motor as he went around them and continued down the road. When Daniel started to laugh, Anna laid her forehead on the steering wheel and joined him. She'd never known anyone who could make her so furious, make her so weak and still make her laugh.

"Daniel, this is the most ridiculous situation I've ever been in." Still chuckling, she lifted her head. "I'd almost believe we could be friends if you'd stop the rest of this business."

"We will be friends." He leaned over and kissed her lightly before she could move away. "I want a wife, a family. There comes a time when a man needs those things, or nothing else is worthwhile."

She folded her arms on the wheel and rested her chin on them. Calm again, she stared off into the tall grass along the road. "I believe that—for you. I also believe that you made up your mind to marry and set out looking for the most suitable woman to fit the bill."

He shifted, uncomfortable. It wouldn't be easy to have a wife who could read you that well. But he'd picked Anna. "Why do you think that?"

"Because it's all business to you." She gave him a steady look. "One way or the other."

He wouldn't evade—couldn't with her. "Maybe so. The thing is, you fit. Only you."

Sighing, she leaned back. "Marriage isn't a business transaction, or it shouldn't be. I can't help you, Daniel." Anna started the car again. "It's time we went back."

He laid a hand lightly on her shoulder before she began the turn. "It's too late to go back, Anna. For both of us."

Chapter Four

Lightning snaked across the sky and thunder rumbled, but the rain held off. The night, though summer had barely begun, was almost sultry. Now and again the wind moved through the trees with no sound and no power to cool the air. Enjoying the heat and the threat of a storm, Myra stopped in front of the Ditmeyers' with a high-pitched squeal of brakes.

"What a dreadful noise." She flipped down the mirror on her visor to check her face. "I really must get that fixed."

"Your face?" Anna's bland smile was answered with easy good humor.

"Before it's over, certainly, but immediately, that nasty noise."

"You might try driving with a bit more...discretion," Anna suggested.

"Now what fun would that be?"

Laughing, Anna stepped from the car. "Remind me not to let you drive my new car."

"New car?" Myra let the door slam, then fussed with the strap of her dress. "When did you get a new car?"

It must be the air, she thought, that made her feel so restless, so reckless. "I was thinking perhaps tomorrow."

"Great. I'll go with you. A new apartment, a new car." Myra linked arms with Anna as they strolled up the walk. The scent of their perfumes, one subtle, one flamboyant, merged. "What's come over our quiet little Anna?"

"A taste of freedom." Tossing her head back, she looked at the sky. It boiled with clouds. Excitement. "One taste and I've discovered I'm insatiable."

It wasn't a word Myra associated with Anna, except when it came to her studies. Unless she missed her guess, her friend's thoughts had strayed from her medical journals. Speculating, she touched her tongue to her top lip. "I wonder just how much Daniel MacGregor has to do with it."

Anna paused to lift a brow before she rang the bell. She recognized the look in Myra's eye and knew just how to handle it. "What would he have to do with my buying a new car?"

"I was thinking about the insatiable."

It was difficult to keep her face sober, but Anna managed to ignore the wicked smile Myra tossed her. "You're looking around the wrong corner, Myra. I've just decided I want to drive back to Connecticut in style."

"Something red," Myra decided. "And flashy."

"No, something white, I think. And classy."

"It'll suit you, won't it?" With a sigh, Myra stepped back to study Anna. Her dress was the color of the inside of a peach, very pale, very warm, with the sleeves thin and cuffed at the wrists. "If I tried to wear a dress that color,

I'd fade into the wallpaper. You look like something in a bakery window."

With another laugh, Anna took her arm again. "I didn't come here to be nibbled on. In any case, flashy suits you, Myra, the way it suits no one else."

Pleased, Myra pursed her lips. "Yes, it does, doesn't it?"

When the Ditmeyers' butler opened the door, Anna swept inside. She couldn't explain why she felt so good. Maybe it was because her routine at the hospital was becoming more and more rewarding. Maybe it was the letter from Dr. Hewitt and the fascinating new surgical technique he'd told her of. It certainly had nothing to do with the white roses that continued to arrive every day.

"Mrs. Ditmeyer."

Stout and formidable in lavender voile, Louise Ditmeyer came to greet both of her guests. "Anna, how lovely you look." She stopped to study Anna's pale peach dress. "Just lovely," she continued. "Pastels are so suitable for a young girl. And, Myra..." She swept a glance down Myra's vivid emerald-green silk. The disapproval was evident in her gaze. "How are you?"

"Very well, thank you," Myra said sweetly. *Silly old fish.*

"You're looking wonderful, Mrs. Ditmeyer." Anna spoke up quickly, well able to read Myra's thoughts. To keep her friend in line, she gave her the tiniest of nudges in the ribs. "I hope we're not too early."

"Not at all. There are several people in the salon. Come along." She swept along ahead of them.

"Looks like a battleship," Myra muttered.

"Then watch your mouth or you'll get torpedoed."

"I do hope your parents are coming." Mrs. Ditmeyer paused in the doorway and took a pleased survey of her guests.

"They wouldn't miss it," Anna assured her, and wondered if anyone would dare tell Louise Ditmeyer that lavender made her look jaundiced.

Mrs. Ditmeyer signaled to a servant. "Charles, some sherry for the young ladies. I'm sure you two can mingle on your own. So much to do." With that, she was bustling off.

Feeling aggressive, Myra sauntered up to the bar. "Make it bourbon, Charles."

"And a martini," Anna put in. "Dry. Behave yourself, Myra. I know she's annoying, but she's Herbert's mother."

"Easy for you to say." With a mumble, Myra took her drink. "As far as she's concerned, you've got halo and wings."

Anna winced at the description. "You're exaggerating."

"All right, just the halo then."

"Would it help if I spilled my drink on the carpet?" Anna plucked out the olive.

"You wouldn't," Myra began, then gasped as Anna tilted her glass. "No!" Myra righted it with a giggle. "I'd forgotten how easily you take a dare." She took the olive from Anna and ate it herself. "I wouldn't mind so much if you spilled it on the dragon, but the carpet's too lovely. Poor Herbert." She turned to study the other guests. "There he is now, cornered by that didactic, man-hunting Mary O'Brian. You know, he is attractive in an intellectual sort of way. It's a pity he's so…"

"So what?"

"Good," Myra concluded. "Now then." She lifted her glass to hide her grin. "There's someone I don't think anyone would call good."

She didn't even have to turn. The room seemed smaller all at once, and warmer. Warmer and charged. She felt the excitement, remembered the thrill. For a moment, she panicked. The terrace doors were to her right. She could be through them and away in an instant. She'd make an excuse later, any excuse.

"My, my." Myra laid a hand on Anna's arm and felt her tremble. "You've got it bad."

Furious with herself, Anna set her glass down then picked it up again. "Don't be ridiculous."

Amusement mixed with concern. "Anna, it's me. The one who loves you best."

"He's persistent, that's all. Outrageously persistent. It makes me nervous."

"All right." Myra knew better than to try to budge Anna off course. "We'll leave it at that for now. But since it seems to me that you need a minute to pull yourself together, let's go rescue Herbert."

Anna didn't argue. She did need a minute. An hour. Maybe years. It didn't matter that she'd considered and weighed her reaction to Daniel and had judged it to be purely physical. The reaction remained, and it grew each time she saw him. She didn't care for the edgy excitement he could bring to her just by being in the same room, so she would ignore him and relax. It had always been possible for her to control the reactions of her body. Breathe slowly, she told herself. Concentrate on individual muscles. The strain in her shoulders eased. They were, after all, at a very proper dinner party surrounded by other people. It wasn't as if they were sitting in a parked car on a lonely road. Her stomach tightened.

"Hello, Herbert." Myra eased her way to his side. "Mary."

"Myra." Obviously annoyed with the interruption, Mary turned to Anna. As she did, Herbert rolled his eyes. Amused and sympathetic, Myra tucked her arm through his. "Put any good criminals in jail lately?"

Before he could comment, Mary sent Myra a withering look. "Really, you make it sound like a game. Herbert is a very important part of our judicial system."

"Really?" Myra arched a brow as only she could. "And I thought he just tossed crooks in the slammer."

"Regularly." Herbert quipped, his voice dry, his look solemn. He nodded at Myra. "I do my best to make sure the streets are safe. You should see the notches on my briefcase."

Delighted he could play the game, Myra leaned closer and batted her lashes. "Oh, Herbert, I simply *adore* tough guys."

It was, unfortunately, a fiendishly clever mimicry of Cathleen Donahue, Mary's closest friend. She sniffed and stiffened. "If you'll excuse me."

"I think her nose is out of joint." Myra looked wide-eyed and innocent. "Anna, what's your medical opinion?"

"Terminal cattiness." Anna patted Myra's cheek. "Careful, love, it's catching."

"Quite a performance."

Anna froze, then forced herself to relax. How could she have guessed that such a big man could move so quietly?

"Good evening, Mr. MacGregor." Myra held out a friendly hand. The dinner party wouldn't be boring after all. "Did you enjoy the ballet?"

"Very much, but I liked your act every bit as much."

Herbert greeted Daniel with a quick handshake. "You'll find that Myra's never dull."

Flattered and surprised, Myra turned to him. "Why, thank you." Going with impulse, she made up her mind on the spot. She loved Anna like a sister. She decided to do what she thought best for her. "I think I could use another drink before dinner. You, too, Herbert." Without giving him a chance to agree, she pulled him along.

With a shake of his head, Daniel watched her maneuver Herbert through the crowd. "She's something."

Anna watched her steam toward the bar. "Oh, she's definitely something."

"I like your hair."

She nearly reached a hand up to it before she stopped herself. Because she hadn't had the time to fuss with it after her day at the hospital, she'd simply pulled it straight back. She'd hoped to look sophisticated at best, competent at the least. Her face was unframed and vulnerable. "Have you been to the Ditmeyers' before?"

"You're changing the subject again."

"Yes. Have you?"

A smile hovered around his mouth. "No."

"There's a wonderful collection of Waterford in the dining room. You should take a look at it when we go in to dinner."

"You like crystal?"

"Yes. It seems cold until the light hits it and then, there are so many surprises."

"If you agreed to have dinner with me at my home, I could show you mine."

She dismissed the first part of the statement as nonsense, but honed in on the second. "You collect?"

"I like pretty things."

The tone was clear. Her look was as direct and as calm as ever. "If that's a compliment, I'll take it for what it's worth. But I have no intention of being collected."

"I don't want you on a shelf or in a glass case. I just want you." He took her hand, tightening his fingers on hers when she would have drawn away. "You're skittish," he commented, and found that fact pleased him.

"Cautious." Without moving her head, Anna shifted her gaze to their joined hands. "You have my hand."

He intended to keep it. "Have you noticed how well yours fits into it?"

She brought her eyes back to his. "You have very large hands. Anyone's would fit into it."

"I think not." But he released her hand, only to take her arm.

"Daniel—"

"It looks like we're going in to dinner."

She couldn't eat. Anna's appetite was never large, which constantly made Myra grumble, but tonight it was nonexistent. At first, she'd thought it a trick of fate that Daniel was seated next to her at the long banquet table. But one look at his face and she was certain he'd arranged it. He made his way without problem through the seafood appetizer and the soup course while she nibbled for form's sake.

He was attentive, infuriatingly so, while all but ignoring the woman on his right. He leaned close and murmured to her, encouraged her to try a bit more of this, taste a bit of that. Forced by upbringing to keep her manners in place, Anna struggled for composure. Her parents were seated closer to the head of the table. From that direction she saw both speculation and approval. She set her teeth and tried to choke down beef Wellington. It didn't take her long to realize there was speculation going on at other points of the table as well. She caught the smiles, the nods, the whispers behind lifted hands. Daniel was making it clear, publicly, that he considered them a couple.

Her temper, always so well controlled, began to heat. Very deliberately Anna cut a piece of meat. "If you don't stop playing the lovesick suitor," she murmured, sending him a smile, "I'm going to knock my wineglass in your lap. You'll be very uncomfortable."

Daniel patted her hand. "No, you won't."

Anna took a deep breath and bided her time. As dessert

was served, she scooted her hand along the table and nudged. If he hadn't glanced down just at that instant, he'd have missed it and would have had a lapful of burgundy. He made a quick grab. The glass tilted the other way. Before he could right it, half the contents had splatted over the tablecloth. He heard Anna swear under her breath and nearly roared with laughter.

"Clumsy." He sent an apologetic look toward his hostess. "I've such big hands." Unrepentant, he used one of them to pat Anna's leg under the table. He thought, but couldn't be sure, that he heard her grind her teeth.

"Think nothing of it." Mrs. Ditmeyer surveyed the damage and decided it could have been worse. "That's what tablecloths are for. You haven't spilled any on yourself, have you?"

Daniel beamed at her, then at Anna. "Not a drop." As the buzz of conversation picked up again, Daniel leaned toward Anna. "Admirable and very quick. I find you more and more exciting."

"You'd have been more excited if my aim had been better."

He lifted his glass and touched it to hers. "What do you think our hostess would do if I were to kiss you right here, right now?"

Anna picked up her knife and examined it as though admiring the pattern. The look she sent Daniel was as tough as nails. "I know what I'd do."

This time he did laugh, loud and long. "I'll be damned, Anna, you're the only woman for me." His announcement carried easily down both ends of the table. "But I won't kiss you now. I don't want you trying your first surgery on me."

After dinner there was bridge in the parlor. Though she detested the game, Anna considered volunteering to keep herself occupied and in a group. Before she could manage it, she was urged along outside by a half dozen younger people.

The storm still threatened and the moon was covered with clouds, but the air was freshened by the building breeze. As the rain crept closer, the wind began to dance around her skirt. There were lights placed strategically here and there so that the trees and the garden were bathed in a muted glow. Someone had turned on the radio inside so that music flowed through the windows. The group started out wandering aimlessly, then slowly paired off.

"I wonder if you know much about gardens," Daniel asked her.

She hadn't expected to be rid of him easily. With a shrug, Anna kept several of her friends in view. "A bit."

"Steven's a better driver than a gardener." Daniel leaned over to sniff at a fat white peony. "He's neat enough, but he lacks imagination. I was hoping for something more…"

"Showy?" Anna suggested.

He liked the word. "Aye. Showy. Colorful. In Scotland we had the heather, and the brambles were full of wild roses. Not the pretty tame sort you buy at the flower shop, tough ones, with stems as thick as your thumbs and thorns that could rip a hole through you." Ignoring Anna's murmur of disapproval, he plucked off a bloom and tucked it behind her ear. "Delicate flowers are nice for looking at, for seeing in a woman's hair, but a wild rose—they last."

She'd forgotten she didn't want to be alone with him, forgotten to keep within a cautious distance of her friends. She wondered what a wild rose would smell like and if a man like Daniel would rip it out or leave it in the brambles to grow as it chose. "Do you miss Scotland?"

He looked down at her, for a moment lost in his own memories. "Sometimes. When I'm not too busy to think about it. I miss the cliffs and the sea and the grass that's greener than it has a right to be.''

It was in his voice, she realized. Mourning. She'd never thought it possible to mourn for land, only for people. ''Are you going to go back?'' She found herself needing to know and afraid of his answer.

He looked away a moment and the lightning flashed, reflecting fast and sharp on his face. Her heart thudded wildly. He looked the way she'd always imagined Thor would look—bold, ruthless, invulnerable. When he spoke, his voice was quiet and should have soothed her. She felt only more excitement. ''No. A man makes his own home in his own time.''

She ran a finger down a fragile vine of wisteria. Just a trick of the light, she told herself. It was silly to be moved by a trick of the light. ''Don't you have family there?''

''No.'' She thought she heard pain in his voice, pain that went deeper than mourning, but his face was impassive when she looked up. ''I'm the last of my line. I need sons, Anna.'' He didn't touch her. He didn't need to. ''I need sons and daughters. I want you to give them to me.''

Why, when he still spoke the outrageous, did it no longer seem so outrageous? Uneasy, Anna continued along the path. ''I don't want to argue with you, Daniel.''

''Good.'' He caught her around the waist and spun her again. The solemn look that had been in his eyes was replaced by a grin. ''We'll drive to Maryland and be married in the morning.''

''No!'' Though it wounded her dignity, she tried to wiggle away.

''All right. If you want a big wedding, I'll wait a week.''

''No, no, no!'' Why it struck her as funny, she didn't know, but she began to laugh as she pushed at his chest. ''Daniel MacGregor, under all that red hair, you have the hardest head known to man. I will *not* marry you tomorrow. I will not marry you in a week. I will not marry you ever.''

He lifted her off her feet so that their faces were level. When she got over her shock, Anna found it an odd and not entirely unpleasant sensation. ''Bet?'' he said simply.

Her brow lifted and her voice was cool as a mountain stream. ''I beg your pardon?''

''God, what a woman,'' he said, and kissed her hard. The visions that came and went in her head swirled so quickly that she couldn't separate them. ''If I didn't want to do the honorable thing, I swear I'd toss you over my shoulder and be done with it.'' Then he laughed and kissed her again. ''Instead I'll make you a wager.''

If he kissed her just once more, she'd be too giddy to remember her name. Clinging to dignity, she braced her hands on his shoulders and looked stern. ''Daniel, put me down.''

''Damned if I will,'' he said, and grinned at her.

''You'll be lame if you don't.''

He remembered her threat with the wineglass. A compromise, Daniel decided, and set her down, but he kept his hands around her waist. ''A wager,'' he repeated.

''I don't know what you're talking about.''

''You said I was a gambler, and right you were. What about you?''

She discovered her hands were resting against his chest and dropped them. ''Certainly not.''

''Hah!'' There was a dare in his eyes she found hard to resist. ''Now you lie. Any woman who takes herself off to be a doctor, thumbing her nose at the system, has gambling in her blood.''

And right he was. She tilted her head. ''What's the wager?''

''There's a lass.'' He would have lifted her off her feet

again if she hadn't narrowed her eyes at him. "I say you'll have my ring on your finger within the year."

"And I say I won't."

"If I win, you spend the first week as my wife in bed. We'll do nothing but eat, sleep and make love."

If he'd meant to shock her, he'd fallen short of the mark. Anna merely nodded "And if you lose?"

His eyes were alive with the challenge, with the taste of victory. "Name it."

Her lips curved. She believed in making the stakes high. "You give a grant to the hospital, enough for a new wing."

He didn't hesitate. "Done."

If she was sure of anything, it was that he would keep his word, no matter how absurd the circumstances. Solemnly she extended her hand. Daniel took it for the official shake, then brought it to his lips. "I've never gambled for higher stakes, nor will I again. Now let me kiss you, Anna." When she backed away, he caught her again. "We've set the wager and named the stakes, but what are the odds?" He brushed his lips against her temple and felt her shiver. "Aye, Anna, my love, what are the odds?"

Slowly he skimmed his mouth over her skin, teasing, promising, but never quite meeting her mouth. His hands, at once gentle and confident, roamed up her back to toy with the sensitive skin of her neck, then retreat again to her waist. He could feel the instant when her body gave in to its own needs and to his. He could feel his own climb higher. But he continued slowly, effortlessly to seduce.

The thunder rumbled again, but she thought it was her own heartbeat. When lightning flashed, it was like the fire in her own blood. What was passion? What was need? What was emotion? How could she tell when no man had ever brought her any of those things with such intensity before? She knew it was vital to separate them, but they flowed together into one incandescent sensation.

This was beauty. As her body went fluid, she recognized it. This was danger. When her muscles went lax, she accepted it.

His mouth brushed over hers again but didn't linger. Frustrated, edgy, she moaned and strained closer. Did he laugh, or was it the thunder again?

Then the skies opened and rain poured over them. With a curse, Daniel swooped her off her feet. "You owe me a kiss, Anna Whitfield," he shouted. He stood a moment while the rain poured down his wild mane of hair. The lightning was in his eyes. "Don't think I'll forget." With that he bundled her close and ran for the terrace.

Was it any wonder she was distracted in the hospital the next day? Anna found herself walking down corridors, then having to stop and sort out where she was going and what she was doing. It worried her. It infuriated her. What if she had her degree, if she had patients and became so easily rattled? She simply couldn't permit herself to think of anything but her duties as long as she was in the hospital.

But she remembered the wild thrill of being carried in Daniel's arms through the pounding summer storm. She remembered, too, the way he'd burst through the terrace doors and sent the quiet bridge game into chaos by demanding towels and a brandy for her. It should have been humiliating. Anna had found it sweet. That was something else that worried her. Thinking of how Louise Ditmeyer's eyes had widened like saucers, Anna smothered a laugh. He'd certainly added spice to a sedate dinner party.

She spent the majority of her day in the wards, bringing books and magazines to the patients and talking to them as they lay in beds set side by side. Lack of privacy, Anna thought, could be as debilitating as the illnesses that had brought them there. But there was only so much room, so many doctors. She smiled a bit, thinking that the impulsive bet she'd made with Daniel would do some good.

With a glance at her watch, she realized she had less than an hour to meet Myra. Today, she'd pick out her new car. Something practical certainly, she reminded herself. But not dull. Maybe it was foolish to be excited over the purchase of four wheels and an engine, but she kept thinking of the long, solitary drives she'd take. She'd been speaking no less than the truth when she'd told Myra that she wanted freedom. She thought of it now and longed for it. Still, she couldn't leave for the day without stopping in on Mrs. Higgs.

Planning the rest of her day as she went, Anna made her way to the fifth floor. She'd take Myra out to dinner and splurge. There was nothing Myra would like better. Then maybe they'd drive out of town and give the new car a test. Some weekend soon they'd drive out to the beach and spend the day in the sun. Pleased with the idea, Anna swung through the door of 521. Her mouth fell open.

"Oh, Anna, we were afraid you wouldn't come by."

Sitting up in bed, eyes bright, Mrs. Higgs fussed with the edge of her sheet. On the table beside her was a vase of red roses, fresh, flamboyant and fragrant. Sitting beside the bed like a suitor was Daniel.

"I told you Anna wouldn't leave without coming in to see how you were." Daniel rose and offered her a chair.

"No, no, of course I wouldn't." Confused, Anna approached the bed. "You're looking well today."

Mrs. Higgs reached for her hair. The young redheaded nurse had helped her brush it that morning, but she hadn't been able to use a rinse for weeks. "I'd have fixed myself up a bit if I'd known I was having a caller." She looked at Daniel with nothing less than an adoring smile.

"You look lovely." He took one of her thin hands between both of his.

He sounded as though he meant it. What impressed Anna most was the fact that his voice carried none of the patronizing tone that so many people used when speaking with the ill or the old. Something flashed in Mrs. Higgs's eyes. It was both gratitude and pride.

"It's important to look your best when you have a gentleman caller. Isn't that right, Anna?"

"Yes, of course." Anna wandered to the foot of the bed and tried unobtrusively to read the chart. "The flowers are beautiful. You didn't mention you were coming to the hospital, Daniel."

He winked at Mrs. Higgs. "I like surprises."

"Wasn't it nice of your young man to come by and visit me?"

"He's not—" Anna caught herself and softened her voice. "Yes, yes, it was."

"Now I know you two want to run along, and I won't keep you." Mrs. Higgs spoke briskly, but her energy was flagging. "You'll come again?" She reached up for Daniel's hand. "I so enjoyed talking with you."

He heard the plea she tried so desperately to hide. "I'll come again." Leaning over, he kissed her cheek.

When he stepped back, Anna adjusted Mrs. Higgs's pillows and made her more comfortable with a few efficient moves. He saw then that Anna's hands weren't just soft, delicate things made to be kissed, but that they were competent, strong and sure. It brought him a moment's discomfort. "Now you try to rest. You mustn't tire yourself."

"Don't worry about me." Mrs. Higgs sighed. "Go have fun."

She was already dozing when they walked from the room.

"Are you done here for today?" Daniel asked as they started down the hall.

"Yes."

"I'll drive you home."

"No, I'm meeting Myra." As always the elevator was slow and temperamental. Anna pushed the button and waited.

"Then I'll drop you." He wanted her to himself, away from the hospital where she'd looked so efficient and at home.

"No, really. I'm meeting her a couple of blocks away." Anna stepped into the elevator with him.

"Have dinner with me tonight."

"I can't. I have plans." Her hands were locked tightly together as the doors opened again.

"Tomorrow?"

"I don't know, I…" Emotions churning, she walked out into sunshine and fresh air. "Daniel, why did you come here today?"

"To see you, of course."

"You went to see Mrs. Higgs." She continued to walk. She'd only mentioned the name once. How was it he'd remembered? Why should he have cared?

"Shouldn't I have? It seemed to me she looked only the better for a bit of company."

She shook her head, struggling to find the right words. She hadn't known he could be kind, not really kind when the gesture brought no gain. He was in business, after all, where there was profit and loss and accounts to be forever balanced. The price of the roses would have meant nothing to him, but the gift of them everything to Mrs. Higgs. She wondered if he knew.

"What you did means more at this point than any of the medicine they can give her." She stopped then and turned. He could see the swirl of emotion in her eyes, the steady intensity of feeling that locked on him, and demanded. Anna asked, "Why did you do it? To impress me?"

No one could lie to eyes like that. He had done it to impress her, and had been damn pleased with the idea until he'd begun to talk to Mrs. Higgs. He'd seen a mirror of his mother's fading beauty and tired dignity. And he'd go see her again, not for Anna, but for himself. He had no way of explaining it to her, and no intention of exposing feelings that had been private for so long.

"The main idea was to impress you. I also wanted to see what it was about that place that keeps bringing you back. I still don't understand it all, but maybe I see part of it now."

When she said nothing, he stuck his hands in his pockets as they walked. This woman worried him a good bit more than he'd anticipated. He wanted to please her—he was surprised how much. He wanted to see her smile again. He'd have even settled for one of her cool, regal stares. Frustrated, he scowled straight ahead. "Well, damn it, were you impressed or not?"

She stopped to look up at him. Her eyes were cool, but he couldn't read them. Then she took him totally by surprise. She put her hands on both sides on his face. In her strong, unhurried way, she drew his face down until she could touch her lips to his. It was hardly more than a hint of a kiss, but it exploded through him. She held him there a moment, her eyes locked on his. Then saying nothing, she released him and walked away.

For the first time in his life, Daniel found himself speechless.

Chapter Five

Daniel sat in his office in the Old Line Savings and Loan, puffing on his cigar and listening to the long-winded report from his bank manager. The man knew banking, Daniel conceded, and he was a whiz with figures. But he couldn't see more than two feet in front of his face.

"Therefore, in addition to my other recommendations, I further recommend that the bank foreclose on the Halloran property. Auctioning this property off would cover the outstanding principal, plus, in a conservative estimate, yield a five percent profit."

Daniel tapped his cigar in an ashtray. "Extend it."

"I beg your pardon?"

"I said extend the Halloran loan, Bombeck."

Bombeck pushed his glasses up on his nose and fluttered through his papers. "Perhaps you didn't understand that the Hallorans are six months behind on their mortgage payments. In the past two months, they've failed to keep current with the interest. Even if Halloran finds work as he claims he will, we can't expect the loan to be brought up to date within this quarter. I have all the figures here.''

''I don't doubt it,'' Daniel muttered, bored. Your work, he thought, should never bore you, or you lose your touch.

Drawing the papers out, Bombeck placed them on Daniel's desk. They were, as Bombeck was, tidy and assiduously correct. ''If you'll just look them over, I'm sure we can—''

''Give the Hallorans another six months to bring the interest up to date.''

Bombeck blanched. ''Six—'' Clearing his throat, he shifted in his chair. His neat hands worked together. ''Mr. MacGregor, I'm sure your sympathies toward the Hallorans are admirable, but you must understand that a bank can't be run on sentiment.''

Daniel drew on his cigar, paused, then blew out a haze of smoke. There was the slightest of smiles on his mouth, but his eyes, if Bombeck had dared to look at them, were cold as ice. ''Is that so, Bombeck? I appreciate you telling me.''

Bombeck wet his lips. ''As manager of Old Line—''

''Which was about to go belly up one month ago when I bought it.''

''Yes.'' Bombeck cleared his throat again. ''Yes, indeed, Mr. MacGregor, that's precisely the point. As manager, I feel it my duty to give you all the benefit of my experience. I've been in banking for fifteen years.''

''Fifteen?'' Daniel said as if impressed. Fourteen years, eight months and ten days. He had the employment records of everyone who worked for him, down to the cleaning woman. ''That's just fine, Bombeck. Maybe if I give this to you in different terms, you'll understand my way of thinking.'' Daniel leaned back in his chair so that the sun shooting through the window behind him turned his hair to fire. Though he hadn't planned it that way, he'd have been more than satisfied with the effect. "You estimate a five percent profit if we foreclose and auction the Halloran prop erty. Have I got that right?"

Sarcasm skimmed over Bombeck's head. "Exactly so, Mr. MacGregor."

"Good. Good. However, over the remaining twelve years of the Halloran mortgage, we would see a long-term profit of, conservatively speaking, triple that."

"Over the long-term, of course. I could get you the exact figures, but—"

"Excellent. Then we understand each other. Extend it." Because he enjoyed doing so, Daniel waited a beat before dropping his bomb. "We'll be lowering the mortgage rates by a quarter percent starting next month."

"Lowering, but Mr. MacGregor—"

"And raising the interest on savings accounts to the highest allowable rate."

"Mr. MacGregor, that will throw Old Line deeply in the red."

"In the short-term," Daniel agreed briskly. "In the long-term—you were understanding the long-term, weren't you, Bombeck?—in the long-term we'll make up for it with volume. Old Line will have the lowest mortgage rates in the state."

Bombeck felt his stomach churn and swallowed. "Yes, sir."

"And the highest rates on savings accounts."

He could almost see dollar bills flying away on little wings. "It will cost the bank,." Bombeck couldn't even imagine. "I could work up the figures in a few days. I'm sure you'll see what I'm trying to say. With a policy like that, in six months—"

"Old Line will be the biggest lending institution in the

state," Daniel finished mildly. "I'm glad we agree. We're going to advertise in the papers."

"Advertise," Bombeck murmured as if in a dream.

"Something big—" Daniel measured with his hands, enjoying himself "—but distinguished. Why don't you see what you can come up with and get back to me? Say, by ten tomorrow."

It took Bombeck a few seconds to realize he'd been dismissed. Too dazed to argue, he tidied his papers and rose. As he walked out, Daniel ground his cigar in the ashtray.

Dim-witted, nearsighted dunderhead. What he needed was someone young, fresh out of college and eager. He could salvage Bombeck's pride by making up a new position for him. Daniel felt strongly about loyalty, and dunderhead or not, Bombeck had been with Old Line for nearly fifteen years. It was something he might just discuss with Ditmeyer. That was a man whose opinion Daniel trusted.

Bankers had to realize it was their business to gamble. It was certainly Daniel's. Rising, he walked to the window behind his desk and looked at Boston. At this point, his whole life was a gamble. The money he'd earned could be lost. He shrugged at that. He'd earn more again. The power he now wielded could fade. He'd build it back up again. But there was one thing he was coming to understand, that if lost, couldn't be replaced. Anna.

When had she stopped being part of his master plan and become his life? When had he lost track of the deal and fallen in love? He could pinpoint it to the instant—the instant she'd taken his face in her hands, looked so solemnly into his eyes and touched her mouth to his. He'd gone beyond attraction, beyond desire, beyond the challenge.

His systematic courtship had been blown to bits. The blueprint so carefully drawn was in tatters. From that moment, he'd become only a man totally bewitched by a woman. So now what? That was one question he had no answer for. He'd wanted a wife who would sit patiently at home while he took care of business. That wasn't Anna. He'd wanted a wife who wouldn't question his decisions, but go quietly about making them into fact. That wasn't Anna. There was a part of her life that would always remain separate from him. If she succeeded in her ambition, and he was coming to believe she would, she'd have *Doctor* in front of her name before a year was out. To Anna, it wouldn't simply be a title, but a way of life. Could a man whose business made such demands, took such long hours out of his day, have a wife whose profession did exactly the same?

Who would make the home? he wondered, pulling his fingers through his hair. Who would tend the children? Better if he turned his back on her now and found a woman who'd be content to do those things and nothing else. Better, if he followed the advice she'd given him and chose a woman who had no windmills to battle.

He needed a home. It was difficult for him to admit, even to himself, just how desperately he needed one. He needed family— the scent of bread baking in the kitchen, flowers sitting in bowls. Those were the things he'd grown up with; those were the things he'd done too long without. He couldn't be sure he would have them with Anna. And yet… If he found them without her, he didn't think they would matter.

Damn woman. He looked at his watch. She'd be nearly finished at the hospital now. He had a meeting across town in just under an hour. Determined not to let his life be run by someone else's schedule, he sat behind his desk again and picked up Bombeck's report. After one paragraph, he slammed it down again. Grumbling and swearing, he stalked out of his office.

* * *

She'd spent five hours on her feet. With a tired satisfaction, Anna thought about a long hot bath and a quiet evening with a book. Perhaps she'd just soak and plan how she'd decorate her apartment. In two weeks she'd have the keys in her hand and rooms to furnish. If her feet weren't certain to object, she'd poke around a few antique stores now. With pleasure, she thought of the shiny white convertible waiting for her in the lot next door. The car meant more than the fact that she didn't have to walk home. It meant independence.

Taking the keys out of her purse, she jiggled them in her hand and felt on top of the world. Anna had never considered her ego very large, but when her father had all but drooled on the upholstery, then demanded a ride, she'd felt her head swell. He'd approved finally. She'd used her own money, her own judgment, and there had been no criticism. She remembered the way he'd dragged her mother outside and pulled her into the back seat with him. Anna had tooled around Boston for nearly an hour with her parents as cozy as teenagers behind her.

She'd understood that they'd begun to think of her as something more than a little girl who needed guidance. Whether they'd realized it yet or not, they'd accepted her as an adult. Maybe, she thought, just maybe, there would be pride when she earned her diploma.

Giddy with success, Anna tossed her keys into the air and caught them again. She walked straight into Daniel.

"You weren't looking where you were going."

She'd been happy before, but was happier yet to have seen him. She could almost admit it. "No, I wasn't."

He'd already decided on the way to deal with her. His way. "You're having dinner with me tonight." When she opened her mouth, he took her by the shoulders. His voice was loud enough to turn heads, his eyes fierce enough to turn them forward again. "I won't have any arguments. I'm tired of them and don't have time at the moment, anyway. You're having dinner with me tonight. Be ready at seven."

There were a number of things she could do. In the space of seconds, Anna thought of them all. But she decided the best way was the least expected. "All right, Daniel," she said very demurely.

"I don't care what… What?"

"I said I'd be ready." She looked at him, her eyes calm, her smile serene. It threw him completely off balance, as she'd been certain it would.

"I— All right, then." He scowled and stuck his hands in his pockets. "See that you are." He'd gotten precisely what he'd wanted, but he stopped halfway to his car and looked back. Anna was standing just where she'd been, in a pool of sunlight. Her smile remained as quiet and sweet as an angel's kiss. "Damn women," Daniel mumbled as he yanked open the door of his car. You couldn't trust them.

Anna waited until he'd pulled off, then rocked with laughter. Seeing him stumble and stutter had been better than any argument. Still laughing, she went to her car. An evening with Daniel, she admitted, would certainly be more interesting than a book. Turning the key in the ignition, she felt the power. She had control. And she liked it.

He brought her flowers. Not the white roses he still insisted on sending her day after day, but some tiny, impudent violets from his own garden. It pleased him to watch her arrange them in a little glass vase as he spoke with her parents. He looked big and brash in her mother's dainty parlor. He felt as nervous as a scrawny boy on his first date. Edgy, he sat on a chair he felt better suited to a dollhouse and shared a tepid cup of tea with Mrs. Whitfield.

"You must come to dinner soon," Mrs. Whitfield told him. The constant delivery of roses had made her quite hopeful. It had also given her something to brag about over bridge. The truth was she didn't understand her daughter and never had. Of course, she could tell herself that Anna had always been a sweet, lovely child, but she herself was simply out of her depth when doing something other than choosing material for a dress or a meal from a menu. Anna, with her calm stubbornness and unshakable ambitions, was completely beyond her scope.

Still, Mrs. Whitfield wasn't a fool. She saw the way Daniel looked at her daughter and understood very well. With a strange mixture of relief and regret, she pictured Anna married and raising her own family. If Daniel's manners were a bit rough, she knew her Anna would smooth them out quickly enough. Perhaps she'd be a grandmother in a year or two. It was another thought that brought mixed feelings. Sipping her tea, Mrs. Whitfield studied Daniel.

"I realize you and John are business associates now, but we'll have to keep that in the office. Of course, I know nothing about the business anyway." She reached over to pat Daniel's hand. "John won't tell me a thing, no matter how I badger him."

"And badger, she does," Mr. Whitfield put in.

"Now, John." With a light laugh, she aimed a killing look. If this man had serious intentions toward her daughter, and she was certain he did, she meant to find out everything there was to find out about him. "Everyone's curious about Mr. MacGregor's dealings. It's only natural. Why just the other day, Pat Donahue told me you'd bought some property of theirs in Hyannis Port. I hope you're not thinking of leaving Boston."

Daniel didn't have to scent the air to know which way the wind blew. "I'm fond of Boston."

Deciding she'd let him sweat long enough, Anna handed Daniel her wrap. Grateful, he was up like a shot and bundling her into it.

"You children have a lovely evening." Mrs. Whitfield would have risen to walk them to the door, but her husband put a hand on her shoulder.

"Good night, Mother." Anna kissed her mother's cheek, then smiled up at her father. She'd never realized he was so perceptive. With a smile, she kissed him, as well.

"Enjoy yourself." In an old habit, he patted her head.

Daniel felt he could finally breathe again when they stepped outside. "Your house is very—"

"Crowded," Anna finished, then laughed as she tucked her arm through his. "My mother likes to fill it up with whatever catches her eye. I didn't realize until a few years ago how tolerant my father is." Pleased that he'd brought the blue convertible, she gathered her skirts and slid into her seat. "Where are we going for dinner?"

He took his own seat and let the engine roar. "We're having dinner at home. My home."

Anna felt a quiver of nerves come and go. Using her best weapon, will, she eliminated the fluttering in her stomach. She hadn't forgotten the feeling of control. She'd handle him. "I see."

"I'm tired of restaurants, I'm tired of crowds." His voice was tense and tight. Why, *he's* nervous, she realized, and felt a jolt of pleasure. He towered over her even when sitting. His voice had a timbre that could make the windowpanes rattle, but he was nervous about spending an evening with her. It wasn't easy, but she tried hard not to be smug.

"Oh? I had the impression you enjoyed being around a lot of people," she said very calmly.

"I don't want a bunch of them staring at us while we eat."

"Amazing how rude some people can be, isn't it?"

"And if I want to talk to you, I don't need half of Boston listening to me."

"Naturally not."

He fumed and turned into his driveway. "And if you're worried about propriety, I have servants."

She sent him a bland look. "I'm not worried in the least."

Not sure how to take it, he narrowed his eyes. She was playing games with him, of that he was sure. He just wasn't sure of what kind, or of the rules. "You're mighty sure of yourself all at once, Anna."

"Daniel." She reached for the door handle and let herself out. "I've always been sure of myself."

She decided with one sweeping look that she liked his house. It was separated from the road by a line of hedges that came to her shoulder. The privacy they provided wasn't as cold or impersonal as a wall, but it was just as sturdy. As she looked at the tall windows, some of which were already softly lit behind curtains, she could smell the mixture of scents from the side garden.

Sweet peas she recognized, and smiled. She had a weakness for them. He'd chosen an imposing house, large enough for a family of ten, but he hadn't forgotten to make it a home with something as simple as flowers. She waited until he'd joined her on the edge of the walkway.

"Why did you choose it?"

He looked at the house with her. He saw the brick, attractively faded with age, the windows, with their shutters freshly painted. There was no sense of kinship, only of ownership. After all, someone else had built it. As he drew in the evening air, he didn't smell the sweet peas, but her. "Because it was big."

She smiled at that and turned to watch a sparrow on a

branch of a maple in the front yard. "I suppose that's reasonable. You looked uncomfortable in my mother's parlor, as if you thought if you turned around you might knock down a wall. This suits you better."

"For the moment," he murmured. He had other plans. "You can watch the sunset from those windows." He pointed, then took her arm to lead her up the walk. "You won't for very many more years."

"Why?"

"Progress. They're going to toss buildings up and block out the sky. Not everywhere, but enough. I'm breaking ground on one myself next month." Opening the door, he drew her into the hall and waited.

The swords crossed on the wall to her left drew her eyes first. They weren't the delicate, almost feminine foils used in duels by lace-cuffed swashbucklers. They were thick, heavy, deadly broadswords with undecorated hilts and dull, well-used blades. It would take two hands and a strong man to lift one. It would take skill and brute strength to use one to attack or defend. Unable to resist, Anna walked closer. She had no trouble imagining what one of them could do to flesh and bone. Still, though she could term them lethal, she couldn't term them ugly.

"The swords are from my clan. My ancestors used them." There was pride in his voice, and simplicity. "The MacGregors were warriors, always."

Was it a challenge she heard from him? It might have been. Anna stepped closer to the swords. The edges of the blades weren't dulled, but as treacherous as ever. "Most of us are, aren't we?"

Her response surprised him, but perhaps it shouldn't have. He knew she wasn't a woman to shudder and faint over a weapon or spilled blood. "The English king—" he nearly spat it and had Anna's full attention "—he took our name, our land, but he couldn't take our pride. We hacked off heads when we had to.'' His eyes were deep, blue and brilliant when he looked at her. She had no doubt he would wield the sword with a ferocity equal to that of his ancestors if he felt justified. "Mostly the heads of Campbells.'' He grinned at that and took her arm. "They thought to wipe us out of Scotland, but they couldn't.''

She found herself wondering how he'd look in the clothes of his country, the kilt, the plaid, the dirk. Not ridiculous, but dramatic. Anna looked back up at the swords. "No, I'm sure they couldn't. You've good reason to be proud.''

His hand moved up to her cheek and lingered. "Anna…''

"Mr. MacGregor.'' McGee stood still as a stone as Daniel whirled on him. There was a look in Daniel's eyes that would have made a strong man shudder.

"Aye?'' In the one word, Daniel conveyed a thousand pungent curses.

"A call from New York, sir. A Mr. Liebowitz says it's quite important.''

"Show Miss Whitfield into the parlor, McGee. I'm sorry, Anna, I have to take this. I'll be as quick as I can.''

"It's all right.'' Relieved she'd have a few moments alone, Anna watched Daniel stride down the hall.

"This way, miss.''

She noticed the brogue, which was heavier than Daniel's, and smiled. He'd keep his own around him when he could. With a last glance at the swords, she followed McGee's ramrod back into the parlor. It made her mother's look like a closet. If big was what Daniel wanted, big was what he had.

"Would you care for a drink, Miss Whitfield?''

Distracted, Anna turned blankly. "I'm sorry?''

"Would you care for a drink?"

"Oh, no, thank you, I'm fine."

He gave her the smallest and staunchest of bows. "Please ring if you require anything."

"Thank you," she said again, anxious to be rid of him. The minute she was alone, she turned a slow circle. Big, yes—much bigger than the average room. Unless she missed her guess, he'd had walls removed and combined two into one.

The unusual size was complemented by unusual furnishings. There was a Belker table twice the size of the wheel of a car, carved so ornately that the edges looked like lace. A high backed chair done in rich red velvet sat beside it. He could hold court in it, she thought, and smiled at the idea. Why not?

Rather than sit, Anna simply wandered. The colors were flashy and bold, but somehow she felt perfectly comfortable with them. Maybe she'd lived with her mother's pastels long enough. A sofa took up nearly an entire wall and would have required four strong men to move it. With a laugh, she decided Daniel had chosen it for exactly that reason.

Along the west window was a collection of crystal, Waterford, Baccarat. A vase, two feet high, caught the beginnings of the sunset and danced with it. Anna picked up a bowl that fit into the palm of her hand and wondered what it was doing there among the giants.

He found her like that, standing in the western light, smiling at a small piece of glass. His mouth went dry. Though he said nothing, could say nothing, she turned toward him.

"What a wonderful room." Enthusiasm added color to her cheeks, deepened her eyes. "I imagine in the winter, with a fire, it would be spectacular." When he didn't speak, her smile faded. She took a step closer. "The telephone. Was it bad news?"

"What?"

"Your call. Has it upset you?"

He'd forgotten it, just as he'd forgotten everything. It didn't sit well with him that a look from her could tie his tongue and his stomach up in knots. "No. I'll have to go into New York for a couple of days and straighten out a few things." Including himself, he thought ruefully. "I have something for you."

"I hope it's dinner," she said, smiling again.

"We'll have that, too." It occurred to him that he'd never felt awkward around a woman until now. Drawing a box out of his pocket, he handed it to her.

There was a moment of panic. He had no business offering her a ring. Then as common sense took over, panic faded. The box wasn't the small velvet sort that held engagement rings, but an old cardboard one. Curious, Anna opened the lid.

The cameo was nearly as long as her thumb and perhaps twice as wide. Old and lovely, it sat in a little bed of tissue paper. The profile was gentle and serene, but the head was tilted up with just a touch of pride as well.

"It favors you," Daniel murmured. "I told you once."

"Your grandmother's," she remembered. Touched, she lifted a finger to trace the outline. "It's beautiful, really beautiful." It was more difficult than it should have been to close the lid again. "Daniel, you know I can't take this."

"No, I don't." Taking the box from her, he opened it again and drew out the cameo, which he'd attached to a velvet ribbon himself. "I'll put it on for you."

She could almost feel his fingers brush the nape of her neck. "I shouldn't take a gift from you."

He lifted a brow. "You can't tell me you worry about

gossip, Anna. If you concerned yourself with what people said or thought, you wouldn't be going to your school in Connecticut.''

He was right of course, but she tried to stand firm. ''It's an heirloom, Daniel. It wouldn't be right.''

''It's my heirloom and I'm tired of having it shut in a box. My grandmother would want it to be worn by someone who'd appreciate it.'' In a surprisingly smooth manner, he slid the ribbon around her neck and fastened it. It fit into the subtle hollow of her throat as if it had been destined to rest there. ''There now, that's where it belongs.''

Unable to resist, she reached up to touch it. Common sense slipped away. ''Thank you. We'll say I'm keeping it for you. If you want it back—''

''Don't spoil it,'' he interrupted, and took her chin in his hand. ''I've wanted to see you wear it.''

She couldn't stop the smile. ''And you always get what you want?''

''Exactly.'' Pleased with himself he rubbed a thumb over her cheek before he dropped his hand. ''Will you have a drink? There's some sherry.''

''I'd rather not.''

''Have a drink?''

''Drink sherry. Is there another choice?''

He felt his nervousness drop away. ''I've some prime Scotch sent—smuggled if you want the truth —from a friend of mine in Edinburgh.''

She wrinkled her nose. ''It tastes like soap.''

''Soap?'' He looked so astonished that she laughed.

''Don't take it personally.''

''You'll try it,'' he told her as he went to the bar. ''Soap.'' While he poured, his voice dropped to a mutter. ''This isn't the swill you get at one of your stiff-necked Boston parties.''

Damn it, the longer she knew him, the more endearing he became. Anna found her hand had wandered to the cameo again. She took a deep breath and reminded herself of the feeling of being at the wheel. Control. When he handed her a glass, she studied it. It was very dark and, she thought, very likely to be as lethal as the swords on the wall. "Ice?"

"Don't be silly." He tossed back his glass and challenged her. Anna took a deep breath and gulped some down.

Warm, potent and smooth. Frowning a bit, she sipped again. "I stand corrected," she told him, but handed back the glass. "And if I drink all of it, I won't stand at all."

"Then we'll get some food into you."

With a shake of her head, she offered her hand. "If that's your way of saying it's time for dinner, I accept."

He took her hand and held it. "You won't get too many pretty words out of me, Anna. I'm not polished. I don't have any plans to be."

His hair flowed around his face, untamed and magnificent. The beard gave him the look of the warrior they both knew was in his blood. "No, I don't think you should."

No, he wasn't polished, but he surrounded himself with beauty. It wasn't the quiet sort Anna had become used to, but a bold, bracing beauty that could grab you by the throat. He had a shield and a pike on the wall of the dining room and below them was a Chippendale breakfront any collector of fine antiques would have envied. The table itself was massive, but set on it was the loveliest china Anna had ever seen. She sat in a chair that would have suited a medieval castle and found herself completely relaxed.

The sun came in red-gold slants through the windows. As they ate, the light softened and dimmed. With silent efficiency, McGee came to light candles, then left them again.

"If I told my mother about this meal, she'd try to steal your cook." Anna took a bite of chocolate torte and understood the phrase *sinfully rich*.

It gave him a quiet sort of pleasure to watch her enjoy his food, eat from the plates he'd chosen himself. "You can see why I prefer this to a restaurant."

"Absolutely." She took another bite, because some things weren't meant to be resisted. "I'm going to miss home cooking when I move into my apartment."

"What about your own?"

"My own what?"

"Cooking."

"It doesn't exist." Studying him, she took another bite. "Your eyebrows come straight together when you frown, Daniel, but don't worry, I intend to learn my way around a kitchen. Self-preservation." Linking her fingers, she rested her chin on them. "I don't suppose you cook."

He started to laugh, then thought better of it. "No."

She discovered she liked catching him off guard that way. "But, naturally, you find it odd that I, as a woman, don't know how."

It was difficult not to admire her logic even when he was on the wrong end of it. "You've a habit of boxing a man into a corner, Anna."

"I enjoy the way you fight your way out. I know this may be a dangerous boon to your ego, but you're an interesting man."

"I've a very big ego. It takes a lot to fill it. Why don't you tell me how I'm interesting?"

She smiled and rose. "Another time perhaps."

He caught her hand as he stood. "There will be another time."

She didn't believe in lies, and in evasions only when the truth didn't suit. "It seems there will. Mrs. Higgs talked of nothing but you today," she said as they walked back toward the parlor.

"Lovely woman."

She had to grin. He said it with such self-satisfaction. "She expects you to come back."

"I said I would." He saw the question in her eyes and stopped. "I keep my word."

"Yes." She smiled again. "You would. It's very good of you, Daniel. She has no one."

Uncomfortable, he frowned. "Don't put a halo on me, Anna. I intend to win the bet, but I'd as soon do it without false pretenses."

"I've no intention of putting a halo on you." She flicked the hair from her shoulder. "And I've no intention of losing the bet."

At the doorway to the parlor, she stopped again. There were candles, dozens of them, glowing throughout the room. Moonlight spilled in through the window to compete. There was music, quiet, bluesy. It seemed to come from the shadows. Anna felt her pulse race but continued into the room.

"Lovely," she commented, noting the silver coffee urn had been set up near the sofa.

As Daniel went to pour brandy, she stood, looking completely at ease. She wondered if her muscles could knot any tighter. "I like the way you look in candlelight," he told her as he handed her a snifter. "It reminds me of the first night I met you, when you stood on the terrace near the gardens. There were moonbeams on your face, shadows in your eyes." When he took her hand, he thought for a moment that it trembled. But her eyes were so steady. "I knew then when I looked at you that I had to have you. I've thought of you every day and every night since.''

It would have been easy, too easy, to give in to the thoughts bursting in her head. If she did, she could feel his mouth on hers again and wait, tingle for the touch of those big, wide-palmed hands on her skin. It would have been easy. But the life that she'd already chosen, or that had chosen her, wasn't.

"A man in your position must know how dangerous it is to make a decision on impulse.''

"No.'' He lifted her hand and kissed her fingers, slowly, one by one. The breath backed up in her lungs.

Through sheer will she spoke calmly, and she hoped, carelessly. "Daniel, are you trying to seduce me?''

When would he ever, how would he ever, get used to that quiet voice and frank tongue? After a half laugh, he drank some brandy. "A man doesn't seduce the woman he intends to marry.''

"Of course, he does,'' Anna corrected and patted his back when he choked. "Just the same as a man seduces women he doesn't intend to marry. But I'm not going to marry you, Daniel.'' She turned away to walk to the coffeepot, then looked over her shoulder. "And I'm not going to be seduced. Coffee?''

He didn't just love her, he realized. He very nearly adored her. There were a great many things he found he wasn't certain of at that moment, but he knew without a doubt he couldn't live without her. "Aye.'' He walked to her and took the cup. Maybe he was better off with something in his hands. "You can't tell me you don't want me, Anna.''

Her body was tingling. He had only to touch her to feel her need, her weakness. She made herself look at him. "No, I can't. That doesn't change anything.''

He set the coffee down untasted. He'd have preferred throwing it. "The hell it doesn't. You came here tonight."

"For dinner," she reminded him calmly. "And because, for some odd reason, I enjoy your company. There are some things I have to accept. There are others I can't risk."

"I can." He reached out and cupped her neck gently, though it was difficult to be gentle when he wanted to drag her to him and plunder. He felt her quick move of resistance, ignored it and pulled her closer. "I will."

When his mouth was on hers, Anna accepted one more thing. Inevitability. She'd known they couldn't be together without passion rising up. Yet, she'd come to him freely and on equal terms. Between them there was a fire raging that she could only bank for so long. There would come a time, she knew, when nothing would stop it from consuming both of them. She slid her arms up his back and stepped closer to the heat.

When he lowered her to the sofa, she didn't protest but drew him closer. Just for a moment, she promised herself hazily, just for a moment she'd have a taste of what it could be like. His body was so firm against her. She could sense the desperation, sense it, and despite all good judgment, she reveled in it.

His mouth raced over her face. Her name was murmured again and again against her lips, her throat. She could taste the fire of brandy as his tongue met hers. The scent of candlewax surrounded her. With the music came a low, pulsing beat that urged, teased, enticed.

He had to touch her. He thought he'd go mad if he couldn't have more. Then as he slid his hand over her, felt the softness, the race of her heart, he knew he'd never get enough. His hands, so wide, so large, passed over her with a tenderness that made her tremble. When he heard his name in her shaky whisper, he fought to keep himself from grabbing what he longed for. He brought his mouth back and found hers warm, willing and open.

Desperate, he fumbled with the buttons running down the front of her dress. His hands were so large, the buttons so small. The blood began to pound in his head. Then he discovered, to his delight, that his dignified Anna wore silk and lace next to her skin.

She arched when he found her, arched and shuddered, then strained for more. He was taking her beyond the expected, beyond the anticipated and into dreams. Large, wide-palmed hands continued to pass over her with incredible gentleness. They stroked, lingered, tested. Unable to resist, she let him guide her. Control no longer seemed essential. Ambitions became unimportant. Need. There was only one. For one mindless moment, she gave herself to it.

There was a desperation in him that grew sharper each time his heart beat. He knew what he wanted, what he would want until the grave. Anna. Only Anna. Her mouth was hot on his, her body cool and slim. The images that rushed through his mind were as dark and dangerous as any uncharted land. She clung to him and seemed to give everything. His head spun with it. Then she buried her face against his throat and went very still.

"Anna?" His voice was rough, his hands still gentle.

"I can't say this isn't what I want." The tug-of-war going on inside of her left her weak and frightened. "But I can't be sure it is." She shuddered once, then drew back. He could see her face in the candlelight, the skin pale, the eyes dark. Beneath his hand her heartbeat was fast and steady. "I never expected to feel this way, Daniel. I need to think."

Desire burned inside him. "I can think for both of us."

She lifted her hands to his face before he could kiss her again. "That's what I'm afraid of." Shifting, she sat up.

Her dress was open nearly to her waist, with her soft white skin exposed for the first time to a man. But she felt no shame. Steadily she began to hook the buttons. "What is happening between us—what could happen between us—is the most important decision in my life. I have to make it myself."

He took her by the arms. "It's already been made."

Part of her thought he was right. Part of her was terrified he was. "You're sure of what you want. I'm not. Until I am, I can't promise you anything." The fingers that had been steady trembled before she could control them. "I may never be able to promise you anything."

"You know when I hold you that it's right. Can you tell me that when I touch you you don't feel that?"

"No, I can't." The more agitated he became, the calmer she forced herself to be. "I can't, and that's why I need time. I need time because whatever decision I make has to be made with a clear head."

"Clear head." Furious, aching with need, he rose to stalk the room. "My head hasn't been clear since the first time I laid eyes on you."

She rose, as well. "Then whether you like it or not, we both need time."

He picked up the brandy she'd left unfinished and downed it. "Time's what you need, Anna." He turned to her. She'd never seen him look fiercer, more formidable. A smart woman would guard her heart. Anna struggled to remember that. "I'll be in New York for three days. There's your time. When I come back, I'm coming for you. I want your decision then."

Her chin lifted, exposing a slender, elegant neck. Dignity covered her in a cool, silent wave. "Don't give me deadlines and ultimatums, Daniel."

"Three days," he repeated and set down the snifter before he snapped it in two. "I'll take you home."

Chapter Six

When three days turned into a week, Anna didn't know whether to be relieved or infuriated. Trying to be neither, to simply go about her life as she always had, wasn't possible. He'd given her a deadline, then didn't even bother to show up to hear her decision, which, she admitted, she hadn't made yet.

Invariably, whenever Anna set her mind to a problem, she solved it. It was a matter of thinking through all the levels and establishing priorities. There seemed to be too many levels in her relationship with Daniel for her to deal with each or any one of them rationally. On the one hand, he was a rude, boastful annoyance. On the other, he was fun. He could be unbearably arrogant— and unbearably sweet. His rough edges would never be completely smoothed off. His mind was admirably quick and clever. He schemed. He laughed at himself. He was overbearing. He was generous.

If she couldn't successfully analyze Daniel, how could

she hope to analyze her feelings for him? Desire. She'd had very little experience with that feeling, aside from her ambitions, but she recognized it. How would she recognize love? And if she did, what would she do about it?

The only thing Anna became certain of during Daniel's absence was that she missed him. She was certain of it because she'd been so sure she wouldn't even give him a second thought. She thought of little else. But if she gave in, if she threw caution to the winds and agreed to marry him, what would happen to her dream?

She could marry him, have his children, dedicate her life to him—and resent everything they built together because she would have divorced herself from her vocation. That meant living half a life, and Anna didn't think she could do it. If she refused him and went on with her plans, would that mean half a life, as well?

Those were the questions that tormented her at night, that nagged at her throughout the day. Those were the questions she found, then rejected answers for. So she made no decision, knowing once it was made, it would be final.

She forced herself to continue her routine. To tone down speculation and questions, she went to the theater with friends and attended parties. During the day, she threw herself into her work at the hospital with energy born of frustration.

Habitually she visited Mrs. Higgs first. Anna didn't need a degree to see that the woman was fading. Before seeing to all her other duties, Anna could spend as much time in 521 as needed.

A week after she'd last seen Daniel, making certain her smile was in place, Anna opened the door to Mrs. Higgs's room. This time the shades were drawn and there were more shadows than light. They seemed to be waiting. Anna saw Mrs. Higgs was awake, staring listlessly at the faded flowers on her table. Her eyes brightened when she saw Anna.

"I'm so glad you came. I was just thinking of you."

"Of course I came." Anna set the magazines down. Instinct told her that pictures weren't what Mrs. Higgs needed today. "How else could I give you all the gossip about the party I went to last night?" On the pretext of tidying the sheets, Anna scanned the chart. Her heart sank. The deterioration of the past five days was increasing. But she was smiling as she took her seat beside the bed. "You know my friend, Myra?" Anna was aware how much Mrs. Higgs enjoyed stories about Myra's escapades. "Last night she wore a strapless black dress cut two inches past discretion. I thought some of the older ladies would faint."

"And the men?"

"Well, let's just say Myra didn't miss a dance."

Mrs. Higgs laughed, then caught her breath as pain sliced through. Anna was on her feet instantly.

"Lie still. I'll get the doctor."

"No." Surprisingly strong, the thin hand gripped hers. "No, he'll just give me another shot."

Trying to soothe, Anna rubbed the frail hand as she took her pulse. "Just for the pain, Mrs. Higgs. You don't have to be in pain."

Calmer, Mrs. Higgs settled back again. "I'd rather feel pain than nothing. I'm all right now." She managed a smile. "Talking to you is much better than medicine. Did your Daniel come back yet?"

Still monitoring her pulse, Anna sat again. "No."

"It was so kind of him to visit me before he left for New York. Imagine his coming by here before he went to the airport."

The fact that he had was just one of the things that added to Anna's confusion. "He likes visiting you. He told me."

"He'd said he'd come again when he got back from New York." She looked at the week-old roses she refused to let the nurses take away. "It's so special to be young and in love."

Anna felt a stab of pain herself. Did he love her? He'd chosen her, he wanted her, but love was a different matter. She wished she had someone to talk to, but Myra had seemed so preoccupied lately and no one else would understand. She could hardly pour her problems out on Mrs. Higgs when she'd come to comfort. Instead, she grinned and patted her hand. "You must have been in love dozens of times."

"At least. Falling in love, that's the roller coaster, the ups and downs, the thrills. Being in love, that's the carousel—around and around with music playing. But staying in love…" She sighed, remembering. "That's the maze, Anna. There are all the twists and turns and dead ends. You have to keep going, keep trusting. I had such a short time with my husband, and never tried the maze again."

"What was he like, your husband?"

"Oh, he was young, and ambitious. Full of ideas. His father had a grocery store, and Thomas wanted to expand it. He was very clever. If he'd lived… But that wasn't meant. Do you believe some things are meant, Anna?"

She thought about her need to heal, her studies. She tried not to think of Daniel. "Yes. Yes, I do."

"Thomas was meant to die young, like a lovely flash fire. Still, he packed so much into the short years. I admire him more as I look back. Your Daniel reminds me of him."

"How?"

"That drive—the kind you can see on their faces. It tells you they're going to do amazing things." She smiled again, fighting back another surge of pain. "There's a ruthlessness that means they'll do whatever is necessary to accomplish it, and yet there's kindness, very basic kindness. The kind that made Thomas give a handful of candy to a child who didn't have the money. The kind that makes your Daniel visit an old woman he doesn't know. I've changed my will.''

Alarmed, Anna straightened. "Mrs. Higgs—"

"Oh, don't fret." She closed her eyes a moment, willing her body to build back some strength. "I can see on your face you're worried I've tangled you up in it. Thomas left me a nest egg, and I invested. It's given me a comfortable life. I have no children, no grandchildren. It's too late for regrets. I need to give something back. I need to be remembered." She looked at Anna again. "I talked to Daniel about it."

"To Daniel?" Disturbed, Anna leaned closer.

"He's very smart, just like Thomas. I told him what I wanted to do, and he told me how it could be done. I've had my lawyer set up a scholarship. Daniel agreed to let me name him executor so he can handle the details."

Anna opened her mouth to brush the subject of death aside, then realized she would be doing so only for herself. "What kind of scholarship?"

"For young women going into medicine." Pleased with the stunned look on Anna's face, Mrs. Higgs smiled. "I knew you'd like it. I thought about what I could do, then I thought of you, and of all the nurses here who've been so kind to me."

"It's a wonderful thing, Mrs. Higgs."

"I could have died alone, without anyone to sit and talk to me. I was lucky." She reached out and curled her fingers around Anna's hand. Because it was difficult to feel, she tightened them. Anna felt barely any pressure. "Anna, don't make the same mistake I did by thinking you don't need anyone. Take love where it's offered. Let it live with you. Don't be afraid of the maze.''

"No," Anna murmured. "I won't."

There was barely any pain now, barely anything at all. Mrs. Higgs stared at the outline of light around the shades. "Do you know what I'd do if I could start all over again, Anna?"

"What would you do?"

"I'd have it all." The light was blurring, but she managed to smile. "It's so foolish to think you have to settle for pieces. Thomas would have known better." Exhausted, she closed her eyes again. "Stay with me a little while."

"Of course I will."

So she sat in the shadowed room. Keeping the frail hand in hers, she listened to the sound of breathing. And waited. When it was over, she fought back the surge of anger, the wave of denial. Carefully, Anna rose and pressed a kiss to Mrs. Higgs's forehead. "I won't forget you."

Calm, controlled, she walked down the corridor to Mrs. Kellerman. Deluged by five new admissions, the nurse gave her a brief glance. "We're a bit rushed now, Miss Whitfield."

She stood very straight. When she spoke her voice held both authority and patience. "You'll need to call the doctor for Mrs. Higgs."

Instantly alert, Mrs. Kellerman rose. "She's having pain?"

"No." Anna folded her hands. "Not anymore."

Understanding flickered in her eyes, and, Anna thought for a moment, regret. "Thank you, Miss Whitfield. Nurse Bates, call Doctor Liederman immediately. Five twenty-one." Without waiting for an answer, she went down the corridor herself. Anna followed her as far as the door and again waited. Moments later, Kellerman looked back. "Miss Whitfield, you don't need to stay here now."

Determined, Anna kept her hands folded and her eyes direct. "Mrs. Higgs had no one."

Compassion came through, and for the first time, respect. Stepping back from the bed, Kellerman put a hand on her arm. "Please wait outside. I'll tell the doctor you want to speak to him."

"Thank you." Anna walked down the corridor to the little L that was the waiting room and sat. As the minutes passed, she grew calmer. This was what she would face, she reminded herself, day after day for the rest of her life. This was the first time—her stomach knotted and unknotted—but not the last. Death would become an intimate part of her life, something to be fought, something to be faced. Starting now, this minute, she would have to learn to defend herself against it.

On a deep breath she closed her eyes. When she opened them again, she saw Daniel walking toward her.

For a moment, her mind went blank. Then she saw the roses in his hand. Tears welled up, brimmed and were controlled. When she rose her legs were steady.

"I thought I'd find you here." Everything about him was aggressive—his walk, his face, his voice. She thought only briefly of the luxury of throwing herself into his arms and weeping.

"I'm here every day." That wouldn't change. Now, more than ever she knew she couldn't let it.

"It took longer than I thought to work things out in New York." And he'd spent his nights restless and wakeful thinking of her. He started to speak again in the same tough, no-nonsense tone, but something in her eyes stopped him. "What's wrong?" He only had to see her glance at the roses to know. "Damn." With a whispered oath he let them fall to his side. "Was she alone?"

That he would ask that first, that he would think of that first, made her reach out her hand to him. "No, I was with her."

"That's good then." Her hand was icy in his. "Let me take you home."

"No." If he were too kind, her composure would never hold up. "I want to speak with her doctor."

He started to object, then slipped an arm around her shoulders. "I'll wait with you."

In silence, they sat together. The scent of the roses flowed over her. They were young buds, very fresh, still moist. Part of a cycle, she reminded herself. It wasn't possible to appreciate life unless you understood, accepted, the cycle.

Anna rose very slowly when the doctor joined them. "Miss Whitfield. Mrs. Higgs spoke of you to me many times. You're a medical student."

"That's right."

He nodded, reserving judgment. "You're aware that we removed a tumor—a malignant one some weeks ago. There was another. If we had operated again, it would have killed her. Our only choice was to make her as comfortable as possible."

"I understand." She understood, too, that one day she'd have to make such decisions herself. "Mrs. Higgs had no family. I want to make the funeral arrangements."

Her composure surprised him as much as her statement. Studying her face, he decided if she made it through medical school, he'd be interested in having her intern under him. "I'm sure that can be easily done. We'll have Mrs. Higgs's attorney contact you."

"Thank you." She offered her hand. Lieberman found it cool, but firm. Yes, he'd like to watch her train.

"We're leaving," Daniel told her when they were alone.

"I haven't finished my shift."

"And you won't today." Taking her by the arm, he led her to the elevator. "You're allowed to let yourself breathe. Don't argue," he said, anticipating her. "Let's just say you're humoring me. There's something I want to show you."

She could have argued. Just knowing she had the strength to do so made her relent. She'd go with him because she knew she'd come back tomorrow and do whatever needed to be done.

"I'll have my driver take us to my house," he told her as they stepped outside. "We'll want my car."

"I have mine." Daniel only lifted a brow and nodded. "Wait a minute." Walking to the Rolls, he dismissed Steven. "We'll use yours. Do you feel like driving?"

"Yes. Yes, I do." She walked to the little white convertible.

"Very nice, Anna, but then I've always admired your taste."

"Where are we going?"

"North. I'll direct you."

Content to drive, to feel the wind and know no destination, she headed out of town. For a time, he left her to her own thoughts.

"Shedding tears doesn't make you weak."

"No." She sighed and watched the sun slant across the road. "I can't yet. Not yet. Tell me about New York."

"A mad place. I like it." He grinned and threw his arm over the seat. "It's not a place to live, not for me, but the excitement can get into your blood. You know Dunripple Publishing?"

"Yes, of course."

"Now it's Dunripple and MacGregor." He'd been satisfied with the way the deal had swung, or more accurately, the way he'd pushed it.

"Prestigious."

"Prestigious be damned," he told her. "They needed new blood and cold cash."

"What did you need?"

"To diversify. I don't like bundling all my interests together."

She frowned a bit, thinking. "How do you know what to buy?"

"Old companies losing ground, new companies breaking it. The first gives me something to fix, the second something to—" he hesitated, unsure of what word would suit "—explore," he said finally.

"But you can't be sure all the companies you buy will make it."

"All of them won't. That's the game."

"Sounds like a vicious one."

"Maybe; it's life." He studied her. Her face was still a bit too pale, her eyes a bit too calm. "A doctor knows all his patients won't make it. It doesn't stop him from taking a new one."

He understood. She should have expected it. "No, it doesn't."

"We all take risks, Anna, if we're really alive."

She drove mostly in silence, following Daniel's directions. Thoughts rushed in and out of her head, feelings tossed freely inside of her. It was a long quiet drive and should have calmed her. By the time they drove along the coast, she was tight with nervous energy. Spotting a little store, Daniel gave a wave of his hand.

"Stop in here."

Agreeable, Anna pulled into the gravel lot beside it. "Is this what you wanted to show me?"

"No. But you're going to get hungry."

She pressed a hand on her stomach before she opened the door. "I think I already am." Thinking they'd hardly do better than a box of crackers, Anna followed him inside.

It was a crowded little hodgepodge of a store, with canned goods lined on shelves, dry goods packed in doorless cupboards. A freshly waxed floor shone back at her. A fan creaked in slow circles swirling the heat.

"Mr. MacGregor!" With obvious pleasure, a round woman eased herself from a stool behind the counter.

"Ah, Mrs. Lowe. Pretty as ever."

She had a face like a horse and knew it. She greeted the flattery with a loud guffaw. "What can I do for you today?" She gave Anna an unconcealed survey, grinned and showed a missing incisor.

"The lady and I need the makings of a picnic." He leaned over the counter. "Tell me you have some of that mouth-watering roast beef you gave me last time."

"Not an ounce." She winked at him. "But I have some ham that'll make you roll your eyes and thank your Maker."

All charm, he took her pudgy hand and kissed it. "I'll roll my eyes and thank you, Mrs. Lowe."

"I'll make a sandwich for the lady. And two for you." The look she gave him was as shrewd as it was friendly. "I'll throw in a thermos of lemonade—if you buy the thermos."

"Done."

With a cackle, she made her way into a back room.

"You've been here before," Anna said dryly.

"Now and again. Quite a little place." He knew the Lowes ran it themselves and kept it stocked and spotless.

"I'm thinking if they added themselves another room, put in a counter and a grill, Mrs. Lowe could make herself famous with her sandwiches."

She saw the look in his eyes and smiled. "Lowe and MacGregor."

With a laugh, he leaned on the counter. "No, sometimes it's best to be a silent partner."

When Mrs. Lowe came back, she carried a huge wicker basket. "Have your picnic and bring the basket back—it's not new." She winked again. "But the thermos is."

Daniel took out his wallet and pulled out bills. Enough to make Anna's eyebrow lift. "My best to your husband, Mrs. Lowe."

The bills disappeared into some handy pocket. "You and the lady have a good time."

"We will." Toting the basket, Daniel swung through the door. "Do you trust me to drive?"

Anna already had the keys in her hands. She hadn't allowed anyone behind the wheel but herself, though her father had hinted and Myra had nagged. Hesitating only a moment, she handed them to him.

Moments later, they were driving straight up. She'd never seen a road so narrow, so winding. The view over the side took her breath away with its sheer cliffs. There was color among the endless gray: touches of red, hints of green. In places it seemed as though the rock had been hewn away with a broadax, in others hacked at with a pick. Waves crashed free against rock, then washed back only to crash again. There was violence here, she thought. An endless war that was also a cycle. With the smell of the sea around her, she leaned back.

Mile after mile they climbed. Trees that dotted the sides of the road grew slanted, leaning away from the constant wind. Anna wondered what Daniel would do if another car came down the road toward them. It didn't worry her. She watched a sea bird skim over the surface of the water below, then soar up toward the sun.

When the road leveled again, she was almost disappointed. Then she saw the stretch of land ahead. Overgrown, rocky, desolate, it spread out to the very edge of the cliff. Something shot into her, sharp as an arrow, sweet as a kiss. Recognition.

Daniel stopped the car and stood, absorbing everything. As it always did, the wildness of it drew him. He could feel the sea, feel the wind. He was home.

Saying nothing, Anna stepped from the car. She was buffeted by the turbulence there, but she could also sense the peace. Whether it was in the air or the land itself, she knew this sense of constant movement and inner stillness would always remain.

"This is your land," she murmured when he stood beside her.

"Aye."

The wind blew her hair into her face, but she pushed it back, impatient. She wanted to see clearly. "It's beautiful."

She said it so simply that he couldn't speak. Until that moment he hadn't realized just how desperately he wanted her to accept it, to understand it. More, he hadn't known how important it was to him that she love it as he had from the first moment he'd seen it. The sun beat down on his face as he brought her hand to his lips.

"The house will go there." He pointed, and began to walk with her. "Near the cliff, so you'll hear the sea, almost be part of it. It'll be made of stone, tons of it, so it'll rise up and hold its own. Some of the windows will come nearly to the ceiling and the front door will be as wide as three men. Here—" he stopped, gauging the position with his eyes "—there will be a tower."

"Towers?" Almost hypnotized, Anna looked up at him. "You make it sound like a castle."

"That's right. A castle. The MacGregor seal will stand above the door."

She tried to imagine it and shook her head. She found it both exciting and incomprehensible. "Why so much?"

"It'll last. My great-grandchildren will know it." Leaving her, he walked back to the car for the basket.

Unable to judge his mood or her own, Anna helped spread the blanket Mrs. Lowe had provided. Besides the sandwiches, there was a bowl of well-spiced potato salad and two thick slices of cake. With her skirt flowing over her knees, Anna sat cross-legged and ate while she watched the clouds.

So much was happening so fast, and yet it seemed her life was suspended in some kind of limbo. She no longer knew what she'd find if she turned right, if she turned left. The path that had once seemed so clear to her had taken on some odd curves. She couldn't see around them. Because Daniel was quiet, she kept her silence, aware he was no more comfortable than she.

"In Scotland," he began, as if talking to himself, "we lived in a little cottage no bigger than the garage on your house. I was five, maybe six, when my mother took sick. After she'd delivered my brother, she was never really well again. My grandmother would come every day to cook and help tend the baby. I'd sit with my mother, talk to her. I didn't realize then how young she was."

Anna sat with her hands in her lap and her eyes intense. A few weeks before, she would have listened politely if he had spoken of his past. Now, it seemed half her world hinged on what he would say. "Go on, please."

It wasn't easy for him, nor had he planned to speak of it. Now that he'd begun, he discovered he'd needed to tell her all along. "My father would come home from the mines, his skin black, his eyes red. God, how tired he must have been, but he sat with my mother, played with the baby, listened to me. She hung on, nearly five years, and when I was ten, she just slipped away. She was suffering the whole time, but she never complained."

Anna thought of Mrs. Higgs. This time she let the tears fall. Daniel said nothing for a moment but listened to the sea.

"My grandmother came to live with us. Tough old bird. She made me tow the line study in books. When I was twelve I went to work in the mines, but I could read and write and work with figures better than the grown men. I was as big as some of them already." He laughed at that and flexed his hand into a fist. More than once he'd been grateful for it.

"The mines were hell. Dust in your lungs, in your eyes. Every time the earth shook, you waited to die and hoped it'd be quick. I was about fifteen when McBride, who owned the mine, took notice of me. He found out I was clever with numbers, so he used to have me come in and do a bit of figuring for him. In his way, he was a fair man, so I was paid for the extra work. Within a year, I was out of the mines and doing his books. My hands were clean. As soon as I'd started working, my father had me put half my earnings in a tin jar. We could have used the money day to day, but he wouldn't have it. Even when I was making more in the office, he made me put half the money aside in that jar. It was the same with my brother, Alan."

"He wanted you to get out," Anna murmured.

"Aye. He had a dream for me and Alan to get out of the mines, away from everything he'd had to live with."

He turned to her, his eyes hot and angry. "I was twenty when the main shaft caved in. We dug for three days, three nights. Twenty men were gone, my father and my brother with them."

"Oh, Daniel." She reached out, resting her head against his shoulder. It was more than grief. She could feel the fury, the resentments, the guilt. "I'm sorry."

"When we buried them, I swore it wasn't the end. It was the beginning. I'd make enough to get out. By the time I did, it was too late to take my grandmother. She'd lived a long time and only asked me one thing before she died, that I see the line go on, that I not forget where we'd come from. I'm keeping that promise, Anna—" he turned her so she'd look at him "—for her, for me, with every stone that goes into this house."

She understood him now, perhaps too well for her own good. She understood that there on the windswept cliff in the middle of the barren land he'd chosen she'd finally, irreversibly fallen in love with him. But with understanding came only more questions.

Rising, she walked toward the plot of land where he envisioned his home. He'd build it, she knew. And it would be magnificent. "They'd be proud of you."

"I'll go back one day to see it all again, to remember it all. I'll want you with me."

She turned, and as she did, wondered if she'd been waiting to make that move all of her life. Perhaps it was the first step into the maze. "I'm afraid I'll never be able to give you everything you want, Daniel. I'm more afraid that I'll try."

He stood and walked toward her. There was still too much space between them when he stopped. "You told me you needed time. I asked you to make a decision. Now, I'm asking you what it is."

Anna stood, poised on the edge of everything.

Chapter Seven

She wanted to give him everything he asked, to give him things he'd never even dreamed of. She wanted to take everything she could grab and hold on to. In that moment she understood what taking just one step forward could mean to both of them. She wondered if he did. One step forward would irrevocably change their lives even if a step back could somehow be taken later. One step and there would be no altering what was said, what was done or what was given. Anna believed in destiny, destiny met with eyes open and mind clear.

Though common sense fought to remain in charge, her heart slowly, willfully took command. What was love? In that moment she understood only that it was a force larger, stronger than the logic she had always lived by. Love had started wars, toppled empires, driven men mad and turned women into fools. She could reason for hours, but she would never diminish the power of that one all-encompassing force.

They stood on the cliffs, with the wind roaring against the rocks, moaning through the high grass, beating against the land he'd chosen to fulfill a dream and a promise. If Daniel was her destiny, she would meet him head on.

He looked fiercer than ever, almost frightening, with his eyes burning into hers and the sun fiery at his back. Zeus, Thor, he might have been either. But he was flesh and blood, a man who understood destiny and would break mountains to achieve the one he had chosen. He'd chosen her.

She took her time, determined to make her decision with a clear head. But the emotions boiling inside her weren't calm. How could she look at him, read the need in his eyes and be calm? He'd spoken of family, of promises, of a future she wasn't sure she could share with him. But there was something she could share now, something she could give, and give only once. Leading with her heart, Anna stepped forward and into his arms.

They came together like thunder, urgent, tempestuous, strong. Her mouth met his with all the chaotic longing she'd held down. She felt the power soar, the fire spread fast and out of control. There was only here; there was only now.

His hands were in her hair, his fingers raking desperately through it so that the combs she wore fell unheeded to the ground. His mouth was restless and urgent, rushing over her face, meeting her lips, then moving on, as if it were vital that he taste everything at once. She heard her name come low and vibrant, then tasted it herself as he murmured against her mouth. Even as she pressed strongly against him, she felt the give of her own body, the incredible fluid yielding only a woman can experience. Her mind leaped forward with the pleasure of discovering the magic of submission when mixed with demand. Then her thoughts scattered, leaving only one. She was where she wanted to be.

Together they lowered themselves to the grass, wrapped so tightly that even the wind couldn't come between them. Like lovers separated for years, they rushed together with no holding back, no hesitation. Eager to feel the delight of flesh against flesh, she tugged on his shirt. Muscles he'd earned while still a boy corded his arms, rippled over his back. Aroused by the sheer strength of him, she allowed her hands free play, and learned the spiraling joy of having a man—her man—groan at her touch.

He wanted her—here, now, exclusively. She could feel it with every beat of her own pulse. Until that moment she hadn't realized just how important it had been to her to be sure of it. Whatever else he wanted from her, whatever plans he'd scrupulously made were tossed to oblivion by one overpowering force. Desire. It was pure; it was desperate; it was theirs.

He'd wanted to be careful, to be gentle, but she was driving him beyond anything he'd experienced. Fantasies, dreams paled foolishly beside reality. She was much more than a goal to be won or a woman to be wooed. Her hands were slim and strong and curious, her mouth warm and insistent. The need that pounded through him concentrated at the base of his neck so that the sound of it roared through his brain, leaving him deaf to the crash of the waves far below. He could smell the wild grass as he buried his lips at her throat, but her scent, subtle, quiet, was more pervasive. She was so small, so heart-breakingly soft that he fought to keep his work-toughened hands easy as he undressed her, but she arched against each touch, wantonly demanding more.

He couldn't resist her, nor could he resist any longer the pressure building inside him. Racing against passion, he yanked the rest of her clothes aside and gave himself to need. Her skin was pale as milk under the hot summer sun, her body as trim and efficient as her mind. No other woman, no dream had ever aroused him more. With a sound that rumbled deep in his throat, he met her gasp of astonished pleasure.

There was more? She had thought it impossible, but everywhere his lips tarried brought her fresh bursts of unspeakable delight. Should she have known a man and a woman could share something so dark, so sultry under a full sun? Could she have known that she, always so self-disciplined, so rational, would give herself to passion in a field of grass on a cliff top? All she understood was that it didn't matter when, it didn't matter where, it was and would always be Daniel.

Her emotions seemed to race just ahead of reason. She wanted to savor each new experience, but before she could absorb one, another tumbled down on her, layering all into a mass of sensations impossible to separate. With a breathless laugh she realized it wasn't necessary to understand each one, but simply to feel. There was no fear in her as desire began to peak, but a wild anticipation.

The blood pounded in his veins, swam in his head until he thought he'd explode from it. Her body burned with the same fire as his, she moved to the same throbbing music. But she was innocent. He knew, even as he ached to take her with fury and speed, that control was vital. Her arms clutched him, her hips thrust up in uninhibited offering. And the fear of harming something so precious snaked through him. He struggled to catch his breath when she reached for him.

"Anna—"

"I want you." Her murmur was like thunder in his ear. "I need you, Daniel." In hearing it, sweet pain spread through him. In saying it, she felt glorious.

"I won't hurt you." He lifted his head to see her lips curve, her eyes cloud.

"No, you won't hurt me."

He called on all his strength of will as he slipped into her. She was so warm, so moist that his head nearly burst with a new flood of emotion. He'd had women before. But not like this. He'd given himself to passion before. Never, never like this.

She felt him enter her, pierce her, fill her. Her innocence was gone in a heartbeat with a pleasure so vast that all pain was smothered. Power. It swept over her like the wind, like the thunder, eclipsing that first surge of wonder. Drunk with it, she gripped him tighter. She heard him call her name before his mouth fastened on hers. They hurled aside control and took each other.

He knew about the cat that swallowed the canary. As he lay on the wild grass with Anna at his side, Daniel felt like a cat who'd feasted on a baker's dozen. The contentment that had somehow always skidded just out of his reach settled through him with a sleepy sigh.

He'd chosen a lovely, intelligent woman to marry. It was a logical choice for a man who intended to build an empire that would last for generations. Wasn't it lucky he'd fallen in love and discovered she was also caring, sweet and passionate? His wife-to-be, the mother of his yet-to-be-born children fit him like a glove. He decided it paid to be lucky as well as shrewd.

She was quiet beside him but he knew from the easy way she breathed, the content way her hand rested in his that she was lost in thoughts, not in regrets. Her head was nestled in the crook of his shoulder so naturally that he could have sworn they'd lain just like this before, grass soft at their backs, the sky clear and blue above. Cloud watchers, he thought. Children would toss themselves on the ground to find images and dreams in the clouds. He'd never had much time for it as a boy. With Anna, he could make time, and he wouldn't have to look for dreams.

He could have lain there for hours, with the surf and the wind and the sun. He had his woman, his land, and it was only the beginning. But he knew, of course, that they had to leave for the city soon. What he wanted with her and for her couldn't be accomplished in an empty field. But he kept his arm around her and lingered while dozens of plans formed and shifted in his head.

"There's more than enough room for us in the house," he said, half to himself. With his eyes nearly closed and the quiet glow of loving still lingering, he could picture her there. She'd add the touches he too often forgot—bowls of flowers, music. "Of course, you might want to change some things. Flounce it up some."

She watched the way the sun played through leaves. She'd just taken the step forward. It was already time for the step back. "Your house is fine the way it is, Daniel."

"Aye, well it's only temporary." He stroked his fingers through her hair while he looked at the plot where he would build his dream. Their dream now. How much sweeter it was now that he had someone to share it with. "When this one's finished we'll sell the one in Boston. Or maybe we'll keep it for business. I'll be cutting down on my traveling once I have a wife."

Overhead clouds moved slowly, too lofty to be persuaded by the wind that rustled the grass. "Traveling's important to your business."

"For now." She felt his shoulder move under her head in a careless shrug. "Before long, they'll come to me. And they'll come here. I don't intend to marry, then spend my time away from my wife."

Her hand rested lightly on his chest. She wondered if he knew how smugly he used the phrase *my wife*. A man might use the same tone to describe his shiny new car. "I'm not going to marry you, Daniel."

"I'll still have to fly into New York now and again, but you can go with me."

"I said I'm not going to marry you."

With a laugh, he pulled her up until she lay half across him. Her skin was warm from sun and loving. "What do you mean you're not going to marry me? Of course, you are."

"No." She laid a hand on his face. Her touch was as soft as her eyes. "I'm not."

"How can you say that now?" He had her by the shoulders. Panic was his first reaction as he recognized the calm, patient look. Part of his success was the ability to turn panic to anger, and anger to determination. "It's not the time for games."

"No, it's not." Calm, she shifted away and began to dress.

Torn between puzzlement and fury, he grabbed her wrists before she could slip into her blouse. "We've just made love. You came to me."

"I came to you freely," she returned. "We needed each other."

"And we're going to go on needing each other. That's why you're going to marry me."

She tried to let out her breath slowly, soundlessly. "I can't."

"Why in hell not?"

Her stomach muscles were beginning to quiver. Her skin was chilled under the bright summer sun. She wanted him to release her but knew he'd ignore any resistance. Suddenly she wanted to run, to run faster than she ever had,

Instead, she remained still. "You want me to marry you, start a family, pick up and go whenever and wherever your business or whims take you." She had to swallow because she knew she spoke the truth. "To do that I'd have to give up something I've wanted almost as long as I can remember. I won't do it, Daniel, not even for you."

"This is nonsense." To prove it he gave her a brisk shake. "If the damn degree is so important, go on and get it then. You can study just as easily married to me."

"No." Easing away, she busied her hands with her clothes. She wouldn't be bullied, and she wouldn't be charmed, though he seemed to be an expert on both. "If I went back to school as Mrs. Daniel MacGregor, I'd never finish. You'd stop me even if you didn't mean to."

"Damn it, that's ridiculous." He stood naked and glorious with the sun at his back. For a moment Anna wanted to open her arms and invite him back to her, to agree with anything he said. Purposefully she stood.

"It's not. And I'm going to earn my degree, Daniel. I have to."

"So you're choosing your doctoring over me." Hurt, angry, he didn't care if his words were unfair. He saw the one thing that would make his life whole, make it real, slipping away.

"I want you both." She swallowed. How could she judge his reaction when she still wasn't sure of her own? "I won't marry you," she repeated. "But I'll live with you."

His eyes narrowed into slits. "You'll what?"

"I'll live with you in your house in Boston until September. After that we could get an apartment off campus. And then…"

"And then what?" His words shot out like sand from under a tire.

She lifted her hands then let them fall. "Then I don't know."

Her head was thrown back in pride so that the wind tossed her hair. But her face was very pale, her eyes unsure. He loved her to the point of madness and his anger was nearly as great. "Damn you, Anna, I want you for a wife, not for a mistress."

The doubts cleared from her eyes to be replaced by a fury to match his own. No longer pale, her skin glowed with indignation. "And I'm not offering to be one." Turning on her heel, she started back to the car. He grabbed her by the arm and whirled her around so quickly that her feet nearly slid out from under her.

"What the hell are you offering then?"

"To live with you." It wasn't often she shouted, but when she did, she gave it everything. If he hadn't been so angry, there would have been room for respect. "Not be kept by you. I don't want your money or your big house or your dozen roses a day. It's you I want. God knows why."

"Then marry me." Still naked, still raging, he dragged her against him.

"Do you think you can have anything you want just by yelling louder, just by being stronger?" She shoved him away and stood, small and slim and stunning. "I'll give you only so much and no more."

He dragged both hands through his hair. How was a man to deal with such a woman? "If you won't think of your reputation, I have to."

She lifted a brow. "You have to do nothing but think of your own." In the regal manner she could assume so effortlessly, she let her gaze drift over him. "You don't seem very concerned about it now."

In one furious move, he swept up his pants. Another man

might have looked foolish. Daniel looked magnificent. "A few minutes ago I seduced you," he began.

"Don't delude yourself." Cool and confident she picked up his shirt. "A few minutes ago we made love. It had nothing to do with seduction."

He took the shirt from her and slipped it on. "You're tougher than you look, Anna Whitfield."

"That's right." Pleased with herself, she started to gather up the picnic things. "You told me once to take you as you are. Now I'm telling you the same. If you want me, Daniel, it has to be on my terms. Think about it." She left him half-dressed and walked to the car.

They barely spoke on the long drive back. Anna was no longer angry, but drained. So much had happened in a short span of time, and none of it had been in her carefully worked out plans. She needed time to think, to evaluate and to recharge. Daniel was electric. He didn't have to speak for her to read his temper.

The hell with his temper, she thought recklessly. Let him be angry. It was something he did well. Not everyone looked magnificent when he ranted and raged.

His mistress. Her own temper began to sizzle but she waited for it to subside. She'd be no man's mistress, Anna told herself as she settled back and folded her arms. And no man's wife until she was ready. She would, though the thought still made her pulse skittish, be one man's lover. In her own quiet fashion, she was as determined as Daniel to have her way.

Live with him. Daniel gripped the wheel tightly as he took a turn faster than a rational man would have dared. He was offering her half of everything he had, half of everything he was. Most importantly, he was offering her his name. And she was tossing it back in his face.

Did she think he would have taken her innocence if he hadn't believed they were committed to each other? What kind of woman would refuse an honest proposal and opt to run off like a renegade child thumbing her nose at what was proper? He wanted a wife, damn it, a family. She wanted a piece of paper that said she could poke needles into people.

He should have taken her advice from the beginning. Anna Whitfield was the last woman in Boston who would make him a suitable wife. So he would forget about her. He'd drop her at her door, say a cool goodbye and drive away. But he could still taste her, still feel the way her skin had slid under his fingers, still smell the scent of her hair as it had floated around her body—and his.

"I won't have it."

With a squeal of brakes he stopped at the curb in front of her house. A few yards away, Anna's mother clipped roses. At the explosion, she looked up and nervously gripped her shears. The fact that a quick glance showed her none of her neighbors were about relieved her only a little as Daniel gunned the convertible's engine.

"That," Anna said with perfect calm, "is your privilege."

"Now you listen to me." Turning slightly, Daniel gripped her by both shoulders. He didn't want to argue, he didn't want to fight; the moment those patient brown eyes met his he wanted to drag her against him and make love with her until they were both too exhausted to speak.

Anna lifted a brow. "I'm listening."

He groped for what needed to be said. "What happened between us doesn't happen with everyone. I know."

She smiled a little. "I'll have to take your word for that."

Frustration boiled. "That's part of the problem," he

mumbled and ordered himself to be as calm as she. "I want to marry you, Anna." In the rose bushes, Mrs. Whitfield dropped her shears with a quiet thump. "I've wanted to marry you from the first minute I saw you."

"That's part of the problem." Because most of her heart was already his, Anna lifted both hands to his face. "You wanted what was suitable and decided I was it. You want me to fit a slot in your life. Perhaps I could, but I won't."

"It's more than that now—much more." As he dragged her closer, she saw the flare of desire in his eyes then tasted it on his lips. Without hesitation, without artifice, Anna met his greed with her own. Yes, it was more than that now— perhaps more than either of them could deal with. When they were together like this, everything else faded into insignificance. That's what frightened her. That's what exhilarated her.

Desperately, he pushed her away again. "You see what we have together. What we could have."

"Yes." Her voice wasn't as steady now, but her determination hadn't wavered. "And I want it. I want you—but not marriage."

"I want you to share my name."

"And I want to share your heart first."

"You're not thinking clearly." Neither was he. Cautious, he dropped his hands from her shoulders. "You need a little time."

"No, I don't." Before he could stop her she slipped from the car. "But it's obvious you do. Goodbye, Daniel."

Mrs. Whitfield watched her daughter stride easily toward the house. Moments later she watched Daniel drive recklessly down the street. Then remembering whose car he was driving, he ground the gears into reverse and backed up as recklessly as he'd gone forward. He slammed the door, shot a ferocious look at the house and stamped away in the opposite direction. Hand to her heart, she dashed up the walk and through the front door.

"Anna!" Fluttering her hands, she caught her daughter at the base of the staircase. "What's going on?"

Anna wanted to be alone. She wanted to go to her room, shut the door and lie on the bed. There was so much to absorb, so much to savor. She needed to weep and wasn't even sure why. Patient, she waited. "Going on?"

"I was clipping the roses." Flustered, Mrs. Whitfield shook her half-filled basket. "And I heard, well I couldn't help but hear..." She let her words trail off, unnerved by Anna's calm brown eyes, which suddenly seemed so mature. To give herself a minute, Mrs. Whitfield carefully pulled off her gardening gloves and laid them on a table.

"I understand you weren't eavesdropping, Mother."

"Of course not! I wouldn't dream—" She caught herself sliding away from the point and straightened her shoulders. "Anna, are you and Mr. MacGregor— Did you...?" The sentence wandered away as she shifted her hands on the basket.

"Yes." With a private smile, Anna stepped from the landing. "We made love this afternoon."

"Oh." It was a feeble response, but the only one she could come up with.

"Mother—" Anna took the basket from her hands "—I'm not a child any longer."

"Obviously." With a deep breath, Mrs. Whitfield faced her duty. "However, if Mr. MacGregor has seduced you, then—"

"He didn't."

Having revved herself up, Mrs. Whitfield could only blink at the interruption. "But you said—"

"I said we made love. He didn't have to seduce me."

Anna took her mother by the arm. "Maybe we should sit down."

"Yes." Shaky, she let herself be led. "Maybe we should."

In the parlor Anna sat beside her mother on the sofa. How should she begin? Never in her wildest dreams had she imagined sitting with her mother in this fussy parlor and discussing romance, love and sex. Taking a deep breath, she plunged. "Mother, I'd never been with a man before. I wanted to be with Daniel. It wasn't something I did impetuously, but something I gave a great deal of thought to."

"I've always said you think too much," Mrs. Whitfield responded automatically.

"I'm sorry." Used to parental criticism, Anna laid her hands quietly in her lap. "I know it's not something you want to hear, but I can't lie to you."

Love, propriety and confusion warred together. Love won. "Oh, Anna." In a rare gesture, Mrs. Whitfield gathered Anna close. "Are you all right?"

"Of course I am." Touched, Anna let her head rest against her mother's shoulder. "I feel wonderful. It's like— I don't know—being unlocked."

"Yes." She blinked back tears. "That's how it should be. I know we've never really talked of such things. We should have, but then you went off to that school and those books...." She remembered her shock when she had picked one up to give it a casual glance. "I suppose it all made me feel inadequate."

"It's nothing like books." Anna discovered she could savor it after all.

"No, it's not." She shifted to take both her daughter's hands. "Books can be closed. Anna, I don't want you to be hurt."

"Daniel won't hurt me." She was warmed even now, remembering how gentle he'd struggled to be. "In fact, he's much too concerned about not hurting me. He wants me to marry him."

Mrs. Whitfield breathed a sigh of relief. "I thought I heard him say so, but you sounded as though you were fighting."

"Not fighting, disagreeing. I'm not going to marry him."

"Anna." When her mother drew away, her face was stern. "What kind of nonsense is this? I admit I don't always understand you, but I know you well enough to be sure nothing would have happened between the two of you if you hadn't cared very deeply."

"I do." Losing some of her composure, Anna pressed her fingers to her eyes. "Maybe too much, it's frightening. He wants a wife, Mother, almost the way a man wants a shoe that fits well."

"That's just their way." On firmer ground, Mrs. Whitfield sat back. "Some men are poets, some are dreamers, but most are just men. I know girls think there should be pretty words and lovely music, but life is much more basic than that."

Curious, Anna studied her. Her mother, she knew from experience, had never been much of a philosopher. "Did you want pretty words?"

"Of course." With a smile, Mrs. Whitfield thought of her past. "Your father is a good man, a very good man, but most of his words come out of law books. I think Mr. MacGregor's a good man."

"He is. I don't want to lose him, but I can't marry him."

"Anna—"

"I'm going to live with him."

Mrs. Whitfield opened her mouth, shut it again and swallowed. "I think I'd like a drink."

Rising, Anna walked to the liquor cabinet. "Sherry?"

"Scotch. A double."

Tension dissolved in amusement as Anna poured. "Daniel had a very similar reaction." She handed her mother the glass and watched her gulp it down. "I've never hidden anything from you."

The Scotch burned through her system. "No, no, you've always been painfully honest."

"I care very much for Daniel." Honest, Anna reminded herself and let out a long breath. "I'm in love with him. That isn't something I chose, so now I feel as though I have to take back some control. If I marry him, I'll lose everything I've been working for."

Mrs. Whitfield set down the empty glass. "Your degree."

"I know you don't understand that, either. No one seems to." She ran her hands through her hair. It fell loose to her shoulders and made her remember that her combs still lay where they had fallen in the grass. The combs didn't matter, they could be replaced. Other things had been lost on that cliff top that couldn't. "What I know, in my heart, is that if I marry Daniel now I'll never finish. And if I don't, I'll never forgive myself or him. Mother, I've tried to explain to you before that being a doctor isn't simply what I want to do, it's what I have to do."

"Sometimes we have to weigh one important thing against another Anna, and choose."

"And sometimes we don't." Desperate for reassurance, she knelt at her mother's feet. "I know it's selfish to want it all, but I've thought it through over and over. I have to be a doctor, and I don't want to live without Daniel."

"And Daniel?"

"He wants marriage. He can't see beyond that, but he will."

"Always so sure of yourself, Anna." She recognized the look in her daughter's eyes: calm, clear and filled with ruthless determination. She nearly sighed. "You would never ask for anything, and I was fooled into thinking you were absolutely content. Then, all at once, you would demand everything."

"I didn't choose to be a doctor any more than I chose to fall in love with Daniel. Both things just are."

"Anna, a step like this can bring you a lot of pain, a lot of unhappiness. If you love Daniel, then marriage—"

"It isn't time, and I can't be sure it ever will be." Frustrated, she rose and paced the room. "I'm terrified to make that kind of mistake—for him, as well as for myself. All I know is that now, right now, I don't want to be without him. Maybe it's wrong, but would it be better, would it be right if we continued to be lovers in secret? Can you tell me it would be more acceptable if we stole a few hours here and there, a night, an afternoon?"

"I could never tell you anything," her mother murmured.

"Oh, please." More frightened than she wanted to admit, Anna went to her mother again. "Now more than ever I want your understanding. It's not just desire, though that's certainly part of it. It's a need to be with him, to share some of his dreams, because I'm not sure I'll be able to share them all. To love him in secret would be hypocrisy. He means too much for that. I won't hide what I feel. I won't hide what I am."

Mrs. Whitfield looked at her only child, at her dark, earnest eyes, her soft, sculpted mouth. She wished she had the answers. "You know what you'll be up against? What people will say?"

"That doesn't matter to me."

"It never has," her mother muttered. "I know how impossible it is to talk you out of anything once your mind's made up, and you're too old for me to forbid anything, but, Anna, you can't ask me to approve.''

''I know.'' For a moment, she laid her head in her mother's lap. ''But if somewhere inside you, if in some little part you could understand, it would be enough.''

Sighing, she touched her daughter's hand. ''I haven't forgotten what it is to be in love. Maybe I do understand, and maybe that's why I'm afraid for you. Anna, you've never been anything but a good daughter, but...''

She had to smile, just a little. ''But?''

''You've also always been a puzzle. I know I've never actually told you I was proud of you, but I am.''

Anna felt a little quiver of relief work through her. ''I know I never actually told you I needed you to be proud, but I do.''

''I have to admit that I always hoped that you'd forget about medicine and settle down into a marriage where I could see you happy, and yet another part of me has watched you and cheered.''

Her fingers curled around her mother's. ''I don't know how to tell you how much that means to me.''

''I think I know. Now your father...'' She closed her eyes, unable to even imagine his reaction.

''He'll be upset, I know. I'm sorry.''

''I'll handle him.'' The words came out on impulse, but she discovered they were true. Mrs. Whitfield straightened her shoulders.

With a smile, Anna lifted her head. For a moment, for the first time, she and her mother looked at each other woman to woman. ''I love you, Mother.''

''And I love you.'' She drew her up on the sofa. ''I don't have to understand you for that.''

With a sigh, Anna laid her head on her mother's shoulder. "Is it too much to ask for you to wish me luck?"

"As a mother, yes." She found herself smiling. "But not as a woman."

Chapter Eight

As the days passed, Anna began to fear that she'd lost. There were no phone calls, no irate visits. No white roses were delivered to the door. The ones still cluttering her room and her mother's parlor were a testimony to what might have been. And they were wilting.

More and more often she caught herself looking out the window at the sound of a car passing, dashing to the phone on the first ring. Each time she did so, she swore at herself and promised not to do it again. But, of course, she did.

She never left the hospital without scanning the lot for the blue convertible. Each time she stepped out of the wide white building she expected to see a big, broad-shouldered, red-bearded man waiting impatiently by the curb. He was never there, but she never stopped looking.

It was disconcerting to learn that she'd come to depend on him, but it was even more disconcerting to discover what she'd come to depend on him for. Happiness. She could be content without him. She could certainly be satisfied with her life and her career. But Anna was no longer sure she could be happy unless Daniel was a part of her day-to-day life.

One day, as she read aloud to a young patient with a broken leg, her mind wandered. To her annoyance she had caught herself daydreaming several times during working hours since Daniel had driven away from her house. Lecturing herself, she brought her attention back to the patient and the story. Like sand, her thoughts scattered again.

The happy-ever-after tale she spun to the sleepy little girl wasn't reality. Certainly the last thing Anna wanted was to sit quietly by and wait for a prince to fit her with a glass slipper. And of course she was too practical to believe in castles in the clouds or magic until midnight. It was nice perhaps, in a story, to dream about white chargers and heroes, but a woman wanted more in real life. In real life, a woman wanted—well, a partner, Anna supposed, not a knight or a prince who would always have to be looked up to and admired. A real woman wanted a real man, and a smart one wasn't going to sit around in a tower and wait for one to come along. She was going to live her own life and make her own choices.

Anna had always been a firm believer in the making of one's own destiny, of fighting—with logic and patience—for one's needs. So why was she waiting around? she asked herself abruptly. If she was as independent as she professed and as she intended to behave, then why was she mooning around and waiting for the phone to ring? Anyone who sat placidly by until someone else called the shots was a fool and a loser. She didn't intend to be either.

Her mind made up, Anna continued to read until the little girl's eyes closed. Shutting the book, she strode out into the hall. On the way down, she passed a frazzled, heavy-eyed intern and nearly smiled. At the moment she was certain he wouldn't understand her twinge of envy. Perhaps no one would but another med student. Still, in a few months she wouldn't be able to leave the hospital on her own whim. It wouldn't hurt to take advantage of the time she had left.

Outside, the weather was nasty. It was gray and stormy and so hot that the rain seemed to steam the moment it hit the concrete. By the time she made it to her car, she was humming and soaked to the skin. She drove across town with the radio turned up as high as her spirits.

The building that housed Old Line Savings and Loan was dignified, staid and trustworthy. As she raced across the little patch of lawn, Anna wondered if Daniel had made any changes. Inside, there was fresh paint and new carpeting but business was still transacted in hushed whispers. Anna ran a hand through her hair, scattering water, then headed for the nearest clerk. She crossed her fingers behind her back.

Upstairs, Daniel looked over the ads that would run in the paper the following week. His manager had cringed when he'd brought in the files, but the young assistant Daniel had hired had been enthusiastic. Some decisions were meant to be made on instinct. Instinct told Daniel that the ads would increase both his business and his reputation. And one was every bit as important as the other. He was not only going to put Old Line back on its feet, he would have a branch in Salem within two years.

Even as the idea germinated, his thoughts drifted away from business. He remembered a windy cliff top and a woman with sable hair and dark eyes. The thrill that rippled through him was as fresh as it had been when his arms had been around her. Her taste was a lingering sensation nothing else had been able to replace. Even here, in the privacy of his office he could smell her, quiet and sweet.

With an impatient mutter, he pushed the papers aside and strode to the window. He should be seeing other women. Hadn't he sworn he would when he'd driven away from Anna? He'd meant to, even started to. But each and every time he tried to so much as think of another woman, Anna was there. She was so firmly planted in his mind that there wasn't room for anyone else. He wasn't going to get over her.

Daniel stared out at the steadily driving rain. From the window, the Boston he looked at seemed gray and depressed. It suited his mood. After he was finished with his stacks of paperwork and meetings, he'd take a walk along the river, fair weather or foul. He needed to be alone, away from servants, employees. But not away from Anna. He could follow the Charles from end to end and never escape Anna. How could you escape what was in your blood, in your bone? And Anna was there. No matter how he tried to pretend he had a choice, Anna was there.

He wanted to marry her. Daniel whirled away from the window to pace the room with his hands thrust in his pockets and his brows lowered. He'd chosen anger over despair and fury over fear. Damn the woman, he thought yet again. He wanted to marry her. He wanted to wake up in the morning and know she was there. He wanted to come home at night and be able to reach for her. He wanted to see his child grow inside her. And he wanted these things with a desperation as foreign to him as failure.

Failure? The word alone had him clenching his teeth. He was far from ready to admit failure. The hell with other women, Daniel decided abruptly. There was only one. He was going after her.

When the phone on his desk rang he was halfway to the door. Cursing all the way he went back to yank it up. "MacGregor."

"Mr. MacGregor, this is Mary Miles, head cashier. I apologize for interrupting you but there's a young woman down in the lobby who insists on seeing you."

"Have her make an appointment with my secretary."

"Yes, sir, I suggested that, but she insists on seeing you now. She says she'll wait."

"I don't have time to see everyone who walks in off the street, Mrs. Miles." Daniel checked his watch. Anna would be out of the hospital. He'd have to catch her at home.

"Yes, sir." The cashier felt herself being squeezed between two ungiving forces. "I explained that to her, but she's very insistent. She's very polite, Mr. MacGregor, but I don't think she's going to budge."

Losing patience, Daniel swore again. "Tell her…" His voice trailed off as the cashier's words formed a picture in his mind. "What's her name?"

"Whitfield. Anna Whitfield."

"What have you got her waiting in the lobby for?" he demanded. "Send her up."

The cashier rolled her eyes and reminded herself of the raise Mr. MacGregor had given across the board when he'd bought the bank. "Yes, sir. Right away."

She'd changed her mind. Victory didn't settle over him. He soared with it. His patience, though it had cost him dearly, had paid off. She was ready to be sensible. True, he hadn't imagined discussing marriage in his office, but he was willing to make some concessions. The plain truth was he was willing to make a great many concessions. But she was coming to him. He would have everything he wanted, including his pride.

The knock on his door was brisk and businesslike before his secretary pushed it open. "Miss Whitfield to see you, sir."

He briefly nodded a dismissal before his gaze and every

thought in his head focused on Anna. She stood on the thick gray carpet he'd recently had installed, dripping from head to foot. The rain had washed her face clean and left her hair dark and shiny and curling to her shoulders. She quite simply took his breath away.

"You're wet." His words came out sounding more like an accusation than a statement of concern. She met it with a smile.

"It's raining." Good God, it was good to see him. For a moment she could only smile foolishly and take him in. His tie was off, his collar open. His hair showed evidence of being combed impatiently with his fingers. She wanted to open her arms and take him to her, where she was beginning to understand he belonged. Instead, she continued to smile and drip quietly on his elegant carpet. While she smiled, he stared. For several humming seconds, neither of them spoke.

Catching himself, Daniel cleared his throat and scowled at her. "Seems to me anybody studying medicine should know better than to run around soaking wet." He pulled open the door to a cabinet and took out a bottle of brandy. "You'll find yourself spending more time in that hospital of yours than you'd like."

"I don't think a little summer shower should do me much harm." For the first time it occurred to her how she must look, with her hair dripping and tangled, her clothes splattered with rain and her shoes damp. She kept her chin up. Wet or not, she had her dignity.

"Drink this, anyway." He thrust a snifter into her hand. "Sit."

"No, I'll ruin—"

"Sit," he repeated in one terse bark.

Lifting a brow, she walked to a chair. "Very well."

She sat, but he didn't. The sweet taste of victory had

already faded. He knew just by looking at her that she hadn't changed her mind. Not Anna. The truth was he never would have fallen so helplessly in love with a woman whose mind could be swayed. She hadn't come to accept his offer of marriage, and he was far from ready to accept her alternative.

His lips curved a bit. His eyes took on a light that those accustomed to doing business with him would have recognized—and been wary of. Stand off, Daniel told himself. But there was no way he would let Miss Anna Whitfield know she had him on edge. He let his gaze run down her once more as she sat ruining the upholstery of his chair.

"Interested in a loan, Anna?"

She sipped and let the brandy calm her sudden nervousness. The easy tone and slight smile didn't fool her for an instant. So, he was still angry. What else should she have expected? Would she have fallen in love with a man who could be too easily cajoled? No, she'd fallen in love with Daniel because he was precisely what he was.

"Not at the moment." To give herself time, she studied the room. "Your office is very nice, Daniel. Dignified but not stuffy." There was a bold abstract on the wall done in different tones and shades of blue. Though it seemed to be no more than random shapes and lines, the sense of sexuality was throbbingly clear. She shifted her gaze from it to his. "Definitely not stuffy."

He'd seen her study the abstract and knew she understood it. He'd paid a stiff price for the Picasso because it had appealed to him and because his instincts had told him the value would skyrocket within a generation. "You're a hard woman to shock, Anna."

"That's true." And because it was, she found herself relaxing. "I've always felt life was too important to go through it pretending to be offended by it. I've missed the roses.''

He leaned a hip against the corner of his massive desk. "I thought you didn't like me sending them to you."

"I didn't. Until you stopped." She left it at that, deciding that even she was entitled to some quirks. "I hadn't heard from you in several days and I wondered if I'd shocked you."

"Shocked me?" A few moments before he'd wavered between tension and boredom. With Anna here, everything seemed settled into place again. "I'm not one to shock easily, either."

"Offended then," she suggested, "because I'd choose to live with you rather than marry you."

He nearly smiled. Had he once said he liked a woman to speak her mind—to a point? It didn't seem odd at all that his opinion on that had already changed radically. "Annoyed," he corrected. "We might even go to infuriated."

She remembered his reaction. "Yes, I think we might. You're still angry."

"Aye. You're still set in your mind?"

"Yes."

Thoughtfully he drew out a cigar, running his fingers over it once before lighting it. In business, he knew how to handle an opponent. Force him to make the pitch. It kept a man in the driver's seat when the other player had to do the explaining. Smoke wreathed over his head as he watched her and waited. "Why did you come here, Anna?"

So, he didn't intend to give an inch. She took another slow sip of brandy. All right then, neither would she. "Because I realized I didn't want to go another day without seeing you." She set the brandy aside as the haze of his smoke billowed then cleared. "Do you mind?"

He let out an impatient huff of breath. Business and personal matters didn't always have the same rules. Still, the aim was to win. "It's hard for a man to mind the woman he intends to marry wanting to be with him."

"Good." She rose then and made a vain attempt to tidy her damp skirts. "Then you'll have dinner with me tonight."

His eyes narrowed. "A man usually likes to do the asking."

She sighed and gave a little shake of her head as she walked to him. "You're forgetting what century you're in again. I'll pick you up at seven."

"You'll—"

"Pick you up at seven," she finished then rose to her toes. When she found his lips with hers, it was soft and easy and completely right. "Thanks for the brandy, Daniel. I won't keep you any longer."

He found his voice by the time she'd walked to the door. "Anna."

She turned, a half smile on her lips. "Yes?"

He saw in the smile that she expected, even anticipated an argument. Change tactics and confuse, Daniel thought, and easily drew on his cigar. "It'll have to be seven-thirty. I have a late meeting."

He had the satisfaction of seeing a quick flicker of doubt cross her face before she nodded. "Fine."

When she shut the door at her back, she let out a long pent-up breath.

By his desk, Daniel grinned, chuckled and ultimately roared with laughter. Though he wasn't sure who'd gotten the best of whom, he discovered it didn't matter. He'd always been one to try a new game, new rules. He'd give Anna the cards and the deal. But, by God, he'd still win.

* * *

The rain had slowed to a drizzle by the time Anna arrived home. She found the house empty, but the scent of her mother's perfume still lingered in the hallway. Pleased to find herself alone, she went upstairs to indulge in a long hot bath. It was a good feeling, she discovered, to have taken the initiative. Once again she was in control, though her foundation was a bit shakier than it could have been.

Daniel MacGregor was not a man who could be manipulated. She'd learned that right from the beginning. But she did believe he was a man who would respond to negotiation. Her main problem would be to keep him from seeing just how much she'd give.

Everything. She closed her eyes as she squeezed the sponge and dripped hot water over her throat and breasts. If he discovered that, if pressed into a corner, she'd give him anything he wanted, he'd press her there without hesitation. A man like Daniel hadn't made it to the top by being a pushover. But she intended to make it to the top in her own profession, as well. So she had to be equally strong, equally determined.

After she picked him up, they'd have a quiet dinner, easy conversation. Over coffee they'd discuss—rationally—their situation. Before it was over, he would understand her feelings and her position. Anna sank down in the waters with a sigh. Who was she trying to fool? That didn't sound like dinner with Daniel MacGregor for a minute.

They'd spar with each other, argue, disagree and probably laugh a great deal. He'd very likely shout. It was entirely possible she'd shout, as well. When it was over, she doubted he'd understand anything, except that he wanted her to marry him.

Something fluttered inside her at the thought. He did want her. She might have gone through her entire life without anyone looking at her in just the way Daniel did. She might have gone through her life without anyone opening those sturdy locks she'd kept on her passion. What would her life have been like then?

Bland. She smiled at the word that sprang to mind. She certainly wouldn't settle for that now. She wanted Daniel MacGregor. And she was going to have him.

Keeping her self-confidence at a peak was half the battle, she realized as she stepped from the tub. It was so easy for it to slip away degree by degree while he looked at her. She wouldn't allow it to happen tonight. With a towel wrapped around her hair, she bundled into a robe. *She* was taking *him* to dinner. Whatever slight edge that gave her, she wouldn't lose it.

Opening her closet, she frowned. Usually she knew precisely what best suited an evening she had planned. Tonight, everything she pulled out seemed too fussy, too plain or simply too ordinary. Calling herself a fool, she grabbed a sea-foam-green silk and laid it on her bed. Perhaps it was almost severely simple, but that was very possibly the best idea for the evening. If she wanted something dashing, she mused, she should have raided Myra's closet. As the thought came and went, she heard the doorbell chime.

She found herself grumbling at the interruption, something so out of character that she lectured herself all the way downstairs. As she opened the door, Myra dashed inside and grabbed both her hands.

"Oh, Anna, I'm so glad you're home."

"Myra, I was just thinking about you." By the time the words were out, she noticed the death grip on her fingers. "What's wrong?"

"I have to talk to you." For perhaps the first time in her life Myra found herself almost beyond words. "Alone. Are your parents in?"

"No."

"Good. I need a drink first. Offer me a brandy."

"All right." Amused, Anna began to lead her to the parlor. "Terrific hat."

"Is it?" Myra lifted a worried hand to the off-white cap and veil. "It's not too fussy?"

"Too fussy?" Anna poured her a double brandy. "Let me get this straight. You're asking me if something you're wearing is too fussy?"

"Don't be cute, Anna." Turning to a mirror, Myra toyed with the veil. "Maybe I should pull out the feather."

Anna glanced at the saucy little feather curling over Myra's ear. "Now I know something's wrong."

"How about the dress?" Myra slipped out of a vivid red raincoat to reveal a trim silk suit with lace at the collar and cuffs.

"It's exquisite. Is it new?"

"It's twenty minutes old."

Anna sat on the arm of a chair while her friend gulped down brandy. "You didn't have to dress up for me."

Myra let out a quick breath and straightened her shoulders before she set the empty snifter down. "This is no time for jokes."

"I can see that." But she smiled anyway. "What is it time for?"

"How soon can you toss on something wonderful and pack an overnight bag?"

"Pack?" She watched as Myra fingered the lace at her throat. "Myra, what's going on?"

"I'm getting married." She said it in a rush, then let out a small explosion of breath. Because her legs were unsteady she dropped onto the sofa.

"Getting married?" Stunned Anna sat exactly where she was. "Myra, I know you work fast and I haven't seen much of you in a couple of weeks, but *married*?"

"It wouldn't hurt to say it a few times so I'd stop losing my breath every time I hear the word. I've already babbled to the clerk in the dress shop and I don't want to do that again. If there's one thing I refuse to do, it's make a fool of myself."

"Married," Anna repeated for both of them. "To whom?" As Myra fastened and unfastened the top button of her jacket, Anna groped for a candidate. "Peter?"

"Who? No, no, of course not."

"Of course not," Anna murmured. "I know, Jack Holmes."

"Don't be ridiculous."

"Steven Marlowe."

Myra fiddled with the hem of her skirt. "Anna, really, I hardly know the man."

"Hardly know him? Why six months ago you—"

"That was six months ago," Myra interrupted, blushing for the first time since Anna had known her. "And I'd appreciate it if you'd forget anything I'd ever written you about him. Better yet, burn those letters."

"Darling, they self-destructed the moment I read them. You should have used fire-proof paper."

Despite herself, Myra grinned. "You're speaking to an engaged woman. I've put all that behind me. Look." Breathy with excitement, Myra held out her left hand.

"Oh." She was usually very casual about jewelry herself, but the simple square-cut diamond on Myra's finger seemed impossibly beautiful. "It's exquisite, really exquisite, Myra. I'm so happy for you." She was up and gathering Myra close for a hug before she laughed. "How do I know I'm happy for you? I don't know who you're going to marry."

"Herbert Ditmeyer." Myra waited for the look of astonishment and wasn't disappointed. "I know, I was pretty damn surprised myself."

"But I didn't think you even...that is you always said he was..." Catching herself, Anna cleared her throat.

"Stuffy," Myra finished and smiled beautifully. "And he is. He's stuffy and rather sober and frustratingly proper. He's also the sweetest man I've ever known. These past couple of weeks..." She sat back, a little dreamy, a little stunned. "I never knew what it could be like to have a man treat you as though you were special. Really special. I went out with him the first time, because he'd had such a hard time asking me and I felt sorry for him. And flattered," she admitted. "I went out with him the second time because I'd had such a good time. Herbert can be so funny. It kind of sneaks up on you."

Touched, Anna watched love bloom in Myra's eyes. "I know."

"You were always such a good friend to him. I'm lucky he didn't fall in love with you. The thing is, he's been in love with me for years." With a little shake of her head, she pulled a cigarette from her purse. "We'd been going out for a couple of weeks when he told me. I was so stunned I could hardly speak. Then I tried to ease myself out gently. After all, he was very sweet and I didn't want to hurt him."

Anna lifted the ringed hand again. "It doesn't appear you eased yourself out."

"No." Still dazed, Myra stared at the diamond winking up at her. "It occurred to me all at once that I didn't want to ease myself out, that I was crazy about him. Isn't that wild?"

"I think it's wonderful."

"Me, too." She stubbed out the cigarette without having taken the first puff. "And tonight. Tonight he put this ring on my finger, told me we were flying to Maryland at eight and getting married.''

"Tonight.'' Anna took Myra's hand again. "Tonight. It's so quick, Myra.''

"Why wait?''

Why wait, indeed? She could think of hundreds of reasons, but none of them would have gotten past that dreamy look in Myra's eyes. "Are you sure?''

"I'm more sure about this than I've ever been about anything in my life. Be happy for me, Anna.''

"I am.'' Tears swam in her eyes as she held Myra again. "You know I am.''

"Then get dressed.'' Half laughing, half crying, Myra pushed her away. "You're my maid of honor.''

"You want me to fly to Maryland tonight?''

"We agreed to elope because it was simpler than dealing with his mother. She doesn't like me and probably never will.''

"Oh, Myra—''

"It doesn't matter. Herbert and I love each other. Anyway, I don't want a big fancy wedding. It takes too long. But I don't want to be married without my best friend there. I really need you, Anna. I want this more than anything in the world, and I'm scared to death.''

Any objections she might have had disappeared. "I can be dressed and packed in twenty minutes.''

Grinning, Myra gave her a last hug. "Because it's you I believe it.''

"Just let me leave a note for my parents.'' She already had the pen in her hand.

"Ah, Anna…'' Myra ran her tongue over her teeth. "I know your sense of honesty won't let you lie—exactly. Could you just not mention what you're going away for?

Herbert and I really want to keep this quiet until we tell his mother."

Anna thought a moment, then began to write. Taking a short trip with Myra. May do some antique shopping—which I may, she added half to herself. I'll be home in a day or two. She signed it and glanced up, showing it to Myra. "Vague enough?"

"Perfectly. Thanks."

"Come on, give me a hand." As she dashed into the hall, she remembered. "Oh, I have to call Daniel and cancel dinner."

"Daniel MacGregor?" Myra's brows arched as only they could.

"That's right." Ignoring the look, Anna headed for the phone. "I'll have to let him know I can't make it tonight."

"You can have dinner with him in Maryland." Myra took the receiver from her and replaced it. "Herbert's asking him to be best man."

"I see." Anna brushed a hand casually down her robe. "Well, that's handy, isn't it?"

"Very." With a grin, Myra pulled her upstairs.

Chapter Nine

.

She'd never flown before. At twenty, Anna had sailed to Europe in luxury and comfort. She'd traveled hundreds of miles on trains, lulled by the swaying motion and watching the landscape whiz by. But she'd never been in the air. If anyone had told her she'd be climbing into a small private plane that looked as though it could land safely in her backyard, she'd have thought them mad.

Love, she thought as she set her teeth and took the last step inside. If she didn't love Myra, she'd turn around and run for her life. She was certain the tin can with propellers could get off the ground. She wished she felt as confident about how it would get down again.

"Quite a machine, isn't it?" Daniel watched Anna take her seat before he settled in his own.

"Quite," she muttered and wondered if it came with parachutes.

"First flight?"

She started to give him a stiff and dignified yes, then

saw he wasn't laughing at her. "Yeah." The word came out on a little breath.

"Try to think of it as an adventure," he suggested.

She glanced at the ground outside the window and wished she were still standing on it. "I'm trying not to think of it at all."

"You've more guts than that, Anna. I should know." Then he grinned at her. "It should be an adventure the first time. After a while flying becomes routine, and you really don't think much about it."

She told herself to relax and used the old trick of starting at her toes and working up. She never got past her knees. "I guess you're used to it. Is this the sort of plane you fly to New York in?"

With a chuckle he fastened her seat belt, then his own. "This is the plane I fly to New York in. I own it."

"Oh." As his words sank in she found that the fact that it was Daniel's plane somehow made flying in it all right. She glanced over to where Myra and Herbert were seated and strapped in, heads together. An adventure, she decided. She'd enjoy one. "So when do we start?"

"There's a lass," he murmured and signaled to the pilot. The engine started with a roar and they were off.

Though her anxiety had passed, there was an air of both celebration and tension all through the flight. Anna saw the tension in Myra as her friend twisted a lace handkerchief into knots as she laughed and talked. Herbert sat, a little pale, a little stiff, and spoke only when prodded. For herself, Anna heard the voices around her, watched the landscape beneath her with a sense of unreality. It was all happening so fast. If it hadn't been for Daniel's easy jokes and constant banter, the celebrational part of the flight might have dissolved into mild hysteria. He was, Anna noted as he flirted outrageously with Myra, enjoying himself. And while he was about it, he was keeping the bride-to-be from climbing the walls of the cabin. He wasn't just an interesting man, she realized. He was a good friend. Pulling herself out of her thoughts, Anna made an effort to be as good.

"You have excellent taste, Herbert."

"What?" He swallowed and straightened his tie. "Oh, yes. Thank you." Then he looked at Myra with his heart in his eyes. "She's wonderful, isn't she?"

"The best. I don't know what I'd have done without her. Life certainly would have been a great deal duller."

"We serious-minded people need someone with a little sparkle in our lives, don't we?" He gave Anna a nervous smile. "Otherwise, we'd just crawl into our careers and forget there was anything else out there."

Serious minded? She let the phrase play in her head. Yes, she supposed she was. In addition, she was coming to understand that Herbert was right. "And people with—sparkle," she murmured with a glance at Myra and Daniel, "need a serious-minded person in their lives to keep them from running off cliffs."

"I'm going to make her happy."

Because his words sounded more like a question than a statement, Anna took his hands. "Oh, yes. You're going to make her very happy."

The small private plane touched down in a rural airport in Maryland. The lingering drizzle had been left behind. Here, the late-evening sky was as clear as glass and crowded with stars. The sliver of moon was like a smile. It might have been a wedding night chosen on impulse, but it was perfect. Taking Myra by the arm, Herbert led the way to the little terminal.

"The justice of the peace who was recommended to me is only about twenty miles from here. I'll check about getting a cab or a car."

"That won't be necessary." When they entered the terminal Daniel quickly scanned it then signaled to a tall uniformed chauffeur.

"Mr. MacGregor?"

"Aye. Give him the directions," he told Herbert. "I took the liberty of arranging for transportation."

Without fuss, the chauffeur gathered the suitcases and led the way outside. At the curb was a pearl-gray stretch limo.

"You didn't give a body much time to come up with a wedding present," Daniel explained. "This was the best I could do."

"It's perfect." With a laugh, Myra swung her arms around him. "Absolutely perfect."

Daniel winked at Herbert over her head. "The best man's supposed to handle the details."

Anna waited until Herbert had helped Myra inside. "This was very sweet of you."

"I'm a sweet man," he told her.

She laughed and accepted his hand. "Maybe. I wouldn't depend on it."

Inside, Myra already had her arm linked through Herbert's. "Two bottles of champagne?"

"One for before." Daniel lifted one from its bucket of ice. "One for after." He let out a cork with a hiss and a pop then poured four glasses. "To happiness."

Four glasses clinked solemnly together, but when Daniel drank, he looked at Anna. As the champagne exploded in her mouth, she realized the adventure was far from over.

By the time they arrived at the little white house, all the champagne and the lingering tension had been drained. With her usual aplomb, Myra tidied her hair and makeup in a powder room off the hall while Anna stood by and held her hat. She took her time, but Anna noted that her hands were steady.

"How do I look?" Myra demanded, and managed a quick turn in the cramped room.

"Beautiful."

"I've always been a couple of degrees away from beautiful, but tonight I think I've nearly managed stunning."

Hands firm, Anna turned her toward the mirror again. "Tonight you're beautiful. Take a good look."

Looking at their reflections together, Myra grinned. "He really loves me, Anna."

"I know." She slipped her arm around Myra's shoulder. "You're going to make quite a team."

"Yes, we are." As her chin tilted up, her grin softened into a smile. "I don't think he realizes just how much of a team yet, but he will." On a quick breath she turned and took Anna by the shoulders. "I don't like to get sentimental, but since I only intend to get married once, this seems to be the time. You're my best friend and I love you. I want you to be as happy as I am this minute."

"I'm working on it."

Satisfied, Myra nodded. "Okay then, let's go. And listen—" she put her hand on the knob and paused "—if I stutter, don't tell anyone—especially Catherine Donahue."

Solemn eyed, Anna put a hand over her heart. "I won't tell a soul."

In a parlor with a tiny marble fireplace and summer flowers in glass vases, Anna watched her closest friend promise to love, honor and cherish. When her eyes misted, she felt foolish and tried to blink them clear. It was silly to cry over two adults making a legal contract with each other. Marriage was, after all, a contract. That was why it had to be approached so cautiously, so practically. But the first tear escaped and ran slowly down her cheek. She felt Daniel press his handkerchief into her hand as he'd done once before. Even as she sniffed into it, the ceremony was over and she found herself hugging a dazed Myra.

"I did it," Myra murmured, then laughed and gave Anna a rib-crushing squeeze.

"And without one single stutter."

"I did it," she repeated and held out her hand. Snuggled next to the diamond was a slim gold band. "Engaged and married within five hours."

Daniel took the hand she was admiring and kissed it formally. "Mrs. Ditmeyer."

Chuckling, Myra curled her fingers around his. "Be sure to call me that several times this evening so I'll learn to answer to it. Oh, Anna, I'm going to cry and destroy my mascara."

"It's all right." Anna handed her Daniel's already crumpled handkerchief. "Herbert's stuck with you now." Anna wound her arms around him and held tight.

He laughed and gave Anna a long, hard squeeze. "And she's stuck with me."

"She'll complicate your life."

"I know."

"Isn't it wonderful?" Anna kissed him hard. "I don't know about you, but I'm starving. The wedding supper is on me."

Through the recommendation of the justice of the peace and the help of the chauffeur, they found a country inn at the peak of a wooded hill. It was, as they'd been told, small, quaint and possibly closed. With a little persuasion, and the exchange of a few bills, they persuaded the owner to open the restaurant and wake up the cook. While the others were led into the dining room, Anna made an excuse about freshening up and slipped aside. Moments later, she waylaid the owner again.

"Mr. Portersfield, I can't thank you enough for accommodating us."

Though he was always glad to receive paying guests, the lateness of the hour had put him a bit out of sorts. He found it difficult, however, to resist the smile Anna sent him. "My doors are always open," he told her. "Unfortunately the kitchen closes at nine, so the meal may not quite live up to our reputation."

"I'm sure everything will be wonderful. As a matter of fact, I can almost promise that my friends will tell you it's the best meal they've ever eaten. You see—" linking her arm through his, she strolled a little farther away from the others "—they were just married a half hour ago. That's why you and I have to arrange a few things."

"Newlyweds." Mr. Portersfield wasn't a man completely without romance. "We're always pleased to have newlyweds at the inn. If we'd had just a bit of notice—"

"Oh, I'm sure the few things we need won't be too much bother. Did I mention that Mr. Ditmeyer is the district attorney in Boston? I'm sure when he gets back from his honeymoon with his new bride, he's going to praise your inn to all his friends. And Mr. MacGregor—" she lowered her voice "—well, I don't have to tell you who he is."

He didn't have the vaguest idea, but implied importance was enough. "No, of course, not."

"A man in his position doesn't often find a quiet place like this to relax. Home cooking, country air. I can assure you he's very impressed by your establishment. Tell me, Mr. Portersfield, do you have a record player?"

"A record player? I have one in my room, but—"

"Perfect." Anna patted his hand and tried the smile again. "I knew you'd be able to help me."

Fifteen minutes later, she was back in the dining room.

At the table was a loaf of crusty bread, a pot of butter and little else.

"Where'd you disappear to?" Daniel asked as she took her seat.

"Details. To the bride and groom," she said and lifted her water glass.

As they toasted, Myra laughed. "And I was just about to say to Herbert that he can look forward to many meals just like this—" she indicated the bread and water "—until we get a cook."

He took her hand and brought it to his lips. "I didn't marry you for your culinary prowess."

"A good thing," Anna said, then added, "she hasn't any."

A sleepy boy of about fifteen came into the room with a vase of wildflowers. A look at the dew on the petals told Anna they'd just been picked. It looked as if Mr. Portersfield was going to come through.

"Oh, how pretty." Myra reached to pluck one out as the boy wandered away and began to pull tables across the floor. Loudly. Mr. Portersfield shuffled into the room, lugging a phonograph. Within moments, there was music.

"The first dance for the Herbert Ditmeyers," Anna stated, and gestured to the space the boy had cleared on the floor. When they were alone at the table, Daniel buttered a chunk of bread and handed it to her. "You accomplished quite a lot in a short time."

Hungry, Anna bit into the bread. "Just the beginning, Mr. MacGregor."

"You know, when you asked me to dinner tonight, I had no idea we'd be having it in a country inn in Maryland."

Anna broke off another hunk of bread, buttered it and handed it to him. "I'd intended to keep things a bit closer to home myself."

"They look happy."

She glanced over to see Myra and Herbert smiling at each other as they moved around the tiny cleared space. "Yes, they do. Funny, I never pictured them together. Now that I see them, it seems so perfect."

"Contrasts." He took his palm and pressed it against hers. His was wide and hard, hers narrow and soft. "They make life more interesting."

"I've come to believe it." She linked fingers with him. "Lately."

With a smile that spread from ear to ear, Mr. Portersfield brought over a tray of salad. "You'll enjoy this," he told them as he served. "Everything straight from our own garden. The dressing is an old family recipe." After setting down the salad bowls, he fussed briefly with the flowers and then was off again.

"He certainly looks more cheerful," Daniel commented.

"And so he should," Anna murmured thinking just how much she'd paid to put a smile on his face. "Daniel..." Thoughtfully, she stabbed her fork into the salad. "About that loan you mentioned this afternoon." She took her first bite of the salad and found it as good as advertised. "I might want to take you up on it—just until we get back to Boston."

Daniel glanced over in time to see Portersfield heading into the kitchen, then looked back to see Anna's eyes dark with humor. He'd never needed anyone to add two and two for him. On a roar of laughter, he took her face in his hands and kissed her. "Interest free for you, love."

There was champagne—the only two bottles to be had at the inn. There was pot roast that melted on the fork and a scratchy Billie Holiday record. When Daniel took Myra to the impromptu dance floor, she didn't waste time beating around the bush.

"You're in love with Anna."

Because he saw no reason to deny it, he ignored her bluntness. "Aye."

"What do you intend to do about it?"

He looked down. In the comfort of his beard, his lips twitched. "I could say that was none of your business."

"You could," Myra agreed. "But I intend to find out, anyway."

After a moment's thought he decided it was best to have her on his side. "I'd have married her tonight, but she's too damn stubborn."

"Or smart." Myra smiled when she saw the heat flash in his eyes. "Oh, I like you, Daniel. I did right away. But I know a steamroller when I see one."

"Like recognizes like."

"Exactly." Pleased rather than insulted, Myra matched her steps to his. "Anna's going to be a doctor, probably the best surgeon in the country."

He scowled down at her. "What would you know about doctors?"

"I know about Anna," she said easily. "And I think I know enough about men to guess that that doesn't suit you very well."

"I want a wife," he muttered, "not a knife wielder."

"I imagine you'd have more respect for a surgeon if you needed your appendix out."

"I wouldn't want my wife to do the cutting."

"If you want Anna, you'd better be prepared to take her career. Have you asked her to marry you?"

"You're nosy."

"Of course. Have you?"

American women, he thought. Would he ever acclimatize? "I did."

"And?"

"She says she won't marry me, but she'll live with me."

"That sounds sensible."

Daniel drew her hand down so they both could see the ring gleam on Myra's finger.

"Oh, that's entirely different. I love Herbert very much, but I wouldn't have married him unless I was certain he accepted me for what I am."

"Which is?"

"Nosy, meddling, flamboyant and ambitious." Her gaze drifted toward the table. "I'm going to make him a hell of a wife."

Daniel looked down at her. Her eyes might have been dewy with love, but her chin was set. "I believe you will."

Daniel had just pulled back Myra's chair when Portersfield wheeled up a cart with a small layer cake with frothy white icing and pink rosebuds. With considerable charm, he handed Myra a silver flat-edged knife.

"With the compliments of the inn," he told her, knowing he could afford to be generous. "Our best wishes to both of you for a long and happy marriage."

"Thank you." Finding herself near tears, Myra waited until Herbert wrapped his fingers around hers on the handle.

Anna waited until the champagne was empty and the cake little more than crumbs. "One more thing." She took a key from her purse and gave it to Herbert. "The bridal suite."

He slipped it into his pocket with a grin. "I didn't think a little place like this would have one."

"It didn't until a couple of hours ago." She accepted the hugs then watched the newlyweds walk away together.

"I like your style, Anna Whitfield."

"Do you?" Buoyed by success and champagne, she smiled at him. With her eyes on his she reached in her purse again. "I have another key."

Daniel glanced down to the single key in her palm. "You tend to take matters in your own hands."

Lifting a brow, she rose. "If it doesn't suit you, you can wake Porterfield up again. I'm sure he can find you another room."

He stood, took her wrist and plucked the key from her hand. "This'll do."

With her hand in his, they left the remains of the wedding supper behind.

They didn't speak as they climbed the stairs, which creaked slightly under their weight. There was a light at the top to guide them, shielded in beveled glass and dim. All the doors they passed were closed. The inn, so recently disturbed for a celebration, was quiet. When Daniel unlocked the door to their room, he smelled the spicy mix of potpourri. It made him think of his grandmother, of Scotland, of all he'd left behind. When Anna closed the door behind them, he thought of nothing but her. Still they didn't speak.

She turned the key on a little globed lamp by the door. Subtle light spilled into the room and pooled at their feet. The windows were open to let in the warm summer air. Thin curtains stirred with it. And just barely audible, from the woods beyond came the melancholy song of a night bird.

She waited. Once, on a cliff top, she'd gone to him. Now she needed him to turn to her. Her heart was already his, though she feared to tell him. Her body would never belong to another. But she waited, touched by lamplight, surrounded by summer air.

He thought she'd never looked more lovely, though he already had dozens of memories of her locked in his mind. Dozens of fantasies. Passion, needs, love, dreams—she was all of them. His heart took the first step, and he followed.

His hands cupped her face gently, so gently that she could barely feel the pressure of his fingers on her skin. Still, the touch rippled through her. His eyes never left hers as he lowered his mouth. The kiss was soft, a bare meeting of lips, a mingling of breath. Eyes open, bodies close, they explored the sensations evoked by the teasing and brushing of mouth against mouth, the tangling and retreating of tongues.

He touched only her face; she touched him not at all, and yet in seconds two hearts were pounding.

How long they stood like that she couldn't be sure. It might have been hours or only seconds while their needs built and twisted together into a desire that bordered on pain. With a moan of delight, she let her head fall back. Her arms came around him. For an instant, the kiss deepened toward delirium. She felt her bones liquefy from her toes up until her body was a fluid mass of sensation. Reveling in it, she went limp in his arms in unqualified surrender.

It nearly drove him mad. To have Anna, strong and eager, made his blood heat and his passion soar. But to have Anna, soft and pliant, was devastatingly arousing. It made him weak. It made him strong. She seemed to seep into him degree by degree until there was no room for anything but her.

He drew back, shaken by the intensity, wary of the merging. But she stood as she was, head thrown back, arms twined around him. It was more than need he saw in her eyes, more even than knowledge. It was acceptance. He waited, his body pulsing, until his mind was nearly clear again. Then he undressed her.

The thin, almost transparent jacket she wore over her dress slid away like an illusion. He let his hands roam up her arms, over her shoulders and back again so that he could feel the skin, the muscles, the texture. And as he lingered, bewitched by the thrill of his flesh against hers, she loosened his tie then tossed it aside. Slowly, while her own blood heated to his touch, she drew his jacket from his shoulders.

He was losing himself in her again but now it didn't seem to matter. While the summer breeze sighed through the windows behind them, he pulled down the zipper of her dress. Like the breeze, it drifted to the floor.

She heard him catch his breath and felt a wild, almost wanton pride in her own body. While she stood, he seemed to drink in the sight of her, inch by inch. Her skin hummed as though his hands had stroked it. The cameo he had given her nestled in the hollow of her throat. He could trace it with his finger and feel her profile come to life. The lacy fantasy she wore was caught snug at her breast and draped lazily at her thighs. The lamplight threw her silhouette into relief and made him hunger for what he already had.

Her fingers weren't steady as she unbuttoned his shirt, but her eyes never left his. More from desire than confidence, her palms stroked over him as his shirt joined her dress on the floor.

Somewhere in the inn a clock rang out the hour, but they'd long since forgotten such things as time and place. In unspoken agreement, they lowered themselves to the bed.

Under their weight, the old mattress creaked softly. Feather pillows yielded. He braced himself above her, needing to see her, all of her. He might have stayed like that for hours, but she reached for him.

Mouth against mouth, heated, impatient. Flesh to flesh, trembling, sensitive. The lamplight cast their shadows on the wall. The breeze carried off their sighs. The night bird still sang plaintively in the woods. They no longer heard.

The world they both knew so much of, the world they both were so determined to discover had been whittled down to one room. Ambitions faded and died in the face of more desperate desires. To give, to take and to experience. To possess and to be possessed.

He buried his face against her skin and no longer noticed the scent of spices and dried flowers that wafted through the room. There was no fragrance but Anna, no taste but Anna, no voice but Anna's. Slowly, but not so gently, he took his mouth on a searing journey down her throat, over the lace and silk clinging to her breasts. Need thundered in his blood as she strained against him. With their hands caught tightly together, he let his tongue lap at the subtle curve just above the lace. With their legs tangled, he let his teeth scrape lightly over her flesh. When she called out his name, he vowed to bring her the thrill and the glory of madness.

Through the silk, his lips pulled and tugged on her nipple until it was hard and hot in his mouth and her body was as taut as a bowstring. He heard her breath tremble when he paused, then heard it catch in her throat as he turned all his skill to her other breast.

Just as slowly, just as ruthlessly, just as devastatingly, he worked his way over her body, touching off fires she hadn't known were there to be kindled. With his tongue and wide-palmed hands he took her again and again to the edge of release. She'd never known torture could be so glorious or pleasure so painful. Her skin was damp when he pulled the last barrier away from it.

She was caught in a haze of delights—dark, secret, desperate delights. The air was heavy and tasted of him as she drew in labored breaths. Everywhere he touched, flames burned. His beard brushed over the soft skin of her belly and set off an inferno of sensation. Her hands found his hair and stroked it as the lamplight turned even this to fire.

Her mind spinning, she locked her arms around his waist. Still riding a crest of sensation she rolled with him, her hands seeking, reaching, finding. She felt him quiver and pressed her mouth to his skin, tasting desire. Before he could anticipate, before he could prepare, she slid down and took him into her.

Sounds burst in her head. Perhaps it was her name on Daniel's lips. Chills coursed along her flesh. They might have been his strong fingers caressing her. As she threw her head back, abandoned, delighted, she saw his eyes on hers. The deep brilliant blue held its own fire, hotter, stronger than any other. Love. Clinging to it, she took them both beyond reason.

Sated and breathless, she still held tight, and with her eyes closed, locked everything into her: the scent of him, the feel of his skin warmed from hers, the sound of his breathing, fast and harsh in her ear, the look of his hand closed tight around hers.

It was here she wanted to stay. And if the rest of the world and all other needs could be ignored, she would. If he were to ask now, if he were even to demand now, she was afraid she would give him all.

A hand moved down her back in one long stroke. Possession. She trembled a bit and knew she could do little to prevent it. Whatever else she wanted, whatever else she was, she belonged to him.

Her body was so small that it seemed almost weightless as she lay on him. He could feel the slight trembles, the aftershocks of passion. He couldn't live without her. He could wheel and deal and blithely slit the throat of a competitor, but he couldn't function any longer without the small serious woman whose hand was still locked in his.

Your way then, damn it. Even as he cursed her, he hooked an arm around her.

"You'll move in with me tomorrow." Grabbing a handful of hair he drew her head back. Her way, but he wasn't giving in. "You'll pack what you have when we get back to Boston. I won't spend another night without you."

Unable to speak, she stared at him. There were dregs of desire in his eyes mixed with the fury just breaking. How did she handle a man like Daniel? Anna had a feeling it would take more than a few weeks to learn. "Tomorrow?"

"That's right. You move into my house tomorrow. Do you have anything to say about it?"

She thought a moment, then smiled. "You'd better make room in your closet."

Chapter Ten

Anna had her first tour of her new home under the guidance of a stiff-backed, tight-lipped McGee. She wondered which of them was more uncomfortable. Her bags had barely been carried upstairs when Daniel had been called to the bank on urgent business. He'd left, annoyed, with a quick kiss of reassurance for her and an absentminded order to McGee to show her around. So she was there alone with a politely indignant butler and a cook who had yet to poke her head out of the kitchen.

Her first reaction was to think of an excuse and go to the hospital where she belonged. Taking the afternoon off hadn't been anything she could afford to do any more than Daniel could. Now he was gone, and she was here. Something about the straight, unyielding back of the man who led her up the stairs had her holding her ground. For Anna, pride went hand in hand with dignity. She'd made her decision, and if a butler happened to be the first to disapprove, she'd accept it. More, she was going to learn to live with it. Starting now.

"We have several guest rooms on this floor," McGee told her in his low, rolling brogue. "Mr. MacGregor also keeps his office on this level, as he finds it convenient."

"I see."

McGee tested a small tilt-top table for dust as they went. Anna had a moment to reflect that it was fortunate for who-ever was in charge of the dust department that McGee didn't find any. "Mr. MacGregor entertains out-of-town business associates from time to time. We keep two guest rooms prepared. This is the master bedroom." So saying he opened a thick, hand-tooled door.

The room was large, as Daniel seemed to prefer, but sparsely decorated, as though he spent little time there. She imagined his office would be cluttered with furniture and piled with papers, more revealing of the inner man than his bedroom, which should have been the more personal room. There were no photographs, no mementos. The paint was new and the curtains stiff with starch. She wondered if he'd ever pushed them aside to look at the view. The bed was big enough for four and of lovingly carved oak. Her bags sat neatly at the foot.

She'd expected to feel odd, walking into this intimate room for the first time. She felt little but a sense of vague curiosity. There was more of Daniel MacGregor on a cliff above the sea than there was in the room where he spent his nights. But this wasn't the time to try to dissect a puzzle where she hadn't expected to find one. Her chin was lifted just a tad higher than usual when she turned back to McGee.

"Mr. MacGregor wasn't clear on the housekeeping ar-rangements. Is that your responsibility?"

If McGee could have stiffened his already ramrod-straight back, he would have. "A day maid comes in three times a week. Otherwise, I oversee the housekeeping. However, Mr. MacGregor informed both myself and the cook that you may wish changes."

If Daniel had walked in the door at that moment, Anna would cheerfully have strangled him. Instead, she took another deliberate study of the room. "I hardly think that will be necessary, McGee. You seem to be not only a man who knows his job, but his own worth."

Her coolly delivered compliment didn't soften him a whit, nor was it intended to. "Thank you, miss. Would you care to see the rest of the second floor?"

"Not at the moment. I think I'll unpack." And be alone, she thought desperately.

"Very well, miss." With a bow he walked to the door. "If you need anything you've only to ring."

"Thank you, McGee. I won't."

The moment he shut the door, she sank down on the enormous bed. What had she done? Every doubt she'd been able to hide, thrust aside or bury until that point came rushing out. She'd moved out of her childhood home, not into her own pretty little apartment, but into a big, rambling house where she was a stranger. A usurper. And to the stiff-lipped McGee, obviously a Jezebel. If she hadn't had her own nerves to deal with, that one point might have amused.

She'd left a nervous mother and a stunned father and had come to a huge half-empty room. She wasn't at the hospital, where the hurdles she had to navigate were at least familiar, if difficult. Nothing here belonged to her but what was in the bags at the foot of the bed.

Slowly she ran her hand over the thick white bed cover. Now, night after night, she thought, she'd be sharing this bed with Daniel. Sleeping with him, waking with him,

There'd be no more simple good-nights and a retreat into privacy. He'd be there, within reach. And so would she.

What had she done? Panic rose. Gamely, Anna swallowed it. Her hand still stroked the cover. In a mirror on the far wall she saw herself—small, pale and wide-eyed on the too-big bed. She saw, too, the reflection of an oak chest of drawers, clean lined and masculine. Her legs were a little shaky as she rose to walk to it. Her fingers seemed a bit numb as she slipped the lid from a bottle of cologne. Then she smelled him—brash, vivid and very male. Her world seemed to steady. When she replaced the lid, her hands were firm and competent again.

What had she done? she asked herself for the last time. Exactly what she'd wanted to do. With a little laugh of relief, she began to unpack.

It didn't take long to distribute her things throughout the room. She'd taken little more than clothes and a few favorite pictures from her room. Still, after her things were tidied away, she felt more at ease, and somehow more at home. Of course, they would have to see about getting a dresser to match the nineteenth-century oak furniture Daniel had chosen for the room. The curtains would have to go in favor of something softer and more friendly.

Pleased, she glanced around again. It had never occurred to her that she would get such a charge out of making a few basic domestic decisions. Perhaps it wasn't anything like deciding whether to operate or treat internally, but it did bring a sense of satisfaction. Perhaps she could indeed have everything. At the moment, she thought, she was going to start by cornering McGee and going in search of a couple of comfortable chairs for the master bedroom. And a good reading lamp, she thought as she walked into the hall. If possible, she'd add a small desk for herself. The room was certainly big enough. Surely in a house this size they could find a few things that would suit. If they couldn't, she'd simply do a bit of shopping after her shift at the hospital the next day.

Once on the first floor, she was tempted to poke into the parlor or library and do some shifting herself. She held herself back for the simple reason that she understood pride. If she were to take on the project herself, it would surely damage McGee's. She would find a way to tactfully change what she wanted changed without damaging his butlerly ego. McGee was part of Daniel's life. If she were to make a success out of her decision, she would have to see that he was a part of hers.

Because she could think of no other logical place to find him, she headed for the kitchen. A few steps away from the door, she heard the voices and paused.

"If the lass is good enough for the MacGregor, she's good enough for me." It was a feminine voice but as musically Scottish as the butler's. "I see no reason for your griping, McGee."

"I don't gripe." Even through the wood, Anna detected the cool indignation. "The girl has no business here without a marriage license."

"Pish posh."

With that chuckled exclamation, Anna decided she could like the cook very well.

"Since when are you judge and confessor, I'd like to know. The MacGregor knows his mind, and so, I'd wager, does the lass, or he wouldn't give her the time of day. It's what she looks like that I want to know. Is she pretty?"

"Pretty enough," McGee muttered. "At least she has the good sense not to flaunt herself."

"Flaunt herself," the cook repeated even as Anna indignantly mouthed the phrase. "A woman makes herself up for a man and she's flaunting herself. She doesn't and she has good sense. I don't know which is more of the insult. Now go on about your business and I'll be about mine, or I'll be too busy to have a look at her before dinner.''

Anna was trying to decide whether to retreat or brazen it out when a cry of pain made her rush into the room. McGee was already bending over a plump white-haired woman. On the floor between them was a long-handled knife smeared with blood. Even as Anna dashed toward them, more blood was pooling at their feet.

"Let me see."

"Miss Whitfield—"

"Move!" Abandoning propriety, she shoved the butler aside. It only took a glance to show her that a slip of the knife had gashed the cook's wrist and knicked an artery. In an instant she presed her fingers over it and stopped the pump of blood.

"It's nothing, miss." But tears were coursing down the woman's face. "I'll make a mess of you."

"Hush." Anna plucked up a dry dishcloth and tossed it at McGee. "Tear this into strips then go bring my car around."

Used to responding to authority, he began to rip. Still holding the cook's wrist, Anna led her to a chair. "Just be calm," she soothed.

"Blood," the cook managed, and went parchment white.

"We're going to take care of it." Anna continued to talk calmly, knowing how difficult it would be to manage the big woman if she keeled over. "McGee, tie a strip on her arm, just here." She indicated where he should fasten the tourniquet while she continued to close the artery with her fingers. "All right now, what's your name?"

"Sally, miss."

"All right, Sally, I want you just to close your eyes and

relax. Not too tight," she cautioned McGee. "Bring the car around quickly. I'll want you to drive."

"Yes, miss." At twice his normal gait and none of his usual dignity, he scurried from the room.

"Now, Sally, can you walk?"

"I'll try. I feel light-headed."

"Of course you do," Anna murmured. "Lean on me. We're going right out the kitchen door to the car. We'll be at the hospital in five minutes."

"To the hospital." Beneath Anna's hand the woman's arm began to shake. "I don't like hospitals."

"There's nothing to worry about. I'll stay with you. I work there. Some of the doctors are very handsome." As she spoke, she eased the cook up and began to help her to the door. "So handsome you'll ask yourself why you didn't cut yourself before." By the time they got through the door, McGee was there to take most of the woman's weight.

"A fine job of emergency first aid, Miss Whitfield." Dr. Liederman rinsed his hands in a basin as he spoke to Anna. "Without it, I'd wager that woman would have bled to death before she made it to the hospital."

Anna had gotten a good look at the wound and estimated the need for ten stitches once the artery had been sealed. "A bad place for the knife to slip."

"We get suicides that don't do that good a job. A lucky thing for her you didn't panic."

Anna lifted a brow, wondering if he considered that a compliment. "If blood made me panic, I'd make a poor surgeon."

"Surgery, is it?" She hadn't chosen an easy road. He glanced over his shoulder as he finished scrubbing the cook's blood from his hands. "It takes more than skill to use a scalpel, you know. It takes confidence."

"I thought it was arrogance," she said with a small smile.

It took him several seconds before he returned the smile. "A more accurate term. Now as to our patient, she'll be weak for a day or two and probably favor that hand for two or three weeks."

"You want the dressing changed every day?"

"Yes and kept dry. I'll want her back in a couple of weeks to take the stitches out." He turned then, drying his hands. "Though I don't imagine you'd have any trouble doing that for her."

She smiled again. "I wouldn't think of it—for another few months."

"You know, Miss Whitfield, you have a good reputation in this hospital."

That surprised her, but she reserved the pleasure. "Do I?"

"Yes, you do. And that's from the horse's mouth." He tossed the towel aside when she only stared. "The nurses."

The pleasure came now. "I appreciate that."

"You're going into your last year of medical school. I've seen enough to judge your...confidence. How are your grades?"

Pride lifted her chin. "Excellent."

With a little laugh, he studied her. "I appreciate that. Where do you want to intern?"

"Here."

He held out a hand. "Look me up."

Anna accepted it. "I'll do that."

So where in hell was everybody? Daniel had come home to find the house empty. Impatient to be with Anna, he'd taken the steps two at a time and burst into the master bedroom. He'd had to look at the closet to assure himself she'd actually been there. Though he'd found himself pleased to see her clothes hanging neatly beside his, it wasn't quite the welcome he'd had in mind. After a quick check of the second floor, he'd started down again.

"McGee!" Cursing all servants, he came to a halt on the landing and scowled. Bad enough his woman wasn't home, but now his butler had disappeared. "McGee!"

Opening and slamming doors as he went, he worked his way down the hall. He hadn't expected a brass band, but he'd thought someone might have found the time to be around when he got home. By the time he had entered the kitchen door, his temper was peaking.

"Where the devil is everyone?"

"Will you stop shouting?" Her voice pitched low, Anna stepped into the room. "I've just this minute gotten her into bed."

"A man ought to be able to shout in his own home," Daniel began, then his temper cleared enough for him to see the blood splattered over Anna's blouse and skirt. "Sweet God!" He closed the distance between them in two steps then swept her against him. "What have you done to yourself? Where are you hurt? I'll get you to the hospital."

"I've just been there." But she wasn't quick enough to stop him from taking her up in his arms. "Daniel, it's not my blood. I'm not hurt. Daniel!" He was nearly out the kitchen door before she could stop him. "Sally had an accident, not me."

"Sally?"

"Your cook," she began.

"I know who Sally is," he snapped at her, then gathered her close as relief shuddered through him. "You're not hurt?"

"No." Her tone softened. He was trembling. Who would have expected it? "I'm fine," she managed to tell him just before his mouth closed over hers. Passion soared, and through it she felt his relief, which was nearly as wild. Moved, she let him take whatever comfort he wanted. "Daniel, I didn't mean to frighten you."

"Well, you did." He kissed her again, hard, and was steadier. "What happened to Sally?"

"Apparently her hands were wet and she wasn't paying as close attention to her chopping as she might have been. The knife slipped and slashed her at the wrist. She hit an artery. That's why there's so much blood. It's a serious cut, but McGee and I got her to the hospital. She's resting now. She'll need a couple of days off."

For the first time he noticed the chopping knife and the blood on the floor by the sink. With an oath, he tightened his grip on Anna. "I'll go in to her."

"No, please." From her position in his arms, she managed to stop him. "She's sleeping. It would really be better to wait until morning."

His cook, like his butler, like every one of his employees was his responsibility. He glanced at the knife again and swore. "You're sure she's all right."

"I'm sure. She lost a good bit of blood, but I was right outside the door when it happened. Then once McGee realized I knew what I was doing, he couldn't have been more helpful."

"And where is he?"

"Parking my car. Here he is now," Anna corrected herself as the butler came through the kitchen door.

"Mr. MacGregor—" a bit pale, but as proper as ever, McGee stopped just inside the door "—I'll have this mess cleaned up right away. I'm afraid dinner will be delayed."

"So I'm told. Miss Whitfield said you were very helpful, McGee."

Something—it might have been an emotion—flickered

across his face. "I'm afraid I did very little, sir. Miss Whitfield was very efficient, and if I may say so, sir, plucky."

Anna had to swallow a chuckle. "Thank you, McGee."

"Don't worry about dinner. We'll see to ourselves."

"Very good, sir. Good night, miss."

"Good night, McGee." The kitchen door swung shut behind them. "Daniel, you can put me down now."

"No." Easily he started up the stairs. "This isn't the welcome I'd wanted for you."

She hadn't realized how good it could feel to be carried as though you were something precious. "I hadn't planned it this way myself."

He paused on the stairs to nuzzle her neck, "I'm sorry."

"It wasn't anyone's fault."

God, she tasted so good. Every hunger he had could be sated with her alone. "You've ruined your blouse."

"Now you sound like Sally. She muttered about that all the way to the hospital."

"I'll buy you a new one."

"Thank goodness," she said and laughed at him. "Daniel, don't we have anything more important to do than worry about my blouse?"

"Do you know what I was thinking of the entire time I sat through that damned meeting?"

"No. What?"

"Making love to you. In my bed. Our bed."

"I see." As he pushed open the door, she linked her hands behind his head. Her pulse was already beginning to race. Anticipation. Imagination. "Do you know what I thought about as I was unpacking my things?"

"No. What?"

"Making love to you. In your bed. Our bed."

Hearing her say that made the room he rarely noticed seem special. "Then we should do something about it."

With her hands still linked behind his head, he tumbled with her onto the thick white cover.

It was easier to live with Daniel, to wake with him, to sleep with him than Anna could have imagined. It seemed to her that the part of her life she had lived without him had been no more than anticipation. Yet their first weeks together weren't without adjustments. Though she had lived most of her life with her parents and the rest in the regimentation of college, Anna had always managed to move at her own pace and protect her privacy.

It was an entirely different matter to wake up with someone beside her. Especially when that someone was a man who viewed the hours spent in sleep as a waste of vital time. Daniel MacGregor wasn't one to loiter in bed or to linger over coffee. Mornings were for business, and morning started the moment his eyes opened.

Because her system was on a different time clock, she usually found herself wandering down for her first cup of coffee when Daniel was finishing his second and last cup. Goodbyes were brief and hurried and anything but romantic. Daniel and his briefcase were out the door before her mind was completely ready to function. Not exactly a honeymoon, she'd thought more than once when she settled down to a solitary breakfast, but it was a routine she could live with.

By the time she drove to the hospital, Daniel was already wheeling and dealing. While she folded linens and read to patients, he played the stock market and planned mergers and takeovers. In living with him, Anna had a better view of just how powerful Daniel was and how potentially powerful he could become. She herself had taken a call from a senator and relayed a message from the governor of New York.

Politics, she began to realize, was an aspect of his career she had never considered. He also had contacts and interests in the entertainment field. A telegram from a well-known producer or a fledgling playwright wasn't uncommon. Though he rarely attended the ballet or the opera, she learned that he made enormous contributions to the arts. It would have pleased her more if she hadn't understood they were made for business purposes.

Culture, politics, stock-market ventures or housing projects—it was all business to Daniel. And though she learned that business consumed his time and his life, he passed off her inquiries into it with the equivalent of a pat on the head. Each time he did, she tried to ignore the little twinge of frustration. In time, she told herself, he'd share. In time, he'd give her both his trust and respect.

Her life and her time were consumed by the hospital, her studies and her preparation for her final year of medical school. Daniel rarely asked her about her hours involving medicine. When and if he did, Anna took it as no more than polite interest and said little.

They spent their evenings lingering over a meal or over coffee in the parlor. Neither of them spoke of ambitions, of what drove them or of professional needs. While they were content just being with each other, it seemed to both as though a shade had been drawn over a part of their lives. Neither of them wanted to be the first to lift it.

They became misers with their social time, spending most of it alone at home. When they did socialize, it was with the newlywed Ditmeyers. Now and again there was a film, and they could sit in a darkened theater holding hands, forgetting about the pressures of the day or the uncertainty of the future. They learned of each other, of habits, whims and annoyances. Love, soothed and left to itself, deepened. But even as it did, they both fretted about what was missing from their relationship. Daniel wanted marriage. Anna wanted partnership. They hadn't yet discovered how to combine the two.

Summer heat soared in August. It boiled in the streets and hung mistily in the air. Those who could escaped to the shore. On the weekends Daniel and Anna took drives out of the city, with the top down. Twice they picnicked on Daniel's lot in Hyannis Port. They could make love there as freely and unrestrainedly as they had the first time. They could laugh or simply doze in the grass. And it was there, unexpectedly, that Daniel began to pressure her again.

"They'll be breaking ground here next week," Daniel told her one day as they shared the last of a bottle of Chablis.

"Next week?" Surprised, Anna glanced over to see him staring at the empty plot where his house would be. He could see it, she knew, as though there were already stone and mortar standing sturdy in the sun. "I didn't realize it would be so soon." He hadn't told her, she thought. He hadn't shown her, though she'd asked, any of the plans of blueprints for the house that was so important to him.

He merely moved his shoulders. "It would have been sooner, but I had some other things to tidy up first."

"I see." And he hadn't considered the other things worth mentioning, either. Anna bit back a sigh and tried to accept it. "I know the house is important to you, and it'll be beautiful, but I'll miss this." When he looked at her, she smiled and reached out to touch his face. "It's so peaceful here, so isolated—just water and rock and grass."

"It'll be all of those things after the house is up. After we're living in it." Because he felt her slight withdrawal, he took her hand. "It won't be quick—the best things aren't. It may be two years before the house is ready for us. But our children will grow up here.''

"Daniel—"

"They will." His fingers tightened on hers as he cut her off. "And whenever we make love in that house, I'll remember our first time here. Fifty years from now I'll still remember our first time here.''

It was all but impossible to resist him when he was like this. He was more dangerous when he spoke quietly, when his voice flowed over her. For a moment she almost believed him. Then she thought about how very far they had to go. "You're asking for promises, Daniel."

"Aye. I expect promises."

"Don't."

"And why not? You're the woman I want, the woman who wants me. It's time for promises between us." Keeping a firm hold on her hand, he reached into his pocket and drew out a small velvet box. "I want you to wear this, Anna." With a flick of his thumb, he opened the box to reveal a fiery pear-shaped diamond.

Something caught in her throat. Part of it was astonishment at the sheer beauty of the ring. The rest was fear of what the symbol meant: promises, vows, commitments. She wanted, she yearned, she feared.

"I can't."

"Of course, you can." When he started to pluck the ring from the box, she put both hands over his.

"No, I can't. I'm not ready for this, Daniel. I've tried to explain to you."

"And I've tried to understand." But his patience was wearing thin. Every day he lived with her he had to accept half of what he needed. "You don't want marriage—at least, not yet. But a ring's not marriage, just a promise."

"A promise I can't give you." But she wanted to. With

each day that passed she wanted to more. "If I took the ring, I'd be giving you a promise that might be broken. I can't do that with you. You're too important."

"You don't make sense." He'd expected to feel frustration. Even when he'd bought the ring he'd known she wouldn't wear it. In some odd way, he'd even known she'd be right. But that knowledge didn't soothe the hurt. "I'm important to you, but you won't accept a ring from me."

"Oh, Daniel, I know you." Regrets washed over her as she took his face in her hands. "If I took this ring, you'd be pressuring me to accept a wedding ring in a month's time. Sometimes, I think you look at the two of us like a merger."

"Maybe I do." Anger flared in his eyes but he controlled it. He'd discovered he could when it was Anna he was angry with. "Maybe it's the only way I know."

"Maybe it is," she agreed quietly. "And maybe I'm trying to understand that."

"You look at it as a trial." He said it flatly. When she looked up, stunned, he continued in the same tone. "I'm not sure whether I'm on trial, Anna, or you are."

"It's not like that. You make it sound so cold and calculated."

"No more calculated than a merger."

"I'm not looking at what's between us as a business, Daniel."

Was he? He realized uncomfortably that he had been, but he wasn't so sure any longer. "Maybe it's time you told me just how you're looking at it."

"You frighten me." Her words came out so fast and strong that both of them sat in silence for several moments.

"Anna—" because her statement was the last response he'd expected from her, his voice was low and tentative "—I'd never do anything to hurt you."

"I know." She thought of the ring in the box, of the image of the house at their backs and rose with her nerves jumping. "If you could, I believe you'd treat me like glass, like something to be protected, cared for and admired. Somehow, it's easier for me when you lose sight of that and shout at me."

He couldn't pretend to understand her. But he rose and stood behind her. "Then I'll shout more often."

"I'm sure you will," she murmured, "when I frustrate you or disagree. But what happens when I give you everything you want?" She turned then, and her eyes were glowing with emotion. "What happens when I say all right, I give up?"

He grabbed her hands for fear she'd turn away again. "I don't know what you're talking about."

"I think you do, deep down. I think you know that part of me wants just what you want. But do either of us know if I want it for myself or just to please you? If I said yes and married you tomorrow, I'd have to toss away everything else."

"I'm not asking for that. I wouldn't."

"Wouldn't you?" She closed her eyes a moment and struggled for composure. "Can you tell me, can you be sure that you'll accept, care for, Dr. Anna Whitfield the same way you do for me now?"

He started to speak quickly, but her eyes were too dark, too vulnerable. There could be nothing with Anna but the truth. "I don't know."

She let out a quick, quiet sigh. Would he have lied if he'd known how much she'd wanted to hear it? And if he had lied, would she have taken the ring and given the promise? "Then give us both the time to be sure." Because he'd released her hands, her arms were free to go around him. "If I accept your ring, it'll be with my whole heart, with everything I am, and it'll be forever. Once it's there, Daniel, it's there to stay. That I can promise you. We both have to be sure it belongs there.''

"It'll keep." The ring was back in his pocket. Anna was in his arms. They were alone, and the air was swirling with summer. When she lifted her face, he crushed his mouth to hers. ''This won't,'' he murmured and drew her down with him.

Chapter Eleven

Anna took the news that they would be entertaining the governor calmly enough. Both her parents and her grandparents had entertained dignitaries from time to time. She'd been trained how to prepare a properly impressive menu, what wines to order and what brandy to serve. It really wasn't the doing it that bothered her. It was the fact that Daniel had simply assumed she would.

She could have told him no. Anna lectured herself on this as she drove home from the hospital. She could have reminded him that she put in a full day between the hospital and her studies and didn't have the time or inclination to plan whether to serve oysters Rockefeller or coquilles St. Jacques as an appetizer. She could have and would have gained a brief moment of self-satisfaction. Then she would have spent the rest of her time feeling guilty for being petty and mean.

It would, after all, be their first dinner party as a couple. And it was so important to him. He wanted, she knew, to show her off as much as he wanted to give the governor a memorable meal. It should have infuriated her. Somehow she found it endearing. With a shake of her head, Anna admitted that loving Daniel could do strange things to common sense. So he could show her off; she wouldn't disappoint him. The time it took to plan the evening would be as much fun as work.

To be honest, she had to admit that preparing for a dinner party came as naturally to her as reciting the names of bones in the hand. Which reminded her, she wanted to look at Sally's the moment she got home.

Home. It made her smile. Only three weeks had passed since she'd unpacked in what had been Daniel's bedroom. It was their bedroom now. She might have her doubts about tomorrow, next week, next year, but she had none about today. She was happy. Living with Daniel had added a dimension to her life she had never expected. Because that was true, how could she explain that going on just as they were seemed the best way? The thought of marriage still sent a chill of unease down her back. And of distrust, she admitted. But whom did she distrust, Daniel or herself? She hadn't forgotten that he'd accused her of putting them both on trial. Perhaps she was, but only because she feared hurting him as much as she feared being hurt.

There were moments when it all seemed so clear to her. She'd marry him, bear his children, share his life. She'd be a doctor and develop her skill to the very height of its potential. He would be every bit as proud of her accomplishments as she was of his. She would have everything any woman could ever want, and so much more. It could happen. It would happen.

Then she would remember how carelessly uninterested he was in her work at the hospital. She would remember how he closeted himself in his office with business he never discussed with her. And how he never asked about the medical books that now littered the bedroom. Not once had he mentioned the fact that she was due back in Connecticut in a matter of weeks—or if he planned to be with her.

Could two people share a life, share a love and not share what was most vital to them? If she had the answer to that one question, she could stop asking herself any other.

With a shake of her head, Anna pulled into the driveway. She refused to be gloomy now. She was home, and that was enough.

As she walked in the kitchen door, Sally was bending over to pop something into the oven. "You're supposed to rest that hand."

"It's had all the rest it needs." Without turning around, Sally reached for a cup. "You're a bit late today."

"There was a car accident. Lots of bumps and scratches in Emergency. I stayed to hold some hands."

Sally poured coffee and set the cup on the table. "You'd rather have been cutting and sewing."

On a little sigh, Anna sat down with the coffee. "Yes. It's so hard not being allowed to do even the little things I could do. I'm not even allowed to take a blood pressure."

"It won't be long until you'll be doing a great deal more than that."

"I keep telling myself, one more year, just one more. But I'm so impatient, Sally."

"You and the MacGregor have that in common." Knowing she'd be welcome, Sally brought over a cup of her own. "He called to say he'd be late himself and for you to eat your supper if you didn't want to wait—but I could tell he was hoping you'd hold off till he got here."

"I can wait. Are you having any pain in that hand?"

"It's a bit stiff when I wake up, but there's barely a twinge even when I use if heavily." She held it out, admiring the scar that ran down the wrist. "There's a nice neat seam. Don't think I could do better myself." Then with a grin, she lowered her hand. "I don't suppose sewing up flesh is much like mending a tablecloth."

"The technique's pretty close." Anna gave the injured hand a pat. "Since Daniel's going to be late, this might be a good time for us to go over the guest list and menu for next week. I have some ideas, but if you've a specialty you'd rather—" She broke off and sniffed the air. "Sally, what have you got in the oven?"

"Peach pie." She preened. "My grandma's recipe."

"Oh." Anna closed her eyes and let the aroma flow through her. Warm peach pie on a summer's evening. "How late was Daniel going to be?"

"Eight, he said."

Anna glanced at her watch. "You know, I have a feeling that working on this menu is going to take a lot out of me." She smiled as she rose to fetch a pad and pencil. "I'll probably need a bit of something to tide me over."

"A piece of peach pie, perhaps?"

"That should do it."

When Daniel came in, Anna was still in the kitchen. Recipe cards, lists and scraps of paper littered the table where she and Sally sat. Between them was half of a peach pie and the remains of a bottle of white wine.

"I don't care how much we want to impress the governor," Anna said with her head close to Sally's. "We're not serving haggis. I know for a fact I'd turn green if I had to eat anything with entrails."

"A fine surgeon you'll make if you're squeamish."

"I'm not squeamish about what I have to look at or what I have to get my hands in. What goes in my stomach is a different matter. I vote for the coq au vin."

"Good evening, ladies."

Anna's head came up, and the smile that was already on her face grew when she saw him. "Daniel." She was up and taking both his hands. "Sally and I have been planning the dinner party. I'm afraid I may have offended her about the haggis, but I think our guests might be more comfortable with coq au vin."

"I'll leave that to the two of you," he said, and leaned down for a kiss. "Things took longer than I'd thought. I'm glad you didn't wait supper for me."

"Supper?" She still held his hands, as much now for support as anything else. Until she'd stood, she hadn't realized how fuzzy her mind was. "Sally and I were just testing out her peach pie. Would you like some?"

"Later. Though I could use a glass of that wine if you've left any." His eyes were burning from reading pages of fine print.

"Oh." She looked blankly at the bottle, wondering how it had come to be nearly empty.

"I'll have a shower first."

"I'll go up with you." Anna rummaged through the piles of paper until she found the one she wanted. "I'd like to read you this guest list so you can add anyone I've forgotten before we send the invitations out."

"Fine. Go on to bed, Sally. I'll help myself to the pie when I'm ready."

"Yes, sir. Thank you."

"You look tired, Daniel. Was it a difficult day?"

"No more than most." He slipped his arm around her as they started up the stairs. "A few problems with the fine points of a deal I'm working on. I think we ironed them out."

"Can you talk about it?"

"I don't bring my troubles home." He gave her a little squeeze. "I spent the afternoon with your father."

"You did?" She felt a little skip of emotion but kept her voice level. "How is he?"

"Well, and keeping business and personal matters well apart."

"Yes." Her smile was a bit tight when they reached the top landing. "I suppose that's for the best."

"He asked about you." His voice was gentle now because he'd come to know her.

"He did?"

"Aye."

She entered first when Daniel pushed open the door to the bedroom. Because she felt so warm, she walked to the window to lean out. "Maybe if I hired him, he'd stop avoiding me."

"He's just worried about his daughter."

"There's nothing to worry about."

"He'll see that for himself at dinner next week."

Anna looked over, the guest list still clutched in her hand. "He'll come?"

"He'll come."

She let out a quick breath before she smiled again. "I suppose I have you to thank for that."

"Some, but I think your mother had more to do with it." He tossed his jacket and tie on one of the chairs Anna had arranged in front of the fireplace. As he unbuttoned his shirt, he could smell the summery scent of sweet peas that brimmed out of a bowl on a table by the window. Small things. Enormous things. Daniel stopped undressing to fold her tight in his arms.

She sensed the abrupt flurry of intense emotion that had taken hold of him. Anna circled his waist with her arms and let the feeling rush through her. Daniel kissed the top of her head before he drew her away.

"What was that for?"

"For being here," he told her. "For being you." He slid off his shoes with a little sigh of relief. "I won't be long. Why don't you just call out the names on that list to me." With economy of movement, Daniel stripped off the rest of his clothes, then walked into the bath.

With only a small frown, Anna looked at the pile of clothes on the floor. She wondered if she'd ever get used to his carelessness about such things. Ignoring the obvious alternative, she stepped over them. A woman who picked up after a grown man was asking for trouble.

"There's the governor and his wife, of course," she called out. "And Councilman and Mrs. Steers."

Daniel answered with a crude and accurate description of the councilman. Anna cleared her throat and made a note on the list to seat that particular couple at the opposite end of the table from their host.

"Myra and Herbert. The Maloneys and the Cooks." She lifted her voice over the sound of water. Still feeling warm, she unfastened the first three buttons of her blouse. "The Donahues, with John Fitzsimmons to balance out Cathleen." Anna peered at the list, blinking because her vision seemed blurred.

"John who?"

"Fitzspimmons—simmons. Fitzsimmons," she repeated when she managed to get her tongue around it. "And Carl Benson and Judith Mann. Myra told me they're about to be engaged."

"She's built like a—" Daniel caught himself. "Very attractive woman," he amended. "Who else?"

Anna walked into the bathroom with her eyes narrowed. "Built like what?"

Behind the curtain Daniel merely grinned. "I beg your pardon?" To his surprise, Anna drew the curtain back. "Woman, is nothing sacred?"

"Just what is Judith Mann built like?"

"Now how would I know?" For safety's sake, he stuck his head under the spray. "You'd better pull the curtain to. You'll get wet."

"And how *would* you know?" she demanded and stepped, fully dressed, into the shower.

"Anna!" Laughing, he watched the water plaster her blouse against her. "What in hell are you doing?"

"Trying to get a straight answer." She waved the now soaking list at him. "Just what do you know about Judith Mann's anatomy?"

"Only what a man with good eyesight can see." He caught her chin in his hand and took a good look. "Now that I think about it I see something else."

She put a hand to his soapy chest for balance. "And what's that?"

"You're drunk, Anna Whitfield."

Dignity streamed from her as thick as the water. "I beg your pardon?"

Her haughtily delivered reply delighted him. Daniel brushed wet hair out of her eyes. "You're drunk," he repeated.

"Don't be ridiculous."

"It's drunk you are. Drunk as an Irish roof thatcher and twice as pretty. I'll be damned."

"You may well be, but I've never been drunk a day in my life. You're just trying to avoid the question."

"What's the question?"

She opened her mouth, shut it again, then grinned. "I don't remember. Have I ever told you what a magnificent body you have, Daniel?"

"No." He drew her against it before he began the task of peeling off her clothes. "Why don't you?"

"Such well-developed pectoral muscles."

Her blouse fell with a muffled splash. "And where might they be?"

"Just here," she murmured and ran a hand over his chest. "The deltoids are very firm. And of course the biceps are impressive, not obviously bulging, just hard." Her fingers slid over his shoulders and down as he tugged off her skirt. "It shows not simply strength but discipline—like the abdomen—very flat and tight." His breath caught as she explored there.

"Tell me, Anna—" he lowered his mouth to her ear and began to trace it with his tongue "—just how many muscles are there?"

Her head fell back, and the water sluiced over her. Naked, wet, pliant, she smiled up at him. "There are over six hundred muscles in the body, all attached to the two hundred and six bones that make up the skeleton."

"Fascinating. I'm wondering how many of mine you might point out."

"We could start with the muscles of the lower limbs. I admire your walk."

"Do you?"

"Yes, it's very firm and arrogant, but not quite a swagger. This, naturally, has something to do with your personality, but you also need your antigravity muscles, such as the soleus...." She bent down just enough to run a finger up his calf. Water poured over her hair. "The vasti," she continued, running a finger up his thigh, "and..." With a sound of approval, she slid her hands around to his bottom.

He grinned and let himself enjoy. He'd never had a woman give him quite so interesting a lesson. "I thought that muscle had more to do with sitting. The things you learn in anatomy class.''

He switched off the water then reached for a towel to cover both of them.

''The gluteus maximus—'' with an approving murmur, she ran her hands over him again ''—has to stretch sufficiently or else you'd have a tendency to jackknife forward as you walk.''

''Can't have that,'' he murmured as he gathered her up in his arms. ''Especially when you're carrying precious cargo.''

''And this is one of your most attractive muscles.''

''Thank you.'' Flinging the towel aside, he lay with her on the bed. Warm night air played over damp skin.

''Now the adductors, the muscles on the inside of the thighs…''

''Show me.''

''Just here.'' Her fingers reached down and skimmed over him just as his mouth closed over hers.

With her eyes half shut, she sighed and nuzzled into him. ''I don't think you're paying attention.''

''Oh, but I am. The adductors. Just here.'' Strong fingers pressed into firm thighs. ''Just here,'' he repeated, ''where your skin's like silk and already warm for me. And here.'' His hand journeyed up to tease the sensitive area where hip and thigh joined. ''What are these muscles here?''

''They're—'' But she could only moan and arch against him.

He caught the lobe of her ear in his teeth. ''Have you forgotten?''

''Just touch me,'' she whispered. ''It doesn't matter where.''

With a sound of triumph, he took his hands over her, skimming, caressing, kneading, arousing. Like putty, she seemed willing to be molded. Like fire, she tempted and dared. Like a woman, she softened and tensed and gave. Her hands were as eager as his, her lips as hungry. Their skin dried in the warm summer air, then became damp again with excitement.

Each time, she thought hazily, each time they made love, it was more thrilling, more beautiful. The first time, the hundredth time, the edge of desire was never dulled. In a field of grass, on feather pillows it was just as volatile. In the bright light of day, in the dark secret night it was just as frenzied. She'd never stop wanting him. Of all the questions she'd asked herself, she was sure of that answer. Need for him would never fade.

They rolled over the big bed, frantic for each other, lost in each other. Trapped in pleasure, she rose up, back arched, eyes closed, her hair a wild, wet tangle. The sliver of light from the next room shot a nimbus around her that seemed to shiver with her ecstasy. Half-mad he came to her, so that kneeling on the bed they could pour pleasures over each other. Weak, vibrating, they tumbled down again and took the last step into passion.

Her limbs were wrapped around him. Her face was buried against his throat as her breath heaved in and out. Her fingers dug into his back and felt hard flesh and sweat. And as he moved into her, moved with her, she rode on the carousel, flew on the roller coaster and lost herself in the maze.

"You're stunning." Daniel stared at her as she studied herself in the mirror. "Absolutely stunning."

It pleased her to hear it, though she'd never thought much of compliments. The dress left her shoulders bare and fell in a loose sweeping line to just above her ankles. Pearls crusted the bodice and danced along the skirt. Myra had talked her into it, though she'd needed little persuasion. True, it had taken a healthy chunk out of the money she'd put aside for board during the fall, but she was confident she'd find a way to balance her books. The look on Daniel's face, and the satisfaction she felt seeing her own reflection made it worthwhile.

"You like it?"

How could he explain that, though he knew every intimate inch of her, just looking at her could still take his breath away? She'd been right when she'd thought he wanted to show her off. When a man had something exquisite, he needed to share it. No, he couldn't explain. "I like it so well I'm wishing the evening was already over."

She gave a last swirl, as much for herself as for him. "You look wonderful in a dinner jacket. Elegantly barbarian."

His brow lifted. "Barbarian?"

"Never change that." She held out both hands and took his. "No matter what else has to change, don't change that."

He brought her hands to his lips, kissed one, then the other. "I doubt I could, any more than you could change being a lady—even after too much wine and peach pie."

She tried to look stern but laughed. "You'll never let me forget that."

"God, no. It was one of the most fascinating evenings of my life. I'm crazy about you, Anna."

"So you've said." She lifted their joined hands to her cheek. "That's something else I don't want you to change."

"I won't. I like seeing you wear the cameo." He brushed a finger over it as was his habit.

"It means a great deal to me."

"You wouldn't take my ring."

"Daniel—"

"You wouldn't take my ring," he continued, "but you took the cameo. I'd like you to take this." Drawing a box out of his pocket, he waited.

Anna folded her hands together. "Daniel, you don't have to buy me presents."

"I think I've figured that out." But he'd yet to figure out how to accept that fact. "It might be why I want to. Humor me," he said, and made her smile.

"You've said that before." Because he smiled back, she accepted the box. "Thank you." Then she opened the box and found she could say nothing.

"Is something wrong with them?"

She managed to shake her head. Pearls and diamonds, pure in simplicity, arrogant in beauty, the earrings lay against black velvet and nearly breathed with life. From the simple orbs of milky white pearls dripped the tear-shaped glamour of diamonds. One gleamed, the other flashed and together they made a stunning unit.

"Daniel, they're…" She shook her head and looked back up at him. "They're absolutely beautiful. I don't know what to say."

"You just said it." Relieved, he took the box and removed the earrings. "I suppose you'll have to thank Myra. I asked her advice. She said something about class and flash making the best team."

"Did she?" Anna murmured as Daniel fastened the earrings on her himself.

"There now." Pleased, he stepped back to inspect. "Yes, they'll do nicely. Now maybe they'll draw the attention and keep men's eyes off all that beautiful skin you've exposed."

Laughing again, Anna lifted a hand to her ear. "Ah, an ulterior motive."

"It's hard not to worry that you'll take a good look around and see someone who appeals to you more."

"Don't be silly." Taking it as a joke, she linked arms with him. "I suppose we'd better go down or the guests will be arriving. Then McGee will scowl at us for being late and unpardonably rude."

"Hah." As they walked through the door, Daniel found her hand with his. "As if you hadn't twisted him around your finger already."

Anna gave him an innocent look as they started downstairs. "I don't know what you mean."

"Fixes scones for you in the middle of the week. Never did that for me."

"Ah, there's the door now." She paused on the bottom landing. "Promise not to glare—even at Councilman Steers."

"I never glare," he lied easily, and led her down the hall to greet the first guests.

In less than twenty minutes the big parlor was crowded with bodies and buzzing with conversation. Though Anna was perfectly aware that she and Daniel were often the topic of the moment, she made her way calmly from group to group. She hadn't needed her mother's warning to know that her decision would alienate her from some. But her choices were never made with other people's opinions in mind.

Louise Ditmeyer's greeting was a bit stiff, but Anna ignored it and chatting, steered her to a group of friends. More than once she caught someone aiming a speculative look in her direction. It was easy enough to meet this calmly. That was her way. Anna had no idea that her cool confidence and natural graciousness did more to squelch gossip than Daniel's power or her own family name.

If there was a shadow on the evening, it came from the

governor's careless request for her opinion on Daniel's projected textile factory. How could she have an opinion or even an intelligent comment? Daniel had never mentioned it to her, and she was faced with the governor's glowing praise of a project that would bring employment to hundreds and fat revenues to the state. Training kept her smile in place and brought easy answers. There was no time for anger as she introduced the governor and his wife to another couple. There was time for only a moment's envy that the governor's wife appeared to be deeply involved in his work. Pressed by her duties as hostess, Anna pushed personal disappointment to the back of her mind.

Not until her parents arrived did she feel any real tension. Holding her breath, she approached her father.

"I'm so glad you came." She rose on her toes to kiss his cheek, though she was far from sure of her reception.

"You look well." He didn't speak coldly, but she felt his reserve.

"So do you. Hello, Mother." She pressed her cheek against her mother's and smiled at the encouraging squeeze.

"You look beautiful, Anna." She shot her husband a quick look. "Happy."

"I am happy. Let me get you both a drink."

"Now don't fuss with us," her mother told her. "You have all these guests. There's Pat Donahue, I see. Just run along. We'll be fine."

"All right, then." As she started to turn away, her father caught her hand.

"Anna…" As he hesitated, he felt her hand tighten on his. "It's good to see you."

It was enough. She wrapped her arms around his neck and held for just a moment. "If I came by your office one day, would you play hooky and go for a ride with me?"

"You going to let me drive your car?"

She smiled brilliantly. "Maybe."

He winked and patted her head as he'd always done. "See to your guests."

When she turned it was to see Daniel a few feet away, smiling at her. She walked to him with her heart in her eyes. "Now you look even more beautiful," he murmured to her.

"What's all this?" Myra came up to stand between them. "The host and hostess aren't even supposed to have time to speak to each other at an affair like this. Daniel, I really believe you should go rescue the governor from our esteemed councilman before he loses his appetite. The governor, that is." When Daniel muttered something rude, she merely nodded. "Just so. Now, Anna, why don't we walk over to where Cathleen is boring the daylights out of the Maloneys. I'm dying to see her gag over your earrings."

"Subtle, Myra," Anna warned as they maneuvered through the groups. "Remember the beauty of subtlety."

"Darling, of course. But I'd really appreciate it if you'd be sure to toss your head just a little now and then. Why, Cathleen, what a nice dress."

Cathleen stopped her dissertation on her summer schedule to study Myra. Anna wasn't sure, but she thought the Maloneys sighed in unison. "Thank you, Myra. I suppose congratulations and best wishes are in order. I haven't seen you since you and Herbert ran away."

"No, you haven't." Myra sipped her drink and ignored the less than complimentary description of her marriage. Envy was the simplest of things to ignore when you were happy.

"I suppose there's something to be said for elopements, though for myself, I'd find it a rather cut-and-dry way of marrying."

"To each his own," Myra returned, and tried to remember it was Anna's dinner party.

"Oh, indeed." Cathleen gave a little nod. "But what a shame you and Herbert have decided to be hermits even after cheating us all out of a big wedding."

"I'm afraid Herbert and I haven't entertained on a grand scale yet. We want to finish our redecorating before we have more than our most intimate friends over. You understand."

Seeing the need to intervene, Anna stepped a bit closer. "I'm sure you've had a busy summer, Cathleen."

"Oh, quite busy." She gave Anna a cool smile. "Though others seem to get more accomplished in a shorter time. I took a little trip to the shore, and when I got back to Boston I learned Myra and Herbert had run off and you'd changed addresses. Are congratulations of a different sort in order?"

Anna laid a hand on Myra's arm to silence her. "Not at all. You've brought back a beautiful tan. I'm sorry I missed getting to the beach. I didn't seem to find the time."

"I'm sure you didn't." Lifting her drink, Cathleen took a long, slow sip. It wasn't easy to accept that two of the women she'd debuted with had snagged two of the most influential men in the city—particularly when she'd all but decided to set her sights on Daniel. "Tell me, Anna, just how do I introduce you and Daniel if the occasion comes up? I'm afraid I'm naive about these things."

Even Anna's patience only lasted so long. "Why should it matter?"

"Oh, it does. As a matter of fact, I'm thinking of giving a little dinner party myself. I haven't a clue how to write your invitation."

"I wouldn't worry about it."

"Oh, but I do." Her eyes widened and rounded. "I'd hate to make a faux pas."

"What a pity."

If Cathleen couldn't get a rise one way, she'd get one another. "Well, after all, one doesn't know how to politely address a man's mistress." Then she let out a gasp and squeal as Myra's drink ran down her bodice.

"Oh, how dreadfully clumsy of me." Rocking back on her heels, Myra surveyed the damage to Cathleen's pink crepe de chine. It was almost enough to satisfy Myra. "I feel like such a mule," she said lightly. "Come, I'll go up with you, Cathleen. I'll be more than happy to sponge you off."

"I can take care of myself," she said between gritted teeth. "Just keep away from me."

Myra lit a cigarette and blew smoke at the ceiling. "Whatever you say."

Feeling obligated, Anna started to take her arm. "Here, let me take you up."

"Keep your hands off me," she hissed. "You and your imbecile friend." Skirts swirling, she was pushing herself through the crowd.

"Subtlety," Anna sighed. "Didn't we speak of subtlety?"

"I didn't toss it in her face," Myra said. "And to tell the truth, I've been wanting to do that for so long. This was the first time I could and feel absolutely justified." She gave Anna a wide grin. "Do I have time for another drink before dinner?"

Chapter Twelve

Perhaps if Daniel hadn't overheard the incident with Cathleen Donahue he would have handled things differently. But he had. Perhaps if his anger at the insult hadn't eaten away at him, their relationship could have continued smoothly enough. But it didn't. Throughout the rest of the evening, he managed to remain the congenial host. Guests left his home well fed and content. He could barely wait to close the door behind the last of them.

"We need to talk," he told Anna before she could take her first sigh of relief.

Though she was wilting a bit around the edges, she nodded. Others might have been fooled by Daniel's easy conversation and careless generosity through the evening, but she had sensed both strain and anger. In tacit agreement, they walked upstairs to the privacy of the bedroom.

"Something has upset you," she began, and sat on the arm of chair, though she longed to take off her clothes and fall mindlessly into bed. "I know you had business with the governor. Did something go wrong?"

"My business is fine." He paced to the window and pulled out a cigar. "It's my personal life that's the problem."

She folded her hands in her lap, a sure sign of annoyance or nerves. "I see."

"No, you don't." He turned to her then, ready to snipe or charge. "If you understood, there'd be no argument about marriage. It would simply be a fact."

"Simply a fact," she repeated and struggled to remember how unproductive anger was. "Daniel, our biggest problem seems to stem from our diverse outlooks on marriage. I don't see it as simply a fact, but as the biggest step one person can take with another. I can't take that step with you until I'm ready."

"If you ever are," he shot back.

She moistened her lips. Behind her growing temper were regrets. "If I ever am."

The anger he'd held in all evening gnawed at him. "So, you'll give me no promises, Anna. Nothing."

"I told you before I wouldn't give a promise I may have to break. I'll give you everything I can, Daniel."

"It's not enough." He drew on the cigar then watched her through a haze of smoke.

"I'm sorry. If I could, I'd give you more."

"If you could?" Fury whipped through him, blinding him to reason. "*If* you could? Nothing's stopping you but your own stubbornness."

"If that were true, I'd be a fool." She rose because it was time to face him. Time, in fact, to face herself. "And perhaps I am, because I expect you to give my needs and ambitions as much respect as you give your own."

"What in hell does that have to do with marriage?"

"Everything. In nine months I'll have my degree."

"A piece of paper," he shot back.

Everything about her turned cold: her skin, her voice, her eyes. "A piece of paper? I wonder if you would call your deeds and stocks and contracts pieces of paper— pieces of paper too lofty, too important to ever be discussed with me. Or perhaps, as with the textile factory the governor asked me about tonight, you don't consider me intelligent enough to understand your work."

"I've never doubted your intelligence," he shot back. "What do deeds and stock have to do with us?"

"They're part of you, just as my degree will be part of me. I've devoted years of my life to earning it. I would think you could understand that."

"I'll tell you what I understand." Rigid with anger, he crushed out his cigar. "I understand I'm tired of coming in second place to this precious degree."

"Damn you, Daniel, no one can tell you anything." Fighting for control, she leaned both hands on her dresser. "It isn't a matter of places; it isn't a competition."

"What is it then? Just what in hell is it?"

"A matter of respect," she said more calmly, and turned to him again. "It's a matter of respect."

"And what about love?"

He spoke of love so seldom that his question nearly broke her. Tears swam in her eyes and smothered her voice. "Love is an empty word without respect. I'd rather not have it from a man who can't accept me for what I am. I'd rather not give it to a man who won't share his problems with me as well as his successes."

His pride was as strong as hers. Even as he felt her slip away from him, he gripped his pride as though it were all he had left. "Then perhaps you'd prefer it if I stopped loving you. I'll do my best.'' With that, he turned on his heel. Moments later, Anna heard the front door slam.

She could have fallen on the bed and given in to tears. She wanted to—maybe too much. Because she couldn't, there seemed to be only one thing left to do. Mechanically she began to pack.

The drive to Connecticut was a long and lonely one. Weeks later, Anna could remember it vividly. She drove through the night until her eyes were gritty and the sun was up. Exhausted, she checked into a motel and slept until dusk. When she woke, she tried to forget what she'd left behind. The first few days were spent finding a small apartment near the campus. She needed privacy, and indulged herself by having her own place. Her days were full with planning, preparing. Anna thought it a pity that her nights couldn't be full as well.

Anna could block Daniel out of her mind for long stretches during the day, but at night she would lie in her bed and remember what it had been like to curl up against him. She would eat alone at her little table in her little kitchen and remember how she and Daniel had lingered over coffee in the dining room simply because it was so comfortable just to talk.

She deliberately refused to install a phone. It would have made it too easy to call him. When classes began, she fell into them with an almost desperate relief.

Her fellow students noticed a change in her. The usually friendly, if slightly reserved Miss Whitfield was now completely withdrawn. She rarely spoke unless it was to ask or answer a question in class. Those who happened to drive by her apartment in the evening or late on a Saturday night invariably saw a light burning in her window. Incessant study brought shadows to eyes that even her professors began to note. She blocked any comment or question with polite but firm withdrawal.

The days blurred together as she wanted them to. If she studied hard enough, long enough, she could fall into oblivion for six hours a night and not think at all.

Connecticut in mid-September was brisk and beautiful, but Anna had taken little time to notice the foliage. The strong colors and rich scents of fall were bypassed in favor of medical journals and anatomy classes. In previous years, she'd managed to enjoy her surroundings while devoting herself to her studies. Now, if she stopped for a moment to admire the wild riot of leaves, she would think only of a cliff top and the roar of water on rock. And she would wonder, in that moment before she pulled herself away, if Daniel was building his house.

In defense, she had even avoided contacting Myra, though her friend sent her long, annoyed letters. When the telegram arrived, Anna realized she couldn't hide forever. It read simply: IF YOU DON'T WANT ME ON YOUR DOORSTEP IN TWENTY-FOUR HOURS CALL STOP MYRA STOP.

With the telegram mixed in with her notes on the circulatory system, Anna stopped between classes at a pay phone in the student lounge. Armed with change, she put the call through and waited.

"Hello."

"Myra, if you arrived on my doorstep you'd have to sleep there. I don't have an extra bed."

"Anna! Good God, I was beginning to think you'd slid into the Atlantic." Anna heard the quick snap of a lighter and an indrawn breath. "That was easier to believe than that you'd been too rude to answer my letters."

"I'm sorry. I've been busy."

"You've been hiding," Myra corrected. "And I'll tol-

erate that as long as it's not from me. I've been worried
about you.''

"Don't be. I'm fine.''

"Of course.''

"No, I'm not fine,'' she admitted because it was Myra.
"But I am busy, up to my ears in books and notes.''

"You haven't called Daniel?''

"No, I can't.'' She closed her eyes and rested her forehead against the cool metal of the phone. "How is he?
Have you seen him?''

"Seen him?'' Anna could almost see Myra roll her eyes.
"He went crazy the night you left. Woke Herbert and I up
after two a.m., demanding if you were here. Herbert calmed
him down. The man's positively amazing—Herbert that is.
We haven't seen a great deal of Daniel since, but I hear
he's spending a lot of time in Hyannis Port supervising the
building of his house.''

"Yes, he would.'' And she could see him there, watching the machines dig and the men laying stone.

"Anna, did you know that Daniel overheard that little
incident with Cathleen the night of the dinner party?''

She caught herself wallowing in self-pity and shook her
head. "No. No, he didn't tell me. Oh…'' She remembered
the underlying fury she'd sensed in him—the same fury
he'd turned on her. It explained a great deal.

"I heard him tell Herbert he'd like to wring her skinny
neck. Though I approved, Herbert talked him out of it. It
did seem though that the entire business had thrown him
off. The man has the idea that you should be protected from
any kind of insult. It's sweet really, though we can certainly
take care of ourselves.''

"I can't marry Daniel in order not to be insulted,'' she
murmured.

"No. And though I'm sure he deserves a kick in the

behind, darling, I'd swear his heart's in the right place. He loves you, Anna.''

"Only part of me." She closed her eyes and willed herself to be strong. "I'm sorry we involved you."

"Oh, please, you know I thrive on being involved. Anna, do you want to talk about it? Would you like me to come?"

"No, really. At least not yet." Though she rubbed at her temple, Anna laughed. "I'm glad I didn't answer your letters. Talking to you has done me more good than anything else."

"Then give me your number. There's no reason why we can't talk instead of writing."

"I don't have a phone."

"No phone?" There was a shocked and pregnant pause. "Anna, darling, how do you survive?"

She stopped rubbing at her temple and really laughed. "I'm very primitive here. You'd be shocked if you saw my apartment." And she wondered if even Myra would understand the enthusiasm she'd felt while spending the best part of the afternoon with a dozen other students and a cadaver. Some things were best left unsaid. "Look, I promise, I'll sit down and write you a long letter tonight. I'll even call again next week."

"All right, then. But one word of advice before you go. Daniel's a man, so he starts with one strike against him. Just try to remember that."

"Thanks. Give my love to Herbert."

"I will. I'm counting on that letter."

"Tonight," she promised again. "Bye, Myra."

When Anna hung up, she felt truly steady for the first time in weeks. True, she'd taken charge of her own life when she'd left Boston. She'd leased her own apartment, registered for classes. She set her own study time and was responsible for her own success, her own failure. But she hadn't been happy. She was responsible for that, as well, she reminded herself as she walked back down the hall. It was time to face the fact that she'd made her choice. If she had to live as it seemed she did—alone—then she had to make the best of it.

A glance at her watch showed her she had ten minutes before her next class. This time she'd step outside and enjoy the autumn weather instead of hurrying to the next building and burying her face in a book.

Outside, she saw the symphony of color she had almost deliberately ignored for weeks. She saw other students hurrying to class or stretched on the grass reading by sunlight. She saw the slight slope and the old red brick of the hospital. And she saw the blue convertible at the curb.

For an instant, she couldn't move. Weeks peeled away and she was coming out of the hospital in Boston to find Daniel waiting for her. Her fingers tightened on the books she carried. But it wasn't Boston, she thought more calmly. And Daniel's wasn't the only blue convertible on the east coast. It was simply a mean twist of fate that had made her walk out and see it. Pulling herself together, she started to walk away. Seconds later, she was going back to the car for a closer look.

"Want a ride?"

At the sound of his voice, she felt her heart roll over in her chest. When she turned, her face was touched with both wariness and pleasure. "Daniel, what are you doing here?" And what did she care? It was enough just to look at him.

"It appears I'm waiting for you." He wanted to touch her, but if he touched, he'd grab. Deliberately he kept his hands in his pockets. "What time is your last class over?"

"Last class?" She'd forgotten what day it was. "Ah, an hour or so. I only have one more today."

"All right, then, I'll be back."

Be back? Dazed, she watched him walk around the hood and open the driver's door. Before she realized she intended to do it, Anna pulled open the passenger's.

"What are you doing?"

"I'm going with you," she blurted out.

He gave her a long, cool stare. "What about your class?"

She gave a desperate look around the campus before she climbed in the car. "I'll borrow someone's notes. I can make it up." But she couldn't make up another hour away from him.

"You're not the type to skip classes."

"No, I'm not." Giddy, she set her books in her lap. "My apartment isn't far. We can have some coffee. Just turn left past the hospital then—"

"I know where it is," he interrupted, but didn't add he'd known almost before the ink had dried on the lease.

The five-minute drive went quickly as dozens of thoughts ran through her head. How should she treat him? Politely? Was he still angry? For the first time since she'd known him, Anna couldn't gauge his mood. Her nerves were jumping by the time he stopped the car again. He seemed perfectly calm.

"I wasn't expecting anyone," she began as they walked up the steps to her apartment on the second floor.

"A person might be able to call if you had a phone."

"I hadn't given it much thought," she told him, then unlocked the door. "Come in," she invited.

The moment he stepped inside she realized how impossibly small the apartment was. In the living area, Daniel could all but touch the walls if he were to spread out his arms. She had a divan, a coffee table and a lamp, and hadn't seen the necessity for anything else.

"Sit down," she offered, discovering she desperately needed a moment to herself. "I'll make coffee."

Without waiting for his answer, she fled to the kitchen. When he was alone, Daniel unclenched his hands. He didn't see simply a small room, but the touches of charm. She had colorful pillows tossed on the couch and a bowl of shells on the coffee table. More than that, the tiny sun-washed room carried her scent—the same scent that had faded from their bedroom. He couldn't sit, and he couldn't stand alone. Clenching his hands again, he followed her into the kitchen.

He couldn't tell how much cooking she did in the cramped space, but she obviously worked here. On the table by the window was a portable typewriter and stacks of notes and books. Pencils worn down to nubs and freshly sharpened ones were held in a china cup. He was out of his element. He felt it. He fought it.

"Coffee will just be a minute," she said to fill the silence. He was there again, and she hadn't had enough time. She couldn't know that he was feeling precisely the same. "I don't have anything else to offer you. I haven't shopped this week."

She was nervous, he realized, hearing the jumps in her usually smooth voice. Curious, he watched and saw her hands tremble lightly as she reached for cups. He felt the knots in his stomach loosen just a little. How did he approach her? Daniel pulled up a chair and sat.

"You're looking pale, Anna."

"I haven't been getting much sun. The schedule's always frantic the first few weeks."

"And weekends?"

"There's the hospital."

"Mmm. If you were a doctor, you might diagnose overwork."

"I'm not a doctor yet." She set the coffee down, then hesitated. After a moment, she sat across from him. It was so much like their time together before. Yet it was nothing like it at all. "I happened to talk to Myra today. She said that you've started the house in Hyannis Port."

"That's right." He'd watched them break the ground, seen the foundation rise. And it had meant nothing. Nothing at all. "If we stay on schedule, the main part will be livable by next summer."

"You must be pleased." Her coffee tasted like mud, and she pushed it aside.

"I have the blueprints in the car. You might like to see them."

Her chest was tight as she lifted her head. He saw the surprise in her eyes and cursed himself for a fool. "Of course, I would."

For a moment he scowled down at his own hands. He was a gambler, wasn't he? It was time to take another chance. "I'm thinking of buying an office building downtown. Small businesses and low rent, but I think the property value should double in five to seven years." He added a lump of sugar to his coffee but didn't stir it. "I've run into some problems with the textile factory. Your father's working on the kinks so we can be in production by spring."

She kept her gaze steady on his. "Why are you telling me?"

He took a minute. Confessions didn't come easily to him. But her eyes were so dark, so patient. Hard as it was, he'd realized he needed her as much as his own pride. "A man doesn't like to admit he was wrong, Anna. But more than that, he doesn't like to face that his woman turned away from him because he couldn't admit it."

He could have said nothing that could have made her love him more. "I didn't turn away from you, Daniel."

"Ran away."

She swallowed. "All right, I ran away. From both of us. Do you realize you've offered me more of yourself in the last five minutes than you did the entire time we lived together?"

"It never occurred to me that you'd want to know about factories and interest rates." He started to rise, then changed his mind when he saw the impatience in her eyes. "You'd better say what's on your mind."

"The first time I walked into the bedroom, I saw how little of yourself was there. After a while, I figured out why. You were so determined to go forward. Daniel, as much as you spoke of the home and family you wanted, you've had it in your head to do it yourself. I was to be swept along."

"There'd be no family without you, Anna."

"But you wanted to give, not to share. You never offered to show me the blueprints of the home you said you wanted for both of us. You never asked for an opinion or a suggestion."

"No. And as I watched them build the foundation, I realized I was going to have the house I wanted, but not the home I needed." He set down his spoon with a snap. "I never thought it really mattered to you."

"I didn't know how to show you." She smiled a little. "Stupid." Because she needed just a bit of distance, she rose to stand at the window. Strange, she realized, she worked here every evening and hadn't noticed the big red maple that spread in the yard. It was beautiful. How much beauty was she cutting out of her life? "Part of me wanted to share that home with you. More than anything."

"But only part."

"I guess it's the part you can't accept that held me back.

That held us both back. Do you know, you never asked about my work at the hospital, about the books or about why I want to be a surgeon.''

He rose, too. He'd already faced himself. Now he had to face her. "A man doesn't ask the woman he loves about her other lover."

Torn between anger and confusion, she turned. "Daniel—"

"Don't ask me to be reasonable," he interrupted. "I'm damn near ready to crawl if I have to, but don't ask me to be reasonable."

On a huff of breath, she shook her head. "All right, I won't. Let's just say then that some women can have two lovers and be happy spending their lives trying to give each what they need."

"It's a hard life."

"Not if the woman has two lovers that are willing to give her back what she needs."

There was no room to pace in the little kitchen. Instead, Daniel rocked back on his heels, his hands still clenched in his pockets. "You know, I did a lot of thinking about your doctoring these last few weeks. More, I guess, than I've wanted to do since I first saw you. There were times, Anna, when I could see you were meant for something more, but I managed to block it out. When you left and I spent my nights alone, I didn't have any choice but to think. I remembered the way you'd been with Mrs. Higgs. And the way you'd look when you'd walk out of the hospital in the evening. I remembered how you'd stood in the kitchen with blood on your blouse and explained, very calmly, how you'd dealt with Sally's wrist. She told me the doctor said you'd saved her life. Something you'd learned in one of these," he said, indicating the stack of books. "Not so hard to learn, maybe, but I wouldn't think so easy to do." He picked up a book and held it as he faced her. "No, I haven't asked you before why you want to be a surgeon. I'm asking now."

She hesitated, afraid he might make some cutting, or worse, patronizing remark. He'd come to her—a gamble. She could gamble as well. "I have a dream," she told him quietly. "I want to make a difference."

He studied her in silence, his eyes narrowed, the irises a deep, intense blue. "I have a dream," he said at length then set the book down again. For the first time, he stepped toward her. "It's a small apartment, Anna. But I think there's room enough for two."

He heard her long broken breath before she wrapped her arms around him. "We'll need a bigger bed."

"There's a lass." On a laugh, he picked her up off the floor and gave himself the pleasure of her mouth. Relief poured through him like wine until he was drunk with it. "I've missed you, Anna. I can't do without you again."

"No." With her face buried against his throat, she drew in his scent and filled herself with it. "Not again. Daniel, I've only been half-alive here without you. I tried to crowd the day with studies, to work harder, longer at the hospital, but it just didn't mean anything. I want you with me, need you with me."

"You'll have me. A bigger bed and three phones should do it."

With a laugh, she found his lips with hers. He could have his phones as long as she had him. "I love you."

"You never told me that." Unsteady, he drew her away. "You never once told me that before."

"I was afraid to. I thought if you knew how much I loved you, you might use it to make me give up the rest."

He started to deny it, then swore at himself because it was true. "And now?"

"The rest doesn't mean much if you're not with me."

He drew farther away. "Once I told you I'd thought of you looking around and seeing someone who appealed to you more. I wasn't joking."

She gave him a little shake. "You should have been."

Didn't she realize how lovely she was, how regal? Didn't she know how clumsy she could make a man feel with just a smile? "Don't believe I've taken you for granted or ever will. I may act like it, but it won't be true. You're my answer, Anna, and I want to be yours."

She rested her cheek on his shoulder a moment. It had never occurred to her that his confidence would ever waver. She loved him more knowing it could. "You are, Daniel. I haven't been sure I could give you what you seemed to want."

"I wanted a wife, a woman who'd be there at night when I came home. One who'd keep flowers in the vases and lace at the windows. One who'd be content with whatever I could give her."

She looked at the books stacked on the table, then at the man standing in front of her. "And now?"

"I'm beginning to think a woman like that would bore me within a week."

She pressed her fingers to her eyes to hold back the tears. "I'd like to think so."

"I'm not backing down." His voice was suddenly rough as he dragged her back against him. "You're going to marry me, Anna, the day after you have that degree. You'll be Dr. Whitfield for less than twenty-four hours."

Her fingers curled into his shirt. "Daniel, I—"

"Then it's Dr. MacGregor."

Her fingers froze. She took three quiet breaths before she dared to speak. "Do you mean that?"

"Aye. I always mean what I say. And you'll have to put

up with me introducing my wife as the best surgeon in the country. I want to share your dream, Anna, as much as I want you to share mine.''

''It won't be easy for you. While I'm an intern, the hours will be hateful.''

''And in twenty years, we'll look back and wonder how we got through them. I like the long view, Anna. I wanted you to marry me because I thought you fit a slot. You didn't fit it.'' He took her hands in his. ''Now I'm asking you to marry me because I love you exactly as you are.''

She took a long time to study him. This time there would be no stepping back. ''Do you still have the ring?''

''Aye.'' He reached in his pocket. ''I got into the habit of carrying it with me.''

Laughing, she lifted both hands to his face. ''I'll take it now.'' As he started to slip it on, she closed her hand over his. ''Here's a promise for you, Daniel. I'll do my best.''

The ring slid on. ''That's good enough.''

Epilogue

Anna had slept in snatches through the night, rejecting the cot an orderly had brought her, preferring the chair beside Daniel's bed. From time to time during the night, he'd murmured in his sleep. Whenever she'd heard her name, she tried to soothe him, talking to him, reminiscing until he was restful again.

Only once did she leave him to go down and check on Shelby. The rest of the time she sat watching him sleep and listening to the all too familiar beeps and clicks of machines.

The nurses changed shifts. Someone brought her coffee before going off duty. The moon began to set. She thought of the man she loved, of the life they'd built and sat in silence to wait.

Just before dawn, she leaned over to rest her head on the bed beside his hand. When Daniel woke, he saw her first. She was sleeping lightly.

He was disoriented for only a moment. Even though the

drugs were still swimming in his system, he remembered the accident with perfect clarity. He thought briefly of his car. He was very fond of that particular toy. Then he felt the pressure in his chest, saw the tubes running from his arm.

He remembered more than the accident now. He remembered Anna leaning over him, talking, reassuring him as he was being wheeled on a gurney down the hospital corridor. He remembered the fear he'd read in her eyes, and before he slipped into unconsciousness, his one moment of blind, naked terror that he was being taken away from her.

Oddly, he thought he remembered looking down at himself from somewhere while doctors and nurses scrambled around. Then it seemed he'd been sucked back into his body, but the sensation was too vague to pinpoint. He remembered one more thing. Anna again, leaning over him, cursing at him, kissing his hand. Then he had simply dreamed.

She looked so tired, he realized. Then it came home to him how old and battered his own body felt. Furious at his weakness, he struggled to sit up and couldn't. Because the effort it cost him embarrassed him, he reached out to touch Anna's cheek. She was awake in an instant.

"Daniel." Her fingers curled around his. In a matter of seconds, he saw it all on her face: terror, relief, grief, weariness and strength. Through sheer will she controlled the need to simply drop her head to his chest and weep. "Daniel—" her voice was as cool and calm as the first time he'd ever heard it "—do you know me?"

Though it cost him, he lifted a brow. "Why in hell wouldn't I know the woman I've lived with for almost forty years?"

"Why in hell not," she agreed and gave herself the pleasure of pressing her lips to his.

"You might be more comfortable if you climbed in here with me."

"Maybe later," she promised, and lifted one of his eyelids to study his pupil.

"Don't start poking and prodding at me. I want a real doctor." He managed to grin at her.

She pressed a button beside the bed. "Is your vision blurred?"

"I can see you well enough. You're as pretty as you were the first night we waltzed."

"Hallucinating," she said dryly, then looked up as a nurse came in. "Please call Dr. Feinstein. Mr. MacGregor is awake and requesting a real doctor."

"Yes, Dr. MacGregor."

"I love it when they call you that," he murmured, and shut his eyes for just a minute. "How much damage did I do, Anna?"

"You were concussed. You've broken three ribs, and—"

"Not to me," he said impatiently, "to the car."

Setting her teeth, she folded her arms. "You never change. I don't know why I bothered to worry. I'm terribly sorry I disturbed the children."

"The children." The light in his eyes wasn't as fierce as it might have been, but it was there. "You called the children?"

He'd given her precisely the reaction she'd needed for her own reassurance. Anna pretended indifference. "Yes, I must apologize to them."

"They came?"

She knew his tactics too well. "Of course."

"What were you going to do, have a wake?"

She tidied his top sheet. "We wanted to be prepared."

He scowled at her and nearly managed to gesture toward the door. "Well, send them in."

"I wouldn't have them spend the night here. They're at home."

His mouth dropped open. "Home? You mean they didn't stay here? They left their father on his deathbed and went to drink his Scotch?"

"Yes, I'm afraid they're very feckless children, Daniel. Take after their father. Here's Dr. Feinstein now." She gave his hand a quick pat before she walked to the door. "I'll leave you two alone."

"Anna."

She paused at the door and smiled back at him. "Yes, Daniel?"

"Don't stay away long."

She saw him then as he'd been so many years before: indomitable, arrogant and strong enough to need. "Do I ever?"

She walked straight out of Intensive Care to her own office. Locking the door, she gave herself the luxury of a twenty-minute weeping spell. She'd cried there before, after losing a patient. This time she wept from a relief too great to measure and a love too strong to soothe. After rinsing her face several times in cold water, she went to the phone.

"Hello."

"Caine."

"Mom, we were just about to call. Is he—"

"Your father wants to see you," she said easily. "He's afraid you've been drinking his Scotch."

He swore, and she heard his momentary struggle for control. "Tell him we didn't put much of a dent in it. Are you okay?"

"I'm terrific. Ask Rena to bring me a change of clothes when you come."

"We'll be there in a half hour."

* * *

"It's a shame when a man has to all but die to get his children to visit him." Propped on pillows, swathed in bandages, Daniel held court.

"A couple of broken ribs," Serena said lightly and tweaked his toe from her position at the foot of the bed. She'd lain wakeful through the night in Justin's arms.

"Hah! Tell that to the doctor who put this tube in my chest. And you didn't even bring my grandson." He glared briefly at Serena before turning to Caine. "Or my granddaughter. They'll be in college before I see them again. Won't even know who I am."

"We show Laura your picture once a week," Caine offered. He continued to hold Diana's hand, wondering if he would have made it through the past twenty-four hours without her quiet, unflagging strength. "Don't we, love?"

"Every Sunday," Diana agreed.

With a grumpy mutter he turned to Grant and Gennie. "I suppose your sister has an excuse for not coming up," he said to Grant. "And it's only right Alan's with her, though he's my firstborn. After all, she's due to give me another grandchild in a couple of weeks."

"Any excuse," Grant said smoothly as Caine grinned and examined his nails.

"You're looking well, lass," he told Gennie. "A woman just blooms when she's carrying a child."

"And spreads," Gennie returned, touching a hand to her rounded stomach. "Another couple of months and I won't be able to reach my easel."

"See that you use a stool," he ordered. "A pregnant woman shouldn't be on her feet all day."

"And see that you're out of this place and on your own feet by spring," Grant told him as he slipped an arm around his wife. "You'll have to come to Maine to be the baby's godfather."

"Godfather." He preened. "It's a sad thing for a MacGregor to be godfather to a Campbell." He ignored Grant's grin, though it made his lips twitch, and looked at Gennie. "But I'll do it for you. Are you getting enough rest?"

Anna slipped a hand to his wrist to unobtrusively monitor his pulse. "He forgets that I was pregnant with Alan the last three months I interned. Never felt better in my life."

"I felt wonderful during pregnancy myself," Serena commented. "I suppose that's why I'm doing it again."

It only took Daniel a minute. "Again?"

Serena rose on her toes to kiss Justin before she smiled at her father. "Again. Seven months to go."

"Well now—"

"No Scotch, Daniel," Anna said, anticipating him. "At least not until you're out of Intensive Care."

He scowled, muttered, then opened his arms as best he could. "Come here then, little girl."

Serena leaned over the bed and held him as hard as she dared. "Don't you ever scare me like this again," she whispered fiercely.

"Now, now, don't scold," he murmured and stroked her hair. "Bad as your mother. You take good care of her," he ordered Justin. "I don't want my next grandchild born in front of a slot machine."

"Eight to five this one's a girl," Justin answered.

"You're on." Grinning, he turned to Diana. "You have to catch up."

"Don't be greedy," she told him and took his hand.

"A man's entitled to greed when he reaches a certain age, isn't that right, Anna?"

"A woman's entitled to make her own decisions—at any age."

"Hah!" Enormously pleased with himself, he surveyed

the room. ''I never mentioned that your mother picketed for equal rights before it was stylish, did I? Living with her's been nothing but a trial. And stop taking my pulse, woman. No better medicine for a man than family.''

''Then maybe we should give you a bit more.'' Anna nodded to the nurse outside the door. With a sigh, she leaned against the bed. They were breaking all manner of hospital rules already. What was one more? She felt Daniel's fingers tighten on hers as Alan wheeled Shelby into the room.

''What's this?'' he demanded and would have attempted to sit up if Anna hadn't eased him back.

''This,'' Shelby began, uncovering the bundle in her arms, ''is Daniel Campbell MacGregor. He's eight hours and twenty minutes old and wanted to see his grandpa.''

Alan took his son to set him in his father's arms. He'd spent the night praying he'd be able to do just that.

''What a sight,'' Daniel murmured, not bothering to blink the tears from his eyes. ''A grandson, Anna. He has my nose. Look, he smiled at me.'' As Anna leaned down, he laughed. ''And don't give me that hogwash about gas. Doctors. I know a smile when I see one.'' Looking up, he grinned at his son. ''Fine job, Alan.''

''Thanks.'' Still awed by his son, Alan sat on the edge of the bed. With one hand he covered his father's over the baby's. For a moment, three generations of MacGregor males were content.

''Campbell,'' Daniel said abruptly. ''Did you say, Campbell?'' His gaze locked on Shelby.

''I most certainly did.'' Her hand slipped into Alan's as she rose. She might be less than nine hours out of the delivery room, but she felt as strong as a bull. Certainly as strong as a MacGregor. ''You'd better accept the fact that he's half Campbell, MacGregor.'' At her brother's chuckle, her chin lifted higher. ''Very possibly the best half.''

His eyes flashed. Anna took note of his color and approved. He opened his mouth, then laughed until he was weak from it. ''What a tongue the girl has. At least you had the good sense to name him Daniel.''

''I named him after someone I love and admire.''

''Flattery.'' He signaled, reluctantly, for Alan to take the baby. Taking Shelby's hand he held it between both of his. ''You look beautiful.''

She smiled, a bit stunned by the tears that swam in her eyes. ''I feel beautiful.''

''You should have heard her swear at the doctor.'' Delighted with her, Alan pressed a kiss to her temple. ''She threatened to get up and go home to have the baby without his interference. She would have, too, if young Daniel hadn't had different ideas.''

''Good for you,'' Daniel decided, and thought his name suited his grandson very well. ''Nothing worse than having a doctor fussing around when you just want to get on with your business.'' After sending Anna a bland smile, he turned back to Shelby. ''Now, I want you to get back in bed where you belong. I don't want to worry about you. You've given us all a gift.''

She leaned down to kiss his cheek. ''You gave me one. Alan. I love you, you old badger.''

''Just like a Campbell. Go to bed.''

''I'm afraid you're all going to have to run along before the hospital board calls me on the carpet.''

''Now, Anna.''

''If your father gets enough rest—'' she turned to give him a telling look ''—he'll be moved out of ICU in the morning.''

It wasn't quick, and it wasn't quiet, but Anna finally

managed to clear the room. She pretended not to hear Daniel's muttered request to Justin for a game of poker later or his demand to Caine for the cigars Daniel had hidden in his office. If he hadn't made the demands, she'd have worried. No matter how Daniel had protested, she knew visits were as much a strain as a blessing. Until she was satisfied with his condition, she'd keep the future ones short. The trick would be making him think it was his idea. She'd had years of practice.

"Now—" she walked back to the bed and smoothed the hair from his brow "—I've a dozen things to see to that I let go while I was fussing unnecessarily over you. I want you to sleep."

He could be weaker now, now that it was only her. "I don't want you to go yet, Anna. I know you're tired, but I need you to stay just a little longer."

"All right." Dropping the bed guard again, she sat beside him. "Just rest."

"We did a good job, didn't we?"

She smiled, knowing he spoke of the children. "Yes, we did a very good job."

"No regrets?"

Puzzled, she shook her head. "What a foolish question."

"No." He took her hand in his. "Last night I dreamed. I dreamed of you. It started on the night we met, that first waltz."

"The summer ball," she murmured. She had only to smile to see the moonlight, smell the flowers. Odd, it had been in her dreams as well. "It was a beautiful night."

"You were beautiful," he corrected. "And I wanted you more than I'd ever wanted anything in my life."

"You were arrogant," she remembered, smiling. "And desperately attractive." Leaning over, she kissed him softly, lingeringly. The same passion that they'd felt in the beginning hovered over them. "You still are, Daniel."

"I'm old, Anna."

"We're both old."

He pressed her hand to his lips. The ring he'd given her so many years before was cool against his skin. "And I still want you more than I've ever wanted anything in my life."

Ignoring rules and procedure, Anna lay next to him and rested her head on his shoulder. "I'll lose my reputation for this." She closed her eyes. "It's worth it."

"A fine one you are to talk of reputations." He brushed his lips over her hair. The scent was the same after all the years. "It's a funny thing, Anna. I keep having this fierce craving for peach pie."

She lay still a minute, drifting, then her eyes opened on a laugh. They were young and wicked as she tilted her head toward his. "The minute you have a private room."

*   *   *   *   *

IN FROM THE COLD

Chapter One

His name was MacGregor. He clung to that even as he clung to the horse's reins. The pain was alive, capering down his arm like a dozen dancing devils. Hot, branding hot, despite the December wind and blowing snow.

He could no longer direct the horse but rode on, trusting her to find her way through the twisting paths made by Indian or deer or white man. He was alone with the scent of snow and pine, the muffled thud of his mount's hooves and the gloom of early twilight. A world hushed by the sea of wind washing through the trees.

Instinct told him he was far from Boston now, far from the crowds, the warm hearths, the civilized. Safe. Perhaps safe. The snow would cover the trail his horse left and the guiding path of his own blood.

But safe wasn't enough for him. It never had been. He was determined to stay alive, and for one fierce reason. A dead man couldn't fight. By all that was holy he had vowed to fight until he was free.

Shivering despite the heavy buckskins and furs, teeth chattering now from a chill that came from within as well as without, he leaned forward to speak to the horse, soothing in Gaelic. His skin was clammy with the heat of the pain, but his blood was like the ice that formed on the bare branches of the trees surrounding him. He could see the mare's breath blow out in white streams as she trudged on through the deepening snow. He prayed as only a man who could feel his own blood pouring out of him could pray. For life.

There was a battle yet to be fought. He'd be damned if he'd die before he'd raised his sword.

The mare gave a sympathetic whinny as he slumped against her neck, his breathing labored. Trouble was in the air, as well as the scent of blood. With a toss of her head, she walked into the wind, following her own instinct for survival and heading west.

The pain was like a dream now, floating in his mind, swimming through his body. He thought if he could only wake, it would disappear. As dreams do. He had other dreams—violent and vivid. To fight the British for all they had stolen from him. To take back his name and his land— to fight for all the MacGregors had held with pride and sweat and blood. All they had lost.

He had been born in war. It seemed just and right that he would die in war.

But not yet. He struggled to rouse himself. Not yet. The fight had only begun.

He forced an image into his mind. A grand one. Men in feathers and buckskins, their faces blackened with burnt cork and lampblack and grease, boarding the ships *Dartmouth*, *Eleanor* and *Beaver*. Ordinary men, he remembered, merchants and craftsmen and students. Some fueled with grog, some with righteousness. The hoisting and smashing of the chests of the damned and detested tea. The satisfying splash as broken crates of it hit the cold water of Boston Harbor at Griffin's Wharf. He remembered how disgorged chests had been heaped up in the muck of low tide like stacks of hay.

So large a cup of tea for the fishes, he thought now. Aye, they had been merry, but purposeful. Determined. United. They would need to be all of those things to fight and win the war that so many didn't understand had already begun.

How long had it been since that glorious night? One day? Two? It had been his bad luck that he had run into two drunk and edgy redcoats as dawn had been breaking. They knew him. His face, his name, his politics were well-known in Boston. He'd done nothing to endear himself to the British militia.

Perhaps they had only meant to harass and bully him a bit. Perhaps they hadn't meant to make good their threat to arrest him—on charges they hadn't made clear. But when one had drawn a sword, MacGregor's weapon had all but leaped into his own hand. The fight had been brief—and foolish, he could admit now. He was still unsure if he had killed or only wounded the impetuous soldier. But his comrade had had murder in his eye when he had drawn his weapon.

Though MacGregor had been quick to mount and ride, the musket ball had slammed viciously into his shoulder.

He could feel it now, throbbing against muscle. Though the rest of his body was mercifully numb, he could feel that small and agonizing pinpoint of heat. Then his mind was numb, as well, and he felt nothing.

He woke, painfully. He was lying in the blanket of snow, faceup so that he could see dimly the swirl of white flakes against a heavy gray sky. He'd fallen from his horse. He wasn't close enough to death to escape the embarrassment of it. With effort, he pushed himself to his knees. The mare was waiting patiently beside him, eyeing him with a mild sort of surprise.

"I'll trust you to keep this to yourself, lass." It was the weak sound of his own voice that brought him the first trace of fear. Gritting his teeth, he reached for the reins and pulled himself shakily to his feet. "Shelter." He swayed, grayed out and knew he could never find the strength to mount. Holding tight, he clucked to the mare and let her pull his weary body along.

Step after step he fought the urge to collapse and let the cold take him. They said there was little pain in freezing to death. Like sleep it was, a cold, painless sleep.

And how the devil did they know unless they'd lived to tell the tale? He laughed at the thought, but the laugh turned to a cough that weakened him.

Time, distance, direction were utterly lost to him. He tried to think of his family, the warmth of them. His parents and brothers and sisters in Scotland. Beloved Scotland, where they fought to keep hope alive. His aunts and uncles and cousins in Virginia, where they worked for the right to a new life in a new land. And he, he was somewhere between, caught between his love of the old and his fascination with the new.

But in either land, there was one common enemy. It strengthened him to think of it. The British. Damn them. They had proscribed his name and butchered his people. Now they were reaching their greedy hands across the ocean so that the half-mad English king could impose his bloody laws and collect his bloody taxes.

He stumbled, and his hold on the reins nearly broke. For a moment he rested, his head against the mare's neck, his eyes closed. His father's face seemed to float into his mind, his eyes still bright with pride.

"Make a place for yourself," he'd told his son. "Never forget, you're a MacGregor."

No, he wouldn't forget.

Wearily he opened his eyes. He saw, through the swirling snow, the shape of a building. Cautious, he blinked, rubbed his tired eyes with his free hand. Still the shape remained, gray and indistinct, but real.

"Well, lass." He leaned heavily against his horse. "Perhaps this isn't the day to die after all."

Step by step he trudged toward it. It was a barn, a large one, well built of pine logs. His numb fingers fumbled with the latch. His knees threatened to buckle. Then he was inside, with the smell and the blessed heat of animals.

It was dark. He moved by instinct to a mound of hay in the stall of a brindled cow. The bovine lady objected with a nervous moo.

It was the last sound he heard.

Alanna pulled on her woolen cape. The fire in the kitchen hearth burned brightly and smelled faintly, cheerfully, of apple logs. It was a small thing, a normal thing, but it pleased her. She'd woken in a mood of happy anticipation. It was the snow, she imagined, though her father had risen from his bed cursing it. She loved the purity of it, the way it clung to the bare branches of trees her father and brothers had yet to clear.

It was already slowing, and within the hour the barnyard would be tracked with footprints, hers included. There were animals to tend to, eggs to gather, harnesses to repair and wood to chop. But for now, for just a moment, she looked out the small window and enjoyed.

If her father caught her at it, he would shake his head and call her a dreamer. It would be said roughly—not with anger, she thought, but with regret. Her mother had been a dreamer, but she had died before her dream of a home and land and plenty had been fully realized.

Cyrus Murphy wasn't a hard man, Alanna thought now. He never had been. It had been death, too many deaths, that had caused him to become rough and prickly. Two bairns, and later, their beloved mother. Another son, beautiful young Rory, lost in the war against the French.

Her own husband, Alanna mused, sweet Michael Flynn, taken in a less dramatic way but taken nonetheless.

She didn't often think of Michael. After all, she had been three months a wife and three years a widow. But he had been a kind man and a good one, and she regretted bitterly that they had never had the chance to make a family.

But today wasn't a day for old sorrows, she reminded herself. Pulling up the hood of her cape, she stepped outside. Today was a day for promises, for beginnings. Christmas was coming fast. She was determined to make it a joyful one.

Already she'd spent hours at her spinning wheel and loom. There were new mufflers and mittens and caps for her brothers. Blue for Johnny and red for Brian. For her father she had painted a miniature of her mother. And had paid the local silversmith a lot of pennies for a frame.

She knew her choices would please. Just as the meal she had planned for their Christmas feast would please. It was all that mattered to her—keeping her family together and happy and safe.

The door of the barn was unlatched. With a sound of annoyance, she pulled it to behind her. It was a good thing she had found it so, she thought, rather than her father, or her young brother, Brian, would have earned the raw side of his tongue.

As she stepped inside the barn, she shook her hood back and reached automatically for the wooden buckets that hung beside the door. Because there was little light she took a lamp, lighting it carefully.

By the time she had finished the milking, Brian and Johnny would come to feed the stock and clean the stalls. Then she would gather the eggs and fix her men a hearty breakfast.

She started to hum as she walked down the wide aisle in the center of the barn. Then she stopped dead as she spotted the roan mare standing slack hipped and weary beside the cow stall.

"Sweet Jesus." She put a hand to her heart as it lurched. The mare blew a greeting and shifted.

If there was a horse, there was a rider. At twenty, Alanna wasn't young enough or naive enough to believe all travelers were friendly and meant no harm to a woman alone. She could have turned and run, sent up a shout for her father and brothers. But though she had taken Michael Flynn's name, she was born a Murphy. A Murphy protected his own.

Head up, she started forward. "I'll have your name and your business," she said. Only the horse answered her. When she was close enough she touched the mare on her nose. "What kind of a master have you who leaves you standing wet and saddled?" Incensed for the horse's sake, she set down her buckets and raised her voice. "All right, come out with you. It's Murphy land you're on."

The cows mooed.

With a hand on her hip, she looked around. "No one's begrudging you shelter from the storm," she continued. "Or a decent breakfast, for that matter. But I'll have a word with you for leaving your horse so."

When there was still no answer, her temper rose. Muttering, she began to uncinch the saddle herself. And nearly tripped over a pair of boots.

Fine boots at that, she thought, staring down at them. They poked out of the cow stall, their good brown leather dulled with snow and mud. She stepped quietly closer to see them attached to a pair of long, muscled legs in worn buckskin.

Sure and there was a yard of them, she thought, nibbling on her lip. And gloriously masculine in the loose-fitting breeches. Creeping closer, she saw hips, lean, a narrow waist belted with leather and a torso covered with a long doublet and a fur wrap.

A finer figure of a man she couldn't remember seeing. And since he'd chosen her barn to sleep, she found it only right that she look her fill. He was a big one, she decided, tilting her head and holding the lamp higher. Taller than either of her brothers. She leaned closer, wanting to see the rest of him.

His hair was dark. Not brown, she realized, as she narrowed her eyes, but deep red, like Brian's chestnut gelding. He wore no beard, but there was stubble on his chin and around his full, handsome mouth. Aye, handsome, she decided with feminine appreciation. A strong, bony face, aristocratic somehow, with its high brow and chiseled features.

The kind of face a woman's heart would flutter over, she was sure. But she wasn't interested in fluttering or flirting. She wanted the man up and out of her way so that she could get to her milking.

"Sir." She nudged his boot with the toe of hers. No response. Setting her hands on her hips, she decided he was drunk as a lord. What else was there that caused a man to sleep as though dead? "Wake up, you sod. I can't milk around you." She kicked him, none too gently, in the leg and got only a faint groan for an answer. "All right, boy-o." She bent down to give him a good shake. She was prepared for the stench of liquor but instead caught the coppery odor of blood.

Anger forgotten, she knelt down to carefully push aside the thick fur over his shoulders. She sucked in a breath as she saw the long stain along his shirtfront. Her fingers were wet with his blood as she felt for a pulse.

"Well, you're still alive," she murmured. "With God's will and a bit of luck we might keep you that way."

Before she could rise to call her brothers, his hand clamped over her wrist. His eyes were open now, she saw. They were green, with just a hint of blue. Like the sea. But there was pain in them. Compassion had her leaning closer to offer comfort.

Then her hand plunged deep into the hay as he tugged her off balance so that she was all but lying on him. She had the quick impression of a firm body and raging heat. Her sound of indignation was muffled against his lips. The kiss was brief but surprisingly firm before his head fell back again. He gave her a quick, cocky smile.

"Well, I'm not dead anyway. Lips like yours would have no place in hell."

As compliments went, she'd had better. Before she could tell him so, he fainted.

Chapter Two

He drifted, on a turbulent sea that was pain and relief and pain. Whiskey, the good, clean kick of it, warming his belly and dulling his senses. Yet over it he remembered a searing agony, a hot knife plunged into his flesh. Curses raining on his head. A warm hand clutching his, in comfort. In restraint. Blissfully cool cloths on his fevered brow. Hateful liquid poured down his throat.

He cried out. Had he cried out? Had someone come, all soft hands, soft voice, lavender scent, to soothe him? Had there been music, a woman's voice, low and lovely? Singing in Gaelic? Scotland? Was he is Scotland? But no, when the voice spoke to him, it was without that soft familiar burr, but instead with the dreamy brogue of Ireland.

The ship. Had the ship gone astray and taken him south instead of home? He remembered a ship. But the ship had been in port. Men laughing among themselves, their faces blackened and painted. Axes swinging. The tea. The cursed tea.

Ah, yes, he remembered. There was some comfort in that. They had taken their stand.

He had been shot. Not then, but after. At dawn. A mistake, a foolish one.

Then there had been snow and pain. He had awakened to a woman. A beautiful woman. A man could ask for little more than to wake to a beautiful woman, whether he awakened live or dead. The thought made him smile as he opened his heavy eyes. As dreams went, this one had its virtues.

Then he saw her sitting at a loom beneath a window where the sun was strong. It glistened on her hair, hair as black as the wing of any raven that flew in the forest. She wore a plain wool dress in dark blue with a white apron over it. He could see that she was wand slender, her hands graceful as they worked the loom. With a rhythmic click and clack she set a red pattern among deep green wool.

She sang as she worked, and it was her voice he recognized. The same voice had sung to comfort him when he had toiled through the hot and the cold of his dreams. He could see only her profile. Pale skin of white and rose, a faint curve to a mouth that was wide and generous, with the hint of a dimple beside it, a small nose that seemed to tilt up just a bit at the tip.

Peaceful. Just watching her gave him such a full sense of peace that he was tempted to close his eyes and sleep again. But he wanted to see her, all of her. And he needed her to tell him where he was.

The moment he stirred, Alanna's head came up. She turned toward him. He could see her eyes now—as deep and rich a blue as sapphires. As he watched, struggling for the strength to speak, she rose, smoothed her skirts and walked toward him.

Her hand was cool on his brow, and familiar. Briskly,

but with hands that were infinitely gentle, she checked his bandage.

"So, have you joined the living, then?" she asked him as she moved to a nearby table and poured something into a pewter cup.

"You'd know the answer to that better than I," he managed. She chuckled as she held the cup to his lips. The scent was familiar, as well, and unwelcome. "What the devil is this?"

"What's good for you," she told him, and poured it ruthlessly down his throat. When he glared she laughed again. "You've spit it back at me enough times that I've learned to take no chances."

"How long?"

"How long have you been with us?" She touched his forehead again. His fever had broken during the last long night, and her gesture was one of habit. "Two days. It's the twentieth of December."

"My horse?"

"She's well." Alanna nodded, pleased that he had thought of his mount. "You'd do well to sleep some more and I'll be fixing you some broth to strengthen you. Mr...?"

"MacGregor," he answered. "Ian MacGregor."

"Rest then, Mr. MacGregor."

But his hand reached for hers. Such a small hand, he thought irrelevantly, to be so competent. "Your name?"

"Alanna Flynn." His was a good hand, she thought, not as rough as Da's or her brothers', but hard. "You're welcome here until you are fit."

"Thank you." He kept her hand in his, toying with her fingers in a way that she would have thought flirtatious—if he hadn't just come out of a fever. Then she remembered he had kissed her when he'd been bleeding to death in her barn, and carefully removed her hand. He grinned at her. There was no other way to describe that quick curve of lips.

"I'm in your debt, Miss Flynn."

"Aye, that you are." She rose, all dignity. "And it's Mrs. Flynn."

He couldn't remember a swifter or weightier disappointment. Not that he minded flirting with married women, if they were agreeable. But he would never have considered taking it further than a few smiles and murmurs with another man's woman. It was a bloody shame, he thought as he studied Alanna Flynn. A sad and bloody shame.

"I'm grateful to you, Mrs. Flynn, and to your husband."

"Give your gratitude to my father." She softened the order with a smile that made her dimple deepen. He was a rogue, of that she hadn't a doubt. But he was also a weak one and, at the moment, in her care. "This is his house, and he'll be back soon." With her hands on her hips, she looked at him. His color was better, she noted, though the good Lord knew he could use a good clipping on that mane of hair he wore. And a shave wouldn't have hurt him. Despite it, he was an excellent-looking man. And because she was woman enough to have recognized the light in his eyes when he looked at her, she would keep her guard up.

"If you're not going to sleep, you might as well eat. I'll get that broth."

She left him to go into the kitchen, her heels clicking lightly on the plank floor. Alone, Ian lay still and let his gaze wander over the room. Alanna Flynn's father had done well for himself, Ian mused. The windows were glazed, the walls whitewashed. His pallet was set near the fire and its stone hearth was scrubbed clean. Above it was a mantelpiece of the same native stone. On it candles were set and a pair of painted china dishes. There were two fowling pieces above it all and a good flintlock, as well.

The loom was under the window, and in the corner was a spinning wheel. The furniture showed not a speck of dust and was brightened a bit by a few needlepoint cushions. There was a scent—apples baking, he thought, and spiced meats. A comfortable home, he thought, hacked out of the wilderness. A man had to respect another who could make his mark like this. And a man would have to fight to keep what he had made.

There were things worth fighting for. Worth dying for. His land. His name. His woman. His freedom. Ian was more than ready to lift his sword. As he tried to sit up, the cozy room spun.

"Isn't it just like a man?" Alanna came back with a bowl of broth. "Undoing all my work. Sit still, you're weak as a babe and twice as fretful."

"Mrs. Flynn—"

"Eat first, talk later."

Out of self-defense, he swallowed the first spoonful of broth she shoveled into his mouth. "The broth is tasty, mistress, but I can feed myself."

"And spill it all over my clean linens in the bargain. No, thank you. You need your strength." She placated him as she would have her own brothers. "You lost a great deal of blood before you got to us—more when the ball was removed." She spoke as she spooned up broth, and her hand didn't tremble. But her heart did.

There was the scent of herbs and her own lavender fragrance. Ian began to think being fed had its advantages.

"If it hadn't been so cold," she continued, "you would have bled all the quicker and died in the forest."

"So I've nature as well as you to thank."

She gave him a measured look. "It's said the Lord works

in mysterious ways. Apparently he saw fit to keep you alive after you'd done your best to die.''

"And put me in the hands of a neighbor.'' He smiled again, charmingly. "I've never been to Ireland, but I'm told it's beautiful.''

"So my father says. I was born here.''

"But there's Ireland on your tongue.''

"And Scotland on yours.''

"It's been five years since I've seen Scotland this time.'' A shadow came and went in his eyes. "I've been spending some time in Boston. I was educated there and have friends.''

"Educated.'' She had already recognized his schooling by his speech and envied him for it.

"Harvard.'' He smiled a little.

"I see.'' And she envied him all the more. If her mother had lived... Ah, but her mother had died, and Alanna had never had more than a hornbook to learn to write and read. "You're a ways from Boston now. A day's ride. Would you be having any family or friends who will worry?''

"No. No one to worry.'' He wanted to touch her. It was wrong, against his own code of honor. But he wanted to see if her cheek could be as beautifully soft as it looked. If her hair would feel as thick and heavy. Her mouth as sweet.

Her lashes lifted, and her eyes, clear and cool, met his. For a moment he could see only her face, drifting over his. And he remembered. He had already tasted those lips once.

Despite his best intentions, his gaze lowered to them. Lingered. When she stiffened, his eyes flickered up. There was not so much apology in them as amusement.

"I must beg your pardon, Mrs. Flynn. I was not myself when you found me in the barn.''

"You came to yourself quickly enough," she snapped back, and made him laugh until he winced at the pain.

"Then I'll beg your pardon all the more and hope your husband won't call me out."

"There's little danger of that. He's been dead these three years."

He looked up quickly, but she only shoveled another spoonful of broth in his mouth. Though God might strike him dead, he couldn't say he was sorry to hear Flynn had gone to his Maker. After all, Ian reasoned, it wasn't as if he had known the man. And what better way to spend a day or two than recovering in the lap of a pretty young widow?

Alanna scented desire the way a hound scents deer and was up and out of reach. "You'll rest now."

"I feel that I've rested weeks already." Lord, she was a lovely thing, all curves and colors. He tried his most ingratiating smile. "Could I trouble you to help me to a chair? I'd feel more myself if I could sit, perhaps look out the window."

She hesitated, not because she was afraid she couldn't move him. Alanna considered herself strong as an ox. But she didn't trust the gleam she'd seen come and go in his eyes.

"All right then, but you'll lean on me and take it slow."

"With gladness." He took her hand and raised it to his lips. Before she could snatch it away, he turned it over and brushed his lips, as no man ever had, over the cup of her palm. Her heart bounded into her throat. "You have eyes the color of jewels I once saw around the neck of the queen of France. Sapphires," he murmured. "A seductive word."

She didn't move. Couldn't. Never in her life had a man looked at her this way. She felt the heat rush up, from the knot in her belly along her suddenly taut breasts, up her throat where her pulse hammered and into her face. Then he smiled, that quick, crooked shifting of lips. She snatched her hand away.

"You're a rogue, Mr. MacGregor."

"Aye, Mrs. Flynn. But that doesn't make the words less true. You're beautiful. Just as your name says. Alanna." He lingered over each syllable.

She knew better than to fall for flattery. But the center of her palm still burned. "It's my name, and you'll wait till you're asked to use it." It was with relief that she heard the sounds outside the house. Her brow lifted a bit when she saw that Ian had heard them as well and braced. "That'll be my father and brothers. If you'd still be having a mind to sit by the window, they'll help you." So saying, she moved to the door.

They would be cold and hungry, she thought, and would gobble down the meat pies and the apple tarts she had made without a thought for the time and care she had given them. Her father would fret more over what hadn't been done than what had. Johnny would think about how soon he could ride into the village to court young Mary Wyeth. Brian would put his nose into one of the books he loved and read by the fire until his head drooped.

They came in bringing cold and melting snow and loud masculine voices.

Ian relaxed as he noted it was indeed her family. Perhaps it was foolish to think the British would have tracked him all this way in the snow, but he wasn't a man to let down his guard. He saw three men—or two men and a boy nearly grown. The elder man was barely taller than Alanna and toughly built. His face was reddened and toughened by years of wind and weather, his eyes a paler version of his daughter's. He took off his work cap and beneath it his hair was thin and sandy.

The older son had the look of him but with more height and less bulk. There was an ease and patience in his face that his father lacked.

The younger matched his brother inch for inch, but there was the dew of youth still on his cheeks. He had the same coloring as his sister.

"Our guest is awake," Alanna announced, and three pairs of eyes turned to him. "Ian MacGregor, this is my father, Cyrus Murphy, and my brothers, John and Brian."

"MacGregor," Cyrus said in a voice that rumbled. "An awkward name."

Despite the pain, Ian stiffened and pushed himself as straight as possible. "One I'm proud of."

"A man should be proud of his name," Cyrus said as he took Ian's measure. "It's all he's born with. I'm glad you decided to live, for the ground's frozen and we couldn't have buried you till spring."

"It's a bit of a relief to me, as well."

Satisfied with the answer, Cyrus nodded. "We'll wash for supper."

"Johnny." Alanna detained her brother with a hand on his arm. "Will you help Mr. MacGregor into the chair by the window before you eat?"

With a quick grin, Johnny looked at Ian. "You're built like an oak, MacGregor. We had the very devil of a time getting you into the house. Give me a hand here, Brian."

"Thanks." Ian bit back a groan as he lifted his arms over the two pairs of shoulders. Cursing his watery legs, he vowed to be up and walking on his own by the next day. But he was sweating by the time they settled him into the chair.

"You're doing well enough for a man who cheated death," Johnny told him, understanding well the frustrations of any sick man.

"I feel like I drank a case of grog then took to the high seas in a storm."

"Aye." Johnny slapped his good shoulder in a friendly manner. "Alanna will fix you up." He left to wash for supper, already scenting the spiced meat.

"Mr. MacGregor?" Brian stood in front of him. There was both a shyness and intensity in his eyes. "You'd be too young to have fought in the Forty-five?" When Ian's brow lifted, the boy continued hurriedly. "I've read all about it, the Stuart Rebellion and the bonny prince and all the battles. But you'd be too young to have fought."

"I was born in '46," Ian told him. "During the Battle of Culloden. My father fought in the rebellion. My grandfather died in it."

The intense blue eyes widened. "Then you could tell me more than I can find in books."

"Aye." Ian smiled a little. "I could tell you more."

"Brian." Alanna's voice was sharp. "Mr. MacGregor needs to rest, and you need to eat."

Brian edged back, but he watched Ian. "We could talk after supper if you're not weary."

Ian ignored Alanna's stormy looks and smiled at the boy. "I'd like that."

Alanna waited until Brian was out of earshot. When she spoke, the barely controlled fury in her voice surprised Ian. "I won't have you filling his head with the glory of war and battles and causes."

"He looked old enough to decide what he wants to talk about."

"He's a boy yet, and his head is easily filled with nonsense." With tense fingers, she pleated the skirt of her apron, but her eyes remained level and uncompromising. "I may not be able to stop him from running off to the village green to drill, but I'll have no talk of war in my house.''

''There will be more than talk, and soon,'' Ian said mildly. ''It's foolish for a man—and a woman—not to prepare for it.''

She paled but kept her chin firm. ''There will be no war in this house,'' she repeated, and fled to the kitchen.

Chapter Three

Ian awoke early the next morning to watery winter sunlight and the good yeasty smell of baking bread. For a moment he lay quiet, enjoying the sounds and scents of morning. Behind him the fire burned low and bright, shooting out comforting heat. From the direction of the kitchen came Alanna's voice. This time she sang in English. For a few minutes he was too enchanted with the sound itself to pay attention to the lyrics. Once they penetrated, his eyes widened first in surprise, then in amusement.

It was a bawdy little ditty more suitable to sailors or drunks than a proper young widow.

So, he thought, the lovely Alanna had a ribald sense of humor. He liked her all the better for it, though he doubted her tongue would have tripped so lightly over the words if she had known she had an audience. Trying to move quietly, he eased his legs from the pallet. The business of standing took some doing and left him dizzy and weak and infuriated. He had to wait, wheezing like an old man, one big hand pressed for support against the wall. When he had his breath back he took one tentative step forward. The room tilted and he clenched his teeth until it righted again. His arm throbbed mightily. Concentrating on the pain, he was able to take another step, and another, grateful that no one was there to see his tedious and shambling progress.

It was a lowering thought that one small steel ball could fell a MacGregor.

The fact that the ball had been English pushed him to place one foot in front of the other. His legs felt as though they'd been filled with water, and a cold sweat lay on his brow and the back of his neck. But in his heart was a fierce pride. If he had been spared to fight again, he would damn well fight. And he couldn't fight until he could walk.

When he reached the kitchen doorway, exhausted and drenched with the effort, Alanna was singing a Christmas hymn. She seemed to find no inconsistency in crooning about amply endowed women one moment and heralding angels the next.

It hardly mattered to Ian what she sang. As he stood, watching, listening, he knew as sure as he knew a Mac-Gregor would always live in the Highlands that her voice would follow him to his grave. He would never forget it, the clear, rich notes, the faint huskiness that made him imagine her with her hair unbound and spread over a pillow.

His pillow, he realized with a quick jolt. It was there he wanted her without a doubt, and so strongly that he could all but feel the smooth, silky tresses shift through his fingers.

Most of those thick raven locks were tucked under a white cap now. It should have given her a prim and proper look. Yet some strands escaped, to trail—seductively, he thought—along the back of her neck. He could easily imagine what it would be like to trail his fingers just so. To feel her skin heat and her body move. Against his.

Would she be as agile in bed as she was at the stove?

Perhaps he wasn't so weak after all, Ian mused, if every time he saw this woman his blood began to stir and his mind shot unerringly down one particular path. If he hadn't been afraid he would fall on his face and mortify himself, he would have crossed the room and spun her around, against him, into him, so that he could steal a kiss. Instead he waited, hopefully, for his legs to strengthen.

She kneaded one batch of dough while another baked. He could see her small, capable hands push and prod and mold. Patiently. Tirelessly. As he watched her, his rebellious mind filled with such gloriously lusty thoughts that he groaned.

Alanna whirled quickly, her hands still wrapped around the ball of dough. Her first thoughts shamed her, for when she saw him filling the doorway, dressed in rough trousers and a full open shirt, she wondered how she might lure him to kiss her hand again. Disgusted with herself, she slapped the dough down and hurried toward him. His face was dead white and he was beginning to teeter. From previous experience, she knew that if he hit the ground she'd have the very devil of a time getting him back into bed.

"There now, Mr. MacGregor, lean on me." Since the kitchen chair was closer, and he was of a considerable weight, she led him to that before she rounded on him. "Idiot," she said with relish more than real heat. "But most men are, I've found. You'd best not have opened your wound again, for I've just scrubbed this floor and wouldn't care to have blood on it."

"Aye, mistress." It was a weak rejoinder, but the best he could do when her scent was clouding his mind and her face was bent so close to his. He could have counted each one of her silky black eyelashes.

"You had only to call, you know," she said, mollified a bit when she noted his bandage was dry. As she might have for one of her brothers, Alanna began to fasten his shirt. Ian was forced to suppress another groan.

"I had to try my legs." His blood wasn't just stirring now but was racing hot. As a result, his voice had a roughened edge. "I can hardly get on my feet again by lying on my back."

"You'll get up when I say and not before." With this she moved away and began to mix something in a pewter cup. Ian caught the scent and winced.

"I'll not have any more of that slop."

"You'll drink it and be grateful—" she slapped the cup on the tabletop "—if you want anything else in your belly."

He glared at her in a way he knew had made grown men back away or run for cover. She simply placed her fisted hands on her hips and glared back. His eyes narrowed. So did hers.

"You're angry because I talked with young Brian last night."

Her chin lifted, just an inch, but it was enough to give her anger an elegant haughtiness. "And if you'd been resting instead of jabbering about the glory of war, you'd not be so weak and irritable this morning."

"I'm not irritable or weak."

When she snorted, he wished fervently that he had the strength to stand. Aye, then he'd have kissed her to swooning and shown her what a MacGregor was made of.

"If I'm irritable," he said between clenched teeth, "it's because I'm near to starving."

She smiled at him, pleased to hold the upper hand.

"You'll get your breakfast after you've drained that cup, and not a moment before." With a twitch of her skirts she returned to her bread making.

While her back was turned, Ian looked around for a handy place to dump the foul-tasting liquid. Finding none, he folded his arms and scowled at her. Alanna's lips curved. She hadn't been raised in a house filled with men for naught. She knew exactly what was going through Ian's mind. He was stubborn, she thought as she pushed the heels of her hands into the dough. But so was she.

She began to hum.

He no longer thought about kissing her but gave grave consideration to throttling her. Here he sat, hungry as a bear, with the enticing smell of bread baking. And all she would give him was a cup of slop.

Still humming, Alanna put the bread into a bowl for rising and covered it with a clean cloth. Easily ignoring Ian, she checked the oven and judged her loaves were done to a turn. When she set them on a rack to cool, their scent flooded the kitchen.

He had his pride, Ian thought. But what good was pride if a man expired of hunger? She'd pay for it, he promised himself as he lifted the cup and drained it.

Alanna made certain her back was to him when she grinned. Without a word, she heated a skillet. In short order she set a plate before him heaped with eggs and a thick slab of the fresh bread. To this she added a small crock of butter and a cup of steaming coffee.

While he ate, she busied herself, scrubbing out the skillet, washing the counters so that not a scrap of dough or flour remained. She was a woman who prized her mornings alone, who enjoyed her kitchen domain and the hundreds of chores it entailed. Yet she didn't resent his presence there, though she knew he watched her with his steady, sea-

colored eyes. Oddly, it seemed natural, even familiar somehow, that he sit at her table and sample her cooking.

No, she didn't resent his presence, but neither could she
relax in it. The silence that stretched between them no
longer seemed colored by temper on either side. But it was
tinted with something else, something that made her nerves
stretch and her heart thud uncomfortably against her ribs.

Needing to break it, she turned to him. He was indeed
watching her, she noted. Not with temper but with...
interest. It was a weak word for what she saw in his eyes,
but a safe one. Alanna had a sudden need to feel safe.

"A gentleman would thank me for the meal."

His lips curved in such a way that let her know he was
only a gentleman if and when he chose to be. "I do thank
you, Mrs. Flynn, most sincerely. I wonder if I might beg
another cup of coffee."

His words were proper enough, but she didn't quite trust
the look in his eyes. She kept out of reach as she picked
up his cup. "Tea would be better for you," she said almost
to herself. "But we don't drink it in this house."

"In protest?"

"Aye. We won't have the cursed stuff until the king sees
reason. Others make more foolish and dangerous protests."

He watched her lift the pot from the stove. "Such as?"

She moved her shoulders. "Johnny heard word that the
Sons of Liberty arranged to destroy crates of tea that were
sitting in three ships in Boston Harbor. They disguised
themselves as Indians and boarded the ships all but under
the guns of three men-of-war. Before the night was done,
they had tossed all of the East Indian Company's property
into the water."

"And you think this foolish?"

"Daring, certainly," she said with another restless movement. "Even heroic, especially in Brian's eyes. But foolish

because it will only cause the king to impose even harsher measures.'' She set the cup before him.

"So you believe it best to do nothing when injustice is handed out with a generous hand? Simply to sit like a trained dog and accept the boot?''

Murphy blood rose to her cheeks. "No king lives forever.''

"Ah, so we wait until mad George cocks up his toes rather than stand now for what is right.''

"We've seen enough war and heartache in this house.''

"There will only be more, Alanna, until it's settled.''

"Settled,'' she shot back as he calmly sipped his coffee. "Settled by sticking feathers in our hair and smashing crates of tea? Settled as it was for the wives and mothers of those who fell at Lexington? And for what? For graves and tears?''

"For liberty,'' he said. "For justice.''

"Words.'' She shook her head. "Words don't die. Men do.''

"Men must, of old age or at sword's point. Can you believe it better to bow under the English chains, over and over until our backs break? Or should we stand tall and fight for what is ours by right?''

She felt a frisson of fear as she watched his eyes glow. "You speak like a rebel, MacGregor.''

"Like an American,'' he corrected. "Like a Son of Liberty.''

"I should have guessed as much,'' she murmured. She snatched up his plate, set it aside, then, unable to stop herself, marched back to him: "Was the sinking of the tea worth your life?''

Absently he touched a hand to his shoulder. "A miscalculation,'' he said, "and nothing that really pertains to our little tea party.''

"Tea party." She looked up at the ceiling. "How like a man to make light of insurrection."

"And how like a woman to wring her hands at the thought of a fight."

Her gaze flew back down and locked with his. "I don't wring my hands," she said precisely. "And certainly wouldn't shed a tear over the likes of you."

His tone changed so swiftly she blinked. "Ah, but you'll miss me when I've gone."

"The devil," she muttered, and fought back a grin. "Now go back to bed."

"I doubt I'm strong enough to make it on my own."

She heaved a sigh but walked to him to offer him a shoulder. He took the shoulder, and the rest of her. In one quick move she was in his lap. She cursed him with an expertise he was forced to admire.

"Hold now," he told her. "Differences in politics aside, you're a pretty package, Alanna, and I've discovered it's been too long since I've held a warm woman in my arms."

"Son of a toad," she managed, and struck out.

He winced as the pain shimmered down his wounded arm. "My father would take exception to that, sweetheart."

"I'm not your sweetheart, you posturing spawn of a weasel."

"Keep this up and you'll open my wound and have my blood all over your clean floor."

"Nothing would give me more pleasure."

Charmed, he grinned and caught her chin in his hand. "For one who talks so righteously about the evils of war, you're a bloodthirsty wench."

She cursed him until she ran out of breath. Her brother John had said nothing but the truth when he'd claimed that Ian was built like an oak. No matter how she squirmed— absolutely delighting him—she remained held fast.

"A pox on you," she managed. "And on your whole clan."

He'd intended to pay her back for making him drink the filthy medicine she'd mixed. He'd only pulled her into his lap to cause her discomfort. Then, as she'd wiggled, he'd thought it only right that he tease her a little and indulge himself. With just one kiss. One quick stolen kiss. After all, she was already fuming.

In fact, he was laughing as he covered her mouth with his. It was meant in fun, as much a joke on himself as on her. And he wanted to hear the new batch of curses she would heap on his head when he was done.

But his laughter died quickly. Her struggling body went stone still.

One quick, friendly kiss, he tried to remind himself, but his head was reeling. He found himself as dizzy and as weak as he'd been when he'd first set his watery legs on the floor.

This had nothing to do with a wound several days old. Yet there was a pain, a sweet ache that spread and shifted through the whole of him. He wondered, dazedly, if he had been spared not only to fight again but to be given the gift of this one perfect kiss.

She didn't fight him. In her woman's heart she knew she should. Yet in that same heart she understood that she could not. Her body, rigid with the first shock, softened, yielded, accepted.

Gentle and rough all at once, she thought. His lips were cool and smooth against hers while the stubble of his beard scraped against her skin. She heard her own sigh as her lips parted, then tasted his on her tongue. She laid a hand on his cheek, adding sweetness. He dragged his through her hair, adding passion.

For one dazzling moment he deepened the kiss, taking

her beyond what she knew and into what she had only dreamed. She tasted the richness of his mouth, felt the iron-hard breath of his chest. Then heard his sharp, quick curse as he dragged himself away.

He could only stare at her. It unnerved him that he could do little else. He had dislodged her cap so that her hair streamed like black rain over her shoulders. Her eyes were so dark, so big, so blue against the creamy flush of her skin that he was afraid he might drown in them.

This was a woman who could make him forget—about duty, about honor, about justice. This was a woman, he realized, who could make him crawl on his knees for one kind word.

He was a MacGregor. He could never forget. He could never crawl.

"I beg your pardon, mistress." His voice was stiffly polite and so cold she felt all the warmth leach out of her body. "That was inexcusable."

Carefully she got to her feet. With blurred vision she searched the floor for her cap. Finding it, she stood, straight as a spear, and looked over his shoulder.

"I would ask you again, MacGregor, to go back to your bed."

She didn't move a muscle until he was gone. Then she dashed away an annoying tear and went back to work. She would not think of it, she promised herself. She would *not* think of him.

She took out her frustrations on the newly risen dough.

Chapter Four

Christmas had always given Alanna great joy. Preparing for it was a pleasure to her — the cooking, the baking, the sewing and cleaning. She had always made it a policy to forgive slights, both small and large, in the spirit of giving. She looked forward to putting on her best dress and riding into the village for Mass.

But as this Christmas approached, she was by turns depressed and irritated. Too often she caught herself being snappish with her brothers, impatient with her father. She became teary over a burnt cake, then stormed out of the house when Johnny tried to joke her out of it.

Sitting on a rock by the icy stream, she dropped her chin onto her hands and took herself to task.

It wasn't fair for her to take out her temper on her family. They'd done nothing to deserve it. She had chosen the easy way out by snapping at them, when the one she truly wanted to roast was Ian MacGregor. She kicked at the crusty snow.

Oh, he'd kept his distance in the past two days. The coward. He'd managed to gain his feet and slink out to the barn like the weasel he was. Her father was grateful for the help with the tack and animals, but Alanna knew the real reason MacGregor had taken himself off to clean stalls and repair harnesses.

He was afraid of her. Her lips pursed in a smug smile. Aye, he was afraid she would call down the wrath of hell on his head. As well she should. What kind of man was it who kissed a woman until she was blind and deaf to all but him—then politely excused himself as if he had inadvertently trod on her foot?

He'd had no right to kiss her—and less to ignore what had happened when he had.

Why, she had saved his life, she thought with a toss of her head. That was the truth of it. She had saved him, and he had repaid her by making her want him as no virtuous woman should want a man not her husband.

But want him she did, and in ways so different from the calm, comforting manner she had wanted Michael Flynn that she couldn't describe them.

It was madness, of course. He was a rebel, once and forever. Such men made history, and widows out of wives. All she wanted was a quiet life, with children of her own and a house to tend to. She wanted a man who would come and sleep beside her night after night through all the years. A man who would be content to sit by the fire at night and talk over with her the day that had passed.

Such a man was not Ian MacGregor. No, she had recognized in him the same burning she had seen in Rory's eyes. There were those who were born to be warriors, and nothing and no one could sway them. There were those who were destined, before birth, to fight for causes and to die on the battlefield. So had been Rory, her eldest brother, and the one she had loved the best. And so was Ian MacGregor, a man she had known for days only and could never afford to love.

As she sat, brooding, a shadow fell over her. She tensed, turned, then managed to smile when she saw it was her young brother, Brian.

"It's safe enough," she told him when he hung back a bit. "I'm no longer in the mood to toss anyone in the stream."

"The cake wasn't bad once you cut away the burnt edges."

She narrowed her eyes to make him laugh. "Could be I'll take it in my mind to send you swimming after all."

But Brian knew better. Once Alanna's hot temper was cooled, she rarely fired up again. "You'd only feel badly when I took to bed with a chill and you had to douse me with medicine and poultices. Look, I've brought you a present." He held out the holly wreath he'd hidden behind his back. "I thought you might put ribbons on it and hang it on the door for Christmas."

She took it and held it gently. It was awkwardly made, and that much more dear. Brian was better with his mind than with his hands. "Have I been such a shrew?"

"Aye." He plopped down into the snow at her feet. "But I know you can't stay in a black mood with Christmas almost here."

"No." She smiled at the wreath. "I suppose not."

"Alanna, do you think Ian will be staying with us for Christmas dinner?"

Her smile became a frown quickly. "I couldn't say. He seems to be mending quickly enough."

"Da says he's handy to have around, even if he isn't a farmer." Absently, Brian began to ball snow. "And he knows so much. Imagine, going to Harvard and reading all those books.''

''Aye.'' Her agreement was wistful, for herself and for Brian. ''If we've a good harvest the next few years, Brian, you'll go away to school. I swear it.''

He said nothing. It was something he yearned for more than breath, and something he'd already accepted he would live without. ''Having Ian here is almost as good. He knows things.''

Alanna's mouth pursed. ''Aye, I'm sure he does.''

''He gave me the loan of a book he had in his saddlebag. It's Shakespeare's *Henry V*. It tells all about the young King Harry and wonderful battles.''

Battles, she thought again. It seemed men thought of little else from the moment they were weaned. Undaunted by her silence, Brian chattered on.

''It's even better to listen to him,'' Brian continued enthusiastically. ''He told me about how his family fought in Scotland. His aunt married an Englishman, a Jacobite, and they fled to America after the rebellion was crushed. They have a plantation in Virginia and grow tobacco. He has another aunt and uncle who came to America too, though his father and mother still live in Scotland. In the Highlands. It seems a wondrous place, Alanna, with steep cliffs and deep lakes. And he was born in a house in the forest on the very day his father was fighting the English at Culloden.''

She thought of a woman struggling through the pangs of labor and decided both male and female fought their own battles. The female for life, the male for death.

''After the battle,'' Brian went on, ''the English butchered the survivors.'' He was looking out over the narrow, ice-packed stream and didn't notice how his sister's gaze flew to him. ''The wounded, the surrendering, even people who were working in fields nearby. They hounded and chased the rebels, cutting them down where they found them. Some they closed up in a barn and burned alive.''

"Sweet Jesus." She had never paid attention to talk of war, but this kept her riveted, and horrified.

"Ian's family lived in a cave while the English searched the hills for rebels. Ian's aunt—the one on the plantation— killed a redcoat herself. Shot him when he tried to murder her wounded husband.''

Alanna swallowed deeply. "I believe Mr. MacGregor exaggerates.''

Brian turned his deep, intense eyes on her. "No," he said simply. "Do you think it will come to that here, Alanna, when the rebellion begins?"

She squeezed the wreath hard enough for a sprig of holly to pierce through her mittens. "There will be no rebellion. In time the government will become more reasonable. And if Ian MacGregor says any different—''

"It isn't only Ian. Even Johnny says so, and the men in the village. Ian says that the destruction of tea in Boston is only the beginning of a revolution that was inevitable the moment George III took the throne. Ian says it's time to throw off the British shackles and count ourselves for what we are. Free men."

"Ian says." She rose, skirts swaying. "I think Ian says entirely too much. Take the wreath in the house for me, Brian. I'll hang it as soon as I'm done."

Brian watched his sister storm off. It seemed that there would be at least one more outburst before her black mood passed.

Ian enjoyed working in the barn. More, he enjoyed being able to work at all. His arm and shoulder were still stiff, but the pain had passed. And thanks to all the saints, Alanna hadn't forced any of her foul concoctions on him that day.

Alanna.

He didn't want to think about her. To ease his mind, he set aside the tack he was soaping and picked up a brush. He would groom his horse in preparation for the journey he had been putting off for two days.

He should be gone, Ian reminded himself. He was surely well mended enough to travel short distances. Though it might be unwise to show his face in Boston for a time, he could travel by stages to Virginia and spend a few weeks with his aunt, uncle and cousins.

The letter he had given Brian to take to the village should be on its way by ship to Scotland and his family. They would know he was alive and well—and that he wouldn't be with them for Christmas.

He knew his mother would weep a little. Though she had other children, and grandchildren, she would be saddened that her firstborn was away when the family gathered for the Christmas feast.

He could see it in his mind—the blazing fires, the glowing candles. He could smell the rich smells of cooking, hear the laughter and singing. And with a pang that was so sudden it left him breathless, he hurt from the loss.

Yet, though he loved his family, he knew his place was here. A world away.

Aye, there was work to do here, he reminded himself as he stroked the mare's coat. There were men he had to contact once he knew it was safe. Samuel Adams, John Avery, Paul Revere. And he must have news of the climate in Boston and other cities now that the deed was done.

Yet he lingered when he should have been away. Daydreamed when he should have been plotting. He had, sensibly, he thought, kept his distance from Alanna. But in his mind she was never more than a thought away.

"There you are!"

And she was there, her breath puffing out in quick white streams, her hands on her hips. Her hood had fallen from her head and her hair swung loose, inky black against the plain gray fabric of her dress.

"Aye." Because his knuckles had whitened on the brush, he made an effort to relax his hand. "It's here I am."

"What business are you about, filling a young boy's head with nonsense? Would you have him heave a musket over his shoulder and challenge the first redcoat he comes to?"

"I gather you are speaking of Brian," he said when she stopped to take a breath. "But when I go a step further than that, I lose my way."

"Would you had lost it before you ever came here." Agitated, she began to pace. Her eyes were so hot a blue he wondered they didn't fire the straw underfoot. "Trouble, and only trouble from the first minute I came across you, sprawled half-dead in the hay. If I'd only known then what I've come to know now, I might have ignored my Christian duty and let you bleed to death."

He smiled—he couldn't help it—and started to speak, but she plunged on.

"First you nearly pull me down in the hay with you, kissing me even though you'd a ball in you. Then, almost on the moment when you open your eyes, you're kissing my hand and telling me I'm beautiful."

"I ought to be flogged," he said with a grin. "Imagine, telling you that you're beautiful."

"Flogging's too kind for the likes of you," she snapped with a toss of her head. "Then two days ago, after I'd fixed you breakfast—which is more than a man like you deserves—"

"Indeed it is," he agreed.

"Keep quiet until I'm done. After I'd fixed you breakfast, you drag me down on your lap as though I were a—a common..."

"Do words fail you?"

"Doxy," she spit out and dared him to laugh. "And like the great oaf you are, you held me there against my will and kissed me."

"And was kissed right back, sweetheart." He patted his horse's neck. "And very well, too."

She huffed and stammered. "How dare you?"

"That's difficult to answer unless you're more specific. If you're asking how I dared kiss you, I'll have to confess it was more a matter of not being able to stop myself. You've a mouth that's made for it, Alanna."

She felt herself go hot and began to pace again on unsteady legs. "Well, you got over it quickly enough."

His brow lifted. So she wasn't in a temper over the kiss but over the fact that he'd stopped. Looking at her now, in the dim light of the barn, he wondered how he'd managed to do so. And knew he wouldn't again.

"If it's my restraint that troubles you, sweetheart—"

"Don't call me that. Not now, not ever."

Gamely, he swallowed a chuckle. "As you wish, Mrs. Flynn. As I was saying—"

"I told you to be still until I've finished." She stopped to catch her breath. "Where was I?"

"We were talking about kissing." Eyes glowing, he took a step toward her. "Why don't I refresh your memory?"

"Don't come near me," she warned, and snatched up a pitchfork. "I was simply using that as a reference to the trouble you've caused. Now, on top of everything else, you've got Brian's eyes shining over the thought of a revolution. I won't have it, MacGregor. He's just a boy.''

"If the lad asks questions, I'll give him true answers."

"And make them sound romantic and heroic in the bargain. I won't see him caught up in wars others make and lose him as I did my brother Rory.''

"It won't be a war others make, Alanna." He circled her carefully, keeping away from the business end of the pitchfork. "When the time comes we'll all make it, and we'll win it."

"You can save your words."

"Good." Quick as a flash he grabbed the staff of the pitchfork, dodged the tines and hauled her against him. "I'm tired of talking."

When he kissed her this time, he was prepared for the jolt. It was no less devastating, no less exciting. Her face was cold and he used his lips to warm it, running them over her skin until he felt them both begin to shudder. He dragged a hand through her hair until he cupped the back of her neck. His other arm banded her hard against him.

"For God's sake, kiss me back, Alanna." He murmured it against her mouth. His eyes were open and hot on hers. "I'll go mad if you don't, mad if you do."

"Damn you then." She threw her arms around him. "I will."

She all but took him to his knees. There was no hesitation, no demur. Her lips were as hungry as his, her tongue as adventurous. She let her body press to his and thrilled at the sensation of his heart hammering against her.

She would never forget the scent of hay and animals, the drifting motes of dust in the thin beams of sunlight that broke through the chinks in the logs. Nor would she forget the strong, solid feel of him against her, the heat of his mouth, the sound of his pleasure. She would remember this one moment of abandonment because she knew it could never last.

"Let me go," she whispered.

He nestled into the sweet, fragrant curve of her neck. "I doubt I can."

"You must. I didn't come here for this."

He trailed his mouth to her ear and smiled when she shivered. "Would you really have stabbed me, Alanna?"

"Aye."

Because he believed her, he smiled again. "Here's a likely wench," he murmured, and nipped at her ear.

"Stop it." But she let her head fall back in surrender. Lord help her, she wanted it to go on. And on, and on. "This isn't right."

He looked at her then, his smile gone. "I think it is. I don't know why or how, but I think it's very right."

Because she wanted so badly to lean against him, she stiffened. "It can't be. You have your war and I have my family. I won't give my heart to a warrior. And there's the end of it."

"Damn it, Alanna—"

"I would ask you for something." She eased quickly out of his arms. Another moment in them and she might have forgotten everything—family and all her secret hopes for her own future. "You could consider it your Christmas gift to me."

He wondered if she knew that at that moment he would have pledged her all that was his, even his life. "What is it you want?"

"That you'll stay until Christmas is passed. It's important to Brian. And," she added before he could speak, "that you will not speak of war or revolts until the holy day is over."

"It's very little to ask."

"Not to me. To me it is a very great deal."

"Then you have it." She took a step back, but with a lift of his brow he took her hand firmly in his, raised it to his lips and kissed it.

"Thank you." She regained her hand quickly and hid it behind her back. "I have work to do." His voice stopped her as she hurried toward the door.

"Alanna...it is right."

She pulled the hood over her head and hurried out.

Chapter Five

The snow that fell on Christmas Eve delighted Alanna. In her heart she held the hope that the storm would rage for days and prevent Ian from traveling, as she knew he planned to do in two days' time. She knew the hope was both selfish and foolish, but she hugged it to her as she bundled into scarf and cloak to walk to the barn for the morning milking.

If he stayed, she would be miserable. If he left, she would be brokenhearted. She allowed herself the luxury of a sigh as she watched the flakes whirl white around her. It was best if she thought not of him at all, but of her responsibilities.

Her footsteps were the only sound in the barnyard as her boots broke through the new dusting to the thin crust beneath. Then, in the thick hush, the door creaked as she lifted the latch and pulled it open.

Inside, she reached for the buckets and had taken her

first step when a hand fell on her shoulder. With a yelp, she jumped, sending the buckets clattering to the floor.

"Your pardon, Mrs. Flynn." Ian grinned as Alanna held both hands to her heart. "It seems I've startled you."

She would have cursed him if there had been any breath remaining in her lungs. Not for a moment could she have held her head up if he'd known she'd just been sighing over him. Instead, she shook her head and drew air in deeply. "What are you doing, sneaking about?"

"I came out of the house moments behind you," he explained. He had decided, after a long night of thought, to be patient with her. "The snow must have masked my approach."

Her own daydreaming had prevented her from hearing him, she thought, irritated, and bent down to snatch the buckets just as he did the same. When their heads bumped, she did swear.

"Just what the devil would you be wanting, MacGregor? Other than to scare the life from me?"

He would be patient, he promised himself as he rubbed his own head. If it killed him. "To help you with the milking."

Her narrowed eyes widened in bafflement. "Why?"

Ian blew out a long breath. Patience was going to be difficult if every word she spoke to him was a question or an accusation. "Because, as I have observed over the past days, you've too many chores for one woman."

Pride was stiff in her voice. "I can care for my family."

"No doubt." His voice was equally cool. Again, they reached down for the buckets together. Ian scowled. Alanna straightened to stand like a poker as he retrieved them.

"I appreciate your offer, but—"

"I'm only going to milk a damn cow, Alanna." So much for patience. "Can't you take the help in good grace?"

"Of course." Spinning on her heel, she stalked to the first stall.

She didn't need his help, she thought as she tugged off her mittens and slapped them into her lap. She was perfectly capable of doing her duty. The very idea of his saying she had too much to do. Why, in the spring there was twice as much, with planting and tending the kitchen garden, harvesting herbs. She was a strong, capable woman, not some weak, whimpering girl.

He was probably used to *ladies*, she thought with a sneer. Polished sugar faces that simpered and fluttered behind fans. Well, she was no lady with silk dresses and kid slippers, and she wasn't a bit ashamed of it. She sent a glare in Ian's direction. And if he thought she pined for drawing rooms, he was very much mistaken.

She tossed her head back as she began the tug and squeeze that squirted the brindled cow's milk into the bucket.

Ungrateful wench, Ian mused as he, with less ease and finesse, milked the second cow. He'd only wanted to help. Any fool could see that her duties ran from sunup to sundown. If she wasn't milking she was baking. If she wasn't baking she was spinning. If she wasn't spinning, she was scrubbing.

The women in his family had never been ladies of leisure, but they had always had daughters or sisters or cousins to help. All Alanna had were three men who obviously didn't realize the burdens that fell on her.

Well, he was going to help her if he had to throttle her into accepting.

She finished her bucket long before Ian and stood impatiently tapping her foot. When he was done, Alanna reached for the bucket, but he held it away from her.

"What are you doing?"

"I'm carrying the milk in for you." He took up the other bucket.

"Now why would you be doing that?"

"Because it's heavy," he all but bellowed, then muttering about stubborn, empty-headed women, he marched to the door.

"Keep swinging those buckets like that, MacGregor, and you'll have more milk on the ground than in your belly." She couldn't quite catch what he muttered at her, but it wasn't complimentary. Suspicious, she brushed snow from her face. "Since you insist on carrying the milk, I'll just go gather the eggs."

They stalked off in different directions.

When Alanna returned to her kitchen, Ian was still there, feeding the fire.

"If you're waiting for breakfast, you'll wait a while longer."

"I'll help you," he said between gritted teeth.

"Help me what?"

"With breakfast."

That did it. With little regard for how many eggs cracked, she slammed down the bucket. "You find fault with my cooking, MacGregor?"

His hands itched to grab her shoulders and give her a brisk shake. "No."

"Hmm." She moved to the stove to make coffee. Turning, she all but plowed into him. "If you're going to be standing in my kitchen, MacGregor, then move aside. You're not so big I can't push you out of my way."

"Are you always so pleasant in the morning, Mrs. Flynn?"

Rather than dignify the question with an answer, she took the slab of ham she'd gotten from the smokehouse and began to slice. Ignoring him as best she could, she began to mix the batter for the pancakes she considered her specialty. She'd show Ian MacGregor a thing or two about cooking before she was done.

He said nothing but clattered the pewter dishes he set on the table to make his point. By the time her family joined them, the kitchen was filled with appetizing smells and a tension thick enough to hack with an ax.

"Pancakes," Johnny said with relish. "Sure and it's a fine way to start Christmas Eve."

"You look a bit flushed, girl." Cyrus studied his daughter as he took his seat. "You're not coming down sick, are you?"

"It's the heat from the stove," she snapped, then bit her tongue as her father narrowed his eyes. "I've applesauce made just yesterday for the pancakes." She set the bowl she was carrying on the table, then went back for the coffee. Flustered because Ian had yet to take his eyes from her, she reached for the pot without remembering to wrap a cloth around the handle. As she singed the tips of two fingers, she let out a cry and followed it with an oath.

"No use bringing the Lord into it when you've been careless," Cyrus said mildly, but he rose to smear cooling butter on the burns. "You've been jumpy as a frog with the hiccups these past days, Alanna."

"It's nothing." She waved him back to the table with her good hand. "Sit, the lot of you, and eat. I want you out of my kitchen so I can finish my baking."

"I hope there's a fresh raisin cake on the list." Johnny grinned as he heaped applesauce on his plate. "No one makes a better one than you, Alanna. Even when you burn it."

She managed to laugh, and nearly mean it, but she had little appetite for the meal as she joined the table.

It was just as well, she decided some time later. Though

the men in her life had chattered like magpies through breakfast, they hadn't left a scrap for the rest of the birds. With relief she watched them bundle up for the rest of the day's work. She'd have the kitchen, and the rest of the house, to herself in short order. Alone, she should be able to think about what and how she felt about Ian MacGregor.

But he had been gone only minutes when he returned with a pail of water.

"What are you up to now?" she demanded, and tried in vain to tuck some of her loosened tresses into her cap.

"Water for the dishes." Before she could do so herself, he poured the water into a pot on the stove to heat.

"I could have fetched it myself," she said, then felt nasty. "But thank you."

"You're welcome." He shrugged out of his outer clothes and hung them on a hook by the door.

"Aren't you going to go with the others, then?"

"There are three of them and one of you."

She tilted her head. "That's true enough. And so?"

"So today I'm helping you."

Because she knew her patience was thin, she waited a moment before speaking. "I'm perfectly capable—"

"More than, from what I've seen." He began to stack the dishes she'd yet to clear. "You work like a pack mule."

"That is a ridiculous and a very uncomplimentary description, boy-o." Her chin jutted forward. "Now get out of my kitchen."

"I will if you will."

"I've work to do."

"Fine. Then let's be at it."

"You'll be in my way."

"You'll work around me." When she drew her next breath he cupped her face in his hands and kissed her, hard and long. "I'm staying with you, Alanna," he said when she managed to focus on him again. "And that's that."

"Is it?" To her mortification, her voice was only a squeak.

"Aye."

"Well, then." She cleared her throat, stepped back and smoothed her skirts. "You can fetch me apples from the storage cellar. I've got pies to bake."

She used the time it took him to return to try to compose herself. What was becoming of her when she lost her brains and every other faculty over a kiss? But it wasn't an ordinary kiss, not when they were Ian's lips doing the work. Something strange was happening when one moment she was pinning her heart on the hope that he would stay a while longer—the next she was resenting him so that she wished him a thousand miles away. And a moment later, she was letting him kiss her, and hoping he'd do so again at the first opportunity.

She'd been born in the Colonies, a child of a new world. But her blood was Irish—Irish enough that words like fate and destiny loomed large.

As she began to scrub dishes, she thought that if her destiny was in the shape of one Ian MacGregor, she was in trouble deep.

"It's simple enough to peel an apple," she insisted later, fuming over Ian's clumsy, hacking attempts. "You put the knife under the skin."

"I did."

"And took most of the meat with it. A little time and care works wonders."

He smiled at her, all too strangely for her comfort. "So I'm thinking, Mrs. Flynn. So I'm thinking."

"Try again," she told him as she went back to her piecrusts and rolling pin. "And you'll be cleaning up all those peelings you're scattering on my floor."

"Aye, Mrs. Flynn."

Holding the rolling pin aloft, she glared at him. "Are you trying to rouse my temper, MacGregor?"

He eyed the kitchen weaponry. "Not while you're holding that, sweetheart."

"I've told you not to call me that."

"So you have."

He watched her go back to her pies. She was a pleasure to watch, he thought. Quick hands, limber fingers. Even when she moved from counter to stove and back again, there was a nimbleness in her movements that sent his heart thudding.

Who would have thought he'd have had to be shot, all but bleed to death and end up unconscious in a cow stall to fall in love?

Despite her criticism, and her tendency to jump whenever he got too close, he was having the best day of his life. Perhaps he didn't want to make a habit out of peeling apples, but it was a simple way to be near her, to absorb that soft lavender scent that seemed to cling to her skin. It melded seductively with the aromas of cinnamon, ginger and cloves.

And in truth, though he was more at home in political meetings or with a sword in his hand than in the kitchen, he had wanted to ease what he saw as an unfair burden of responsibility.

She didn't appear to deem it so, he mused. Indeed, she seemed content to toil away, hour by hour. He wanted — needed, he admitted—to show her there was more. He imagined riding with her through the fields of his aunt's plantation. In the summer, he thought, when the rich green might remind her of an Ireland she'd never seen. He wanted to take her to Scotland, to the glory of the Highlands. To lie with her in the purple heather by a loch and listen to the wind in the pine.

He wanted to give her a silk dress, and jewels to match her eyes. They were sentimental, romantic notions, he knew. Surely he would have choked on the words if he had tried to express them.

But he wanted to give, that much he knew. If he could find a way to make her take.

Alanna felt his stare on her back as though it were tickling fingers. She'd have preferred the fingers, she thought. Those she could have batted away. Struggling to ignore him, she covered the first pie, fluted and trimmed the crust and set it aside.

"You'll slice a finger off if you keep staring at me instead of watching what you're about."

"Your hair's falling out of your cap again, Mrs. Flynn."

She took a hand and shoved at it, only succeeding in loosening more curls. "And I don't think I care for the tone you use when you call me Mrs. Flynn."

Merely grinning, Ian set aside a pared apple. "What should I call you then? You object to sweetheart, though it suits so nicely. Your nose goes in the air when I call you Alanna—without your permission. Now you're ready to spout into temper when I, very respectfully, call you Mrs. Flynn."

"Respectfully, hah! You'll go to hell for lying, Ian MacGregor." She waved the rolling pin at him as she turned. "There's not a dab of respect in your tone when you use it—not with that smug smile on your mouth and that gleam in your eye. If you don't think I know just what that gleam means, you're mistaken. Other men have tried it and gotten a good coshing for their pains."

"It gratifies me to hear it…Mrs. Flynn."

She made a sound he could only describe as hot steam puffing out of a kettle. "You'll call me nothing at all. Why I took Brian's part and asked you to stay for Christmas will always be a mystery to me. The good Lord knows I don't want you here, cluttering up my kitchen, giving me another mouth to cook for, grabbing me and forcing your unwelcome attentions on me at every turn."

He leaned against the counter. "You'll go to hell for lying, sweetheart."

It was the reflex of the moment that had the rolling pin flying out of her hand and toward his head. She regretted it immediately. But she regretted it even more when he snagged the flying round of wood the instant before it cracked into his forehead.

If she had hit him, she would have apologized profusely and tended his bruise. The fact that she'd been foiled changed the matter altogether.

"You cursed Scotsman," she began, lathering up. "You spawn of the devil. A plague on you and every MacGregor from now till the Last Reckoning." Since she'd missed with the rolling pin, she grabbed the closest thing at hand. Fortunately, the heavy metal pie plate was empty. Ian managed to bat it away from his head with the rolling pin.

"Alanna—"

"Don't call me that." She hefted a pewter mug and tried her aim with that. This time Ian wasn't so quick and it bounced off his chest.

"Sweetheart—"

The sound she made at that would have caused even a battle-tried Scotsman to shudder. The plate she hurtled struck Ian's shin. He was hopping on one leg and laughing when she reached for the next weapon.

"Enough!" Roaring with laughter, he grabbed her and

swung her around twice, even when she bashed him over the head with the plate.

"Damned hardheaded Scot."

"Aye, and thank God for it or you'll have me in my grave yet." He tossed her up and caught her nimbly at the waist. "Marry me, Mrs. Flynn, for your name was meant to be MacGregor."

Chapter Six

It was a close thing as to whom was the most shocked.
Ian hadn't realized he'd meant to ask her. He'd known he
was in love, was both amused and dazzled by it. But until
that moment his heart hadn't communicated to his brain
that marriage was desired. Marriage to Alanna, he thought,
and let loose another laugh. It was a fine joke, he decided,
on the pair of them.

His words were still echoing in Alanna's head, bouncing
from one end of her brain to the other like balls in a wheel.
Marry me. Surely she hadn't mistaken what he'd asked her.
It was impossible, of course. It was madness. They had
known each other only days. Even that was long enough
for her to be certain Ian MacGregor would never be the
life companion of her dreams. With him, there would never
be peaceful nights by the fire but another fight, another
cause, another movement.

And yet... Yet she loved him in a way she had never
thought to love. Wildly, recklessly, dangerously. Life with

him would be…would be… She couldn't imagine it. She put a hand to her head to still her whirling brain. She needed a moment to think and compose herself. After all, when a man asked a woman to marry him, the very least she could do was…

Then it occurred to her that he was still holding her a foot off the floor and laughing like a loon.

Laughing. Her eyes narrowed to sharp blue slits. So it was a great joke he was having at her expense, tossing her in the air like a sack of potatoes and chortling. Marry him. Marry him indeed. The jackass.

She braced a hand on his broad shoulder for balance, rolled the other into a fist and struck him full on the nose.

He yelped and set her down so abruptly she had to shift to keep upright. But she recovered quickly and, feet planted, stuck her hands on her hips and glared at him.

Tentatively, he touched his fingers to his nose. Aye, it was bleeding, he noted. The woman had a wicked right. Watching her warily for any sudden moves, he reached for his handkerchief.

"Is that a yes?"

"Out!" So deep was her rage her voice shook even as it boomed. "Out of my house, you pox-ridden son of Satan." The tears that sprang to her eyes were tears of righteous fury, she assured herself. "If I were a man I'd murder you where you stand and dance a jig on your bleeding body."

"Ah." After an understanding nod, he replaced his handkerchief. "You need a bit of time to think it over. Perfectly understandable."

Speechless, she could only make incoherent growls and hisses.

"I'll speak with your father," he offered politely. She shrieked like a banshee and grabbed for the paring knife.

"I will kill you. On my mother's grave, I swear it."

"My dear Mrs. Flynn," he began as he cautiously clamped a hand on her wrist. "I realize a woman is sometimes overcome with the proposal or marriage, but this..." He trailed off when he saw that tears had welled from her eyes and run down her cheeks. "What is this?" Uncomfortable, he brushed a thumb over her damp cheek. "Alanna, my love, don't. I'd rather have you stab me than cry." But when he gallantly released her hand, she tossed the knife aside.

"Oh, leave me be, won't you? Go away. How dare you insult me this way? I curse the day I saved your miserable life."

He took heart that she was cursing him again and pressed a kiss to her brow. "Insult you? How?"

"How?" Behind the veil of tears her eyes burned like blue suns. "Laughing at me. Speaking of marriage as if it were a great joke. I suppose you think because I don't have fine clothes or fancy hats that I have no feelings."

"What do hats have to do with it?"

"I suppose all the elegant ladies in Boston just smile indulgently and rap your hand with their fans when you play the flirt, but I take talk of marriage more seriously and won't stand by while you speak of it and laugh in my face at the same time."

"Oh, sweet God." Who would have thought that he, a man reputed to be smooth and clever with the ladies, could muck things up so badly when it mattered? "I was a fool, Alanna. Please listen."

"Was and are a fool. Now take your paws off me."

He gathered her closer. "I only want to explain."

Before he could, Cyrus Murphy pushed open the door. He took one look at the wreckage of the kitchen, at his daughter struggling against Ian, and reached calmly for the hunting knife in his belt.

"Let go of my girl, MacGregor, and prepare to die."

"Da." Eyes widened at the sight of her father, pale as ice with a knife in his hands, Alanna threw herself in front of Ian. "Don't."

"Move aside, lass. Murphys protect their own."

"It isn't the way it looks," she began.

"Leave us, Alanna," Ian said quietly. "I'll have a word with your father."

"The hell you will." She planted her feet. Perhaps she would have shed his blood herself—and had, if one counted his nose—but she wouldn't have her father kill him after she'd worked for two days and nights to keep him alive. "We had an argument, Da. I can handle it myself. He was—"

"He was proposing marriage to your daughter," Ian finished, only to have Alanna round on him again.

"You lying polecat. You didn't mean a word of it. Laughing like a loon while you said it, you were. I won't be insulted. I won't be belittled—"

"But you will be quiet," he roared at her, and had Cyrus raising a brow in approval when she did indeed subside. "I meant every word," he continued, his voice still pitched to raise the roof. "If I was laughing it was at myself, for being so big a fool as to fall in love with a stubborn, sharp-tongued shrew who'd as soon stab me as smile at me."

"Shrew?" Her voice ended on a squeak. "Shrew?"

"Aye, a shrew," Ian said with a vicious nod. "That's what I said, and that's what you are. And a—"

"Enough." Cyrus shook the snow from his hair. "Sweet Jesus, what a pair." With some reluctance, he replaced his knife. "Get on your coat, MacGregor, and come with me. Alanna, finish your baking."

"But, Da, I—"

"Do as I say, lass." He gestured Ian out the door. "With all the shouting and the wailing it's hard for a body to remember it's Christmas Eve." He stopped just outside and planted his hands on his hips in a gesture his daughter had inherited. "I've a job to do, MacGregor. You'll come with me and explain yourself."

"Aye." He cast a last furious look at the window where Alanna had her nose pressed. "I'll come with you."

Ian trudged across the snow and through the billowy cur tain that was still falling. He hadn't bothered to fasten his coat and stuck his ungloved hands in its pockets.

"Wait here," Cyrus said. He went inside a small shed and came out with an ax. Noting Ian's cautious stare, he hefted it onto his shoulder. "I won't be using it on you. Yet." He moved off toward the forest with Ian beside him. "Alanna's partial to Christmas. As was her mother." There was a pang, as there always was when he thought of his wife. "She'll be wanting a tree—and time for her temper to cool."

"Does it ever?"

As a matter of habit, Cyrus studied the forest floor for signs of game. They'd want fresh venison soon. "You're the one who's thinking of shackling his leg to hers. Why is that?"

"If I could think of one good reason, I'd give it to you." He hissed his breath out between his teeth. "I ask the woman to marry me, and she hits me in the nose." He touched the still sore appendage, then grinned. "By God, Murphy, I'm half-mad and in love with the woman—which amounts to the same thing. I'll have her to wife."

Cyrus stopped in front of a pine, studied it, rejected it, then moved on. "That remains to be seen."

"I'm not a poor man," Ian began. "The bloody British didn't get everything in the Forty-five, and I've done well enough with investments. I'll provide well for her."

"Mayhap you will, mayhap you won't. She took Michael Flynn and he had no more than a few acres of rocky land and two cows."

"She won't have to work from dawn to dust."

"Alanna doesn't mind work. She takes pride in it." Cyrus stopped in front of another tree, nodded, then handed the ax to Ian. "This'll do. When a man's frustrated, there's nothing like swinging an ax to sweat it out of him."

Ian spread his legs, planted his feet and put his back into it. Wood chips flew. "She cares for me. I know it."

"Might," Cyrus agreed, then decided to treat himself to a pipe. "'Tis her habit to shout and slap at those she cares for most."

"Then she must love me to distraction." The ax bit into the meat of the pine's trunk. Ian's expression was grim. "I'll have her, Murphy, with or without your blessing."

"That goes without saying." Cyrus patiently filled his pipe. "She's a woman grown and can make up her own mind. Tell me, MacGregor, will you fight the British with as much passion as you'll woo my daughter?"

Ian swung the ax again. The blade whistled through the air. The sound of metal on wood thudded through the forest. "Aye."

"Then I'll tell you now, it may be hard for you to win both." Satisfied the pipe was well packed, he struck a match against a boulder. "Alanna refuses to believe there will be war."

Ian paused. "And you?"

"I've no love for the British or their king." Cyrus puffed

on his pipe and sent smoke drifting through the snow. "And even if I did, my vision's sharp enough yet to see what will come. It may take a year, or two, or more, but the fight will come. And it will be long, and it will be bloody. When it comes I'll have two more sons to risk. Two more sons to lose." He sighed, long and heavy. "I don't want your war, Ian MacGregor, but there will come a point when a man will have to stand for what is his."

"It's already begun, Murphy, and neither wanting it nor fearing it will change history."

Cyrus studied Ian as the tree fell to the cushioning snow. A strong man, he thought, one of those damned Scot giants, with a face and form a woman would find pleasing enough, A good mind and a good name. But it was Ian's restless and rebellious spirit that concerned him.

"I'll ask you this, will you be content to sit and wait for what comes to come, or will you go out in search of it?"

"MacGregors don't wait to stand for what they believe in. Nor do they wait to fight for it."

With a nod, Cyrus helped Ian heft the fallen tree. "I won't stand in your way where Alanna is concerned. You may do that for yourself."

Alanna rushed into the front of the cabin the moment she heard Ian's voice. "Da, I want to… Oh." She stopped short at the sight of her father and Ian with a pine tree held between them. "You've cut a Christmas tree."

"Did you think I'd be forgetting?" Cyrus took off his cap and stuffed it in his pocket. "How could I with you nagging me day and night?"

"Thank you." It was with both pleasure and relief that she crossed the room to kiss him. "It's beautiful."

"And I suppose you'll want to be hanging ribbons and

God knows what else on it.'' But he gave her a quick squeeze as he spoke.

"I have Mama's box of ornaments in my room." Because she understood him so well, she kissed him again. "I'll fetch it after supper."

"I've other chores to see to. You can devil MacGregor about where you want the thing." He gave her hand a quick pat before he went out again.

Alanna cleared her throat. "By the front window, if you please."

Ian dragged it over, balancing it on the flat wooden boards Cyrus had hammered to the trunk. The only sound was the rustling of needles and the crackle of the fire.

"Thank you," she said primly. "You can go about your business now."

Before she could escape to the kitchen again, he took her hand. "Your father has given me permission to wed you, Alanna."

She tugged once on her hand, then wisely gave up. "I'm my own woman, MacGregor."

"You'll be mine, Mrs. Flynn."

Though he stood a foot over her head, she managed to convey the impression of looking down her nose at him. "I'd sooner mate a rabid skunk."

Determined to do it right this time, he brought her rigid hand to his lips. "I love you, Alanna."

"Don't." She pressed her free hand to her nervous heart. "Don't say that."

"I say it with every breath I take. And will until I breathe no more."

Undone, she stared at him, into those blue-green eyes that had already haunted her nights. His arrogance she could resist. His outrageousness she could fight. But this,

this simple, almost humble declaration of devotion left her defenseless.

"Ian, please…"

He took heart because she had, at long last, called him by his given name. And the look in her eyes as the word left her lips could not be mistaken. "You will not tell me you're indifferent to me."

Unable to resist, she touched a hand to his face. "No, I won't tell you that. You must see how I feel every time I look at you."

"We were meant to be together." With his eyes on hers, he pressed the palm of her hand to his lips. "From the moment I saw you bending over me in the barn I felt it."

"It's all so soon," she said, fighting both panic and longing. "All so quick."

"And right. I'll make you happy, Alanna. You can choose whatever house you want in Boston."

"Boston?"

"For a time, at least, we would live there. I have work to do. Later we could go to Scotland, and you could visit your homeland."

But she was shaking her head. "Work. What work is this?"

A shield seemed to come down over his eyes. "I gave you my word I would not speak of it until after Christmas."

"Aye." She felt her bounding heart still and freeze in her breast. "You did." After a deep breath, she looked down at their joined hands. "I have pies in the oven. They need to come out."

"Is that all you can say?"

She looked at the tree behind him, still bare, but with so much promise. "I must ask you for time. Tomorrow, on Christmas, I'll give you my answer."

"There is only one I'll take."

That helped her to smile. "There's only one I'll give."

Chapter Seven

There was a scent of pine and wood smoke, the lingering aroma of the thick supper stew. On the sturdy table near the fire Alanna had placed her mother's prized possession, a glass punch bowl. As had been his habit for as long as Alanna could remember, her father mixed the Yuletide punch, with a hand generous with Irish whiskey. She watched the amber liquid catch the light from the fire and the glow from the candles already lighted on the tree.

She had promised herself that this night, and the Christmas day to follow, would be only for joy.

As well it should be, she told herself. Whatever had transpired between her father and Ian that morning, they were thick as thieves now. She noted that Cyrus pressed a cup of punch on Ian before he ladled one for himself and drank deeply. Before she could object, young Brian was given a sample.

Well, they would all sleep that night, she decided, and

was about to take a cup herself when she heard the sound of a wagon.

"There's Johnny." She let out a huff of breath. "And for his sake he'd best have a good excuse for missing supper."

"Courting Mary," Brian said into his cup.

"That may be, but—" She broke off as Johnny came in, with Mary Wyeth on his arm. Automatically, Alanna glanced around the room, relieved everything was as it should be for company. "Mary, how good to see you." Alanna went quickly to kiss the girl's cheek. Mary was shorter and plumper than she, with bright gold hair and rosy cheeks. They seemed rosier than usual, Alanna noted—either with cold from the journey from the village, or with heat from Johnny's courting.

"Merry Christmas." Always shy, Mary flushed even more as she clasped her hands together. "Oh, what a lovely tree."

"Come by the fire, you'll be cold. Let me take your cape and shawl." She shot her brother an exasperated look as he just stood by and grinned foolishly. "Johnny, fetch Mary a cup of punch and some of the cookies I baked this morning."

"Aye." He sprang into action, punch lapping over his fingers in his rush. "We'll have a toast," he announced, then spent considerable time clearing his throat. "To my future wife." He clasped Mary's nervous hand in his. "Mary accepted me this evening."

"Oh." Alanna held out her hands, and since Mary didn't have one to spare, grabbed the girl by the shoulder. "Oh, welcome. Though how you'll stand this one is beyond me."

Cyrus, always uncomfortable with emotion, gave Mary a quick peck on the cheek and his son a hearty slap on the back. "Then we'll drink to my new daughter," he said. "'Tis a fine Christmas present you give us, John."

"We need music." Alanna turned to Brian, who nodded and rushed off to fetch his flute. "A spritely song, Brian," she instructed. "The engaged couple should have the first dance."

Brian perched himself with one foot on the seat of a chair and began to play. When Ian's hand came to rest on her shoulder, Alanna touched her fingers briefly, gently, to his wrist.

"Does the idea of a wedding please you, Mrs. Flynn?"

"Aye." With a watery smile, she watched her brother turn and sway with Mary. "She'll make him happy. They'll make a good home together, a good family. That's all I want for him."

He grinned as Cyrus tossed back another cup of punch and began to clap his hands to the music. "And for yourself?"

She turned, and her eyes met his. "It's all I've ever wanted."

He leaned closer. "If you gave me my answer now, we could have a double celebration this Christmas Eve."

She shook her head as her heart broke a little. "This is Johnny's night." Then she laughed as Johnny grabbed her hands and pulled her into the dance.

A new snow fell, softly, outside the cabin. But inside, the rooms were filled with light and laughter and music. Alanna thought of her mother and how pleased she would have been to have seen her family together and joyful on this most holy of nights. And she thought of Rory, bright and beautiful Rory, who would have outdanced the lot of them and raised his clear tenor voice in song.

"Be happy." Impulsively she threw her arms around Johnny's neck. "Be safe."

"Here now, what's all this?" Touched, and embarrassed, he hugged her quickly then pulled her away.

"I love you, you idiot."

"I know that." He noted that his father was trying to teach Mary to do a jig. It made him almost split his face with a grin. "Here, Ian, take this wench off my hands. A man's got to rest now and then."

"No one can outdance an Irishman," Ian told her as he took her hand. "Unless it's a Scotsman."

"Oh, is that the way of it?" With a smile and a toss of her head, she set out to prove him wrong.

Though the candles had burned low before the house and its occupants slept, the celebrations began again at dawn. By the light of the tree and the fire, they exchanged gifts. Alanna gained a quiet pleasure from the delight on Ian's face as he held up the scarf she had woven him. Though it had taken her every spare minute to work the blue and the green threads together on her loom, the result was worth it. When he left, he would take a part of her.

Her heart softened further when she saw that he had gifts for her family. A new pipe for her father, a fine new bridle for Johnny's favorite horse and a book of poetry for Brian.

Later, he stood beside her in the village church, and though she listened to the story of the Savior's birth with the same wonder she had had as a child, she would have been blind not to see other women cast glances her way. Glances of envy and curiosity. She didn't object when his hand closed over hers.

"You look lovely today, Alanna." Outside the church, where people had stopped to chat and exchange Christmas greetings, he kissed her hands. Though she knew the gossips would be fueled for weeks, she gave him a saucy smile. She was woman enough to know she looked her best in the deep blue wool dress with its touch of lace at collar and cuffs.

"You're looking fine yourself, MacGregor." She resisted the urge to touch the high starched stock at his throat. It was the first time she'd seen him in Sunday best, with snowy lace falling over his wrists, buttons gleaming on his doublet and a tricornered hat on his mane of red hair. It would be another memory of him to treasure.

"Sure and it's a beautiful day."

He glanced at the sky. "It will snow before nightfall."

"And what better day for a snowfall than Christmas?" Then she caught at the blue bonnet Johnny had given her. "But the wind is high." She smiled as she saw Johnny and Mary surrounded by well-wishers. "We'd best get back. I've a turkey to check."

He offered his arm. "Allow me to escort you to your carriage, Mrs. Flynn."

"Why that's kind of you, Mr. MacGregor."

He couldn't remembered a more perfect day. Though there were still chores to be done, Ian managed to spend every free moment with Alanna. Perhaps there was a part of him that wished her family a thousand miles away so that he could be alone with her at last and have her answer. But he determined to be patient, having no doubt what the answer would be. She couldn't smile at him, look at him, kiss him that way unless she was as wildly in love as he. He might have wished he could simply snatch her up, toss her on his horse and ride off, but for once, he wanted to do everything properly.

If it was her wish they could be married in the church where they had observed Christmas. Then he would hire— or better, buy—a carriage, blue picked out in silver. That would suit her. In it they would travel to Virginia, where he would present her to his aunt and uncle and cousins.

Somehow he would manage a trip to Scotland, where she would meet his mother and father, his brothers and sisters. They would be married again there, in the land of his birth.

He could see it all. They would settle in Boston, where he would buy her a fine house. Together they would start a family while he fought, with voice or sword, for the independence of his adopted country.

By day they would argue and fight. By night they would lie together in a big feather bed, her long slender limbs twined around him.

It seemed since he had met her he could see no further than life with her.

The snow did fall, but gently. By the time the turkey and potatoes, the sauerkraut and biscuits were devoured, Ian was half-mad with impatience.

Rather than join the men by the fire, he grabbed Alanna's cloak and tossed it over her. "I need a moment with you."

"But I haven't finished—"

"The rest can wait." As far as he could see, her kitchen was already as neat as a pin. "I will speak with you, in private."

She didn't object, couldn't, because her heart was already in her throat when he pulled her out into the snow. He'd barely taken time to jam on his hat. When she pointed out that he hadn't buttoned his coat against the wind, he swept her up in his arms and with long strides carried her to the barn.

"There's no need for all of this," she pointed out. "I can walk as well as you."

"You'll dampen your dress." He turned his head and kissed her snow-brushed lips. "And I like it very well."

After he set her down inside, he latched the door and lighted a lamp. She folded her hands at her waist. It was now, Alanna told herself firmly, that the Christmas celebration had to end.

"Ian—"

"No, wait." He came to her, put his hands gently on her shoulders. The sudden tenderness robbed her of speech. "Did you not wonder why I gave you no gift this morning?"

"You gave me your gift. We agreed—"

"Did you think I had nothing more for you?" He took her hands, chilled because he had given her no time for mittens, and warmed them with his. "On this, our first Christmas together, the gift must be special."

"No, Ian, there is no need."

"There is every need." He reached into the pocket of his doublet and withdrew a small box. "I sent a village lad into Boston for this. It was in my quarters there." He placed the box in her hand. "Open it."

Her head warned her to refuse, but her heart—her heart could not. Inside she saw a ring. After a quick gasp, she pressed her lips together. It was fashioned of gold in the shape of a lion's head and crown.

"This is the symbol of my clan. The grandfather whose name I carry had it made for his wife. Before she died, she gave this to my father to hold in trust for me. When I left Scotland, he told me it was his hope I would find a woman as strong, as wise and as loyal to wear it."

Her throat was so tight the words hurt as she forced them out. "Oh, Ian, no. I could not. I don't—"

"There is no other woman who will wear it." He took it from the box and placed it on her finger. It might have been made for her, so perfect was the fit. At that moment, he felt as though the world were his. "There is no other woman I will love." He brought her ring hand to his lips, watching her over it. "With this I pledge you my heart."

"I love you," she murmured as she felt her world rip in two. "I will always love you." There would be time, she knew, as his mouth came to hers, for regrets, for pain, for tears. But tonight, for the hours they had, she would give him one more gift.

Gently, she pushed his coat from his shoulders. With her mouth moving avidly beneath his, she began to unbutton his doublet.

With unsteady hands, he stilled hers. "Alanna—"

She shook her head and touched a finger to his lips. "I am not an untried girl. I come to you already a woman, and I ask that you take me as one. I need you to love me, Ian. Tonight, this Christmas night, I need that." This time it was she who captured his hands and brought them to her lips. It was reckless, she knew. But it was right. "And I need to love you."

Never before had he felt so clumsy. His hands seemed too big, too rough, his need too deep and intense. He swore that if he accomplished nothing else in his life he would love her gently and show her what was written in his heart.

With care, he lowered her onto the hay. It was not the feather bed he wished for her, but her arms came willingly around him, and she smiled as she brought his mouth to hers. With a sound of wonder, he sank into her.

It was more than she'd ever dreamed, the touch of her love's hands in her hair, on her face. With such patience, with such sweetness, he kissed her until the sorrows she held in her heart melted away. When he had unbuttoned her frock, he slipped it from her shoulder to kiss the skin there, to marvel at the milky whiteness and to murmur such foolish things that made her want to smile and weep at once.

He felt her strong, capable fingers push aside his doublet, unfasten his shirt, then stroke along his chest.

With care he undressed her, pausing, lingering, to give pleasure and to take it. With each touch, each taste, her response grew. He heard her quick, unsteady breath at his ear, then felt the nip of her teeth as he gave himself over to the delights of her body.

Soft, lavender scent twining with the fragrance of hay. Smooth, pale skin glowing in the shadowed lamplight. Quiet, drifting sighs, merging with his own murmurs. The rich shine of her hair as he gathered fistfuls in his hands.

She was shuddering. But with heat. Such heat. She tried to say his name but managed only to dig her nails into his broad shoulders. From where had come this churning, this wild river that flowed inside her? And where would it end? Dazzled, desperate, she arched against him while his hands traveled like lightning over points of pleasure she hadn't known she possessed.

Her mouth was on his, avid, thirsty, as he pushed her to the first brink, then beyond. Her stunned cry was muffled against his lips and his own groan of satisfaction.

Then he was inside her, deep. At the glory of it, her eyes flew open. She saw his face above her, the fire of his hair glinting in the lamplight.

"Now we are one." His voice was low and harsh with passion. "Now you are mine."

And he lowered his mouth to hers as they gave each other the gift of self.

Chapter Eight

Tney dozed, turned to each other, her cloak carelessly tossed over their tangled forms, their bodies warmed and replete from loving.

He murmured her name.

She woke.

Midnight had come and gone, she thought. And her time was over. Still, she stole a bit more, studying his face as he slept, learning each plane, each angle. Though she knew his face was already etched in her head, and on her heart.

One last kiss, she told herself as she brushed her lips to his. One last moment.

When she shifted, he mumbled and reached out.

"You don't escape that easily, Mrs. Flynn."

Her heart suffered a new blow at the wicked way he said her name. "'Tis almost dawn. We can't stay any longer."

"Very well then." He sat up as she began to dress. "I suppose even under the circumstances, your father might pull his knife again if he found me naked in the hay with his daughter.'' With some regret he tugged on his breeches. He wished he had the words to tell her what the night had meant to him. What her love meant to him. With his shirt unbuttoned, he rose to kiss the back of her neck. ''You've hay in your hair, sweetheart.''

She sidestepped him and began to pluck it out. ''I've lost my pins.''

''I like it down.'' He swallowed and took a step forward to clutch handfuls of it. ''By God, I like it down.''

She nearly swayed toward him before she caught herself. ''I need my cap.''

''If you must.'' Obliging, he began to search for it. ''In truth, I don't remember a better Christmas. I thought I'd reached the peak when I was eight and was given a bay gelding. Fourteen hands he was, with a temper like a mule.'' He found her cap under scattered hay. With a grin, he offered it. ''But, though it's close in the running, you win over the gelding.''

She managed to smile. ''It's flattered I am, to be sure, MacGregor. Now I've breakfast to fix.''

''Fine. We can tell your family over the meal that we're to be married.''

She took a deep breath. ''No.''

''There's no reason to wait, Alanna.''

''No,'' she repeated. ''I'm not going to marry you.''

For a moment he stared, then he laughed. ''What nonsense is this?''

''It isn't nonsense at all. I'm not going to marry you.''

''The bloody hell you aren't!'' he exploded, and grabbed both her shoulders. ''I won't have games when it comes to this.''

''It's not a game, Ian.'' Though her teeth had snapped together, she spoke calmly. ''I don't want to marry you.''

If she had still had the knife in her hand and had plunged

it into him, she would have caused him less pain. "You lie. You look me in the face and lie. You could not have loved me as you did through the night and not want to belong to me."

Her eyes remained dry, so dry they burned. "I love you, but I will not marry you." She shook her head before he could protest. "My feelings have not changed. Nor have yours—nor can yours. Understand me, Ian, I am a simple woman with simple hopes. You'll make your war and won't be content until it comes to pass. You'll fight in your war, if it takes a year or ten. I cannot lose another I love, when I have already lost so many. I will not take your name and give you my heart only to see you die."

"So you bargain with me?" Incensed, he paced away from her. "You won't share my life unless I'm content to live it ignoring all I believe in? To have you, I must turn my back on my country, my honor and my conscience?"

"No." She gripped her hands together tightly and fought not to twist them. "I offer you no bargain. I give you your freedom with an open heart and with no regrets for what passed between us. I cannot live in the world you want, Ian. And you cannot live in mine. All I ask is for you to give me the same freedom I give you."

"Damn you, I won't." He grabbed her again, fingers that had been so gentle the night before, bruising. "How can you think that a difference in politics could possibly keep me from taking you with me? You belong with me, Alanna. There is nothing beyond that."

"It is not just a difference in politics." Because she knew she would weep in a moment, she made her voice flat and cold. "It is a difference in hopes and in dreams. All of mine, and all of yours. I do not ask you to sacrifice yours, Ian. I will not sacrifice mine." She pulled away to stand rigid as a spear. "I do not want you. I do not want to live my life with you. And as a woman free to take or reject as she pleases, I will not. There is nothing you can say or do to change that. If in truth you do care for me, you won't try.''

She snatched up her cape and held it balled in her hands. ''Your wounds are healed, MacGregor. It's time you took your leave. I will not see you again.''

With this, she turned and fled.

An hour later, from the safety of her room, she heard him ride off. It was then, and only then, that she allowed herself to lie on the bed and weep. Only when her tears wet the gold on her finger did she realize she had not given him back his ring. Nor had he asked for it.

It took him three weeks to reach Virginia, and another week before he would speak more than a few clipped sentences to anyone. In his uncle's library he would unbend enough to discuss the happenings in Boston and other parts of the Colonies and Parliament's reactions. Though Brigham Langston, the fourth earl of Ashburn, had lived in America for almost thirty years, he still had high connections in England. And as he had fought for his beliefs in the Stuart Rebellion, so would he fight his native country again for freedom and justice in his home.

''All right, that's enough plotting and secrets for tonight.'' Never one to pay attention to sanctified male ground, Serena MacGregor Langston swept into the library. Her hair was still fiery red as it had been in her youth. The few strands of gray didn't concern a woman who felt she had earned them.

Though Ian rose to bow to his aunt, the woman's husband continued to lean against the mantel. He was, Serena thought, as handsome as ever. More perhaps. Though his hair was silver, the southern sun had tanned his face so that it reminded her of oak. And his body was as lean and muscular as she remembered it from nearly thirty years before. She smiled as her eldest son, Daniel, poured her brandy and kissed her.

"You know we always welcome your delightful company, Mama."

"You've a tongue like your father's." She smiled, well pleased that he had inherited Brigham's looks, as well. "You know very well you wish me to the devil. I'll have to remind you again that I've already fought in one rebellion. Isn't that so, *Sassenach*?"

Brigham grinned at her. She had called him by the uncomplimentary Scottish term for the English since the first moment they had met. "Have I ever tried to change you?"

"You're not a man who tries when he knows he must fail." And she kissed him full on the mouth. "Ian, you're losing weight." Serena had already decided she'd given the lad enough time to stew over whatever was troubling him. As long as his mother was an ocean away, she would tend to him herself. "Do you have a complaint for cook?"

"Your table, as always, is superb, Aunt Serena."

"Ah." She sipped her brandy. "Your cousin Fiona tells me you've yet to go out riding with her." She spoke of her youngest daughter. "I hope she hasn't done anything to annoy you."

"No." He caught himself before he shifted from foot to foot. "No, I've just been a bit, ah, distracted. I'll be sure to go out with her in the next day or so."

"Good." She smiled, deciding to wait until they were alone to move in for the kill. "Brig, Amanda would like you to help her pick out a proper pony for young Colin. I thought I raised my eldest daughter well, but she apparently thinks you've a better eye for horseflesh than her mama.

Oh, and, Daniel, your brother is out at the stables. He asked me to send for you.''

"The lad thinks of little but horses,'' Brigham commented. ''He takes after Malcolm.''

"I'd remind you my younger brother has done well enough for himself with his horses.''

Brigham tipped his glass toward his wife. "No need to remind me.''

"I'll go.'' Daniel set down his snifter. "If I know Kit, he's probably working up some wild scheme about breeding again.''

"Oh, and, Brig. Parkins is in a lather over something. The state of your riding jacket, I believe. I left him up in your dressing room.''

"He's always in a lather,'' Brigham muttered, referring to his longtime valet. Then he caught his wife's eye, and her meaning. "I'll just go along and see if I can calm him down.''

"You won't desert me, will you, Ian?'' Spreading her hooped skirts, she sat, satisfied that she'd cleared the room. "We haven't had much time to talk since you came to visit. Have some more brandy and keep me company for a while.'' She smiled, disarmingly. It was another way she had learned—other than shouting and swearing—to get what she wanted. "And tell me about your adventures in Boston.''

Because her feet were bare, as she had always preferred them, she tucked her legs up, managing in the wide plum-colored skirts to look both ladylike and ridiculously young. Despite the foul mood that haunted him, Ian found himself smiling at her.

"Aunt Serena, you are beautiful.''

"And you are trying to distract me.'' She tossed her head so that her hair, never quite tamed, flowed over her shoulders. "I know all about your little tea party, my lad." She toasted him with her snifter. "As one MacGregor to another, I salute you. And," she continued, "I know that the English are already grumbling. Would that they would choke on their own cursed tea." She held up a hand. "But don't get me started on that. It's true enough that I want to hear what you have to say about the feelings of those in New England and other parts of America, but for now I want to know about you."

"About me?" He shrugged and swirled his drink. "It's hardly worth the trouble to pretend you don't know all about my activities, my allegiance to Sam Adams and the Sons of Liberty. Our plans move slowly, but they move."

She was nearly distracted enough to inquire further along these lines, but Brigham, and her own sources, could feed her all the information she needed. "On a more personal level, Ian." More serious, she leaned forward to touch his hand. "You are my brother's first child and my own godchild. I helped bring you into this world. And I know as truly as I sit here that you're troubled by something that has nothing to do with politics or revolutions."

"And everything to do with it," he muttered, and drank.

"Tell me about her."

He gave his aunt a sharp look. "I have mentioned no 'her.'"

"You have mentioned her a thousand times by your silence." She smiled and kept his hand in hers. "'Tis no use trying to keep things from me, my lad. We're blood. What is her name?"

"Alanna," he heard himself saying. "Damn her to hell and back."

With a lusty laugh, Serena sat back. "I like the sound of that. Tell me."

And he did. Though he had had no intention of doing

so. Within thirty minutes he had told Serena everything from his first moment of regaining hazy consciousness in the barn to his furious and frustrated leave-taking.

"She loves you very much," Serena murmured.

As he told his tale, Ian had risen to pace to the fire and back, to the window and back and to the fire again. Though he was dressed like a gentleman, he moved like a warrior. He stood before the fire now, the flames snapping at his back. She was reminded so completely of her brother Coll that her heart broke a little.

"What kind of love is it that pushes a man away and leaves him with half a heart?"

"A deep one, a frightened one." She rose then to hold out her hands to him. "This I understand, Ian, more than I can tell you." Pained for him, she brought his hands to her cheeks.

"I cannot change what I am."

"No, you cannot." With a sigh, she drew him down to sit beside her. "Neither could I. We are children of Scotland, my love. Spirits of the Highlands." Even as she spoke, the pain for her lost homeland was ripe. "We are rebels born and bred, warriors since time began. And yet, when we fight, we fight only for what is ours by right. Our land, our homes, our people."

"She doesn't understand."

"Oh, I believe she understands only too well. Perhaps she cannot accept. By why would you, a MacGregor, leave her when she told you to? Would you not fight for her?"

"She's a hardheaded shrew who wouldn't listen to reason."

"Ah." Hiding a smile, she nodded. She had been called hardheaded time and again during her life—and by one man in particular. It was pride that had set her nephew on his horse and had him licking his wounds in Virginia. Pride was something she also understood very well. "And you love her?"

"I would forget her if I could." He ground his teeth. "Perhaps I will go back and murder her."

"I doubt it will come to that." Rising, she patted his hand. "Take some time with us here, Ian. And trust me, all will be well eventually. I must go up now and rescue your uncle from Parkins."

She left him scowling at the fire. But instead of going to Brigham, she went into her own sitting room and composed a letter.

"I cannot go." Cheeks flushed, eyes bright and blazing, Alanna stood in front of her father, the letter still clutched in her hand.

"You can and will," Cyrus insisted. "The Lady Langston has invited you to her home to thank you in person for saving the life of her nephew." He clamped his pipe between his teeth and prayed he wasn't making a mistake. "Your mother would want this for you."

"The journey is too long," she began quickly. "And in another month or two it will be time for making soap and planting and wool carding. I've too much to do to take such a trip. And...and I have nothing proper to wear."

"You will go, representing this house." He drew himself up to his full height. "It will never be said that a Murphy cowered at the thought of meeting gentry."

"I'm not cowering."

"You're shaking in your boots, girl, and it makes me pale with shame. Lady Langston wishes to make your acquaintance. Why, I have cousins who fought beside her clan in the Forty-five. A Murphy's as good as a MacGregor any day—better than one if it comes to that. I couldn't give you the schooling your good mother wanted for you—"

"Oh, Da."

He shook his head fiercely. "She will turn her back on me when I join her in the hereafter if I don't push you to do this. 'Tis my wish that you see more of the world than these rocks and this forest before my life is done. So you'll do it for me and your mother if not for yourself."

She weakened, as he'd known she would. "But... If Ian is there..."

"She doesn't say he is, does she?"

"Well, no, but—"

"Then it's likely he's not. He's off rabble-rousing somewhere more like."

"Aye." Glumly, she looked down at the letter in her hand. "Aye, more like." She began to wonder what it would be like to travel so far and to see Virginia, where the land was supposed to be so green. "But who will cook? Who will do the wash and the milking. I can't—"

"We're not helpless around here, girl." But he was already missing her. "Mary can help, now that she's married to Johnny. And the Widow Jenkins is always willing to lend a hand."

"Aye, but can we afford—"

"We're not penniless, either," he snapped. "Go and write a letter back and tell Lady Langston you kindly accept her invitation to visit. Unless you're afraid to meet her."

"Of course I'm not." That served to get her dander up. "I will go," she muttered, stomping up the stairs to find a quill and writing paper.

"Aye," Cyrus murmured as he heard her door slam. "But will you be back?"

Chapter Nine

Alanna was certain her heart would beat so fast and hard that it would burst through her breast. Never before had she ridden in such a well-sprung carriage with such a fine pair of matched bays pulling it. And a driver all in livery. Imagine the Langstons sending a carriage all that way, with a driver, postilions and a maid to travel all the miles with her.

Though she had traveled by ship from Boston to Richmond, again with a companion the Langstons had provided, she would journey by road the remainder of the way to their plantation.

They called it Glenroe, after a forest in the Highlands.

Oh, what a thrill it had been to watch the wind fill the sails of the ship, to have her own cabin and the dainty maid to see to her needs. Until the maid had taken sick from the rocking of the boat, of course. Then Alanna had seen to *her* needs. But she hadn't minded a bit. While the grateful lass had slept off her illness, Alanna had been free to walk

the decks of the great ship and watch the ocean, glimpsin
occasional stretches of coastland.

And she wondered at the vastness and beauty of th
country she had never truly seen.

It was beautiful. Though she had loved the farm, th
forest and the rocks of her native Massachusetts, she foun
the land even more glorious in its variety. Why, when sh
had left home, there had still been snow on the ground. Th
warming days had left icicles gleaming on the eaves of th
house and the bare branches of the trees.

But now, in the south, she saw the trees greening an
had left her cloak unfastened to enjoy the air through th
carriage window. In the fields there were young calves an
foals, trying out their legs or nursing. In others she sa
dozens and dozens of black field hands busy with sprin
planting. And it was only March.

Only March, she thought again. Only three months sinc
she had sent Ian away. In a nervous habit, she reached u
to touch the outline of the ring she wore on a cord und
her traveling dress. She would have to give it back, c
course. To his aunt; for surely Ian wouldn't be on the pla
tation. Couldn't be, she thought with a combination of reli
and longing. She would return the ring to his aunt wit
some sort of explanation as to her possession of it. Not th
full truth, she reflected, for that would be too humiliatin
and painful.

She wouldn't worry about it now, she told herself, an
folded her hands in her lap as she studied the rolling hil
already turning green in Virginia's early spring. She wou
think of this journey, and this visit, as an adventure. Or
she would not likely have again.

And she must remember everything to tell Brian, th
curious one. She would remember everything, she thoug

with a sigh, for herself. For this was Ian's family, people who had known him as a babe, as a growing lad.

For the few weeks she remained on the plantation with Ian's family, she would feel close to him again. For the last time, she promised herself. Then she would return to the farm, to her family and her duties, and be content.

There was no other way. But as the carriage swayed, she continued to hold her fingers to the ring and wish she could find one.

The carriage turned through two towering stone pillars with a high iron sign that read Glenroe. The maid, more taxed by the journey than Alanna, shifted in the seat across from her. "You'll be able to see the house soon, miss." Grateful that the weeks of traveling were almost at an end, the maid barely restrained herself from poking her head out the carriage window. "It's the most beautiful house in Virginia."

Heart thudding, Alanna began to fiddle with the black braid that trimmed the dove-gray dress she had labored over for three nights. Her busy fingers then toyed with the ribbons of her bonnet, smoothed the skirts of the dress, before returning to pluck at the braid again.

The long wide drive was lined with oaks, their tiny unfurling leaves a tender green. As far as she could see, the expansive lawns were tended. Here and there she saw trimmed bushes already in bud. Then, rising over a gentle crest, was the house.

Alanna was struck speechless. It was a majestic structure of pristine white with a dozen columns gracing the front like slender ladies. Balconies that looked like black lace rimmed the tall windows on the second and third stories. A wide, sweeping porch skirted both front and sides. There were flowers, a deep blood red, in tall urns standing on

either side of stone steps that led to double doors glittering
with glass.

Alanna gripped her fingers together until the knuckles
turned as white as the house. It took all her pride and will
not to shout to the driver to turn the carriage around and
whip the horses into a run.

What was she doing here, in such a place? What would
she have to say to anyone who could live in such richness?
The gap between herself and Ian seemed to widen with
each step of the prancing bays.

Before the carriage had drawn to a halt at the curve of
the circular drive, a woman came through the doors and
started down the porch. Her billowing dress was a pale
watery green trimmed with ivory lace. Her hair, a lovely
shade of red gold, was dressed simply in a coil at her neck
and shone in the sunlight. Alanna had hardly alighted with
the assistance of a liveried footman when the woman
stepped forward, hands extended.

"Mrs. Flynn. You're as beautiful as I expected." There
was a soft burr to the woman's speech that reminded
Alanna painfully of Ian. "But I will call you Alanna, because I feel we're already friends." Before Alanna could
decide how to respond, the woman was smiling and gathering her into an embrace. "I'm Ian's aunt, Serena. Welcome to Glenroe."

"Lady Langston," Alanna began, feeling dusty and
crumpled and intimidated. But Serena was laughing and
drawing her toward the steps.

"Oh, we don't use titles here. Unless they can be of
some use to us. Your journey went well, I hope."

"Aye." She felt she was being borne away by a small
red-haired whirlwind. "I must thank you for your generosity in asking me to come, in opening your home to me."

"'Tis I who am grateful." Serena paused on the thresh-

old. "Ian is as precious to me as my own children. Come,
'll take you to your room. I'm sure you'll want to refresh
ourself before you meet the rest of the family at tea. Of
course we don't serve the bloody stuff," Serena continued
blandly as Alanna gaped at the entrance hall with its lofty
ceilings and double curving stairs.

"No, no of course not," Alanna said weakly as Serena
took her arm to lead her up the right-hand sweep of the
stairs. There was a shout, a yell and an oath from somewhere deep in the house.

"My two youngest children." Unconcerned, Serena continued up. "They squabble like puppies."

Alanna cleared her throat. "How many children do you
have, Lady Langston?"

"Six." Serena took her down a hall with pastel wall
covering and thick carpeting. "Payne and Ross are the ones
you hear making a din. They're twins. One minute they're
bashing each other, the next swearing to defend each other
to the death."

Alanna distinctly heard something crash, but Serena
didn't blink an eye as she opened the door to a suite of
rooms.

"I hope you'll be comfortable here," she said. "If you
need anything, you have only to ask."

What could she possibly need? Alanna thought dumbly.
The bedroom was at least three times the size of the room
she had slept in at home. Someone had put fresh, fragrant
flowers into vases. Cut flowers in March.

The bed, large enough for three, was covered in pale blue
silk and plumped with pillows. There was a wardrobe of
carved wood, an elegant bureau with a silver-trimmed mirror, a dainty vanity table with a brocade chair. The tall
windows were open so that the warm, fragrant breeze ruf-

fled the sheer white curtains. Before she could speak, a
maid scurried in with a steaming pitcher of water.

"Your sitting room is through there." Serena moved pas
a beautifully carved fireplace. "This is Hattie." Seren
smiled at the small, wiry black maid. "She'll tend to you
needs while you're with us. Hattie, you'll take good car
of Mrs. Flynn, won't you?"

"Oh, yes, ma'am." Hattie beamed.

"Well, then." Serena patted Alanna's hand, found i
chilled and unsteady and felt a pang of sympathy. "Is ther
anything else I can do for you?"

"Oh, no. You've done more than enough."

I've not even begun, Serena thought but only smiled
"I'll leave you to rest. Hattie will show you down when
ever you're ready."

When the door closed behind the indomitable Lad
Langston, Alanna sat wearily on the edge of the bed an
wondered how she would keep up.

Because she was too nervous to keep to her rooms
Alanna allowed Hattie to help her out of the traveling dres
and into her best frock. The little maid proved adept a
dressing hair, and with nimble fingers and a chattering sing
song voice, she coaxed and brushed and curled unti
Alanna's raven locks were draped in flirty curls over he
left shoulder.

Alanna was just fastening her mother's garnet eardrop
and drumming up her courage to go downstairs when ther
were shouts and thumping outside her door. Intrigued, sh
opened her door a crack, then widened it at the sight c
two young male bodies rolling over the hall carpet.

She cleared her throat. "Good day to you, gentlemen."

The boys, mirror images of each other with ruffled blac
hair and odd topaz eyes, stopped pummeling each other t

study her. As if by some silent signal, they untangled themselves, rose and bowed in unison.

"And who might you be?" the one with the split lip asked.

"I'm Alanna Flynn." Amused, she smiled. "And you must be Payne and Ross."

"Aye." This came from the one with the black eye. "I'm Payne, and the eldest, so I'll welcome you to Glenroe."

"I'll welcome her, as well." Ross gave his brother a sharp jab in the ribs with his elbow before he stepped forward and stuck out a hand.

"And I'll thank both of you," she said, hoping to keep the peace. "I was about to go down and join your mother. Perhaps you could escort me."

"She'll be in the parlor. It's time for tea." Ross offered his arm.

"Of course we don't drink the bloody stuff." Payne offered his, as well. Alanna took both. "The English could force it down our throats and we'd spit it back at them."

Alanna swallowed a smile. "Naturally."

As the trio entered the parlor, Serena rose. "Ah, Alanna, I see you've met my young beasts." With a considering look, she noted the black eye and bloody lip. "If it's cake the pair of you are after, then you'll wash first." As they raced off, she turned to introduce Alanna to the others in the room. There was a boy of perhaps eighteen she called Kit, who had his mother's coloring and a quick smile. A young girl she measured as Brian's age, with hair more blond than red, dimpled prettily.

"Kit and Fiona will drag you off to the stables at every opportunity," Serena warned. "My daughter Amanda hopes to join us for dinner tonight with her family. They live at a neighboring plantation." She poured the first cup

of coffee and offered it to Alanna. "We won't wait for
Brigham and the others. They're off overseeing the planting
and the good Lord knows when they might come in."

"Mama says you live on a farm in Massachusetts,"
Fiona began.

"Aye." Alanna smiled and relaxed a little. "There was
snow on the ground when I left. Our planting season is
much shorter than yours."

The conversation was flowing easily when the twins
came back, apparently united again as their arms were
slung around each other's shoulders. With identical grins
they walked to their mother and kissed each cheek.

"It's too late," Serena told them. "I already know about
the vase." She poured two cups of chocolate. "It's a good
thing it happened to be an ugly one. Now sit, and try not
to slop this over the carpet."

Alanna was at ease and enjoying her second cup of coffee when a burst of male laughter rolled down the hall.

"Papa!" The twins cried and leaped up to race to the
door. Serena only glanced at the splotch of chocolate on
the rug and sighed.

Brigham entered, ruffling the hair of the boys on either
side of him. "So, what damage have you done today?"
Alanna observed that his gaze went first to his wife. There
was amusement in it, and something much deeper, much
truer, that lighted a small spark of envy in her breast. Then
he looked at Alanna. Nudging the boys aside, he crossed
the room.

"Alanna," Serena began, "this is my husband,
Brigham."

"I'm delighted to meet you at last." Brigham took her
hand between both of his. "We owe you much."

Alanna flushed a little. Though he was old enough to be
her father, there was a magnetism about him that set a

woman's heart aflutter. "I must thank you for your hospitality, Lord Langston."

"No, you must only enjoy it." He shot his wife a strange and, what seemed to Alanna, exasperated look. "I only hope you will remain happy and comfortable during your stay."

"How could I not? You have a magnificent home and a wonderful family."

He started to speak again, but his wife interrupted. "Coffee, Brig?" She had already poured and was holding out the cup with a warning look. Their discussions over her matchmaking attempt had yet to be resolved. "You must be thirsty after your work. And the others?"

"Were right behind me. They stopped off briefly in the library."

Even as he spoke, two men strode into the room. Alanna only vaguely saw the tall, dark-haired man who was a younger version of Brigham. Her stunned eyes were fixed on Ian. She wasn't even aware that she had sprung to her feet or that the room had fallen into silence.

She saw only him, dressed in rough trousers and jacket for riding, his hair windblown. He, too, had frozen into place. A dozen expressions crossed his face, as indeed they crossed hers. Then he smiled, but there was an edge to it, a hardness that cut her to the quick.

"Ah, Mrs. Flynn. What an...unusual surprise."

"I—I—" She stumbled to a halt and looked around wildly for a place to retreat, but Serena had already risen to take her hand. She gave Alanna's fingers a short, firm squeeze.

"Alanna was good enough to accept my invitation. We wanted to thank her in person for tending you and keeping you alive to annoy us."

"I see." When he could tear his gaze from Alanna, he

sent his aunt a furious look. "Clever, aren't you, Aunt Serena?"

"Oh, aye," she said complacently. "That I am."

At his side, Ian's hands curled into fists. They were twins of the one in his stomach. "Well, Mrs. Flynn, since you're here, I'll have to welcome you to Glenroe."

"I..." She knew she would weep and disgrace herself. "Excuse me, please." Giving Ian a wide berth, she raced from the room.

"How gracious of you, Ian." With a toss of her head Serena went after her guest.

She found Alanna at the wardrobe, pulling out her clothes.

"Now, what's all this?"

"I must go. I didn't know—Lady Langston, I thank you for your hospitality, but I must go home immediately."

"What a pack of nonsense." Serena took her firmly by the shoulders and led her toward the bed. "Now sit down and catch your breath. I know seeing Ian was a surprise but—" She broke off as Alanna covered her face with her hands and burst into tears.

"Oh, there, there, sweetheart." In the way of all mothers she put her arms around Alanna and rocked. "Was he such a bully, then? Men are, you know. It only means we must be bigger ones."

"No, no, it was all my fault. All my doing." Though humiliated, she couldn't stem the tears and laid her head on Serena's shoulder.

"Whether it was or not, that's not something a woman should ever admit. Since men have the advantage of brawn, we must use our better brains." Smiling, she stroked Alanna's hair. "I wanted to see for myself if you loved him as much as I could see he loved you. Now I know."

"He hates me now. And who could blame him? But it's for the best," she wept. "It's for the best."

"He frightens you?"

"Aye."

"And your feelings for him frighten you?"

"Oh, aye. I don't want them, my lady, I can't have them. He won't change. He'll not be happy until he gets himself killed or hanged for treason."

"MacGregors don't kill easily. Here now, have you a handkerchief? I can never find one myself when it's most needed."

Sniffling, Alanna nodded and drew hers out. "I beg your pardon, my lady, for causing a scene."

"Oh, I enjoy a scene, and cause them whenever possible." She waited to be sure Alanna was more composed. "I will tell you a story of a young girl who loved very unwisely. She loved a man who it seemed was so wrong for her. She loved in times when there was war and rebellion, and death everywhere. She refused him, time and time again. She thought it was best."

Drying her eyes, Alanna sighed. "What happened to them?"

"Oh, he was as pigheaded as she, so they married and had six children. Two grandchildren." Her smile blossomed. "I've never regretted a single moment."

"But this is different."

"Love is always the same. And it is never the same." She brushed the hair from Alanna's cheek. "I was afraid."

"You?"

"Oh, aye. The more I loved Brigham, the more frightened I was. And the harder I punished us both by denying my feelings. Will you tell me of yours? Often it helps to speak with another woman."

Perhaps it would, Alanna thought. Surely it could hurt

no more than it already did. "I lost my brother in the war with the French. I was only a child, but I remember him. He was so bright, so beautiful. And like Ian, he could think of nothing but to defend and fight for his land, for his beliefs. So he died for them. Within a year, my mother slipped away. Her heart was broken, and it never mended. I've watched my father grieve for them, year after year."

"There is no loss greater than that of ones you love. My father died in battle twenty-eight years ago and I still see his face, so clear. I left my mother in Scotland soon after. She died before Amanda was born, but still lives in my heart." She took both of Alanna's hands, and her eyes were damp and intense. "When the rebellion was crushed, my brother Coll brought Brigham to me. He had been shot and was near death. In my womb I carried our first child. We were hiding from the English in a cave. He lingered between life and death."

So Ian's stories to Brian were true, she thought as she stared at the small, slender woman beside her. "How could you bear it?"

"How could I not?" She smiled. "He often says I willed him back to life so that I could badger him. Perhaps it's true. But I know the fear, Alanna. When this revolution comes, my sons will fight, and there is ice in my blood at the thought that I could lose them. But if I were a man, I would pick up a sword and join them."

"You're braver than I."

"I think not. If your family were threatened, would you hide in a corner, or would you take up arms and protect them?"

"I would die to protect them. But—"

"Aye." Serena's smile bloomed again, but it was softer, more serious than before. "The time will come, and soon, when the men of the Colonies will realize we are all one,

As a clan. And we will fight to protect each other. Ian knows that now. Is that not why you love him?''

''Aye.'' She looked down at their joined hands.

''If you deny that love, will you be happier than if you embraced it and took what time God grants you together?''

''No.'' She closed her eyes and thought of the past three months of misery. ''I'll never be happy without him—I know that now. And yet, all of my life I dreamed of marrying a strong, quiet man, who would be content to work with me and raise a family. With Ian, there would be confusion and demands and risks. I would never know a moment's peace.''

''No,'' Serena agreed. ''You would not. Alanna, look into your heart now and ask yourself but one question. If the power were yours, would you change him?''

She opened her mouth prepared to shout a resounding ''Aye!'' But her heart, more honest than her head, held another answer. ''No. Sweet Jesus, have I been so much a fool not to realize I love him for what he is, not for what I wish he might be?''

Satisfied, Serena nodded. ''Life is all risk, Alanna. There are those who take them, wholeheartedly, and move forward. And there are those who hide from them and stay in one place. Which are you?''

For a long time Alanna sat in silence. ''I wonder, my lady—''

''Serena.''

''I wonder, Serena,'' she said, and managed a smile, ''if I had had you to talk with, would I have sent him away?''

Serena laughed. ''Well, that's something to think about. You rest now, and give the lad time to stew.''

''He won't want to talk to me,'' she muttered, then set her chin. ''But I'll make him.''

''You'll do,'' Serena said with a laugh. ''Aye, you'll do well.''

Chapter Ten

Ian didn't come to dinner, nor did he appear at breakfast the next morning. While this might have discouraged most women, for Alanna it presented exactly the sort of challenge she needed to overcome her own anxieties.

Added to that were the Langstons themselves. It was simply not possible to be in the midst of such a family and not see what could be done with love, determination and trust. No matter what odds they had faced, Serena and Brigham had made a life together. They had both lost their homes, their countries and people they loved, but had rebuilt from their own grit.

Could she deny herself any less of a chance with Ian? He would fight, certainly. But she began to convince herself that he was too stubborn to die. And if indeed she were to lose him, was it not worth the joy of a year, a month or a day in his arms?

She would tell him so. If she ever ran the fool to ground

She would apologize. She would even, though it grated, beg his forgiveness and a second chance.

But as the morning whiled away, she found herself more irritated than penitent. She would apologize, all right, Alanna thought. Right after she'd given him a good, swift kick.

It was the twins who gave her the first clue as to where to find him.

"You were the one who spoiled it," Payne declared as they came poking and jabbing at each other into the garden.

"Hah! It was you who set him off. If you'd kept your mouth shut we could have gone off with him. But you've such a bloody big—"

"All right, lads." Serena stopped clipping flowers to turn to them. "Fight if you must, but not here. I won't have my garden trampled by wrestling bodies."

"It's his fault," they said in unison, and made Alanna smile.

"I only wanted to go fishing," Ross complained. "And Ian would have taken me along if *he* hadn't started jabbering."

"Fishing." Alanna crushed a blossom in her hand before she controlled herself. "Is that where Ian is?"

"He always goes to the river when he's moody." Payne kicked at a pebble. "I'd have convinced him to take us, too, if Ross hadn't started in so Ian was snarling and riding off without us."

"I don't want to fish anyway." Ross stuck up his chin. "I want to play shuttlecock."

"*I* want to play shuttlecock," Payne shouted, and raced off to get there first.

"I've a fine mare in the stables. A pretty chestnut that was a gift from my brother Malcolm. He knows his horseflesh." Serena went on clipping flowers. "Do you like to ride, Alanna?"

"Aye. I don't have much time for it at home."

"Then you should take advantage of your time here." She gave her young guest a sunny smile. "Tell Jem at the stables I said to saddle Prancer for you. You might enjoy riding south. There's a path through the woods just beyond the stables. The river's very pretty this time of year."

"Thank you." She started to dash off, then stopped. "I—I don't have a riding habit."

"Hattie will see to it. There's one of Amanda's in my trunk. It should suit you."

"Thank you." She stopped, turned and embraced Serena. "Thank you."

Within thirty minutes, Alanna was mounted.

Ian did indeed have a line in the water, but it was only an excuse to sit and brood. He'd given brief consideration to strangling his aunt for her interference, but before he'd gotten the chance she had burst into his room and raked him so completely over the coals that he'd had nothing to do but defend himself.

Aye, he'd been rude to her guest. He'd meant to be.

If it didn't smack so much of running away, he'd have been on his horse and headed back to Boston. He'd be damned if he'd ride away a second time. This time, she could go, and the devil take her.

Why had she had to look so beautiful, standing there in her blue dress with the sun coming through the window at her back?

Why did it matter to him how she looked? he thought viciously. He didn't want her any longer. He didn't need a sharp-tongued shrew of a woman in his life. There was too much work to be done.

By God, he'd all but begged her to have him. How it grated on his pride! And she, the hussy, had lain with him in the hay, given herself to him, made him think it mattered to her. He'd been so gentle, so careful with her. Never before had he opened his heart so to a woman. Only to have it handed back to him.

Well, he hoped she found some weak-kneed spineless lout she could boss around. And if he discovered she had, he would cheerfully kill the man with his own two hands.

He heard the sound of a horse approach and swore. If those two little pests had come to disrupt his solitude, he would send them packing soon enough. Taking up his line, he stood, feet planted, and prepared to roar his nephews back to the house.

But it was Alanna who came riding out of the woods. She was coming fast, a bit too fast for Ian's peace of mind. Beneath the jaunty bonnet she wore her hair had come loose so that it streamed behind her, a midnight flag. A few feet away, she reined the horse. Even at the distance, Ian could see her eyes were a brilliant and glowing blue. The mare, well used to reckless women riders, behaved prettily.

When he got his breath back, Ian shot her a killing look. "Well, you've managed to scare away all the fish for ten miles. Don't you have better sense than to ride through unfamiliar ground at that speed?"

It wasn't the greeting she'd hope for. "The horse knew the way well enough." She sat, waiting for him to help her dismount. When he merely stood, glaring, she swore and struggled down herself. "You've changed little, Mac-Gregor. Your manners are as foul as ever."

"You came all the way to Virginia to tell me so?"

She fixed the mare's reins to a nearby branch before she whirled on him. "I came at your aunt's kind invitation. If I had known you were anywhere in the territory, I wouldn't have come. Seeing you is the only thing that has spoiled my trip, for in truth, I'll never understand how a man such as yourself could possibly be related to such a fine family. It would be my fondest wish if you would—'' She caught herself, blew out a breath and struggled to remember the resolve she had worked on all through the night. "I didn't come here to fight with you."

"God help me if that had been your intention, then." He turned back to pick up his line. "You got yourself off the horse, Mrs. Flynn. I imagine you can get yourself back on and ride."

"I will speak with you," she insisted.

"Already you've said more than I wish to hear." And if he stood looking at her another moment, he would crawl. "Now mount and ride before you push me too far."

"Ian, I only want to—"

"Damn you to hell and back again." He threw down the line. "What right have you to come here? To stand here and make me suffer? If I had murdered you before I left I'd be a happy man today. You let me think you cared for me, that what happened between us meant something to you, when all you wanted was a toss in the hay."

Every ounce of color fled from her cheeks, then rushed back again in flaming fury. "How dare you? How dare you speak so to me?" She was on him like a wildcat, all nails and teeth. "I'll kill you for that, MacGregor, as God is my witness."

He grabbed wherever he could to protect himself, lost his balance and tumbled backward with her into the river.

The dunking didn't stop her. She swung, spit and scratched even as he slid on the slippery bottom and took her under with him.

"Hold, woman, for pity's sake. You'll drown us both." Because he was choking, coughing up water and trying to keep her from sinking under again, he didn't see the blow coming until his ears were already ringing. "By God, if you were a man!"

"Don't let that stop you, you bloody badger." She swung again, missed and fell facedown in the river.

Cursing all the way, he dragged her onto the bank, where they both lay drenched and breathless.

"As soon as I've the strength to stand, I'll kill her," he said to the sky.

"I hate you," she told him after she'd coughed up river water. "I curse the day you were born. And I curse the day I let you put your filthy hands on me." She managed to sit up and drag the ruined bonnet out of her eyes.

Damn her for being beautiful even wet and raging. His voice was frigid when he spoke. A dangerous sign. "You asked me to put them on you, as I recall, madam."

"Aye, that I did, to my disgust." She threw the bonnet at him. "'Tis a pity the roll in the hay wasn't more memorable."

"Oh?" She was too busy wringing out her hair to note the reckless light in his eyes. "Wasn't it now?"

"No, it wasn't. In fact, I'd forgotten all about it until you mentioned it." With what dignity she still had in her possession, she started to rise. He had her flat on her back in an instant.

"Well, then, let me refresh your memory."

His mouth came down hard on hers. She responded by sinking her teeth into his lip. He cursed her, gathered her dripping hair in his hand and kissed her again.

She fought herself, all the glorious feelings that poured through her. She fought him, the long firm body that so intimately covered hers. Like scrapping children, they rolled over the grassy bank, blindly seeking to punish for hurts old and new.

Then she whimpered, a sound of submission and of joy. Her arms were around him, her mouth opening hungrily to his. All the force of her love burst out in that one meeting of lips and fueled a fire already blazing.

Frantic fingers tore at buttons. Desperate hands pulled at wet, heavy clothing. Then the sun was steaming down on their damp bodies.

He wasn't gentle now. She didn't wish it. All the frustration and the need they had trapped within themselves tore free in a rage of passion as they took from each other under the cloudless spring sky.

With her hands in his hair, she pulled his mouth to hers again and again, murmuring wild promises, wild pleas. As they lay on the carpet of new grass, he absorbed the scent that had haunted him for weeks. He stroked his hands along the smooth white skin he had dreamed of night after night.

When she arched against him, ruthlessly stoking his fires, he plunged into her. Her name was on his lips as he buried his face in her hair. His was on hers as she wrapped her long limbs around him. Together they raced toward the end they both craved, until at last they lay still, each hounded by their own thoughts.

He drew himself up on his elbow and with one hand cupped her face. As she watched, loving him, she saw the temper return slowly to his eyes.

"I give you no choice this time, Alanna. Willing or weeping we marry."

"Ian, I came here today to tell you—"

"I don't give a bloody damn what you came to tell me." His fingers tightened on her chin. He had emptied himself in her, body and soul. She had left him with nothing, not even pride. "You can hate me and curse me from now until the world ends, but you'll be mine. You are mine. And by God, you'll take me as I am."

She gritted her teeth. "If you'd let me say a word—"

But a desperate man didn't listen. "I'll not let you go again. I should not have before, but you've a way of scraping a man raw. Whatever I can do to make you happy, I'll do. Except abandon my own conscience. That I cannot do, and won't. Not even for you."

"I don't ask you to, and never would. I only want to tell you—"

"Damn it, what is it that's digging a hole in my chest?" Still swearing he reached between them. And held up the MacGregor ring that dangled from a cord around her neck. It glinted in the sunlight as he stared at it. Slowly, he closed his fingers around it and looked down at her. "Why..." He took another moment to be sure he could trust his voice. "Why do you wear this?"

"I was trying to tell you, if you would only let me speak."

"I'm letting you speak now, so speak."

"I was going to give it back to you." She moved restlessly beneath him. "But I couldn't. It felt dishonest to wear it on my finger, so I tied it to a cord and wore it by my heart, where I kept you, as well. No, damn you, let me finish," she said when he opened his mouth. "I think I knew even as I heard you ride away that morning that I had been wrong and you had been right."

The beginnings of a smile teased his mouth. "I have river water in my ears, Mrs. Flynn. Would you say that again?"

"I said it once, I'll not repeat it." If she'd been standing, she would have tossed her head and lifted her chin. "I didn't want to love you, because when you love so much, it makes you afraid. I lost Rory in the war, my mother from grief and poor Michael Flynn from a fever. And as much as they meant to me, I knew that you meant more.''

He kissed her, gently. ''Don't let me interrupt.''

''I thought I wanted a quiet home and a family, a husband who would be content to work beside me and sit by the fire night after night.'' She smiled now and touched his hair. ''But it seems what I wanted all along was a man who would never be content, one who would grow restless by the fire after the first night or two. One who would fight all the wrongs or die trying. That's a man I would be proud to stand beside.''

''Now you humble me,'' he murmured, and rested his brow on hers. ''Only tell me you love me.''

''I do love you, Ian MacGregor. Now and always.''

''I swear to give you that home, that family, and to sit by the fire with you whenever I can.''

''And I promise to fight beside you when the need comes.''

Shifting, he snapped the cord and freed the ring. His eyes were on hers as he slipped it onto her finger. ''Never take it off again.''

''No.'' She took his hand in hers. ''From this moment, I'm a MacGregor.''

Epilogue

Boston, Christmas Eve, 1774

No amount of arguments could keep Ian out of the bedroom where his wife struggled through her first birthing. Though the sight of her laboring froze his man's heart, he stood firm. His aunt Gwen in her quiet, persuasive way had done her best, but even she had failed.

"It's my child, as well," he said. "And I'll not leave Alanna until it's born." He took his aunt's hand and prayed he'd have the nerve to live by his words. "It's not that I don't trust your skills, Aunt Gwen. After all, I wouldn't be here without them."

"It's no use, Gwen." Serena chuckled. "He's as stubborn as any MacGregor."

"Hold her hand then, when the pain is bad. It won't be much longer now."

Alanna managed a smile when Ian came to her side. She

hadn't known it would take so long to bring such a small thing as a child into the world. She was grateful that he was with her and for the comforting presence of Gwen, who had brought so many dozens of babies into the world. Gwen's husband, who was a doctor, would have attended the birth as well, had he not been called away on an emergency.

"You neglect our guests," Alanna said to Ian as she rested between contractions.

"They'll entertain themselves well enough," Serena assured her.

"I don't doubt it." She closed her eyes as Gwen wiped her brow with a cool cloth. It pleased her that her family was here for Christmas. Both the Murphys and the Langstons. She should have been doing her duties as hostess on this first Christmas in the house she and Ian had bought near the river, but the babe, not due for another three weeks, was putting in an early appearance.

When the next pang hit, she squeezed Ian's hand and tensed.

"Relax, relax, mind your breathing," Gwen crooned. "There's a lass."

The pains were closer now, and stronger. A Christmas baby, she thought, struggling to rise over the wave. Their child, their first child, would be a priceless gift to each other on this the most holy night of the year.

As the pain passed, she kept her eyes closed, listening to the soothing sound of Ian's voice.

He was a good man, a solid husband. She felt his fingers twine around hers. True, her life was not a peaceful one, but it was eventful. He had managed to draw her into his ambitions. Or perhaps the seeds of rebellion had always been inside her, waiting to be nurtured. She had come to listen avidly to his reports of the meetings he attended and to feel pride when others sought his advice. She could not but agree with him that the Port Bill was cruel and unjust. Like Ian, she scorned the idea of paying for the tea that had been destroyed in order to escape the penalty.

No, they had not been wrong. She had learned there was often right in recklessness. She had to smile. It was recklessness, and right, that had brought her here to a birthing bed. And she thanked God for it.

And hadn't other towns and provinces rallied to support Boston, just as her family and Ian's had rallied to support them in this, the birth of their first child?

She thought of their honeymoon in Scotland, where she had met his family and walked in the forests of his childhood. One day they would go back and take this child, show him, or her, the place of roots. And to Ireland, she thought as the pain returned, dizzying. The child would not forget the people who had come before. And while the child remembered, he would choose his own life, his own homeland. By their struggles, they would have given him that right.

"The babe's coming." Gwen shot Ian a quick, reassuring smile. "You'll be a papa very soon."

"The birth of our child," Alanna panted, fighting to focus on Ian. "And soon, the birth of our nation."

Though he could taste his own fear, for her, he laughed. "You're becoming more of a radical than I, Mrs. Mac-Gregor."

"I do nothing by half measures. Oh, sweet Jesus, he fights for life." She groped for her husband's hand. "There can be little doubt he will be his father's son."

"Or her mother's daughter," Ian murmured, looking desperately at Gwen. "How much longer?" he demanded. "She suffers."

"Soon." She let out a little sound of impatience as there was a knock on the door.

"Don't worry." Serena pushed at her already rolled-up sleeves. "I'll send them packing." It surprised her to find her husband at the threshold. "Brig, the babe's all but here. I don't have time for you now."

"You'll have time." He stepped inside, tossing one arm around his wife. "I've just gotten a message I've waited for, a confirmation from London I wanted before I spoke to you."

"Damn messages from London," Serena muttered as she heard Alanna groan.

"Uncle, news can wait."

"Ian, you need to hear this as well, tonight of all nights."

"Then say it and be gone," his wife snapped at him.

"Last month a petition was debated by Parliament." Brigham took Serena by the shoulders and looked into her eyes. "The Act of Proscription has been repealed." He cupped her face in his hands as her eyes filled. "The MacGregor name is free."

With her tears fell a weight she had carried all of her life. "Gwen. Gwen, did you hear?"

"Aye, I heard, and I thank God for it, but I've my hands full at the moment."

Dragging her husband with her, Serena hurried to the bed. "Since you're here," she told Brigham, "you'll help."

Within minutes there was the sound of church bells heralding midnight and the birth of a new Christmas. And the sound of a baby's lusty cry, heralding life.

"A son." Gwen held the squirming child in her arms.

"He's all right?" Exhausted, Alanna lay back against Brigham's bracing hands. "Is he all right?"

"He's perfect," Serena assured her, mopping her own tears. "You'll hold him in a moment."

"I love you." Ian pressed Alanna's hand to his lips. "And I thank you for the greatest gift that man can have."

"Here now." Gwen shifted the newly swaddled infant to his father's arms. "Take your son."

"Sweet God." Stunned, he looked from the baby to Alanna. It was an image she would treasure all of her life. "He's so small."

"He'll grow." Serena smiled up at her husband. "They always do." She put an arm around her sister as Ian transferred the baby to Alanna's waiting arms.

"Oh, he's so beautiful." Reaching for Ian, she drew him down beside her. "Last Christmas we were given each other. This Christmas we're given a son." Gently, she stroked the downy dark hair on the baby's head. "I can't wait to see what the years will bring."

"We'll give you time alone—" Brigham took his wife and his sister-in-law by the hand "—and go down and tell the others."

"Aye, tell them." Ian stood, and because she understood, Alanna gave him the child to hold once again. "Tell them that Murphy MacGregor is born this Christmas day." After kissing his son, he held him up for the others to see, and the baby let out a lusty wail. "A MacGregor who will say his name proudly to all that can hear. Who will walk in a free land. Tell them that."

"Aye, tell them that," Alanna agreed as Ian's hand closed around hers. "From both of us."

* * * * *

THE MACGREGORS OF OLD...

#1 *New York Times* bestselling author

NORA ROBERTS

has won readers' hearts with her enormously popular
MacGregor family saga. Now read about the MacGregors'
proud and passionate Scottish forebears in this
romantic, tempestuous tale set against the bloody
background of the historic battle of Culloden.

Coming in July 1999

REBELLION

One look at the ravishing red-haired beauty and Brigham
Langston was captivated. But though Serena MacGregor
had the face of an angel, she was a wildcat who spurned
his advances with a rapier-sharp tongue. To hot-tempered
Serena, Brigham was just another Englishman to be
despised. But in the arms of the dashing and dangerous
English lord, the proud Scottish beauty felt her hatred
melting with the heat of their passion.

Available at your favorite retail outlet.

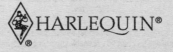

HARLEQUIN®

If you enjoyed what you just read,
then we've got an offer you can't resist!

Take 2 bestselling
love stories FREE!
Plus get a FREE surprise gift!

Of all the unforgettable families created by
#1 *New York Times* bestselling author

NORA ROBERTS

the Donovans are the most extraordinary. For, along with
their irresistible appeal, they've inherited some rather
remarkable gifts from their Celtic ancestors.

Coming in November 1999

THE DONOVAN LEGACY

3 full-length novels in one special volume:

CAPTIVATED: Hardheaded skeptic Nash Kirkland has *always*
kept his feelings in check, until he falls under the bewitching
spell of mysterious Morgana Donovan.

ENTRANCED: Desperate to find a missing child, detective
Mary Ellen Sutherland dubiously enlists beguiling
Sebastian Donovan's aid and discovers his uncommon abilities
include a talent for seduction.

CHARMED: Enigmatic healer Anastasia Donovan would do
anything to save the life of handsome Boone Sawyer's
daughter, even if it means revealing her secret to the man
who'd stolen her heart.

Also in November 1999 from Silhouette Intimate Moments

ENCHANTED

Lovely, guileless Rowan Murray is drawn to darkly enigmatic
Liam Donovan with a power she's never imagined possible. But
before Liam can give Rowan his love, he must first reveal to
her his incredible secret.

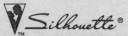

Available at your favorite retail outlet.

Look us up on-line at: http://www.romance.net

PSNRDLR

Coming in May 1999

BABY *Fever*

by
New York Times Bestselling Author

KASEY MICHAELS

When three sisters hear their biological
clocks ticking, they know it's
time for action.

But who will they get to father their babies?

Find out how the road to motherhood
leads to love in this brand-new collection.

Available at your favorite retail outlet.

Send for Julia: The MacGregor Bride today!

"a woman with rose-petal skin and curling, flame-colored hair. Her eyes were chocolate brown...her mouth was wide...her hands narrow...and her curvy body was fueled with an inner energy."

—from *The MacGregor Brides* by **Nora Roberts**

Here's beautiful Julia, cherished granddaughter of the clan patriarch, Daniel MacGregor. Hand-crafted in fine bisque porcelain, Julia is dressed her wedding day in a cream satin gown accented by a wide, graceful sash traditional MacGregor tartan. She carries an exquisite traditional bridal bo quet and wears a cathedral-length dotted Swiss veil. Embroidered flowers cascade down her lace overskirt to the scalloped hemline; underneath all multi-layered crinoline.

Nora Roberts fans will surely want to acquire **Julia: The MacGregor Bride** a collectible to cherish and display with pride!